The Circle of Fire

Owen Elgie

ISBN: 978-1-326-16866-7

PublishNation, London
www.publishnation.co.uk

For Jo

Who helped me to tell the story I've had inside my head all these years and encouraged me to let my mind soar. It's all your fault, you know. Thank you for everything.

1

Slowly easing the door closed behind me, I turned and made my way down the steps from the home of one of my more enthusiastic clients. Lifting my hood up over my head, I braced myself against the fine drizzle which was ever so steadily drenching the city and started to make my way down to street level. I was still two steps short of the pavement when the door was opened behind me.

"Anthony. We haven't booked for our next session yet" practically dribbled down the steps behind me, a torrent of breathless suggestion which had been intended to generate a reaction I was unable to give.

Taking a steadying breath, I slowly turned round to face the owner of the voice fixing that ever so professional smile. She was still dressed as I'd left her, out of breath with her hair soaked from perspiration. Her voice carried that extra huff of breathlessness caused by strenuous activity and she still had that same grin on her face.

"Sorry Mrs. Jones. I ..."

"Please call me Stephanie. We've been doing this for long enough now that you can call me by my first name." The comment was accompanied by a small smile and a wink.

"Stephanie. I'll have to contact you in the next day or so I'm afraid. I have a family issue I need to attend to and I'm not really sure when it will be resolved."

Stephanie beamed again then giggled slightly.

"I'll be looking forward to the call then."

With that, she slowly eased the door closed, all the while keeping a suggestive gaze fixed on me, and I was again back in the rain soaked street, alone.

Thank God.

Walking away from the house of Stephanie Jones, all I could think about was the delight of the having to go through this same dance regarding everything. She had been having sessions with me now for four weeks and her advances were starting to border on the ridiculous.

OK, looking back at that whole exchange, it would be very easy for someone to get the wrong idea about so many things.

First up, I'm Anthony Johns, Personal Trainer, not gigolo. I've been training her at her house for a month, twice a week. She is signed up to do the London Marathon and has been looking for some extra help to be able to be the best she can be. The problem seems to be that she seems to think that her Personal Trainer is also expected to help her with other 'demands'. I'd been forced to walk that wonderful tightrope of keeping the client happy while all the time keeping her at more than arm's length. So far so good but this was getting ridiculous.

I'd been working as a Personal Trainer for years. I spend my working days making Geoff from Accounts and Brian from Human Resources feel terrible all in the name of health and well-being. I also spend a large chunk of my time doing home visits with Mrs Smith or Ms Jackson who have lots of money and enjoy the attentions of an athletic young man. Let me get this straight from the outset, I don't just go around sleeping with my lonely housewife clients. I do flirt with them a bit but that simply works as a way of renewing business. I won't cross that line.

Walking through the rain, which had decided that the slow insidious soaking wasn't good enough and had moved on to the out and out downpour, I ran through different ways I could get her to back off while still maintaining a good, paying client. Maybe this was proof that I had to be more professional than simply making the frustrated housewife think she had a chance.

By the time I'd got to my car, a delightfully aged silver Alfa Romeo which was cheap to buy but kind of still carried that air of 'position', I'd run through at least ten scenarios which would just end up with me getting slapped, wildly insulted or at the barest minimum, fired.

Not good.

What I'd told her had been true regarding the family issue but it hadn't managed to impinge on what was going on in my life up until now. At the very least I could be satisfied that I was telling her the

2

truth regarding the reason for not rushing to book the next session. I really should stop putting things off.

Climbing into the car and starting the engine, I resolved to do some more thinking on the subject and hopefully get to the bottom of things.

It took me about an hour to get back to my flat, park the car and get inside, thanks mainly to the delights of traffic in a big city. I travelled eight miles in an hour and that was pretty good going. Eventually though, the sun having slipped below the horizon, bringing the darkness of a winter early evening, I arrived at my destination.

Depending on the weather, my front door seemed to warp just enough to make getting into the flat become a pain in the neck as it had today, all the way through to practically locking me out. Leaning just that little bit harder than should have been required, I was able to persuade the door open. Mumbling the usual resolution to finally get the thing sorted out, I edged into my home.

I live in a wonderful little second floor flat which is close enough to the inner workings of the city of London to make it easy to reach clients in the city but without having to pay quite the ridiculous rents of a property which was truly in the inner sanctum of the metropolis. It gave me the best of both worlds as far as I could see.

My one bedroom flat had a small bathroom, a pretty small kitchen but a very comfortably spacious living room. Add to that a bedroom which was also much larger than a flat this size had any right to have and I was able to feel that I was living in a home designed for people rather than dogs or cats as some of the properties in London seemed to be.

Working my way out of my coat and my training gear, I could feel the relaxation of being at home start to wind its way through me.

I dug my work phone out of my pocket and plugged it in to charge in its usual spot by the front door. Looking at the screen, I could see that there was already a message waiting for me from Stephanie. I thought that I'd explained the situation to her on the steps to her home but no doubt she was just saying hello, so there was no way to forget that she was a little bit interested in me. Lifting the phone, I played back the message, feeling just a kernel of discomfort returning.

"Anthony, it's Stephanie." I could hear the absolutely overt sexual tones and it made me shiver. Either that or the wet clothes I was still wearing but you get the picture.

"I forgot to tell you before you left, when you book our next, appointment, please can you make certain to avoid Wednesday and Thursday of next week. My husband is home for those days and I don't want to have our time together interrupted. Speak soon."

The click that came to signify her hanging up came as a blessed relief. She really was getting very persistent and I was even considering the idea of saying I couldn't work with her anymore.

Plugging the phone back in to charge, I resolved to spell out the true extent of our relationship the next time I worked with her.

Next it was on to my bedroom. I'd say that this was where the magic happened but this isn't an episode of Cribs. Besides, what magic?

Getting changed hurriedly, throwing on a pair of jeans and a shirt which was probably just about creased enough to look effortless rather than a mess. I picked up my personal phone from its charging point next to my bed and checked the screen.

There were three voicemail messages waiting for me, one from Sarah, one from Kelly and one from Jane. They all had basically the same message, wanting to see me again. I resolved that this situation was another that I needed to get sorted out sooner rather than later.

Look, I'm not the cheating pig everyone would easily think I am. I didn't want to hurt anyone ever and I kind of found my way into this situation. I didn't like the thought of being viewed as the heartless brute so I found it quite difficult to say no. OK, so maybe a little magic.

Pocketing the phone and swearing to whichever higher power was listening at that second that I was going to get this mess sorted, I left the flat again, pulling my hooded jacket around me tightly, and started to walk my way through the soaked streets of the city.

Step by step, street by street, I covered the ground quickly. I didn't have miles and miles to cover in the rain but I was on the verge of being late for an appointment that I had thought would never happen. That and I was also keen to get to the venue.

Superman had the Fortress of Solitude while Batman had the Batcave. Me, I did my best thinking in the bar.

As I walked in I was greeted by that most welcoming of sensations. People in the bar looked towards the noise of the opening door and acknowledged me as I made my way in. I was greeted by nods and smiles from the collection of people I knew. There was Barry and John, a pair of guys in their sixties who told very un-PC jokes to anyone who'd listen, Jeff the Beast, a man who made certain that everyone knew that back in the old days he was considered a 'bit tasty' when it came to fighting, the dominoes boys of Charlie, Dave and Colin (they never actually played a game but they always had the dominoes spread out on the table in front of them) and Big Al, a twenty six stone man who stood five foot four.

Each and every one of these people, and many more besides who weren't currently present, made sure that we were all made to feel welcome and that we had a place to go when we needed to just have a chat and get away from it all.

As the theme song to the 80's TV show Cheers said, "Sometimes you want to go where everybody knows your name".

Making my way to the bar I could see that there was a new face greeting me. She looked young and impressionable with jet black hair and full lips.

Concentrate on the reason you're here, will you, for crying out loud.

Ordering myself a drink, my usual of a bottle of lager, which of course she didn't know, I sat at the bar and let my mind wander over where I was.

I've been coming in here for the last fifteen years. In all that time the decor hasn't changed short of more up to date pictures of sports teams. The place has the look of somewhere which had been very well to do when the doors first opened but that nothing has been done since. There was lots of exposed wood, beams and banisters, around the room but they had all lost their colour in certain spots as, over the years, thousands of hands had slowly worn them down without anyone coming to repair what was being done. The paint work can best be described as smoker's magnolia. The ban may have pushed the smokers outside but the building was still clinging to the proof that it had seen many a nicotine laden cloud over the years. The large single room of the bar was lined with strangely patterned seating set around an array of different sized tables. There was also a scattering of smaller tables around the floor. The floor itself was carpeted in what can only be described as 'pub colours', that remarkable patterned mish mash of colours which no-one ever has in their homes but which can cover a multitude of stains from spilt drinks, food or, well, anything.

The walls were covered in pictures of the local area from times gone past but also with pictures of sporting success – Bobby Moore lifting the World Cup, Eric Bristow celebrating one of his World Darts Championships, Henry Cooper in action against Mohammed Ali, the Welsh Grand Slam team from 2008, even photos of teams and sports from all over the world. I can remember a very odd evening having the finer points of Kabbadi explained to me as a new picture of players engaged in their own gladiatorial combat was hung. Sport did play a big part in the life of this place. In every way this place looked exactly like hundreds of other pubs or bars across the country but this place was like family.

You see, up until recently, this bar had been the place where I had spent many an hour discussing all the most important things in the world with my uncle, David. We had gone all the way through literature in the western world, the socio-political balance being developed in the former Soviet bloc, why there were so many people willing to risk death by eating a potentially poisonous fish in the far east but the majority of our time was spent mulling over the real bedrock of society as a whole, rugby!

In that bar he and I had decided who was the best player from every major rugby playing nation, some of the minor ones too. We discussed why teams did what they did in certain situations and if Wales would ever win the World Cup (if you asked Uncle David it was always when they would win the World Cup, not if! He'd got very drunk after the 2011 World Cup semi-final when one decision had been what had seen us eliminated and had expressed the belief that the referee had been an imp or some other mythical beast, intent on some kind of mischief! A very weird day at the bar and he had sworn not to mix his drinks in that way ever again.) We'd watched the Grand Slam matches that we won and the ones we lost but we had a great time doing it.

My Uncle had always said that despite the fact he was living in England, despite the fact he had been away from home for so long, he could always feel the call to go back to Wales. He had told me that there was always something pulling him back to Wales and that he would always have a connection to where he was from. It probably rubbed off a little on me. I hadn't been in years but there were very fond memories from the trip.

My family comes originally from Wales but my parents moved us away from the Swansea area when I was just a toddler – more money to be made in London. My parents had decided that the life they could provide for their young family could be improved if they left Wales behind. My uncle had told me from quite early on that he hadn't ever understood the reasons for the move but it was my father's decision. We had gone back to Wales for a holiday when I was still very young but after that I never went back. I had asked why there had never been further holidays to Wales as I grew up but things in my life had seemed to get in the way and there was always a good reason not to go.

So my parents brought me and my older brother Steve to where I currently reside. After that, the sheer weight of normality that was our life had taken hold. Both my parents worked in offices doing office things and my brother and I were kids doing kid things. My uncle hadn't been in our lives until my parents were killed in an accident when I was seven and Steve was fourteen but he moved to live with us.

From the outset he and Steve hadn't seen eye to eye. Steve never seemed to enjoy spending time with Uncle David and when they did talk they would always end up shouting at each other. Me on the other hand, all my Uncle and I ever did was have a great time. Where he was always pushing Steve he just wanted me to be happy in whatever I did, hence Steve and David haven't really spoken since Steve left when he was nineteen. This had also meant that Steve and I hadn't spoken since Steve was nineteen either. I was twelve.

After that, life had rumbled on in a non-descript way as I got older and did all those things young people do during the course of school and later life, Uncle David always saying that I should follow whatever it was that was calling to me. I wasn't ever really blessed with what you could call an academic mind. My whole time at school seemed to me to be a collection of events that I wasn't really interested in or that I couldn't work out. None of the teachers seemed

7

to like me and every day felt like a waste of time. My lack of ability coupled with my teachers absolute dismissal of me had made me resent school and all the conformity and constriction that it represented. My Uncle never tried to force the issue, though. He just told me not to worry about it when the letters came home from the school detailing my latest act of sullen rebellion. He must have known that I was really trying but books and study just weren't for me.

School did have the occasional bright spot buried amongst all the drudgery, though. Sport. I really enjoyed playing sport and training so I simply tried to find any way to keep me in that world as I grew up. Working as a trainer seemed a great way for me to keep doing what I liked without the need to fly a desk. The thought of working in an office was my idea of hell on earth.

We occasionally heard word from Steve saying that he was with friends in a certain town or had been working abroad but mainly we got nothing. The older I got, the worse it felt. My closest family had abandoned me. I never let it show but there was always a shadow at the back of my mind about why he'd left. There was always a hole in my life but you just carry on don't you?

I saw that it had hurt my uncle as well but he would never admit it. You see, my uncle was a big brute of a man, old school. Feelings should never be shown and crying made you weak etc. He was well over six feet tall and broad and well muscled with it. I had good genes but really had to work hard in the gym to get half way to what he was. He'd been a farmer in West Wales so had been working very physically for many years. When he moved to look after my brother and I, he organized some people to maintain his business while he drew a salary from it. Despite twenty years away from the day to day needs of his farm and twenty more years on his own body clock, he had somehow managed to maintain the same level of physique. My uncle had some times been called back to Wales for some reason, spending a week or two away at a time, but he in the most part left the farm in the hands of the managers and focussed his attentions on us, leaving the physical work behind.

If I knew the secret of how he maintained himself I could retire as a Personal Trainer and sell the elixir of youth!

We had grown to be more than simply Uncle and Nephew over the years. When he first moved to live with us he hadn't really tried to be my dad, instead trying to be an advisor to me. He was more about encouragement and nudging me in the right direction than ruling with an iron fist. As I had grown up he had taken me to the bar for my first drink, he'd given me advice on what path to take with work and he'd filled me in on the facts of life. He let me explore possibilities and was next to me regardless of the results. All things considered, I had had a great relationship with my Uncle, but this only served to highlight the differences in my Uncle's relationship with my brother. I had spoken to Uncle David about it, asked about the reasons for the break down between them, but I didn't get any real answers. "He needed to grow up but didn't want to, He wouldn't listen to me, He was unwilling to stand up for his responsibilities" seemed to be the central flavour of why, but that was always as far as the conversation went and he was always fast to change the subject to something different.

As the years rolled on and we got closer, I was always aware of the hole in my family. Despite my Uncle being more like a friend, his opinions of Steve had always made me aware that there was something missing and it was always in the back of my mind that I was losing out. This in turn gave me a frustration when it came to family. Why had Steve really left? Why didn't my Uncle tell me the whole story? I didn't ever have the full picture and I felt a bubbling anger about it.

I drained the drink without really paying attention to it or anything else that was going on around me, but found that I had a refill in front of me without having to ask for it. She was good at what she was doing.

Thinking about just how good she could be I got a nudge in the arm from Big Al who had been collecting his drink. Winking conspiratorially, he walked back to his seat giggling to himself. I really should try to make sure I wasn't just the hound of the group.

The excellent service did mean that I was able to remain in my mind rather than being forced to interact with the real world. The trouble with that was it meant I had nothing else to get in the way of going over the worst details of what had happened over the last few weeks. All of the mundane concerns of the day to day fell away as my mind meandered. Stephanie and her obsession with me. The other three ladies. My car not sounding that healthy as I drove through London. All of these thoughts fell away as my mind danced through the details and I was left with the final truth.

The world was now changed.

I was sat in my local having my usual drink, surrounded by the same people, the same sights, sounds and smells yet everything felt different. Up until very recently, all of my focus and energy had been aimed at preparing for the opening match of the Six Nations rugby tournament and watching Wales play against England in Cardiff. That match had been all I could really focus my attention on and the fever for it had been building for weeks, but now, it really didn't seem to matter.

Coming back from a loved one's funeral is something that makes the world seem wrong. You see where they fit into the world on a day to day basis but they aren't there. When you think about events gone by and laugh you catch yourself and feel guilty about even thinking about anything good. All those great memories are now to be put away out of respect. I was sat at the bar having my first drink in my local since my uncle had been killed. A violent attack, a mugging gone wrong. He and I would have spent hours here talking about every aspect of the international match but now I had been left with a hole that nothing would be able to repair. The injustice of the situation had seemed to come to life and crawl into my head. It had been gnawing at me since I had been told what had happened and seemed to have stoked the fire in my temper. I was always angry and regularly found myself drifting through scenarios and ideas of what I would do to the person who had killed my uncle if I ever got my hands on them. The funeral had helped take the edge off my morbid thoughts but they were always there, just scratching at the surface.

The funeral had taken place in West Wales in, what seemed to be, the smallest chapel in the most remote village in the whole of the country. There had seemed to only be enough space for around twenty people in the chapel but it had been full with quite a crowd outside as well. Who knew my uncle knew so many people.

As I sat there contemplating the time I had spent in Wales mourning my family, the familiarity of the bar, the void of the empty stool next to me at the bar, I heard the door to the bar open and the new girl quickly hurried toward the new customer.

The new patron asked quietly for a bottle of beer and settled down on the stool next to me. The void seemed to get filled in a little.

"It sounded urgent" came a deep, familiar voice.

I finished my drink and turned to my right. "It is" and then almost as an afterthought, "How you been Steve?"

2

Steve and I looked slowly at each other, each of us taking in the view of the other and feeling the burn of a myriad of different emotions. It had been almost twenty years since we had last seen each other but there was no way of us missing each other in a crowd. Apart from the extra years that Steve had on me we looked almost like twins, both over six feet tall and well muscled (like I said – good genes) and with the right mix of carefree ruffle and ordered style to our dark brown hair. We would never have been described as the best looking guys in the world but I like to think we scored a decent step above average but I spend my life flirting with desperate housewives so I'm not too sure if my view point is that accurate. Steve did look like he had been training pretty hard though. He was noticeably bigger than me but didn't look comfortable in his own skin. He was carrying himself like someone who didn't like the spotlight of people's gazes which his appearance was sure to bring. He was wearing a dark grey suit, a white shirt but no tie. If he had been aiming for the non-descript, blend into the background look then he really missed. Everyone in the room had at the very least, glanced him up and down. Probably didn't help that he was effectively walking into enemy territory by coming in here. This was Uncle David's refuge from the world and everyone in here must have been aware of the fact that the two of them hadn't got on.

"I'm doing Ok little brother, adventures in far off lands, intrigue and danger" Steve offered as a way of filling in almost two decades of experience as quickly as he could without actually saying anything. In other words living life, now get to the reason I'm here.

"So what is it that I get messages from at least five different sources that you need to see me immediately back home and that it can't wait or be put off?"

"You're a difficult man to reach" I responded, aiming to include a little of my own discomfort into the sentence but I think he missed the tone.

"You have been leaving messages with people I have worked with, roomed with, hell even one guy I met in bar once telling me I'm needed at home for something earth shattering, now tell me what's going on, I have places I need to be."

Good to see you too brother.

"Uncle David is dead. Stabbed during a mugging." I said and beckoned over for two more drinks. The new girl nodded nervously and hurried off.

"Is that all?" Steve replied, slumping his shoulders forward as he leaned on the bar. "You could have left that message with any of the people you called and they would have passed the info on just as well as you telling me. Would have saved me money in plane tickets too." He'd obviously been mulling over different scenarios in his mind as to why I wanted to see him and it looked like this wasn't high on his list.

I could feel my anger rising as my old frustrations rose towards the surface but fought it back as best I could; I needed to talk to Steve not start a fight and watch him walk out of the door.

"Steve, he was family. I know you two didn't see eye to eye about whatever it was that made you leave but please don't tell me that a relative being murdered really doesn't matter to you." The end of the sentence caught a glimpse of the anger I was trying to conceal.

Steve bowed his head slightly as the new drinks arrived and I was again greeted by an odd look from behind the bar. What the hell had everyone told her about me? As we both drank, for a moment there was silence.

"When is the funeral?" Steve started.

"It's already happened, down in Wales. I didn't think you'd want to be involved so I figured I'd let you know afterwards"

Steve looked at me with an expression that was part sadness, part annoyance and part anger. I wasn't really sure which emotion would come out on top but again, I wasn't looking for a fight.

Luckily most of the anger drained away. "Then what is it you need to see me about? Have we just inherited millions of pounds, millions of debts? Come on Anthony it can't simply be that our uncle isn't around anymore and you want a hug."

I took a long slow drink, set the glass down on the bar and tried to settle myself for the story I was about to tell. The mocking tone and confrontational attitude that Steve had brought with him was making me feel that maybe my Uncle had been right about everything he had ever told me. I took a long breath, balled up my anger and frustration, and looked Steve squarely in the eyes and with a mock smile opened with "Are you sitting comfortably? Then I'll begin."

"When I was told that he'd died I didn't know what to do. How do you sort this stuff out? I was contacted by someone from his farm who offered his help – he saw the details on the news or something so gave me a call."

"Why isn't he buried round here? Answering the call of his ancestors?" said Steve without really caring.

"The arrangements were made according to his wishes, service in a specific chapel and then to be buried in a certain place by people he had named in his will. As it turned out I had very little to do with the whole affair –just turn up and watch my family shrink." As soon as I had said it I realised that I was again pushing at Steve but it was a reflex – Steve had walked out of my life and David had stayed. As I looked across towards my brother I realised that we had a very long journey to take if we were going to enter into each others lives again. He looked back and I knew that he was thinking the same thing.

"The service was exactly as you would imagine but was attended by more people than I expected. There were crowds outside of the chapel listening as best they could but they were all keen to pay their respects to the coffin before it left" I described, slowly twisting my glass.

"Well so far you're not really blowing up my skirt with deep and meaningful death bed confessions. He was a crazy old fart from the back of beyond. What was important enough to bring me here?" chided Steve but now with a slightly softer tone to his voice. Maybe he did care?

"Now this is where you come in pal. After the service I was doing the usual hand shaking and thanking everyone for coming when, amongst the locals and farm hands, I was introduced to various different people who weren't from Wales, some Chinese guys who looked like bodyguards round their boss who happened to be a little middle aged lady, a Russian woman (who I really wanted to get to know better), some Americans and an Aussie. They all explained to me that our uncle had been a great man and that he would be sorely missed. Well I got that from the Aussie and the Americans but the others didn't speak a word of English so all I could manage was to stare at them nodding. The thing that got me most puzzled about the whole situation was that they referred to me as the only child and that when they had finished with David they would help me."

"When I filled them in on your sorry tale the mood changed and the farm manager who had done all of the organising, Lloyd something, told me that you really need to pay your respects and that Uncle David's will can only be completed to you, no-one else. No-one would tell me any specifics but they were all very insistent that you attend within two weeks and there was no room for negotiation. He spent the rest of the time in conversation with each of the overseas visitors, looking like he was getting torn a new one for the most part until they each left, and get this, bowing to me on the way out.

"Uncle Dave was a Mason." snorted Steve.

"What?"

"Secret messages passed between people, people who would never come into contact through any normal course of their life. Mason, or some other secret society. Maybe some of the things he used to tell me were part of some weird code. No wonder he thought they were so important. You didn't happen to get any funny handshakes during the day?"

I stared at my brother realising that as I told the story back it did sound a little out there; at least the girl behind the bar wasn't the only one to think I was odd. That said, I don't like being made fun of.

"All you have to do is go down there and pay your respects and collect on his will. Maybe he felt bad that you two didn't get along and he set something up as his way of saying sorry. In any case, one day, two at the most, and you can go back to whatever life you had going on before I interrupted. Just for two days, be my brother, do what needs to be done and then forget all about it."

Steve finished his drink and stood up, stretching his lower back in the process. "It really was good to see you again Anthony, you look well. Maybe one day I'll let you know why David and I didn't get on but for your peace of mind, I'll go and do my duty back in the home land. Jesus, February in Wales, I'm going to freeze out in a random field in the middle of nowhere, no doubt so our uncle can have one last laugh at me. I hope you're happy." The venom in his voice was purely for show. With our uncle gone he could risk coming back here to see me without the weight of their problems. Maybe that meant after almost twenty years I was going to get my brother back.

"I'll let you know how it went when I get back. Speak to you soon" fired back at me as Steve marched across the bar and pushed through the door.

I turned back to the bar and beckoned for another refill but the piercing shatter of glass burst into the quiet murmur of the room before I could get my order placed. That was quickly followed by the screams of the new girl – she really was having a bad day. The other people drinking around me were fast to start shouting and screaming. Glasses were dropped or knocked over and the sounds of smashing rang through the place from all areas. As I turned around to find out what had caused the damage I was confronted by the shattering of not only the glass doors to the bar, but the shattering of my world. I stared towards the source of the terrible sound and fought to focus through the melee of people running for the exit or crowding the doorway.

Propped on what was left of the door frame was the crumpled form of Steve. He had been hurled back through the door he had left less than a minute before but now he was broken and split. The glass had cut into him across the back of his neck and shoulders where he had hit the door but he had also been contorted into an utterly unnatural position. Almost every joint of his body now seemed to be pointing the wrong way. There were no engine sounds of any kind from outside but it looked as if he had been hit by a car doing over a hundred miles an hour. My instinct was to run to him, to give emergency aid, to do something that would keep him alive so we could carry on from where our conversation had finished but as I got closer to him I realised that there was nothing I could do. Aside from the would be impact injuries there were also two huge slashes running from his left shoulder to his stomach which had opened my big brother up down to his rib cage and beyond. I checked for a pulse on his ruined throat more out of reflex and was glad to find none. To feel those injuries would have driven a person mad. There was no air being dragged into his lungs, there were no clouds of breath to indicate life despite the chill of the February night. His stillness had given him an almost model like quality, something from the set of a horror film. I looked up out of the door hoping to see the car that did this leaving the scene in a hurry but was confronted by something very different.

Back from the entrance to the bar stood a man. He stood back away from the lights of the building, utterly enveloped by shadows but I could see his outline. It looked like he was wearing a long coat of some kind; I could see the shape of the material down by his legs but that was all. I stepped toward him, thinking he must have seen something to explain this horror; he would be able to help. He darted away with a movement so fast and fluid that I lost him in the gloom. The one fact I was very sure of was that as he left, he was laughing. The noise didn't sound like anything I had heard before but I could recognise it as a laugh none the less. As I rounded the corner of the building I was still aiming for the sound, I couldn't see a thing through the shadows of the surrounding buildings and low street light but that noise drew me on. I got to the end of the alleyway next to the bar which opened out into the large rear delivery area of the buildings adjacent to the one I had just rushed from, still following that sound. My heart was racing in my chest and I could feel rage building inside me as I slowed towards the centre of the empty loading bay. The laughter continued, but it also continued to move away from me. What I didn't understand was why it was moving straight up.

3

I strained my neck looking up and around hoping to pinpoint where the sound was coming from but the harder I tried to focus, the more elusive it became. Add to that the sound of my own heart now feeling as if it was beating not in my chest but in my ears, I had no real hope of finding him.

I slowly swayed as I scanned the area around and above me but there was nothing. All I could hear was the low hum of road noise and the sound of incoming sirens.

Sirens. My god, Steve.

In the rush to find someone who could explain, who could fill in the blanks, the why and how, I had pushed the horror at the bar to the back of my mind but the sound of the approaching emergency services had reached in and pulled every image and sensation back into sharp focus. I stumbled as I sprinted back to my brother as each fragment of information fell back into place. My tears were streaming by the time I returned to the carnage.

I skidded to a standstill before the demolished entrance to the bar as the headlights of the police and ambulance appeared behind me. I knew what was there but that didn't make it any easier to see.

Two paramedics rushed past me aiming for my brother but their urgency quickly faded as they took in the full details of what lay before them. They both looked around the crowd in the doorway, partly to see if anyone else needed help but also hoping to get some information as to what had taken place. The police were next to arrive. Each took a second to try and comprehend what was presented as their next job, drew themselves together and headed in. They started working their way around the group behind the paramedics – taking stock of what had happened and then started to deal with the situation as they found it. Names and addresses were recorded of the witnesses, proper procedure followed. Through the quiet sobs and heated murmuring, which came from the assembled crowd, I could hear a tone of speculation. The crowd were quite open in their whispered guess work but the Police must have shared the same thoughts. All their questions echoed my own. What had caused the injuries to Steve? Where was the car that had hit him to throw him through the building? What type of weapon had caused the slashes to his chest and abdomen? Why had he been attacked?

As I fell to my knees in front of the activity, I watched on as inch by inch the place started moving from where I had had life experience to becoming part of a group of statistics. Methodically, each of the paramedics and police who were working the site moved from person to person, place to place recording facts, details. The swirl of existence and interaction was being removed. More emergency services started to arrive and the police were starting to speak to everyone who had been present to begin their investigation.

I felt a hand rest gently on my right shoulder as a young police officer leaned over me asking if I was Ok, had I been injured in any way? I shook my head.

"Did you see what happened here?" he asked with real concern in his voice. He had a good bed side manner for someone who looked as if he was at least ten years younger than me. It helped me feel that I wasn't just going to fall to the floor and never move again. In the space of a few days I had lost the only blood relations I had.

"I was in there with my back to the door when whatever happened, happened" I croaked.

"Do you know the name of the man who was attacked?"

"Yes, his name is Steve Johns. He's my brother"

The young officer took in a sharp breath before he could get his business expression in place. We both looked at the paramedics who were slowly putting their equipment away and realised that it had just been made official. Steve was gone.

"I'm very sorry for your loss. I'm afraid we'll need to speak to you regarding the details of the accident so we can try and piece things together," he said robotically as we both stared into the building. I reached as deeply into myself as I could, summoning as much strength as possible so I could stand up. I staggered to my feet and turned to the officer at my right,

"Shall we do this now?" I sighed. Get the interview completed fast then get some rest rather than resting before. Get everything sorted while I was still partly running on adrenaline. As soon as that was gone I wasn't going to want to return to the exact details of this night ever again.

I recounted the full details of the evening to the officer back at the station. A middle aged man of medium height, Officer Pullen had been very matter of fact regarding the information I was giving him. I didn't mean to give it all the full emotional twist of lost family members and fleeting reconciliations but by the look on his face when I had finished I could see that the story had given him a renewed appreciation of the family he had.

He leaned back into his chair and ran both hands through his grey hair as he considered the details now laid out before him.

"So now the inheritance passes to you?" Was his first question, not what I had been expecting it to be!

"I don't know? I hadn't even thought about that" was all I could think to say.

"The man outside the bar that you followed. You couldn't really see him but you could make out that he was wearing a long coat, down to his ankles?"

"Just the shape of him rather than any details but, yes, I could just make out the shape of a long coat around his ankles."

"Can you give us any more information about this person we could use?" Officer Pullen was already several steps ahead in the investigation in his mind. He knew what steps would need to be taken procedurally to be able to identify this mystery man but 'man in long coat' wouldn't really be any use.

I closed my eyes to try and focus, to recall the events from the evening, to clear my view of the past. Hell it worked in films!

"He was stood back out of all of the light so I could barely see him, just his outline really, hence the coat." I opened my eyes and could feel the details slowly slipping as time passes. Soon, as my mind tried to fill in the blanks, if I wasn't careful, I could find myself being confronted by Elvis!

"All I can see is his outline" I repeated, almost pleading with myself to see more. The image hung in my mind as I struggled against it. All that was there was the large black shape.

The really large black shape!

"He was massive!" I exclaimed slamming both hands down onto the desk in front of me. "He must have been over seven feet tall and really broad with it! I couldn't make out any details but unless he was wearing American Football shoulder pads and was stood on a box, his outline was enormous"

This in itself still wasn't the most insightful piece of information but it was something. Officer Pullen looked a little more relaxed – he had something to use – seven foot tall, 300 pound man in coat would be a little more conspicuous.

"But you lost sight of him when you followed him round the building?" There was no leading tone to his voice like you get on TV when they want to imply guilt but I kind of felt it anyway for not being able to catch this person. Pullen must have noticed how I was taking the last comment so did his best to help. He leaned forward and in a very soothing tone "Don't beat yourself up about not catching him, we'll find him". I did feel better. If nothing else I had seen firsthand how the Police were more than just catching the bad guys – another good bed side manner.

Pullen leaned back away from me and returned to his previous tone and demeanour.

"Thank you for your help Mr. Johns." Business as usual. "The investigation will take some time but we will keep you informed when we know more. I am truly sorry for your loss" rolled out of Pullen. It felt very much like he had had to offer his condolences to people on more than one occasion during his career and that he could get the words out without having to think about their meaning. Perk or curse of the job, dependant on your point of view.

"Is there anyone you would like us to contact for you?" was his final question as he stood up to leave the room.

I didn't have any clue where to begin to organise the now billions of things that I would need to do. Steve's funeral, time out of work, the non-collection of Steve's inheritance, any further Police questions which would no doubt need answering, trying to explain to the guys in the bar what had happened.

"Can you call the manager from my Uncle's farm in West Wales please, he will need to know about Steve and he will probably help with the funeral arrangements" was all I could think to say. He was the only person who I knew at this point who could definitely organise what needed to be sorted and I was floundering in the dark.

"What's his name and number?" asked Pullen

Embarrassed, I bowed my head and mumbled "His first name is Lloyd but I never found out his last name. My uncle's farm – it's called..." I fumbled in my pockets for the piece of paper I had written the address down for Steve. He'd told me he knew where he had to go so hadn't needed to take the paper from me, "Gadwyn Ceidwad Y Gwyn."

Officer Pullen looked at me with the usual mix of disbelief and confusion when I told him the name of the farm. The Welsh language is something that my uncle had tried to teach me way back when but he didn't have much success. I was much like Officer Pullen. None of the words looked or sounded right so my grasp was negligible. I could pronounce the words correctly if I heard them spoken – no breaking things down phonetically for me, the mighty academic – but that was as far as things went. Meaning I could pretty much say place names and sound like I knew what I was talking about!

I handed Officer Pullen the piece of paper with the name on it and he half smiled and left the room saying he would get right on it. The sounds of Welsh could confuse the uninitiated at fifty paces and I think Officer Pullen was glad he didn't have to try and repeat what I had told him and that he would now only have to spell it. Uncle David had always delighted in making anyone and everyone he could, struggle with the Welsh language. When asked about Wales he would regale people in the Bar with stories of timeless history and the connection to his 'real' home. He would then 'teach' people small Welsh phrases and sayings so if they ever found themselves in need of it, they would get by. This included telling a young couple that if they were ever lost they should ask any passerby to direct them to the nearest pub or hostelry as "all Welsh villages are based around the pub you know, that and the Chapel". In reality he taught them to say "I'm a little teapot, short and stout!" Genius!

That small memory made a flicker of warmth run through me but in an instant, it was gone again as the icy gloom of present reality returned.

After what felt like at least an hour, but was closer to fifteen minutes, Officer Pullen returned to the small interview room and slowly sat down in the chair opposite from me again. The professionally concerned expression he had been wearing before leaving had now been mixed with a new shade of puzzlement.

"Did you get through?" I asked partly as a courtesy but also out of the slow growing fear which was settling into my stomach at the reality of the situation, I needed Lloyd whoever's help to get through the next few weeks.

"Lloyd Jones - probably should have guessed that! – has said that he is on his way here as fast as he can so he will be able to give you any help you need." started Pullen. "He also asked if you had been hurt at all, to which he was very pleased when I told him that you hadn't but he also wanted to know if your Uncle and Brother died the same way. When I told him that they hadn't, he wouldn't believe me, asking over and over again about the details of their deaths".

For a long minute, we sat in the room in silence. I thought about the violent ends which had claimed my family and the apparently incredibly morbid person who was heading my way to help, Pullen hoping he could call this a night. I went first.

"If that is everything Officer Pullen, can I go? It would appear I am expecting a visitor."

"We're all done here tonight Mr. Johns. Again I am very sorry for your loss and can assure you that we will do all we can". More platitudes which sounded like they were on automatic, how many times had Pullen had to do this? As I moved to leave the room, and the station, Pullen held out his hand and presented me with his business card.

"If you think of anything else which may be of use, give me a call"

I took the card, pushed it into my wallet and offered him my thanks but I really didn't feel that I was going to be of any more use. I barely felt like I'd been of use up to now. All that was left for me was to get home and prepare the sofa bed for my guest tomorrow. It really wasn't fair of course, but right now the only thought going through my mind was – I really need a drink.

4

A restless night led into the following day. The adrenaline that had been coursing through my system the previous night had evaporated but left behind a deep hollow feeling and an almost overwhelming numbness. I was now finding every small movement to be more strenuous, more draining. What a come down. My mind played the events of the previous evening over and over, my mental finger held firmly down on the repeat button. It felt that both my mind and my body were fighting against me, waging a covert war to disrupt everything I was.

"Come on Anthony, you're not going to get any rest. Let's just get the day going" I sighed as I finally admitted defeat to myself. I pushed back the covers and forced myself up. I felt dizzy, thick headed and a little sick. Lack of sleep can have all manner of effects on you but at least I wasn't hallucinating.

The clock next to my bed pulsed out seven o'clock. I had got back to my flat at gone midnight and by the time I felt slightly able to get to sleep it had been close to three. So four hours of bad sleep was going to have to do.

Slowly standing up seemed to make the feelings of exhaustion grow but I still had enough energy to jump when someone started banging on my front door. My door shook under the weight of whoever was knocking and there seemed to be real urgency building the longer it went on.

I stumbled towards the noise and pulled the door open to be confronted by Lloyd Jones from the farm. Jones, I must remember Jones.

"Morning Bach. Just got up have you?" boomed Lloyd in a strong Welsh accent. My head boomed back just a little bit.

"Just coming to. Come in." I offered, rubbing my eyes. Lloyd walked in and started to look around the flat taking in all of the details as they presented themselves to him. Lloyd looked like he had been cast in the same mould as my uncle, tall and powerfully built. He had been managing the farm so had obviously had a demanding physical job so whereas my uncle looked big and well built, Lloyd was that plus about twenty percent. He had wild red hair and a full bushy beard. The sleeves of his sweater and shirt were rolled up over his elbows to complete the quintessential farmer 'look'. It all added up to be quite intimidating up close, I am a big guy but Lloyd was very noticeably bigger.

"Thanks for coming Lloyd, I didn't know who else to speak to about any of this and you were going to need to know about Steve anyway."

"Don't worry, I'd known Dai for years so was happy to help" said Lloyd as he slapped me on the back, a little too hard.

The fugg in my mind was starting to clear a little and I began to get a little more aware of what was going on. "You didn't waste any time getting here did you? Who is going to look after the farm while you're here?"

"Don't worry. I made a few calls last night and the place will be in good hands until I get back. As soon as that was done I got here as fast as I could, it's my job to look after you" he replied with yet another over enthusiastic slap.

"Do you need a hand with any baggage?" I asked, moving a little further out of his reach.

"No, this is it" he gestured to the small rucksack on his back and set it down next to the sofa which would later become his bed. He was carrying his jacket so draped it lazily over the arm of the sofa and sat down. He scanned the main room of the flat that he was sat in and took in all of the details. My flat was populated with striking lines, bold colours and contempory shapes. All of the furniture had been lifted from the pages of an IKEA catalogue and probably looked a little different to what Lloyd had been used to. There were also several large posters framed and hung at strategic locations around the room. Growing up, the chance to disappear into a film for a short period offered me the chance not to be myself amongst the drudgery of school and the loneliness of not having my parents around. As such, my favourites now looked out into my home as a solid comfort against all the horrors of the world. You see, Star Wars works on so many levels.

I leaned against the frame of the door into the kitchen and watched Lloyds eyes pass from object to object taking in all of the detail. He looked uncannily like my uncle as he sat there, examining the way I had chosen to decorate my home. When I had moved into my own place, my Uncle had always told me that my taste in decoration hadn't quite matched his. He had moved into a small flat when I moved out, filling it with all manor of old knick-knacks and objects. After his death, I had decided to keep the place and clear it in my own time, still wanting to clutch at the vestiges of my family. With that thought came the flooding reminder of why Lloyd was here. Lloyd must have noticed the extra weight getting loaded back onto me and was quickly to his feet again.

"I'm sorry for Dai and Steve. You shouldn't have to watch family go like that". He wrapped an arm around my shoulder and gently shook me as way of comfort. It kind of worked.

"Now let's get a cuppa going and we can give your brother the send off he deserved" he said and headed for my kitchen.

Lloyd seemed content to do the honours in there so I got myself ready for the day, showered and dressed in what I thought would be the appropriate attire for spending the day meeting and greeting undertakers and the like. When I re-emerged from the bedroom Lloyd was sat at my sofa with a mug in his left hand, a phone to his ear and he was scribbling wildly into a small notebook with his right.

"Thank you very much, your help is greatly appreciated" and down went the phone. He looked up at me with half a smile on his face. "Everything is taken care of. I've got a date for the funeral and I've e-mailed all of the people that you tried contacting regarding Steve's whereabouts so they could come if they wanted to". Lloyd leaned back in the chair and took a deep swig from the mug and set it down on my window sill and looked back at me.

"You look very smart but we don't need to go to any funeral homes now" he chided.

"You've sorted everything? Are there places open this early? How did you know who I had been contacting to find Steve?" all tumbled out at once.

"You left your computer and e-mail account open so I sent a blanket e-mail to everyone you have over the last week. I have a friend or two around here and one was able to pull strings and grease wheels, so time saved and funeral booked."

"You know people in London?" was all I could muster. He'd taken the fastest route available to him to help minimize the stress to me. Very impressive really. The budding anger I had been starting to feel was quickly draining away.

"Yes I do. The small town farmer who probably never even saw an aeroplane except on the news has friends outside Wales" snorted Lloyd sarcastically but with a big smile on his face. It made me smile too.

"Come on now Anthony, tell me about your brother. Dai didn't even tell me there were two of you." Started Lloyd and he beckoned me to sit next to him.

"I barely knew him. He left home almost twenty years ago after arguing with Uncle David and that was the last I saw of him until last night." I bowed my head thinking about all the things about my brother that I would now never know. "We had the first step to reconciliation and then he gets ripped to pieces in a massive hit and run and the only person who may have seen anything ran off before I could speak to him."

"Hit and run" Lloyd thought out loud. "Not the way I'd choose to go. Not mugged like your uncle but certainly bad enough."

"I never expected there to be so much damage" I continued, feeling my eyes starting to well up. "What kind of vehicle could cut a man almost in half from shoulder to stomach and what kind of person could stand by and watch the whole thing happen and then just leave him there?" The tears had started to flow freely now and the return to the image from the previous night was threatening to really open the flood gates to all the sadness and anger I was feeling.

Lloyd had stiffened slightly next to me at the details of the accident but he was now focussed intently on me. "Someone stood and watched it happen?"

"Yeah, a really big guy in..." I was cut off before I could finish the sentence.

"In a really long coat that went down to his ankles" Lloyd finished for me. I stared at him in disbelief. "How did you know that?" Now I was really starting to feel lost. Images of the character from the mugging drifted around the edges of my mind and I started to run through the different ways I was going to have my pay back with him. Add to this the thought that he had had something to do

27

with the death of my brother as well and all I seemed to have left was a very deeply set hatred.

"Dai's mugging. It was in the paper. One person said that they saw a big bloke in a long coat hanging around there too. Stood out cause he was so big" explained Lloyd but now he was starting to pace the room, slowly rubbing his temples.

"Anthony, you've got to see your family off in Wales like your uncle wanted. The job would have been for Steve but now it will have to fall to you. We can be down and back in a couple of days and you will be able to move on with your life". Lloyd stopped and put both his hands on my shoulders.

"I know this isn't what you want to hear Anthony but we need to complete your uncle's requests quickly. Will you come with me now?"

"Now? I thought there was at least a week left on the clock you gave to Steve". I was really starting to get confused by what I was being told.

"This whole situation is going to weigh you down unless you complete all that is asked of you. Why drag it out when you can get everything tied up quickly" Lloyd nudged me again. It made sense, pull the sticking plaster off quickly rather than slowly and the results speak for themselves. That said, it did feel like Lloyd wanted me to go and get this done sooner rather than later, and he was starting to push a little harder. I didn't have the will to fight it. I still felt dizzy and sick and I just wanted this whole situation to be over. Everything hurt too much.

"Fine, let's go and complete Uncle David's Will so I can get back here to bury my brother" and the last of the fight went out of me. I'd lost everyone.

"Fantastic. Get your stuff together and we'll get going" and Lloyd slapped me on the back again, still just a little too hard.

I shuffled over to the bedroom to get my bags packed and started to think about the funerals. My uncle had what seemed like the population of several villages at his and it was a real possibility that my brother would only have a hand full of people. That thought was still in my mind when I looked back into the living room to see Lloyd looking out of each window in turn quickly and muttering to himself, marching up and down the flat trying to see everything at once. What the hell was he doing, keeping watch?

"You OK Lloyd? You look a little on edge" I probed into the living room. Lloyd stopped still and turned to face me.

"Just looking for the taxi. I just called them and they said they would be here in five minutes" was the reply but Lloyd didn't look at all comfortable. I lifted my now bulging bags and slowly walked out of the bedroom. Lloyd was still pacing the room but before I could ask what was up I heard the sound of a car's horn from below the front window.

Lloyd let out a deep breath.

"The car's here."

We walked down the stairs towards the front of the building, Lloyd striding out in front with me trying to keep up behind. I really was starting to feel like the lost little boy. We walked through the front door towards the taxi. It had pulled up directly outside the doors to the building and the driver had the boot open ready for our bags. Lloyd stepped forward to the driver, shook his hand and gave him a solemn nod.

"Thanks for getting here so fast. Have you contacted everyone yet?" Lloyd almost whispered.

"Don't worry. Get in and we can get moving. I've called ahead already so things will be getting under way" responded the driver and started to load the bags into the car. He was around fifty years of age with white hair tied back into a long ponytail. He was dressed casually in jeans and a white shirt but he carried himself with a confidence, almost seriousness. He was roughly the same size as me, which in normal company would make him well above average but next to Lloyd he looked tiny. Under his shirt you could see the shape of his musculature. I stared at Lloyd still feeling really sick and my head was starting to spin a little more than it had been.

"You two know each other? What's going on Lloyd? I feel like I only know about twenty percent of what is going on around me and everyone else is in on the joke. What's happening?" I could feel the nausea getting worse and my head with it but my anger was starting to build as well.

"Trust me" started Lloyd, "there are bigger things going on around you, of which you will soon be made fully aware. My job was to look after you and get you back home quickly. I know Mike, here." he pointed to the driver of the taxi who nodded in my direction "Like I said before, he helped me pull strings and grease wheels. He's a good friend of mine and of your uncle's before he died."

My head was really turning now and the nausea was building to a level where I thought I wouldn't be able to control myself much more. Add to this the new information from Lloyd and I felt like I was trying to climb a mountain of treacle – I really was flailing in the dark.

"Everything that we are doing now is in your best interests Bach and you are perfectly safe with us. Please get in the car and we can get going." This time there was a level of pleading in Lloyd's voice. He *needed* me to go with him. As I stood there looking at the two men either side of the car my sickness and dizziness rapidly increased and then faded to a pin point of heat at the back of my head. I had already been swaying due to ill feeling but the sudden change caused me to stagger and fall forwards. The sensation in my head wasn't painful, I was just aware of it pushing into the back of my skull. With the nausea and dizziness now removed, I was able to really feel the anger which had been building. Flashes of red started to pulse through me and I could feel an incredible rage growing.

Lloyd and Mike rushed to my side as I crouched on the floor next to the car. They slowly helped me to my feet and started to ask if I was OK but I could barely hear them. Their voices were muffled as if someone had taken all the edges from the sounds. It wasn't just their voices either. My hearing was now totally muffled apart from the low laughter coming from across the forecourt to my flats. It was only then that I realised that my building anger wasn't aimed at the two men with me but at the man standing in the shadows of the large trees which lined the property, less than fifty yards away. The very large man. In a long coat.

Despite clinging to the shadows at the edge of the forecourt, I was now able to make out more detail and my previous estimate of seven feet tall had been off by at least a foot on the small side and he had the width to go with it! In the daylight, he was monstrous. Lloyd and Mike both followed my gaze when I failed to respond to them and took in the detail of our visitor. From what I could make out, he was wearing a battered old leather coat with long ribs down its length and done up to his throat, large work boots and a black wide brimmed hat. He hadn't looked up completely so I could only just see the lower part of his face but that was enough to make me feel nervous, even through the rage. A wide mouth was spread thinly into a wicked smile. He looked every inch the gunslinger. I couldn't make out any more details from the shadows but I knew this man was the one who had killed Steve. I could feel it but not in the usual nebulous way people say they can be aware of things, I could really feel the sensation in my chest running up through the back of my head to crystallize as knowledge. There was no hit and run, he had done the deed and stood by to watch the aftermath unfold.

Either side of me I could feel an increased tension from both men and when I glanced quickly to each of them I could see them slowly coiling into a ready position and muttering under their breath in, what I assumed to be, Welsh. Mike slowly shuffled in front of me still muttering to himself and started to raise his hands up to either side of him at shoulder height. It was then I started to feel that it was more than tension building between us. It started as a buzzing sound in my mind and began to build as a weight, expanding through my consciousness. The temperature around us had increased slightly when I noticed the glow emanating from Mike's hands. The dull white light was only barely visible but it was growing brighter by the second. I risked a glance towards Lloyd to see him doing exactly the same but I was able to see his face whereas Mike was in front of me. Lloyd's eyes had been drained of their entire colour, leaving behind only grey spheres, not even the white which would have at least been a reference point for what should be there remained. His hair was being wildly ruffled by an unseen force and his brow was furrowed deep. His clenched fists had started to randomly spit out small electrical lances, as if whatever was in his hands was fighting to be free of his grasp. I looked back to Mike to see the same happening. The temperature around us continued to grow and I was still aware of the man opposite us, unmoved by the events ahead of him but he wasn't smiling any more.

He took one large stride forward and moved away from the cover afforded him by the trees and I was now able to see more of him. He lifted one hand and slowly removed his hat and let it drop to the floor. The wide mouth was topped by a face which looked as if it had been made from animal hide. Rough, dark, leathery skin which looked like it had been witness to a great many things through the ages, covered his completely bald head. He appeared to be in his late sixties by the condition of his skin but his posture and movement suggested that he was much younger. He looked across at us and focussed on us with almost reptilian eyes, darting between each of us but always returning to me.

The heat around me rose and the mumbling from Lloyd and Mike started to grow louder. The pressure through me grew again and as I locked gazes with our opponent he smiled again, revealing lines of razor sharp, pointed teeth. I could feel the sneer come from him as he took another step towards us.

Then, without warning, Lloyd yelled a deep and primal singular word battle cry and slammed both his hands together in front of him. There was a massive thunder clap as whatever force Lloyd had drawn to him was expelled outward in all directions, accompanied by a blinding white light. I was totally unprepared for what he had done and the force of it knocked me back off my feet and I landed on my back on the floor next to Mike. He hadn't let go of his, whatever was building up, but looked like he was primed to whenever he needed to.

The explosion Lloyd let out had been aimed at the man opposite from us. From my position on the floor I tried to focus in his direction to see what had happened to him. I expected to see him looking much the same way he had left Steve. I wanted him to have been dealt a violent and bloody end but there was nothing opposite us aside from fallen branches and ruffled bushes. He was nowhere to be seen.

"Are you OK?" called Lloyd in a worried tone as he continued to scan the area while reaching forward with his arms and twisting each fist in turn. Mike didn't answer and kept muttering to himself but his head was moving as if taking in every inch of the surrounding area.

"I'm fine" I coughed from the floor and began to pull my senses together. I pulled my legs underneath me and began to stand up; thinking now would be a great time for some real answers.

It was then that the attack rushed towards me.

I hadn't seen or heard anything. There had been no clues that I was in trouble but I 'felt' it again. I let my legs drop from under me and fell back to the floor. The giant reappeared, standing over me as if he had stopped time to position himself before restarting events. He stood above me showing his apparel to not be a coat but what looked like a long cape fastened at the neck by two bony hooks. As I fell, I had avoided his swinging right hand which had been aimed at where my chest would have been had I continued to move upwards. The razor sharp nails on his hand shone brightly as he wound up to deliver the killing blow.

But they weren't just nails, they were too big. They were claws.

I reflexively covered my face with both my arms as some kind of feeble last defence. Before my death came down, Mike flew at our assailant and caught his arm at the wrist. The white fire in his right hand started to burn through the flesh of our assailant and Mike stopped his hand dead. The giant turned towards Mike and screeched at him, a high pitched noise of both violence and the pain he was feeling. Mike didn't stop there and with a wild swing of his free arm he slammed all of the remaining power coursing through him into the chest of the behemoth stood over me. The giant crashed up and away from us and into the wall of the building one hundred yards from where we were stood. His shape fell to the ground behind the tree line.

I looked up at Mike who was breathing heavily and mumbling again. I needed to understand what was happening, but also needed to understand why everyone else already did. I thought of the girl in the bar. If my previous story had made her wary of me, thinking I was nuts, this would have had me locked up in a padded cell. Maybe she was right.

"Will someone please tell me..." I began but was cut short by Lloyd.

"Keep your eyes open, he's coming back." How could he, he'd been thrown one hundred yards into a brick wall. He must be pate by now. People don't get up from that and carry on regardless. That said, I found myself looking around as much as I could. The heat at the back of my head, which had eased after the giant was thrown away, was slowly returning. Mike looked everywhere, again with his arms outstretched, recharging but Lloyd was stood stock still with both his arms out in front of him at chest height. Blue fire was creeping up his arms. Before I could make any further comment about any of the situation the trees directly ahead of us burst apart and the giant flew directly at us, his cape spread out wide so it almost looked like a set of wings.

Lloyd blurred into motion. He leapt forward with inhuman speed and connected with the on rushing giant, hitting both his hands squarely into his victim's chest. For a split second they both hung motionless in mid air, before the giant was engulfed in the blue flame Lloyd had carried and vanished. Lloyd landed with some grace but still fell hard.

"We've got to leave right now" yelled Mike as he headed for the driver's door to the car.

"He'll be able to get back from where I just sent him but it's going to take him some time. We need to get to safety as fast as we can" added Lloyd as he got to his feet.

Lloyd stood over me and reached out a large hand, "You coming with us now?"

I took his hand, got to my feet and headed towards the car. Wherever I was going, they thought it was safer than here with that guy running around. I wasn't sure about what was going on but it seemed that Lloyd and Mike had the answers.

5

Lloyd held the back door open for me while Mike eased into the driver's seat, then climbed into the passenger seat and the car started moving almost before he had closed the door. Mike was pushing the car fast enough for me to recognise that we were in a hurry to be away from my place but also just the right side of that magical line which the authorities seem to use when deciding if they should pull you over.

I leaned back into the seat and started to notice the supreme level of tension which had wrapped its way around my body. A near fatal encounter and the light show from the people in the car with me will do that to you! I was now so far away from anything that I could comprehend that every single part of me was ceasing up in an attempt to desperately cling to the facts of reality as I knew them. My body was taking over where my mind was falling short.

Both Mike and Lloyd were looking around nervously as we travelled along, checking everywhere at once while putting as much distance between us and the events which had unfolded behind us. They were both breathing hard but were trying to appear that all was well. Whatever had taken place back there had been a massive effort for the both of them and now we were running from it.

"Lloyd, Mike" I started and leaned forward to rest my arms on the shoulders of both front seats, my head poking between, allowing me to hold an almost normal conversation with the two men. "I want to know, now, what was that? What's going on?" Lloyd and Mike exchanged a sideways glance, each had deep lines of worry etching their faces and I could see that Lloyd now looked as if he had aged roughly ten years in the last half an hour. With a small sigh of resignation Lloyd turned slightly further to look more directly at me.

"This is a very delicate situation. I don't want to say the wrong thing." My head was slowly starting to spin again and with it was coming the sick feeling again. The adrenaline must be wearing off.

"Give me some information." I shouted, louder than I intended or thought was possible. This startled both driver and passenger and looked like it was having the desired effect.

"You're important to a lot of people, special" began Lloyd. I liked the sound of that even if it still meant absolutely nothing. "But you are also an enemy to a great many others" he finished. Not too keen on that bit.

"So you two think I'm important and our friend, the clawed giant back there isn't that keen. Well now we have a place to begin". I finally had a point on the map. The spinning in my head grew again. "Why am I important and where are we going?" I repeated for what felt like the thousandth time.

"We're taking you home" said Lloyd in an almost reverential tone. "You are about to start a very important journey and we need to get you back to Wales as quickly as we can so things can begin" he finished.

So far I had been given cryptic responses and half answers and despite feeling that I was starting to scrape back the debris covering the facts, there was still a massive part of the information which was missing. My head continued to spin. I needed to be more direct.

"What was the fireworks display you two put on all about? What were you actually doing?" Lloyd didn't hesitate this time. He turned towards me and without pause simply stated "Magic is real Bach". He smiled slightly and turned towards the front again.

"What?" Now they were making fun of me, surely. After a pause, Lloyd turned back to me and started to explain further.

"Magic is real. What you saw us do was defend you against an attack which could have killed you by using a very ancient skill. Mike and I are both *able* when it comes to magical ability, Mike a little more so, but that is all we are – able" This last piece was delivered by a darkened expression rather than the slight smile he had when he started. If he'd intended to make me feel nervous it had worked.

"We had to get away quickly before the fight started again. We only have a small supply of magical energy available to us and each time we use it, it runs down. We need to have time to re-charge" explained Lloyd.

"Magic? How?" was the only place to begin.

"We are all a part of something much greater than ourselves, something which has been in motion for thousands of years. Families have passed on gifts to their children for generations and still do today. We were given some magical power but with the responsibility of carrying out certain tasks so those above us in return. Our responsibilities are things we take very seriously and has been the case for years." Lloyd paused, almost allowing me time to take all the information in and decide what to do next.

"You have a part to play Anthony which is why we are moving so quickly to get you home" added Mike. My head continued to spin wildly and the increase in information was doing nothing to slow it down.

"You two are magical odd job men and your boss wants to see me?" I think I had managed to boil it all down. "In the last week or so I have the only family I knew existed killed in a mugging, I bury him in Wales, get told my estranged brother needs to collect on Uncle David's will in person, speak to my brother for the first time in twenty years, see him get killed by the gunslinger Terminator, get attacked by said gunslinger Terminator myself and then get told that Magic is real." The anger had grown during my overview and was now boiling.

"Do you two really expect me to believe all this?" I asked them both in a low, whispered tone. Red flashes were crossing my sight as I continued to seethe.

"I know this will sound like absolute nonsense but please believe me" replied Lloyd without turning to face me. The anger built, as did the constant spinning in my mind making new waves of nausea flood over me. I started to reflexively grip tightly onto the seats in front of me as I began to shake. I couldn't believe them. They were turning my world to nothing. I was now totally alone in the world and I was being mocked by two old men. The red flashes grew thicker, grew faster, in intensity as my rational mind gave way to the anger searing through me. Every inch of my vision turned a deep blood red, the spinning in my mind built and built and built until it wound itself in to a singular point and I roared forward a cry of all of the frustration and rage in me. I gripped tightly to each of the chairs as I did and poured out every inch of me without thought, care or calculation. I had given in to my animal emotions and discarded reason.

Before all of the energy had left me and I collapsed onto the back seat unconscious, I caught a glimpse of Lloyd's expression. He had been terrified of what I had been doing. He had been gripped by utter terror at the person in the back of his car and he had been powerless to stop me.

When I came to the car was stationary and Lloyd and Mike were nowhere to be seen. I blinked my eyes to try to clear my mind but I felt mentally jumbled. The spinning was still there, less than before but I was struggling to piece together what had happened leading up to my outburst. I felt a residual anger after the conversation I had had with the others but that was being rapidly overtaken by a deep feeling of embarrassment. This whole chain of events was nonsense but whatever was going on, I shouldn't go around screaming at people. I reached out my left arm to grip the seat in front of me so I could lift myself up into a sitting position. My head gave an extra twist of disagreement as I did. As I sat upright I could now see the new damage to the inside of the car. There were now huge swathes of the seats missing on the shoulders in the centre of the car, both the passenger and drivers seats had been forced up and out towards the sides of the car and there was the smell of burnt plastic hanging in the air. As I surveyed the damage I noticed the missing pieces of the front seats were in the back with me, one on the seat to my right, the other on the floor behind the passenger seat. What the hell had happened?

While I sat there lost, I noticed Lloyd and Mike returning to the car. I climbed out into the grey, damp day to meet them, needing to apologise for going off the deep end but also to find out what had happened to the car.

"Welcome back" grinned Lloyd as they approached the car. They both looked contented and relaxed. That made even less sense.

"I'm sorry for going off on one earlier. This whole situation has spun me round completely and I don't know where I am anymore." I had thought I needed to build bridges with them but they were both smiling and relaxed.

"Don't worry Bach" started Lloyd. "You gave us quite a scare for a second but you burnt out quickly. You'll learn the control, just takes time, that's all".

"*I* did that in the car?"

"You're a strong lad Anthony and you used your anger as a fuel source." explained Mike with a smile. "Seems you could tap into that easily and there seemed to be quite a bit there. You learn to aim that and you'll be very interesting."

"You guys seem reasonably calm for people who saw me mangle a car they were in" I pointed out. Neither man was carrying any apprehension. If anything, they looked as if all of the previous worry which they had been carrying with them had melted away.

"Anthony. We are aware of a great deal more which is going on than you are. We have seen things like this before bach so relax, everything is under control" Lloyd reassured me with what seemed to be a habit of his, the just too hard slap on the back.

"Under control? Will you please stop talking in circles and get to the point about what's going on? What did I do to the car?" This whole situation was still marching through the foothills of insane land and I was being made to feel like *I* was the one being stupid.

Both Lloyd and Mike could see that I was getting wound up. The expressions on their faces changed and I could see the apparent smugness drain away."Please understand that this is reasonably familiar territory for us. We've only got your best interests at heart and we will not stand by and let anything bad happen to you." Mike looked sincere as he talked to me.

"You were in more danger in London than now. We're here to look after you bach" said Lloyd adding to what Mike had said. "Don't worry though, we're almost home."

"This is ridiculous guys. I feel rough as hell and as you may be aware, I'm not having the best of times of things at the moment. Answers. Come on." Both of them seemed to be masters of evasion.

"We can't tell you everything bach. We've probably told you too much already. Please trust us that we've only got your best interests at heart" Lloyd explained and I could see the desperation was starting to creep towards the surface. The desperation in his voice was very disarming and his pleading made the frustration I was feeling, ebb.

I let out a deep sigh and let my shoulders sag as I relaxed my stance. The relaxation triggered a slight smile and he reiterated, "Like I said, we're almost home."

I looked around but didn't recognise where we were. It was a relatively modest sized car park on a motorway service station. I could hear the sound of the passing traffic in the distance and could smell a great deal of car fumes and fuel. There weren't many other cars around us.

"Where are we?" I asked, still looking for clues.

"Bridgend services"

"Bridgend? We're in Wales already? We were still in London when I lost it. I've been unconscious for three hours?" I had expected to have at least one cold shoulder from them so their accepting humour knocked me off balance again. Every time I got to some level of control on what was going on around me, a new piece of the puzzle appeared and I slipped back down the slippery slope I was climbing.

"Look fellas, I really need to have the whole story. Will you please let me in on my life?"

My two wards looked at me with an expression halfway between amusement and resignation.

"We can't tell you everything, we don't have all the info but we also aren't allowed to do the telling" was all Lloyd said in reply but I was somehow sure that he was telling the absolute truth and that he probably shouldn't have said as much as he had.

"So when we get to where we're going and I meet up with the people who can tell me I'll be sure to point out the real lack of information you have been." I said with a slight hint of a smile. Lloyd grinned back and I felt the ever present spinning in my brain drop a little.

"Come on then boys, let's get going again. We're almost home," boomed Lloyd and again slapped me on the back a little too hard. "We only stopped so you would be awake when we actually got you back. I don't think the rest would like to see the new powerhouse turn up out cold." We all climbed into the car and Mike turned back onto the M4 West.

"How far have we got to go?" I asked from the back of the car, still looking at the damage that I had apparently done to the car.

"About twenty miles. We're taking you to the hub of everything in Wales, everything in Britain really. Welcome to Neath." Replied Mike with a touch of pride in his voice.

I sat back and pondered.

"Neath? What's in Neath?"

As the car slowed towards the turn off we needed, the weather had turned from a steady fine rain to a full blown storm. Sheets of rain lashed down from what seemed like every direction, given extra impetus by the slowly raising wind. The spray from the road combined with the water from above and the very low lying grey clouds meant that visibility was dramatically reduced and our field of vision was reduced to barely more than the width of the motorway in every direction. Just the greeting I had been hoping for.

The journey continued in silence as we turned towards the town. Neath is a strong little town. It is very near Port Talbot which has been a large commercial port for years and years. Neath has a history of workers staffing the ship yards, the port, mines, the steelworks and many other industrial areas. All those years of very physical people working in and around the area has ingrained a feeling of raw strength into the whole environment. Or so Uncle David had led me to believe, I had never been here before but you listen to your family don't you?

The Neath rugby team had featured heavily in the discussions my uncle and I had had in the past. He had regularly told me stories of watching matches when Neath had simply strong armed anyone they came up against. The teams were famed for their strength. David had said the ground was a fortress, the supporters being so close to the pitch that teams almost felt like they were on top of them.

But things have a habit of changing. The rugby team had maintained a decent level but as time had passed, industry had changed and the forms of heavy labour started to reduce. As economics grew and changed it altered the make-up of areas all over the country and my uncle had told me stories of how large swathes of Wales were now practically derelict as the work had gone. Industry had been pulled out but the scars could be seen everywhere. Uncle David had been very clear on how physicality was wound tightly into the population despite the changes to the economic situation of the country.

It all added up to Neath having that feeling of absolute strength. To me, this town had been built up to be the place where all the strongest people in Wales came from. My Uncle had muttered to everyone who would listen to him, late at night in the bar, when everyone had had far too much to drink, that he had come from a place of ancient strength and power. I was expecting to see every person who walked past the car looking like a professional bodybuilder.

As we drew nearer to the town I was struck by the small scale of the place. There were no large expanses of buildings. Large areas of housing could just be seen on either side of the valley but that was it. For a town that was described by my driver as being *the hub of everything in Wales*" it was pretty underwhelming so far! The journey continued down the link road and I could see areas of old industry crouching down by the river and leaning against each other as shelter against the rain. This wasn't the hub I had expected.

As I stared out of the car feeling quite disappointed at the view which greeted me, Lloyd called out over his right shoulder without turning round,

"You can't really see much at the moment, bloody weather, but on the left here is the old Abbey. You'll feel better when you meet everyone there tomorrow."

I looked out of the window and strained my eyes and my concentration to try and pick out any detail I could but I couldn't make out anything past the edge of the road. Welcome to Wales.

The journey continued at the same steady pace as we headed further into the low cloud and mist. The visibility occasionally improved in patches but the sheeting rain was quick to draw the veil back over us at every opportunity. I slowly leaned back into the back seat of the car and gave up on trying to see through the murk and find any detail of the area we were moving into. My head was still spinning with wild abandon. The whole journey, well, the parts I had seen anyway, had been a real struggle focusing on anything. As we had been travelling my body had slowly started to develop its own set of distractions to work alongside my head. Both of my hands had seized up completely, my arms, chest and shoulders were cramping at every possible site and my throat felt like I had been eating the stones from a particularly warm sauna. Mike nudged Lloyd and gestured towards me.

"You alright back there boy?" Lloyd asked as he turned himself round to face me. Obviously, my discomfort was quite apparent.

"I feel like I have been training too hard, every muscle in my body is cramping and my head is spinning. Must be the stress of the last few days coming out" was my scientific response.

"Aye, something like that" replied Lloyd with an expression on his face that let me know I was probably miles from the real reason and he turned back to face the front. At least he felt comforted by my appearance. My head spun some more and I continued to feel like the dogs favourite chew toy.

We eventually pulled off the link road and started to move through residential streets. All the roads were lined with terraces of solid looking, stone fronted homes. None were new builds but rows and rows of Victorian homes. They had been built when the industry in the area grew wildly and the population had kept pace. Looking out at the small roads and the narrow lanes that seemed to make up every area we passed through I could only feel the stark differences between this place and my home in London. My home hadn't been in the centre of the buzzing metropolis which was England's capital but at least there was a life to the place. You could see people at any time of the day or night. You were always around people and there was always a bustle to the place, everyone going somewhere or doing something. This place had so far looked like there was only a skeleton population at best and everyone was probably in bed by eight o'clock. In London there had been a life to the whole area, here there was barely a human presence at all.

I looked out of the car feeling a steady gloom gathering in my ever spinning mind. The 'hub of everything' was barely a village in terms I could understand. I let out a sigh and sank back into the seat. What was I doing? I was sat in a car being driven through a small collection of buildings in the middle of nowhere by two people who knew more than they were telling me about the whole situation and my head had been rolling wildly since they had turned up. I looked out of the window at the small buildings and roads as they passed by and started to feel that I was being pulled along by a very powerful river without any hope of dragging myself out.

The journey continued and the view of the area we travelled through remained as small and contained as it had since we pulled off the main link road. We travelled through ever shrinking roads out into the middle of the rural countryside. Neath was a small place but we seemed to be moving into even more remote areas. Fields rolled by and civilization melted away.

"Here we are" called Lloyd from the passenger seat as the car slowly turned off the road and into a single lane track. I looked up and forward, suddenly feeling a level of anticipation building in my stomach. I had expected the track we had turned onto to be an ongoing smaller road leading to a run down farm or some other local building halfway up a mountain but the image that greeted me was the last thing I had in mind. The road twisted and turned slowly through a very dense wood, the trees leaned into the road as if investigating the pathway and any vehicles which travelled along it. Some of the branches flicked against the car as we passed, really giving the feeling of the wood closing in on us as a protection for whatever was on the other side. The further we travelled; the more the trees seemed to form tighter and tighter ranks, reducing the amount of space to let in any available sunlight. The atmosphere on the outside of the wood had been overcast and dull with a thick layer of impenetrable low cloud covering everything in and around what felt like the whole county, inside the twisting and turning tunnel of trees, the limited sunlight was rapidly receding almost to the point that our journey felt as if it had taken us into a place of perpetual night. Mike had turned the headlights on which only served to draw more attention to the inherent spookiness of the place.

"Where are we?" was all I could think to ask. To be told we had arrived at our destination only to disappear into the haunted woods sent me off worrying again. With what I had seen so far today, I had images of being dragged into a clearing as a group of naked bearded fools leapt around a large fire and chanted nonsense. My God, they were going to put me in a huge wicker statue and burn me!

Before either Lloyd or Mike could answer, the wood surrounding the road opened up in front of us into a vast clearing with a large stately looking home set in the centre. As we pulled further away from the tree line I was more clearly aware of the vastness of the space ahead and around me. The fog was almost completely clear within the wooded clearing so I was able to see almost all of the detail of the dimensions of the space. The trees were massive in height. As we had entered the wood the tree line had been made up of only moderately sized trees, each standing only twenty feet tall,

44

but as we had travelled further and further into the wood, the trees had grown in size to the point where they now stood towering over everything, the shortest being over one hundred feet tall, the tallest being very much taller. Their vast trunks had worked together to fill the space they inhabited, almost to the point that they looked as if the whole lay out had been carefully planned. The effect became that of a massive natural wall blocking out every shred of evidence of the building inside. From my first view of the area I was certain that no light or sound would get out and that only the most ardent explorers would have ever found their way through the woods.

Either side of the road way were large areas of what may have been called a lawn once. Where there had been vast expanses of pristinely manicured grass, now there was dark, browning scrub. It was still short in most areas, looking as if someone was still trying to tend to the place but was really fighting a losing battle, but there was occasional sprouting which was growing wildly. Ugly, spiny plants sat in amongst the open plains of the gardens desolation and drifted slowly from side to side as an unseen breeze toyed with them. The only other sights on the lawn area were the several dark grey stone statues. They showed the usual mix of griffons, people and the like which you would expect to find in the grounds of a stately home. The car continued slowly along the long driveway towards the main building and I was starting to pick out more details as we got closer. The main body of the building formed a mighty obelisk of dark grey stone and slate. The edges of the building formed a sharp line of stone against the darkness of the tree line behind. The overall architecture of the place looked at first glance as the usual well crafted structure but as you looked closer, there were more rough edges to the place. It had looked as if whoever had put this thing together wasn't truly looking to perfect the aesthetics. Function over style. There was a large, gravel covered space preceding the main entrance, already partially filled by a variety of cars. The many windows covering the front of the building matched the solid designs which were draped over the vast framework of the doorway and the entrance hall. Large shapes, images of trees and local wildlife were roughly carved into the walls surrounding the heavy main door. Perfectly manicured shrubs, bushes and trees were evenly spaced and organised around the edges of the exterior. Small beds of planting

45

and foliage leaned against the building giving the effect of a very well-to-do hotel or country club. The place itself was very different. Rather than the measured exterior there was more of an air of hunched power, as if a large creature was being held down against its will, constantly straining against whatever it was that was keeping it in place.

Planted squarely at the head of the building, fluttering in the breeze, was a massive flag. The Red Dragon standard of Wales held pride of place over the whole estate.

"Impressive hotel. Who is paying for this? Uncle David put some money aside eh?" I probed trying to get some information without being too pushy, neither Lloyd or Mike had responded well to the direct approach.

"This is a private estate" responded Lloyd matter of factly.

The car pulled slowly to a stop alongside a highly polished vintage black Jaguar. We all climbed out of the car and Lloyd moved to my side quickly and gripped my arm tightly, leaning in to whisper in my ear, "This is going to seem very strange, even with what we have told you and what you have seen over the last few days. I'm going to be with you all the time we're here so I'll be able to give you any information you need. Stick with me and we'll get you set." Sounds great. My head got the revs up again just to remind me that it was still there. At least it had stopped raining.

Mike had retrieved the bags from the car and had already started heading towards the main door of the house. Lloyd winked at me and then started to walk in, beckoning me to follow. As we approached the now open door, we were greeted by a tall, lean man who looked like he was about fifty years old but who carried himself with a lithe energy which gave the impression he was much younger. He had grey hair which was cut in a very short, regimented style, a deep tan and very sharp, dark eyes. He gave the very real impression that he was taking in any and every piece of information around him, wary of everything and willing to react to anything without a thought. He wore a well tailored black suit, black shirt and black tie. He also wore them well.

"Lloyd. Michael. Good journey I hope" enquired the man in what sounded to me like it had been a Welsh accent but was now mixed with something else, American maybe. The Welsh was still dominant but the waters had been muddied somewhat.

"Mr. Johns" he started while nodding his head slightly in greeting. "Good to see you. I expect you will be feeling a little lost at the moment, lots of strange people saying lots of strange things." A slight smile played at the corners of his mouth as he started speaking. "My name is Eugene Lunn and I am much the same as you in terms of role but I have been in place a little longer. I look forward to seeing you take up your place in the Circle." I looked back at him and nodded with that usual fixed smile which people use when they have absolutely no idea what the other person in the conversation is talking about.

"Lloyd, do you know where you are going inside? A room has been put aside for you in the East wing of the house, The Goch suite, for Mr. Johns" said Eugene as he turned quickly to face Lloyd.

"The arrangements were made before I left Sir, thank you" responded Lloyd with a slight bow. That wasn't what I had expected to see. *Sir?*

"Excellent. I hope tomorrow will be a good day for you Mr. Johns. Your place is prepared. See you then" and with another nod he moved from us towards the line of cars.

I looked at both Lloyd and Mike hoping that they would give me some clue what was happening but, again, they ignored my silent request and they both just turned from me and headed towards the main door again. I shrugged and followed them into the house. I realised that the only option really open to me at this point was to simply go along with everything as they presented themselves to me. I was too far in now to kick up a fuss when the next piece of unexpected information presented itself or when someone gave me a fragment of fact but left me further from where I needed to go.

I caught up with the others and followed them through the main door. We entered into a wide, triple-height ceiling room which would have passed for a ballroom in most people's experience. There was a central stairway to the balcony of the first floor which wrapped itself totally round the entrance hall we were stood in. The staircase was made of dark stone and took on the feeling of erupting directly from the foundations below us; there were still unfinished edges to the steps and the banisters. The entire structure carried the same 'function over style' aesthetics as the rest of the building. On each of the walls around this mighty space were portraits of people and vistas from history. We were surrounded by hoards of blank stares from faces of men and women of the past. As I looked around to each of them, even through the constant distraction from my head, I began to feel a very real sense of the timeline that was being shown. These all represented someone who had lived here or at least had some serious connection to the site. This private estate had been here a very long time.

Directly overhead there hung a massive metallic dish, which roughly measured fifteen feet across. It looked to be made of brass or something similar rather than gold, so again, looked to be simply serving a purpose rather than having any visual intention. It had been attached to the walls by four thick chains which strained under the weight. At ordered points through the vast disc were cut small shapes, some depicting celestial bodies, stars, moons, suns and the like, while others seemed to be nothing more than spaces to let the light pass through, indistinct shapes which bore no resemblance to anything I could recognise. As I looked up, I realised that the only light source in the room was coming from within the mighty crucible above us despite there being no form of power leading into it. The light from above felt like it was ebbing and flowing as I looked up, gently pulsing as if it were the heartbeat of the entire building.

"This way bach" called Lloyd from the mouth of a corridor off to the right of the room we were stood in. He and Mike had stopped to wait for me while I had stood, slowly spinning, in the centre of the room taking in all of the detail. They both stood there carrying the assorted bags they had dug from the car and were looking at me in the same fashion they had cultivated since the journey had begun, one of silent mocking, like they were amused by my reaction to things they were completely used to. I gathered myself up and headed towards them. My head kicked into a higher gear than I thought I actually had and made me feel that I was about to fall over like all the heavy drinkers you see on the funny CCTV footage. I shook my head a little clearer and pushed on.

We all headed through tall, ornately designed corridors, all decorated with expensive looking paintings and large crystal light fittings. They weren't quite chandeliers but they weren't far off.

Heavy, plush carpet was laid out in every corridor we passed through. It gave the somewhat familiar impression of a well-to-do hotel but I was always aware that this whole estate was so much more. It had spoken to my subconscious mind and I knew that there was more here than was immediately apparent. It was familiar in some way but none the less creepy for it.

As we continued deeper into the building, my head spun even more wildly and the rest of my body continued to feel like I had been thrown around by a very enthusiastic animal. My body and mind felt drained of every shred of energy. My entire world had been turned upside down in the space of a few days and I could feel the despair building along with the dizziness as the last vestiges of my physical and mental fuel ran down. Without really noticing we had arrived at our intended destination, the Goch suite, and we all stopped moving. Lloyd opened the door we stood next to a mighty oak piece decorated with Celtic symbols and images of myth. Mike strode inside carrying my bags.

"This is your room. Mike and I are either side of you. If you need anything, just call" said Lloyd and motioned for me to go in. I stumbled as I started to head for the door, began to fall forwards but didn't have any reserves to steady myself. Lloyd darted to my side and caught me in a vice like grip and prevented me hitting the carpet. Lloyd practically dragged me into the room and laid me on the bed.

"Get some rest, you look terrible and you're going to need to be at your best for tomorrow" said Lloyd by way of, I assumed, gentle reassurance. I closed my eyes as the two men left my room and I was finally alone. Slowly, before I finally lost my battle with the marauding hoards of the forces of sleep, I realised, that whatever was happening here and whatever I had in store tomorrow, something much larger than I had first thought was underway.

6

When I woke up I was feeling worse.

I checked my watch and found that I had slept for over seventeen hours. We had arrived in the afternoon and despite the short winter days I had fallen asleep before the sun had set and had come to well after dawn. I must have needed the rest! Despite the extended period of recuperation the waves of nausea I had been experiencing the previous day had now grown to tidal proportions, every time I moved I was engulfed by an upgraded dizziness which was forcing me to have to reach for any object to support my movement. Sharp, searing pain was snaking through my whole body and was forming into tight, burning knots on the back of my head, on my shoulder blades and in my knees. The attack yesterday morning had obviously given me some injury that I hadn't been aware of but I was really now feeling unbearably ill.

After trying to move around my room with little success I decided that I needed help. I needed a doctor. I called out for Lloyd. Without any warning my door burst open and Lloyd came crashing in, fists raised and eyes tracking around the room preparing for trouble. He quickly realised that I wasn't under attack and I could feel the tension draining away.

"When I said just call if you need anything, I meant use the phone." Lloyd teased me as he sat down on the bed.

"I need a doctor or something. I can barely stand up and I am in real pain. I can't move without being in agony. I need help!" I begged him through gritted teeth.

Lloyd let out a sigh and I saw him shake his head and smile. He leaned forward and placed a hand gently on my shoulder.

"You don't need a doctor. It will be over soon. With everyone coming here today and it following so quickly after what happened with your brother, you are going through something which has usually been prepared for over a lifetime but you are very close to it being complete" explained Lloyd.

"I've been keeping an eye on you and I know you feel like you are in trouble but you will be through it soon and then you'll feel much better."

Before I could ask any further questions or let Lloyd know that he was actually making me feel worse, he stood up and turned towards the door. As he opened it I could see Mike outside with a worried expression on his face. On either side of him I recognised Eugene, the man who had greeted us the day before and a woman I had seen talking to Lloyd during my uncle's funeral, I think she was Russian. She looked up to Lloyd as he walked out and raised her eyebrows in a silent question. Lloyd looked back over his shoulder and slowly pulled the door closed behind him before answering.

I sank deeper into the bed and closed my eyes tightly and tried to create some kind of control over the pain and nausea coursing through my body. I couldn't control my body and felt that I was being broken from the inside out, pulled apart slowly piece by piece and the pain was continuing to grow every minute without any sign of stopping before it had claimed me. I gripped the bed clothes tightly and vainly attempted to remain still, any movement magnified my agony, and I could feel every last fragment of me give out. I arched my back in an involuntary spasm and screamed out all of the frustration and white hot searing terror which was slicing into me. The noise came out in waves of deep, rasping and tearing heat and for a brief second I was aware of the feeling of released pressure as I screamed but it was short lived as the force and pain working at me grew again and finally became too much and I slumped back into unconsciousness.

I had reached the limits of my resolve but there was no respite from the building assault. The pain wracking my body was no longer an issue but there was warfare for the mind continuing. Through my minds eye I was confronted by images of colours, mountains, fire. Buildings of stone and images of people who I didn't recognise blurred through my head. Large periods of blackness were intermingled with the pictures but all the time the sounds kept playing. There was still no order to anything but I could hear voices talking, calling and shouting all in a collection of tongues that I didn't recognise or understand. Occasionally I could pick out snippets of English but they didn't give me any more information.

I had given up. Completely.

My body was beaten and my mind had been taken down only a short time later. But that wasn't the end for me. Dimly, at the edges of my mind, I could hear my name being called. Diffuse sound slowly floated over the images in front of me, whispering my name.

"Anthony. Anthony. Open your eyes and know that you are safe. The pain is gone and you can come out" The end of the sentence grew lighter and I could hear the smile to it. I could feel my awareness slowly returning to me and feel the presence of the room I was staying in poking at my mind. The images in my mind started to wash out of colour and definition as I moved up and out of this enforced dream but before I was totally back, a deep roar pierced my senses and from the murk came an image which threatened to unmake all of the calm which was being built in my mind.

At the centre was a dark figure, dressed wholly in black with a wide brimmed hat covering most of his face. The only part of his face which was visible was his too wide smile, his sharp teeth glinting in an almost menacing fashion. He wore a long, ribbed coat which flapped around his ankles, dark trousers and large heavy boots. I quickly recognised him as the visitor we had encountered at my flat before we had left to come to Wales. He was also the man who had killed my uncle and my brother. He slowly lifted his head to look directly at me revealing the same weathered, leathery skin, the same hairless head and the same almost reptilian eyes. He looked at me and tilted his head to one side, dropped his hat to the ground, and started laughing. Every time I had any dealings with this character he seemed to find me highly amusing. I slowly turned my focus away from him; his image had given me unpleasant flashbacks of the last few days and I didn't feel up to dwelling on them. As I looked past the image of my family's killer I became aware that he wasn't alone in this picture. Behind him was a bright white wall of light. I had been so focussed on the black clad figure in front of me that I hadn't viewed the background framing him as anything more than being a blank canvas. As I looked more closely I could start to make out detail. I could see the faint lines of what looked like large tiles – giving the appearance of a massive kitchen wall! The tiles were perfectly smooth but the layout wasn't the regimented lines you would expect. The wall they all sat on was of irregular shape with large areas bulging out or falling back in massive mounds or troughs. As I casually passed my gaze over the whole area I could make out, the wall moved. But not in the way I was expecting. The tiled surface expanded and stretched, each of the tiles moving smoothly, overlapping in places and becoming more than a covered wall. The entire structure slowly started to move from right to left before me behind the standing figure who was still smiling at me. As I stared, I realised that I was looking at the side of something that was not only vast in size, but also, that it was alive.

My unconscious mind was showing me some very weird things and I told myself that I must speak to Lloyd about this whole situation. I was starting to become more and more aware of the dream state fading and the real world returning when the gunslinger terminator opened his mouth and called out my name. His voice was like tearing sheet metal, a shrieking sound which I felt as much as heard. It was at that moment that I realised that he wasn't simply a part of my mind – he was really there. He spoke directly to me. This was happening in real time and somehow the brute that had killed my family was now in my head and he wanted a chat.

"Anthony. Welcome to the game" he called out. "I've been a fan of your family for some time. I look forward to our next meeting but feel sad that we won't have a third." Before I could really take in what he had said or make any kind of reply, there was a bright blur as he moved from his original position to be directly in front of me. I could feel his searingly hot breath pouring over me as he towered over me. If we had been of equal height we would have been standing nose to nose. As I looked up to him I realised that this wasn't the best way to describe the situation. My attacker had changed.

His face was now that of the darkest nightmares ever experienced. The weathered skin of his head had been replaced by a chitinous mass of both shiny silver/black scales and plate. His now fully reptilian eyes were pushed further apart and seemed to be almost on the sides of his head. Between them gaped what had once been his nose. Instead, he now had a broad and deep hole surrounding a small bony protuberance. There seemed to be no way he would be able to make use of his sense of smell but he seemed to be taking deep breaths through his 'nose' as he looked down at me. Could he smell

53

how scared he was making me? As he continued to examine me I took in more details of his ruined face. His too wide mouth had now lost the last vestiges of human features and was now wrapped almost from ear to ear. Both of his lips were gone resulting in a full view of all of the long razor sharp teeth that filled his mouth. They had grown in length and were now pointed out at irregular angles. His lower jaw was also now more elongated, stretching down to a large point at the chin. I didn't dare look at the rest of him. I shook as I stared straight at him and silently prayed for the outside world to come back to me before something I didn't want to happen took place.

"You aren't ready yet, are you? Such a shame" he whispered and leaned over me, again smelling for something but raising his right hand slowly above his head. This movement was greeted by a new, massive explosion of sound which engulfed every part of my mental landscape. There was complete animal rage throughout the roar. The anger there, combined with the sheer enormity of that sound twisted through me making me want to turn and run despite my location. The force pushed against me and I could feel the weight pressing into me everywhere, body and mind. The monster in front of me seemed unaffected by the wave and I could make out the words *'End it'* buried within the new sound. This made my fear grow even further as I realised that there was something else in my mind and that it was apparently giving the monster who killed my family orders. I tried to run away. I wanted to turn and put any distance I could between myself and whatever was going on in my head. I wanted to shut my brain down and scrub away the memory of what I had just experienced. It had been more than just images, I could hear and smell him. I could feel his breath and I didn't want to have to return to this at any time soon.

As my fear continued to grow I was finally aware of the same voice calling from the real world getting louder. I looked at the horror ahead of me and it suddenly started to dissolve at the edges and the sound began to dissipate. The beast noticed the alteration and lunged towards me, slashing at me with the blade like claws on his right hand. The attack had no effect. I was somehow now out of his range and as the vision of bright light and appalling anger evaporated; my awareness was transported back to my room. I didn't know what had happened but I was sure that something awful had just been avoided.

My body was covered in sweat when I woke up. I was breathing rapidly and my heart was racing. On the other hand, all the pain was gone. I sat up in the bed and felt my body calm slowly. Around me sat Lloyd, Mike and several other people I didn't recognise. The Russian woman stood towards the back of the group, hovering just out of the way of everyone else but watching intently. All of them wore the same expression of worry.

"What happened? Are you alright?" asked Lloyd as he gripped my shoulders tightly. "You were waking up, you actually spoke to me. Then you started shaking and shouting, punching out. What was happening?"

"Really bad dream." was my response. The residual fear was still draining away so I didn't take in much of what Lloyd had just asked me. "That thing we met outside my flat wanted to say hello. *Gasp* He was deformed. *Gasp*. All teeth and insect features. *Gasp*. It's good to be awake."

Lloyd looked around the room at the other people gathered around me and matched their worried expression.

"Did he look like this?" he asked and reached out to colleague. The man passed him something and Lloyd turned back to me and held up a picture. It was a small drawing, completed in charcoal on a very old piece of cloth or parchment. It was a perfect match.

"That's him" I replied, feeling the apprehension of the others taking shape within me. "Who is he?"

Lloyd looked directly at me. "If he is in your head, he's a real problem."

7

Lloyd tugged on my arm and pulled me to my feet. All the agony which had been coursing through my body had subsided completely and as I got to my feet I discovered that it had been replaced by a feeling of buzzing warmth. The spinning in my mind had gone and I felt that my body was stronger than before. The relief had obviously given me a feeling of euphoria.

"Get dressed quickly Anthony, we need to get underway. Everything is set up but it looks like we have to get you into the safest location we can before our friend comes back for you. We'd planned to take you through the facts of your situation before we left but now it looks like we'll fill you in on all of the details when we get to the Abbey" said Lloyd as he started to walk towards the door. The remaining people in the room followed him, each moving like there was a real urgency driving them.

At last, some answers. I enjoyed the knowledge that everything was going to be explained to me but lurking with it was a growing discomfort at the thing that had been in my head. The how and why were coming and at least I was going to the safest place I could.

I washed and got dressed as fast as I could. When I walked back into the main room I found a large platter of breads and fruits waiting for me on a small table at the end of the bed. I started to pick at pieces as I got myself together. The picking soon grew to ravenous gulps. The hunger that I hadn't even noticed up to now was gnawing at me and I felt an incredible pleasure sweep through me as I ate. Outside, I could hear running footsteps and muffled speech. Whatever was going on, someone felt very serious about it. Lloyd came in, looked at me stuffing food into my mouth, and waved his arm at me. We must have been getting going.

"Everyone else has gone. They're getting the Abbey set up for us to start as soon as we arrive. Let's get moving. You can eat on the go."

I picked up two croissants and an apple, slid them into the pockets of my jacket, and followed Lloyd out, eating a piece of toast as I went.

We got to the car and Mike was again waiting to drive us. We quickly got in and started moving down the driveway towards the wall of trees. Lloyd turned to face me, this time making himself comfortable. This was going to be a long story and I felt glad I had a snack with me.

"You already know something about the existence of magic but our world is much bigger than that" he started. "For thousands of years, there has been a balance held through the world. Magical beings have existed in a harmony. No one tried to push to take control of more than they should have and everyone got along. Everyone involved knew that any change in the set up would jeopardize their existence. Basically, the baddies wouldn't try to seize power because the human race – the source of their food in so many ways, would need to be killed in the process, and the goodies, us, wouldn't move for fear of collateral damage in the human race being so vast that it would make any victory worthless."

"Oh come on fellas, magic, monsters, thousands of years ago there was a mystical war! Blah Blah. You really believe this, don't you?" I felt more and more ridiculous that they thought I would go along with this story.

"I agree that I've felt unwell but please, creatures in my head?" Lloyd's expression darkened as a deep frown set on his face.

"We're rushing you through the history here because you need to know and I don't have the time to spoon feed all of this to you and hope you agree with us. This is a very real situation and you are in very real danger" he boomed. The sudden change of tone shook me silent.

"You watched the fight outside your flat didn't you? You saw what was going on? You saw how we beat the creature who was there to do you harm? You saw how your brother died?" I nodded from the deepest reaches of the back seat.

"You saw all of that. Now explain it. Tell me what has been going on and don't include details I've told you. How do you make sense of everything?

I looked at him and pushed my mind to find any alternative to fit the situation. Nothing came. I couldn't rationalize away any of it. Nothing made sense anymore other than the fantastical which the others were treating as being the norm.

Lloyd's gaze didn't waver in the slightest. He believed this, all of it, down to the very tiniest detail and he wasn't going to hang around with me if I wasn't going to take him seriously. I sighed and felt the last of my resistance ebb away. In for a penny... I thought to myself and started to sort through all the information Lloyd had just given me.

"You mean you guys got involved in a supernatural cold war! You fought over the human race without really wanting to risk the possibility of losing" I pointed out feeling a little better that I could still reason with facts I was given. Does this mean I'm not mad?

Lloyd seemed to examine the idea, and then grinned, "I knew you'd pick this up fast" the previous anger now totally gone. He continued with the story.

"That said, this wasn't always the case. A group came to prominence which called for the human race to be treated as nothing more than food. They were the worst of the worst. They viewed the entire world as nothing more than their plaything; everything in it was to be consumed. These beasts didn't want to keep a harmony with anyone; they wanted dominion over everything. When the battle was eventually fought, the damage to humanity was vast, but they survived. The human race found a way through an event which destroyed so much. The creatures that started the conflict were beaten and a new order was established."

"So, basically, the good guys won." I replied.

"Eventually" Lloyd continued "over thousands of years, creatures of magic, demons you could call them, and humans lived together, and in some cases, offspring were produced which had traits from both. We are now in a position where those of us descended from those early mixings look exactly like every other human being, but we have a link to those demon traits."

"Magic." Can I boil a story down or what?

"That and more, it just depends on what line you come from" said Lloyd.

"So the good guys wiped out all of the monsters who wanted to eat the human race and everyone lived happily ever after? Very pretty!" So far I was being told a very interesting history lecture, kind of.

"If that had been the case then you would still be happy in London and your family would be alive and well" Lloyd cut me off. He held my gaze for a second and I could practically feel the twist coming in this tale.

"The strongest and most powerful of the enemy, those who had driven the uprising, couldn't be destroyed, they were too strong. The only course of action available was to bind them and imprison them. There were prisons set up all over the world, separating the creatures as much as we could. We called this central group The Hive. Each one of these tombs was to be guarded to ensure the beasts remained bound and the world as it had become was protected." Lloyd moved in his seat a little.

"The guards were our heavyweights." Lloyd's eyes glinted with something I couldn't place and I could see Mike watching me in the rear view mirror, also with an intensity in his eyes.

"You are about to take up an ancient power and an ancient role. You are going to take control of all of your family power and ensure that one of our most dangerous enemies is kept in the cage we made for him." Lloyd stared at me.

"What in God's name are you talking about Lloyd?" I looked back at him feeling the waves of ignorance starting to lap at my feet again.

"All of the people here are connected to the worldwide control of those who were locked away millennia ago. There is a Circle of twenty one members who hold the abilities to control the prisons and if necessary, recapture the creatures should they ever break free. The Circle moves to ensure the order that has been established, remains. Along with the duties of guarding the bonds of the enemies' leaders, we also move around the world hunting out pockets of demon resistance and searching for artefacts and objects which are valuable, monetarily or, otherwise. The charge is given through bloodlines and has been since the beginning. Children are prepared for years for the day that they will take up the post." Lloyd smiled at me, "You got your power woken up a little faster than is usually expected, though"

Finally, something which related directly to me and it kind of explained why I had been feeling so crappy recently. I still wasn't sure if this was good news or not.

"We're the good guys and we're happy to leave the human race to be food for the things that go bump in the night. This is the better option?!" I had to try and work through the story which was being laid out in front of me.

"I said that the human race was the source of food. In some, very isolated, cases, people are abducted and fed upon but in the most part, those things that are left are simply scavenging on the left over's of human existence. Really, they're just like foxes in a way – rubbish bins etc. but some kinds live off human waste itself, plastics, carpets even glass. We live in a very diverse universe Anthony" Lloyd explained giving me another smile.

"You're Uncle and Brother knew what was expected of them" pointed out Mike without turning his focus from the road.

I'm not sure if Mike had intended his words to have the effect they did but they did none the less. I was being driven to a place I didn't know, by people I had only just met, to become a part of a world I had never heard about and that the things that go bump in the night are really the monsters we think they are. But in the middle of it all were two deaths. My Uncle had known from day one that Steve was supposed to take up the Holy Hand Grenade when his time came and had spent all the time he had preparing him for that day. Steve had wanted nothing to do with any of it, probably thinking that he was being yelled at by a crazy old man.

The value placed on the situation by the closest member of my family would have been enough to drive me on, hell, I was here wasn't I? The final understanding of why the relationship between my Uncle and my Brother had been so strained was enough to erase the last fragments of resistance.

The silence which followed lasted for a short time as the journey continued through the outlying residential streets of Neath. Old terraced houses were everywhere as we moved towards the centre of town. We never made it to the town proper but instead turned off onto a tiny back road which led us towards a modest industrial complex. The car started to slow as we approached an aged low railway bridge which passed over the road and I could see Lloyd getting ready to open his door.

"Where are we now? Is this where everyone is waiting for us?" I asked looking around at the assorted buildings as we passed, feeling very little confidence.

"This is where everything will kick off properly Anthony. The others from the group are already here and will be waiting for us" Lloyd threw over his shoulder as we passed under the low bridge.

"Welcome to Neath Abbey."

8

Neath Abbey wasn't what I had expected.

I had expected to see a vast, ornately carved mass of stone and stained glass looming ahead of us, standing resolute against the effects of all invaders and of time itself. Crowds of tourists taking photographs. Guides leading onlookers around the points of interest. Swathes of visiting people taking in all of the detail and information about this veritable fortress. What greeted us wasn't quite as imposing.

Neath Abbey was a ruin.

It was also a ruin which sat amongst a selection of small industrial buildings. In short, the town had been built right up to the edges of the grounds of this now wrecked religious site. Tall walls of stone were still standing in some areas and some were connected by expanses of stone holding the shapes of window frames. It was apparent that Neath Abbey had been an impressive sight when it had been young but time had not been kind.

"This is your idea of a stronghold?" I leaned forward to direct the question to both of the men. Lloyd again turned to face me as we continued our slow journey around the exterior.

"The building may not look like the seat of ancient power but believe me, this place is mighty in the ways that really matter." replied Lloyd as Mike drew the car to a halt. "Your family built the Abbey as part of the protection system years ago when the forces against us were mobilising a new attack. They had the castle in the town as an outpost years before but needed something a little more subtle."

He casually lifted his hand and pointed over the edge of the ruin at the hillside in the distance.

"You can see where your ancestor quarried the stone." I turned to follow his gesture and laid my eyes on a wide swathe of shattered cliff face. Huge gouges ran through the stone wall of the hill where tonnes and tonnes of stone had been cracked free for the building. As I stared up at the makeshift quarry I was struck by a compelling image of a distant relation of mine doing all of the work himself, Mike had said that my ancestor had quarried the stone.

We all climbed out and I recognised some of the cars we were nestled amongst. I had seen them outside the country house when we had arrived there. Apparently we were among friends. As we moved closer to the building and stepped onto the grass surrounding it, I was forced to stop dead in my tracks and focus my attention on my balance. I felt as if I had walked from a freezing cold exterior into a roasting hot sauna. The air had been blown out of my lungs, my whole body was now as weak as a baby and my head was spinning again. Lloyd and Mike had silently moved to stand either side of me, prepared for my reaction, both aiding my balance with smiles on their faces.

"Feels a little strange the first time you come to this place, if you are able to feel it" grinned Mike. I gathered myself and shook off their guiding arms. I had had enough of being the weakest. The two men swapped a glance and we all started again towards the building as the effects of whatever we had just walked through passed.

We had travelled no more than two steps when my head started to spin wildly again and create a low feeling of nausea. All of the sensations felt like they were moving through me, travelling slowly through my limbs and my body. This wasn't the same as I had just felt but it was something I recognised. The unsettling feeling of familiarity grew as I stood still again, this time with Lloyd and Mike chuckling quietly between themselves.

"I told you Bach, it feels a little strange. The threshold to this site is like a wall of magical energy. Magically speaking, only members from our groups can cross it which makes it something of a fortress against our enemies. Anyone who doesn't have any magical power can pass through harmlessly. You take as long as you need to steady yourself" said Lloyd, folding his arms across his chest, while nodding in sage wisdom.

Before I could answer him, all the waves of sensation rumbling through me snapped to a pin point at the back of my head accompanied by flashes of red in my peripheral vision and I realised where I could remember all this from. I could feel an instinctive hatred and need for violence simmering up steadily as I looked past the two men who were both still relaxed and waiting for me to clear my head. Through this anger, I focussed on the large, wrecked wall of the Abbey which was nearest to us. Nothing was there but I knew it was coming. Lloyd and Mike both noticed the change in me at the same time and lunged forward to grip my arms, evidently expecting me to fall. I continued to stare at the wall ahead of us and reflexively began to crouch slowly, bracing myself.

"What's wrong Anthony? Talk to me Bach" called Lloyd as the air around us began to rapidly cool. Before I could answer, or really be aware of what was unfolding around me, the wall of the Abbey which had held my gaze so intently was slowly torn open.

I had expected to see falling stone, hear rock crashing against rock but instead there were neither. There was only what looked like a tear in fabric, hanging unsupported around five feet from us. Through the tear was blackness. No shapes, no colours, simply nothing I could see. My other senses weren't as lucky. I could hear screams and howls, wails and yells of all kinds, though none had come from any human being. They pushed themselves towards us as if wanting to grip us and pull us to them. They brought with them a thick, rancid odour of stagnant waters, of decaying matter and, simply, of all there was that could rot or putrefy.

The other two turned to face the hole in reality and the temperature around us continued to drop. Lloyd turned to me and yelled, urging me to run towards an opening in the rock wall to our right. He tugged my arm in that direction, almost pleading for me to go but I knew what was happening. Within the tear of sound and smell came a shudder of low light and, practically on top of us, appeared the beast from my dream. He looked at me from under the brim of that wide hat and started to laugh.

Lloyd looked back to me and pushed against my chest, trying to force as much distance between me and the beast. Etched all over his face was absolute terror.

"RUN, NOW" he screamed at me before turning to face our visitor.

"Now, now" hissed the monster slowly, "The boy and I need to get to know each other." His stare didn't once leave me.

"You can't be here" responded Mike in a level tone and raised his hands in a gesture which mirrored what he and Lloyd had used in our first encounter back in London. Lloyd quickly joined him and the temperature around us, which had continued to fall, started to climb rapidly.

Before my companions could respond or defend themselves, though, the monster sharply reached out his hands from under his long cloak and a lance of black fire leapt from each palm, pounding into Lloyd and Mike and smashing them away through the air like a pair of rag dolls. They hit the ground well over on the other side of the road we had travelled in on and lay still, broken limbs fallen at impossible angles.

I turned back to our assailant and drew myself up to my full height, feeling the anger building in me. He looked down at me and continued to laugh as he slowly raised his hands, baring all of his razor sharp claws. "And now to you" he snarled and stepped forward.

I had had enough of being the weakest. The anger had grown and grown to beyond rage. I had known it was him coming through from wherever he had been, even before his 'gateway' had opened and I was going to make him work for my kill. The red flashes had continued to grow and had now flooded my sight completely and all of the primal emotions within me were now to the point where I couldn't, but more importantly, wouldn't, control them.

I threw my arms out and rocked my head back to release a roar of all the terror I had felt and would now be visiting upon him. I rocked forward, dropped down onto all fours and pushed forwards with all the force I could muster, reaching out with my arms as I went to grip onto his head when I landed.

He hadn't been expecting the attack but he reacted quickly. He spread his fingers on both raised hands and forced forwards more shafts of black lightning. His aim had been excellent despite the surprise of the attack and I was hit squarely in the chest by both shards.

Nothing happened.

I continued forwards without any hindrance. I had been prepared for a crushing pain or immediate blackness as my body had given way to his force. The complete absence of any pain had added an unnatural euphoria to me and I knew I was going to enjoy this. I hit my assailant across the chest and gripped tightly to his head, clawing and tearing at his face and eyes, roaring my defiance with every swing of my arms. He staggered back under the weight of my attack and I could feel him clawing at me in much the same way, though he was trying to push me away. I didn't feel any pain at all from his slashing attacks but in my hands I could feel the rotten skin which covered his face peeling away as I tore.

He finally forced both of his hands between himself and me and drove out another black lance against me. Combined with the push from his arms, he had created enough force to part us but he was now drenched in a thick coating of the black material he had been throwing at us. It clung to him like oil, slowly dribbling down him to form growing puddles on the floor.

I crouched down onto all fours again and the anger which had been my driving force had now whirled so far out of my control that I wanted to pull every part of him away from his bones and bathe in his entrails, I wanted to drink his blood and stand over his broken frame.

In front of me, he had steadied himself and was pulling the last vestiges of torn flesh from his face to reveal the deathly image which I had seen in my head. He smiled a, now much too wide, grin at me and raised his hands again.

He was mine.

I clenched onto the ground with my hands and I could feel the temperature plummet to below freezing in an instant. The ground around me took on a wide covering of frost and ice and I could feel fire rising in me. I bounded forward, again using my arms as well as my legs, and roared at him. He hadn't expected to see what came next. Neither had I.

As I leapt forward, I screamed out a searing burst of flame.

The reds and oranges danced out around a central arm of purest white. The heat was unbelievable and I could feel areas of my exposed flesh want to turn and run from the assault. My opponent stood there, unable to move from sheer surprise. The flame crashed into him and ignited all of the oily liquid which covered him. He screamed out in sudden agony and fury as the heat bit into him and I completed my leap by crashing into him again. He staggered back, his body outlined by flame but his cries had ceased.

"Now it's my turn" he croaked from within the flaming, smouldering pile.

His long black cloak dropped open to either side of him, then, rose up and out, to reveal itself as exactly what I had thought outside the flat in London, a vast pair of demonic, leathery wings. His clothes were burnt away to now reveal a chitinous skin covering his entire body, the same as I had seen previously on his face. Both his hands and feet were clawed viciously and it looked as if his legs were jointed in a completely inhuman way. He had gone from being a ghastly figure of shadows to being a true nightmare – he had lost the last vestiges of his humanity.

I didn't care. He was going to be torn to pieces and I was going to be the one to do it.

I reached into the ground and prepared to leap again but faintly became aware of a dark, booming voice calling out to my enemy, "*End it Tyus.*" He grinned again as he stared at me. "With pleasure Master."

Tyus reached down to match my posture and the air began to crackle with power as we both readied ourselves to surge on the other. Before either of us could move there came another roar from nearby, quickly followed by another and another and with a flash of unnatural speed, Eugene and several others appeared around us and took posture to fight.

Tyus, at least I had a name for him now, scanned his opposition quickly. He obviously knew them and they had given him pause enough to mean they could do some real damage. I didn't care. I surged out to him screaming as I went. He had seen that he couldn't win this fight with these odds so simply ducked underneath my attack and slithered back through his tear in reality, closing it behind him.

I landed in a crouch and span round to check on Tyus' position before I realized that he was gone. The others rushed to my side. "What happened? Are you alright? How did he get in here? Where are Lloyd and Mike?" It was that last question which snapped me back to reality from the depths of my blood lust. Where were they? Were they alive? I pointed towards where they had been thrown and waved for everyone to see to them, I was fine despite my heavy breathing and the strange tingling sensation which was running through my mouth. A group set off to the aid of my friends and I caught myself thinking that it hadn't taken long for me to think of

Lloyd and Mike as friends. I pondered that for a second, and passed out.

The next thing I was aware of, I was lying on my back, staring up to the grey sky above me. A steady breath of air washed over me which was more than cool but not quite cold. I blinked and slowly looked around me taking in who was doing what. The majority of the people who had appeared to aid us were still gathering around Mike and Lloyd. A few others still stood staring at where the rent in reality had been, worry and confusion taking up equal measure on their faces. No-one was paying any attention to me. I couldn't have been down for long otherwise people would have been at my side, or at least I thought they would. I pushed myself up onto my elbows and tried to get to my feet but before I could get any further I was knocked back down by the crushing pain coursing through the back of my head, the feeling of razor blades tearing down my throat and the countless bruises and scrapes which were covering my body. Pain and unconsciousness seemed to be all I was feeling over the last few days.

The group of people helping Lloyd and Mike was now starting to break up and I could see Mike being helped to his feet, his eyes were beginning to bruise deeply and blood was still slowly seeping from his nose. He was unsteady on his feet so needed Eugene to help him walk. Lloyd was still on the ground with several people crowding around him. He wasn't moving. I pushed myself up quickly despite the pain I was feeling and lurched as fast as my body could take me towards the group.

I had managed to stumble half way there when I was gripped tightly around my left arm and stopped dead in my tracks. I turned slowly, trying to move faster but not being able to get my body as active as I had before my fracas. I had expected to see one of any number of monstrous images which were tumbling through my mind. Instead, I was greeted by the woman from the country house.

"Come with me, now" she stabbed at me through a thick accent. So she was Russian. She was noticeably shorter than me but still looked to be roughly five foot ten. She had bright white hair pulled tightly into a ponytail which exposed her face. She had sharp features which framed her piercing grey eyes which carried with them a very other worldly sheen. They seemed to draw your attention to them. Attractive. She was wearing a tight fitting black shirt and black combat trousers. Her tight clothing was barely disguising the taught musculature which covered her body. She was moving with a lithe grace and looked like she was more than capable of handling herself in a fight. She looked at me with an expression which told me she was supremely confident and used to getting her own way. Very attractive.

Before I could argue the point, she was dragging me towards the side of the nearest wall of the ruined Abbey and out of sight of everyone else on the grounds.

9

We moved quickly out of sight of the outside world. The inner areas of the Abbey were much the same as its exterior. It had been a mighty building when it was at its peak but now the grass which surrounded the grounds had worked through the whole foot print of the Abbey. Large pieces of stone were strewn through the grounds having fallen from the ever crumbling walls. The building was sitting in its own crumbling remains. It was still making me feel less than overwhelmed at the ability of the people around me to actually mount any long term defence against the things that were coming to pay us a visit. So far, I had done all the work.

The pain was slowly leaving my body and I was now able to keep pace with my Russian comrade without trouble. Before I could ask any of the questions which were coursing through my mind, she stopped walking and thrust an arm out at my chest height. She obviously wanted to stop.

"You are safe now" she growled, staring deep into me.

I didn't feel particularly safe. As far as I could see we were still in the same situation we were a minute before. I started to question her but before I could really argue the point, she closed her eyes and raised her right hand ahead of her. The air crackled around us with sudden static electricity. Small blue sparks spat from her hand as the force she was producing grew and grew. The temperature around us had begun to slowly increase and I scanned the area around us as it was bathed in an increasingly thick heat haze. The heat continued to grow around us until, with a small force of effort, my latest guardian forced out a gout of white/blue energy which landed on the ground no more than ten yards ahead of us. A wide hiss of steam erupted and climbed skywards. My eyes were drawn to the ground directly ahead of us, to the wide area of sheet ice which was now stretching forwards to the base of the slowly retreating jet of steam.

My companion strode out again with confidence over the now treacherous surface and, without being told, I knew I was supposed to be following her.

"Here is our safety" she called over her shoulder. I looked ahead of us and could see that the steam had cleared to reveal a large hole in the ground and we were heading right for it. The space ahead of us wasn't a sheer drop. I could now make out a set of steep stone steps descending into the blackness. The Russian strode in with purpose and disappeared down.

"In for a penny..." I muttered and stepped in after her.

As we walked in, the hole we had walked through sealed in on itself, completely shutting off the outside world. The tunnel we were travelling through looked like it had been carved out of the stone many thousands of years before. It carried the features of the deepest and darkest tunnels you see on the Discovery Channel and was easily big enough to allow both of us to walk upright and with room either side of us to allow people coming in opposite directions to pass without impeding each other. There were smooth edges to all of the steps, to the walls, as if the sharpness had been worn away by years of constant use in the same way rivers and streams cut their paths. The way was being lit by regularly spaced recesses which had been cut into the walls, each throwing out a low, soft light. I idly peered into a few of them as we passed but couldn't see any candles or bulbs which could have been creating the light. Where was she taking me?

The air felt damp and there was a slight breeze coming from up ahead, bringing with it a pleasant warmth. There was a calming woody smell to the air, like we were breathing in from a distant bonfire, but one with a slight hint of something I couldn't quite place. Something spicy, hot. We pushed on and I was aware of the tunnel constantly bearing to the left. It was turning tight enough to feel like a corkscrew, steadily boring deeper into the earth, we were moving straight down.

We continued on for a further ten minutes in silence, me dutifully following my guide, her not even turning to acknowledge my presence, when I noticed a light source ahead. Whatever we were walking towards was creating a bright enough light to illuminate the now expanding tunnel mouth which we were rapidly approaching. The tunnel came to an end and both of us stopped dead in our tracks.

The cavern that the tunnel had led into was immense. We had travelled down behind the wall and had exited on a vast stone ridge which curved around at least a third of the entire oval area. Around

71

the edges of the cavern, I could see different tunnel openings much like the one we had just left. They were different sizes and shapes and had different coloured light sources floating from them but I assumed they led back to the surface. The floor to the cavern stretched down at least thirty feet below the level we currently stood on but it was the distance which stretched out above us which took the breath away. Reaching fifteen or twenty storeys above us was the roof. The whole area looked perfectly smooth, again, as if the movement of something had taken off all the rough edges, all the way from ceiling to floor. I stood staring up with, my mouth wide open, again, feeling totally lost.

I brought my gaze back down and asked where we were but my guide had started walking off again, further down the pathway now leading to the bottom of the cavern. I ran after her, starting to stare into the lower reaches of the gargantuan space as I went.

The floor area was again totally smooth but at the centre, there rose a massive stone obelisk. It was roughly the size of a tennis court and took on the appearance of an island on the floor of the cavern as it commanded the whole space. Anyone and everyone in this space would be able to see it clearly. There was also a steady plume of smoke coming from an orange glowing crack in the centre and I could feel the heat rolling onto me despite the distance. My mouth was wide open again.

I was totally transfixed by the enormity of what I was looking at that I had lost focus on my guide. She had stopped walking. I hadn't stopped running after her. I ran into her as she was turning to face me. Smooth.

We both corrected ourselves, me with the feeling of wonder bouncing round me like a kid on Christmas morning, her with more than mild frustration on her face. I gasped, looking back and forth from the view we were next to and her, my mouth flapping wildly, asking the thousand questions which were fighting for supremacy. I gripped her shoulders and practically shook her as the wonder of it engulfed me,

"Who are you?" was all I could put together.

"My name is Andrea Thomich" she growled and shook herself clear of my grip. She placed distinct emphasis on the pronunciation of her first name, An-dray-a. She must have had enough of being called And-ree-a over the years.

"I am the same as you Mr. Johns. I am a part of the Circle and we have to get you in place quickly". She waved her arm out towards the centre of the cavern and I was now able to see more detail on the central obelisk. Spaced around the outer wall were evenly spaced recesses, each bearing a carved image. There was a wide range of animal carvings depicting various poses and stances. It looked to me like I was staring at a display of people's coat of arms.

As I cast my eyes over the whole space, my attention was drawn to one of the recesses. There was no reason for it that I could see but I just couldn't take my focus from it. Andrea noticed my attention and answered the question which was forming in my mind.

"You can feel the power from your glyph can't you? You have the basis to your strength now. You're feeling the call of your awakening. You'll be taking up your place in the Circle soon."

"My glyph?" I asked, still not turning my attention from the view in front of me.

"The symbol you are looking at. That is your family line seat of power. You have taken a great deal of your power already, that's why you have been doing the things you have over the last few days" she leaned forward and parted her lips slightly into a wicked grin "-strong magical power." I turned to her and she continued, maintaining the expression of quite assurance.

"The family glyphs are shown at each of the prisons around the globe but the power for each line is based in that Guardians home. The complete circle of glyphs surrounding that monument is what the magic of the binding is built on. This is yours. Mine is in Russia – Siberia to be precise."

"Prisons? That monster cold war way back when." Some order forced itself onto the information bouncing round my mind. "This is one of the prisons?"

"This is what your family, and now you, have responsibility for. The whole Circle is here to open the power here for you. You'll then take up Guardianship for this prison."

I stood silent.

I absolutely thought she, and all of the people here were barking mad. Unfortunately, I absolutely knew she was telling the truth.

Before we could continue the conversation, I noticed several people come through one of the tunnels on the other side of the cavern. I couldn't make out who they were from this distance but I hoped that Lloyd and Mike were OK. The scene I had left them in didn't fill me with huge confidence.

We worked our way down and walked across the floor of the cavern, obviously the walkway round the edge wasn't going to be fast enough! As we got closer, Andrea called out a greeting to the people working their way down to meet us. I could now make out Eugene, still helping Mike along, and several other faces I recognised from the mansion and the surface here. I could also see Lloyd being carried down by two huge men on a makeshift stretcher. He was bound and strapped up in gauze bandages at over a dozen points around his body, each depicting the sight of an injury. He was smiling though.

Andrea greeted the group walking towards us, which was being led by an Arab looking man in his late sixties. He had grey hair, flecked through with intermittent shots of black, cut into a short, side parted style and a bushy black moustache. He, again, stood well over six feet tall and moved with both grace and purpose despite his advancing years. He was wearing a black suit and a crisp white shirt and looked as if he had come from money. "Any problems Wagdi?" she asked him.

"He's gone, and however he managed to cross our threshold seems to have gone with him" Wagdi replied. "I've left some of my people up there reinforcing our barriers but also to stand guard. If he comes back, we'll know about it." Andrea nodded in agreement. With that, everyone turned towards the nearest wall of the cavern and started off to a low collection of caves and outlying structures.

Andrea gestured to the nearest hole in the wall. "Stay here. We will come for you when we are prepared. Try to get some rest." She still had a hard expression on her face but I could sense the slight softening of her disposition.

"Who killed my family?" I asked in a low tone. I figured that the direct approach would work best with Andrea. That character had taken two shots at me and invaded my mind. After all of his efforts, I thought that it was only fair that I know who he was.

Andrea looked at me with zero emotion leaking out.

"His name is Tyus. He is thousands of years old and extremely powerful. He is a follower of what we have caged in there" she swept an arm out towards the smoke spewing obelisk in the centre of the cavern. "He has been trying for years to kill the Guardians, mainly here, but also all over the world. He wants his Master and the others, free and we are the ones sworn to stop it. When the war was going on, many of The Hive poured power into generals – creatures with some magical ability who could work in their name. These creatures became known for their skill as assassins and enforcers. Tyus has been killing those connected to our group for generations. His power and that he took from his master make him a perfect killer of a great many of The Circle, you included."

We both looked at each other in silence and I was struck by a brief shadow which passed over her features. She had been doing this for quite some time and by the looks of things, not much had changed despite her efforts.

"This character means business, OK, but when he wandered into my head he was being told what to do. His boss was there too. If you said he was serving whatever you have in Alcatraz out there, how was it that both of them were speaking to me?" The practical question burst to the surface and by the look on her face, Andrea didn't really know.

"The power base for your family line has been passed quickly, you weren't prepared, and so there was a weakness in The Circle. Without an active Guardian to maintain the control of the binding here, our grip on him weakened. It looks like he was able to reach out and work with Tyus. One without the other wouldn't be able to break into your head but our current situation has let them in. We need to move quickly to remove this avenue of attack."

Without another word, she turned on her heel and strode away towards another structure carved into the rock face. I watched her leave and had to shake myself out of the stare I had fixed on her. Concentrate Anthony.

The cave had been set up much like a hotel room. High end fixtures and fittings were all over the room and made the place look incredibly chic, quite at odds with the cavern outside. I lay down on the double bed provided and tried to sift through the facts as they were. I closed my eyes and let my mind drift. Images of people and places swam through my mind, sights, sounds and smells filled my consciousness in the same way they had back in the mansion. The whole sensation was similar to before but this time the pictures were much clearer, the sounds much more coherent but the whole thing was much more familiar. I was again looking upon people I had never seen, of places I had never been but I could feel recognition of every last detail. The speech was again a mixture of languages I didn't know with only the briefest hint of English, but I knew what everyone was saying. I could *feel* what was being talked about.

My mind continued to swim through the now growing sea of awareness that was pouring over my subconscious. Mountains, deserts, forests; different peoples. I recognised Neath Abbey but I was now seeing it whole, before time had ravaged the place. It had really commanded the area. The view quickly changed and as more sights flooded in, I started to see people I had met, places I had really been. A much younger Eugene, a Chinese woman I had seen at my Uncles funeral, Lloyd and finally, my Uncle David were intermingled with views of the mansion, of the now wrecked Abbey and finally of the bar where it seemed, all of this started.

That was the final clear picture I saw before I came to but before I was fully away from my minds eye, a roar of flame poured through my head and the last image became indistinct and broken. All I thought I could recognise was a wide spread of red opening up ahead of me, exactly the same shape as Tyus' wings had made when he had unveiled his true form.

With a final snap of awareness, I jumped up and barged into Mike as he was trying to wake me. We both recovered our momentarily lost composure and looked at each other.

"Come with me" he growled. "It is time."

10

Mike led me out of my room and we stood looking out over the mighty cavern which was now populated by a wide collection of people, all milling around the centre obelisk. As we stepped out into the space before us, everyone turned to face us in unison. Mike was walking freely now. Apparently all of his injuries had been taken care of while I had been 'meditating'.

"Don't worry Anthony, you're amongst friends here" whispered Mike as we made our way out towards the centre of the cavern.

"Are you OK? Is Lloyd OK? You two looked like you had been hit by a train." We were still moving but I needed to find out what had happened to my friends.

"We're both fine, don't worry. As you can see, I'm back to my beautiful best and Lloyd is resting in another room. I'll get him back to the mansion when we are finished here" Mike informed me. "Lloyd took the brunt of the attack but he'll be fine. I was just winged."

It felt good to know that they were both OK. After losing my Uncle and my Brother, I was starting to feel quite alone in the world. I let out a long sigh and turned my mind back to the events at hand.

"So what's going on now? Am I being led off to a sacrifice?" I asked slightly nervously, realising that it was only partly meant as a joke.

"This will finish your power gathering and you'll be in The Circle fully. Just go along with everything that happens and you'll be fine" Mike continued.

"Just go along with everything?" I pulled on Mikes arm. "What's going to happen?"

"Just watch what the others do. You're going to become something special" Mike whispered back with a huge grin on his face and what almost felt like envy floated just behind it.

He led me slowly through the large gathering of people which was drifting both towards the centre of the cavern and towards us. Groups of people were everywhere and all the attention was focussed on me. Everyone was wearing smart clothes and they all looked like they were supremely confident and eager to see what was coming. I started to realise that every person that I had had any contact with since this whole thing started was well muscled, tall and carried the air of absolute strength. I looked back to Mike and realised that he was the same as the others, and as I considered it all, so was Lloyd and so had my Uncle been.

"It's a rather happy side effect from the magic we are all a part of." Mike answered my unspoken question. "We are all meant to serve a purpose so we need to be at our best to do it."

"Who are all these people?" I was surrounded and felt isolated beyond extreme.

"They are all members of staff from each of the prison estates. Each Guardian has brought an honour guard with them. Very ceremonial, but also as protection, just in case."

Protection. Just in case. Just in case of what?

I flicked glances around the gathered throng and smiled nervously. It was too late to worry now.

Mike led me up a stone staircase which led through the wall of the obelisk and up towards the surface above us. No-one else followed us up. We reached the top of the walkway and Mike strode out onto the wide surface ahead of us. I looked around and stepped out after him.

There was one person stood with us, on the far side. I had to look directly through the rising column of smoke but I could make him out clearly none the less. Another very tall man, wearing a long black robe made of heavy, woollen material. It was tied at the waist with a plain dark grey, cloth band and the hood was pulled up to conceal the face of the person ahead of us. Long tresses of grey hair tumbled from underneath the hood in a beard which reached down to the centre of the man's chest.

I was stood still at the top of the stairs but Mike had marched across towards the man on the other side. When he reached the other side, he stopped and bowed in a gesture of absolute respect. The other man nodded his head slightly in response.

I looked around the cavern floor below me at the faces of everyone staring back at me. I could feel the expectation in the group below and scanned the mass of on lookers, trying to pin point any familiar faces. No-one. As my eyes passed over everyone there was a loud roll of thunder behind me and as I turned back towards Mike I could feel a deep, low hum rumbling through the floor. I stared across at Mike and the robed mystery man as a massive jet of smoke and steam blasted from the chasm in the centre of the obelisk and tore up towards the roof of the cavern. It was accompanied by a tearing, grating roar of noise and I knew, I was stood on the threshold of that mighty prison, and that whatever it was that had been imprisoned was nearer the surface than I would have liked and it wanted out. The increasing smoke had also brought with it an all encompassing smell of burning flesh. It filled my nostrils and bored its way into me. That thing wanted it to be me roasting. I could feel the barely caged anger rolling towards me. Not a good feeling.

Mike quickly marched towards me, jumping straight through the venting smoke without any pause. He reached my side and skidded slightly as he came to a stop.

"Come away from the edge, it's starting" said Mike and he pulled me away from the edge. The hum coming from the floor started to increase as we moved and I could feel in my chest as the vibrations grew.

The robed man reached his hands high above his head a poured out a call of power. Despite the elevation in his limbs, he kept his head lowered. It had been more than just noise. I had felt a tangible pull at the edges to my consciousness when he had opened up his call. The beast I knew was below us felt his power as clearly as I had. A fresh gout of smoke, heat and burning flesh leapt from the chasm along with more angry sound.

The hum of power was now forming into a low, pulsating, drum beat. The robed man slowly dropped his arms and I could have sworn that the sound was really filling the whole cavern. Instead, it continued to rise in me.

"Look" said Mike as he leaned into me and pointed out towards the caves we had come from.

A slow, steady column of people was making their way from the caves towards the obelisk in the same way we had. They were all dressed in white cloaks with their hoods up, covering their faces. They kept a steady pace towards us and the masses below us parted to give them clear passage to the centre of the cavern. Everyone down there was staring hard at them but was keeping a clear boundary. The troop of people continued without molestation and I could make out that they were all keeping perfect step to the ever growing beating.

They climbed the stairs slowly and circled out around the edge of the stone platform, each taking up a position they seemed to be drawn to. I looked around the newcomers. Each had their face covered so I couldn't recognise anyone but I could feel several familiar presences around me. Again, I *knew* that Eugene was to my left, that Andrea was two to his left and others I had met were up here as well.

The black robed mystery man called out again in the same booming tone and I could feel every pair of eyes in the vast underground space focus on him.

"This is where I leave you Anthony" whispered Mike as he clasped both of my hands in his and started into my eyes. "Trust it." His eyes narrowed. "I'll see you on the other side. The Mage has done this for years so trust everything he does." He quickly turned and hurried back down the stone stairs, back to where everyone else was watching. I watched him go and hoped that I was in safe hands. Despite the fear that was rolling through me, despite the feeling of terror which was coming from beneath me, I looked around me and felt totally at home. There were suddenly no doubts, no questions about the whys and what's, no uncertainty. I could feel the sensation of apprehension rather than terror. I was in the spotlight and didn't want to blow my lines. This really was going to be the most elaborate school play.

As Mike reached the bottom of the stairway, I noticed, all of the people below us were still locked onto what was going on up here but they were now quickly backing away from the obelisk at a uniform speed. They were creating a virtual moat between themselves and where I was standing. That uncertainty wavered just for a second, but the hum from below me jumped higher in intensity and I turned back to see all of the gathered personnel drop their robes to the ground in unison. Every single person at the edge of the platform was now naked, every inch of their taught bodies on display. I couldn't help myself. I studied Andrea quickly and looked away. I continued my furtive glance around the group to see that one member of the assembled throng was still covered in their robe. That was as much thought on the subject that I could spare as the drum beat of energy suddenly stopped and I could sense that proceedings were really going to kick-off; everyone around me was staring intently at me.

The dark robed man started to call aloud a collection of sentences in a language I didn't understand but again I could *feel* that he was calling into something which bound through all of the twenty people who were standing before me. He raised his hands, again keeping his head down to maintain the cover over his face and boomed out in a deep, resonant tone to the gathered congregation in perfect English,

"I Welcome, and unveil, the Mighty Circle."

He threw his hands down and a new wave of heat and raised sensation grew from the obelisk and into all those people stood with me. Bright columns of light shot from the surface of the monument, underneath where each of the people stood. As it leapt from the stone, I could make out the slightly glowing shapes of the glyphs carved on the walls below etched in the ground. They passed around and through everyone, and each one took on a slightly different colour as they travelled towards the roof. One column remained unfilled. That must have been mine.

The Mage boomed from beneath his hood again, "Members of The Circle, one of our number has fallen. The Circle is broken. So it shall be re-forged. Ready yourselves and give me your power to complete the Awakening of this new guardian." He raised his hands above his head again and all of the light pouring towards the roof turned a uniform dark red and the temperature surrounding me started to slowly climb. I could feel a growing weight starting to settle onto my mind as the temperature rose. I shook my head, trying to keep my attention focussed but the weight grew and the heat rose.

I kept my attention directly on the Mage and tried to push away the now searing sensation covering my whole body, the splitting headache and now, the red flashes which were crossing my vision. This time he lowered his arms more slowly and pointed them towards the nearest people on his left and right. As I stood there, only just able to remain upright, he unleashed a deep roar which seemed to shake the very ground we stood on and caused me to fall to one knee. The Circle all threw their heads back and roared out in

81

unison, the cry of an animal. Each one of them was straining against the ferocity of what they were unleashing and I could make out several of the group who had sunk to their knees. The roar continued, ebbing and flowing through different pitches and I could feel them all calling out to me as one. They were welcoming me into something which was both powerful and ancient. And I wanted to be with them. I wanted to join with all that they were. I wanted to roar.

I rocked my head back and roared out as the red engulfed my vision completely and I felt that my skin was being flayed from my body. The weight in my mind burst forward with the roar.

The rest of The Circle must have been waiting for me to let loose the call to them because they all acted at the same time. What they did next terrified and fascinated me in equal measure. They all leapt into the air, tumbling back off the precipice and started to change. Bodies grew in size, limbs lengthened, joints dislocated, skin became thicker and altered colour, faces changed and the last sign of humanity left them.

One by one, each member of The Circle completed their transformations and stood down off the main obelisk, in the 'moat' which had been created by the others watching from below. They all trained their attention back to the Mage, and to me. I shook as I looked in wonder at the creatures which had replaced the people who had been standing around me. The creatures continued the roaring but now it was accompanied by snarls and truly terrifying resonance to go with their now vastly increased size. I recognised what each of them had become. I had seen pictures of them. They were the stuff of legend.

The Mage called out from under his hood from the other side of the platform only we were now stood on, "Now you will take your place and reform the Circle. We shall awaken what is in you." He thrust out his arms, again, at the nearest two members to him and started to draw in power from the whole Circle. The ever present roaring increased in volume and the cavern began to shake as a shard of red energy drifted from each of the mighty creatures surrounding us towards the outstretched arms of the Mage. They all coalesced in his hands as glowing orbs of power and as the final piece of energy hit him, he thrust forward both hands at me and sent all the energy pouring out.

As I fell to the ground under the impact of the beam of energy, I became more acutely aware of the beasts staring down at me; I could feel their strength, their power, their wisdom and their fury. There was no pain involved, only a sensation of warmth. All the burning had gone and the weight in my mind felt like it was flowering into understanding. The Mage slowly walked across the platform and stood over me and with a heavy voice, ordered,

"Take your place amongst The Circle. Become as the others. Arise, Dragon."

The final word made all of the energy within me pour out in all directions. Deep scarlet filled my vision again and I could feel fire coursing through my veins. I threw my head back, spread my arms wide and roared out to everyone in the cavern. I could feel to my core that I had come home, that I was doing something that had been set down for me. My roar continued but deepened, becoming more animal. A white hot force pummelled at my head, my back and my limbs and I could feel my body undergoing the same changes as the others. I swung my head down to see the Mage moving away and down as I grew. I could feel forces pulling at me, remodelling me as I grew, building me in a different way. I let my body become their clay. I wanted the change to happen and gave myself over to it completely. I wanted to feel the ancient power of what I was now. The energy continued to build within me until I couldn't contain it any more. With a final surge, sparks and flame burst from my skin and the power which had been driving the alterations within me burst out and expanded out through the cavern, boiling into the rocky surfaces all around. The walls and roof glowed with a low orange radiance as the surface settled and smoothed.

After only seconds, I could feel the transformation was complete.

The noise in the cavern had dropped back to nothing more than a background hum of excited whispering and the scraping of massive clawed feet on stone. I looked around the surface of the obelisk and the Mage was nowhere to be seen. I was alone on the mighty stone platform with twenty dragons of various sizes, shapes and colours staring at me. I looked back and realised that I was truly one of them now. But what had I become?

I snapped my hands in front of my face, wanting to see any detail of what had just happened. Two massive, clawed, reptilian hands slowly opened and closed before me as I clenched my fists, unsure of my movements. My skin had been replaced by a covering of rough overlapping scales. I rolled my shoulders against a gathering tension in my now armour covered muscles and took a deep breath, *'in for penny...'* I thought again.

I was pulled from my thoughts by a large yet slender blue/white scaled hand resting lightly on my left arm. As I turned to face the owner of the hand, I came face to face with a lithe creature of an almost glowing blue/white, standing roughly two thirds of my height. The Dragon looked up to me with fierce grey eyes embedded in a long face that had bony, horned outcroppings along its jaw that spread towards the back of its head. A large fan of what looked like bone plate and horns spread out across the back of its head. They shimmered in the light of the cavern which made them take on the appearance of a crown or tiara. I took in all of the detail and knew that I was looking at Andrea.

I looked her up and down slowly, taking in every tiny detail of the now mighty Dragon. Her scaled skin was stretched taught over her still powerfully sculpted muscles and her whole body ebbed and flowed as she transferred her weight from foot to foot. The bobbing of her body hadn't reached her head though. Her elongated neck swayed in reaction to her movement but her head remained completely still, eyes maintaining an unwavering focus of attention. She truly was a predator. There was the same intensity to her as before her transformation, but with that intensity coming from within the huge reptile face before me, the effect was greatly magnified. She had large, leathery wings which were folded neatly behind her, taking on the appearance of a full length cloak. She had made her new limbs fold away in a similar way as Tyus had each time he had mingled with people when he was tracking after my family.

Other Dragons started to move around the edge of the obelisk, gesturing towards each other and looking up onto the platform we stood on. Another two climbed up to stand with us, a much smaller and thinner creature of blue/black with a wider snout, longer, more snake like body, shorter limbs and no wings; and one of a deep green colour which was only a head smaller than me and looked as if it had stepped off the pages of a mythology book, large wings and pointy horns. The green one was Eugene but I hadn't been introduced to the other.

"How do you feel?" asked Andrea. Her voice was instantly recognisable, accent and all, but it was now folded together with a deep, growling quality which was underlying all of her speech. She was in there but she was now very different. If I hadn't been a little scared of her before, this would have done the trick perfectly.

"What are you?" I asked her and then followed quickly with "What am I?" and I held up my now reptile hands in front of her to emphasise the point. The same underlying growl touched my voice when I spoke.

"We are the Guardians of The Hive prisoners" she started. "The things we have bound, out of harms way, are the leaders of the demon forces that were too strong to be killed all those thousands of years ago. They are the immortal leaders of the forces who stood against us all those millennia ago. We used the most powerful magics to put them where they are but they have always needed to have a guard ready to defend the prison and return them should they ever get free."

"I know that, family line responsibility etc. but no-one said anything about this. Look at me. How can I do anything but sit in this cavern for the rest of my life? I can't go back to my life looking like this." I shouted back at her. As my anger grew, I started to see steady plumes of grey smoke rising up in front of my eyes.

"Calm down, please" Andrea soothed. "You really don't want to start pouring fire out all over us do you?" and she reached up to touch my mouth. The smoke cleared quickly as I realised that I was the one producing it.

"We can all change back and forth between our human form and our Dragon form at will" assured Eugene from ahead of me through a similar, but more subtle, growl. "The Dragon is the creature which stood on the front line of the battle against the forces that were going to enslave the human race. Our ancestors were from this line and carried a charge to always stand guard over these animals. We were the only creatures throughout the whole world strong enough to do any good should any of them get out."

I stared at the three of them in turn, kicking the facts around my mind, trying to put things together. I pondered slowly and came to a

85

halt at the, as I could see it, most important fact, I could turn into a real fire breathing Dragon. How cool was I?

I stretched myself up and flexed my now mighty muscles. Without meaning to, this action had caused a large pair of wings I didn't even know I had to reach out to their full span. I almost knocked Andrea and Eugene off the platform and had to steady myself as I tried to balance with the new weight spreading out either side of me.

The others let me drop my wings back down and fold them back in place at my back. This was really blowing my mind.

Despite the inhuman faces which were staring back at me, I could sense the grins on Andrea and Eugene's faces. The third Dragon that stood with us, the shortest of us all, wasn't grinning though. I could feel the frustration pouring off it and its posture showed that it had no time for me flapping about wildly. It slithered towards me and lifted itself up onto its back legs and started to jab a finger into my belly.

"Do not think you have been given this gift solely to drive your need for pleasure boy. You have a great deal to prepare for. The creature beneath us will require your utmost skill to defeat should he ever escape." By the sounds of the voice, the accent, this was a woman from the Far East. I could only just make out a human voice but this time it had been overlaid by an added whispering breath. There was much more of an animal call in the sound she was calling speech, almost like the human part of her was having difficulty getting through. I scrambled back through my memories and finally remembered her from my Uncles funeral, the tiny Chinese woman who looked at least fifty years old. And now I could understand what she was saying.

Andrea and Eugene had straightened ever so slightly so I knew that she meant business. So far, Andrea and Eugene had been marching round as the top of the pile but, by the looks of things, there was someone above them.

"Dragon! You are now whole in spirit. You have completed The Circle and will not break it until your death" she continued. It wasn't a question. "The Mage has declared that Andrea should be your guide as you learn the powers and responsibilities you now answer to." Her tone and gestures indicated that she didn't agree with The

Mage's choice but she stopped short of actually saying anything. We all looked at each other, each hoping for the conclusion of this ceremony.

For the longest heartbeat, silence hung between all of us and I felt the tension rising as her cold steel stare continued. I could feel barely contained fury pouring from her. I met her gaze more out of sheer stubbornness but this seemed to have a positive effect. She narrowed her eyes, raised her right arm and called out to everyone else who was gathered there in, again, more of an animal tone than human. As one, all of the other Dragons let out another roar of pure beastly rage which seemed to shake the ground we were all stood on. It was a call of unity. As this faded away I was aware of all of the other people in the cavern, those who had gathered further away from the centre, cheering and applauding. I looked out into the sea of faces and realised that there were hundreds of people who were all looking to me. They were all looking on without any fear or apprehension. They were all familiar with what was going on. It seemed again that I was the only person who was learning things on the fly.

Andrea led me from the obelisk to stand in amongst the other Dragons as our Chinese acquaintance slipped back off in the other direction, growling as she went. I took in as much detail as I could of the group. There were a multitude of colours, sizes and types. Some looked similar to Eugene, what I would have called a 'classic' Dragon, some looked like Andrea, with a much longer neck, there was even one which looked like a massive snake, coiled and ready to strike, but none looked like our small Chinese friend.

All but two were of a similar height to me or smaller. The two bigger ones stood towards the back of the group and were both at least a head taller than me. Along with the height, they both looked like they were packed tightly with dense muscle. On almost every surface on their bodies were spines or bony protuberances and on their heads were a large array of horns sprouting from any and every available point. The smaller of the two was a harsh yellow colour, whereas the larger was a deep, dark orange. Both looked like they could happily pull the entire cavern to pieces with their bare hands. They welcomed me to The Circle in the same enthusiastic way as all of the others but they both looked like walking thunder, as if they were angry at life itself.

Andrea must have picked up on my apprehension. She took hold of my right hand and began to lead me away from the group. Without any signal, the gathered masses of people had parted to create a pathway for us to follow across to the opposite end of the cavern to where we had started. As we neared the wall, Andrea lifted her left hand and created a blast of white light which wafted more than flew towards the cavern wall we were travelling towards. The beam of light seemed to be made up of millions of smaller parts rather than being one single jet. It drifted all over the wall and started to coalesce over an area large enough to reach from the floor up to well above me eye line. I became more aware of the unusual nature of the rock surface as we closed the distance. It was smooth in the same way as the rest of the rock walls surrounding us, but Andrea's power had started to alter it and it looked as if it had been highly polished. It was now being covered in a thick, yet pristine wall of ice. As we approached I could make out gentle carvings in the frozen wall which created a boundary of ornate and elaborate artwork.

Andrea finished her outpouring of energy and lowered her hand to her side. As the last of the light reached the frozen wall, a small glow of blue power flashed through the shapes which created the outer boundary of the icy shape and the surface became that of a perfectly polished mirror.

Andrea looked up to me as we closed in on the wall. "This isn't an illusion. Don't you want to see what you look like? You need to understand what you are." She took a step back from me and I took the final few steps on my own. I stopped and stared. I could see the image which was being shown to me and I knew from the events up to now that it was me but nothing can prepare you for the total absence of self you get when you are confronted by a new reflection. My new form was terrifying but felt comfortable. I looked as if I could fill people's hearts with horror but also create reassurance. I had become a mighty, powerful, brutal monster. I stared deep into the mirrored surface at what was looking back at me. Aside from my newly acquired height, which, from the other people in the area and the layout of the cavern, I could estimate at around forty feet, I had two large horns which peeled out from the back of my head and curled round to points at either side of my face. My face had been stretched forward into an elongated snout with my nostrils now set flush on the top. My jaw line was covered in small but wickedly sharp looking spurs of bone which grew in length as they neared the point of my chin. Each was flat and pointed, giving them the appearance of animal teeth. This drew my attention to my mouth. It was now filled with a collection of razor sharp teeth which made my jaw line decoration look timid. I blinked my yellow reptilian eyes in amazement as the detail began to sink in. I lifted both of my hands up to my face to make sure it really was me. My reflection did the same. My whole body was covered in deep red scales which undulated as I moved. I was effectively, armour plated.

I looked at my whole image. I was still broad across the chest, but it now looked like I had taken on the ratios of a body builder, my arms were as muscled as my legs and as I stood there I realised that, following a few joint alterations in my legs, I could now move around on all fours just as comfortably as I could on two legs. All of these facts joined together to form an image which was truly incredible. To top it all off, I now had the chance to get a good look at my wings. They hung down, neatly folded in on themselves when they weren't in use, giving the impression of a full length cape. I still couldn't quite take it all in. I looked into my reflection and, from behind me, caught Andrea staring. We locked gazes for a split second, before she snapped her eyes away. I could feel a slight smile creep across my face as I noticed her apparent discomfort – even as a monster, I've still got it.

I threw my arms out and flexed through my back and two mighty wings snapped into view. Thin leathery membrane was pulled taught between bony ribs which spread through each wing. I let them hang out at their full extent for a short while, feeling their weight pulling on my body in ways which I could never have ever been able to describe without the practical experience. I was enjoying this. I folded my wings away and turned to look over my shoulder at them. How did they fold down? How long were they? I absorbed the detail of my rear view and only then did I notice the large tail I had acquired. Running down the upper edge of my tail were large pieces of what looked like bone plate. My eyes followed the line down the full length of my new appendage until they finished at my tails tip. A large, flat, irregularly shaped piece of serrated bone grew directly out from the tip and carried the authority of some kind of heavy medieval weapon, a mace or battleaxe. All in all I had become something which I felt not only looked like it could do the job but was really cool to look at.

I turned back to Andrea feeling like the kid who had just got the keys to his dads Porsche. Thinking about my appearance, I was more akin to a Hummer than the sporty car. An unnatural pride was pouring through me at what I now was but by the look on her face, this was all the admiring time I was going to get.

"We need to get you out of here and back to the mansion house so we can get you used to your new body. You will need to understand how to do things in your new form but I've got to let you know all of the details on your charge." Andrea turned and dropped to all fours and bounded across the cavern floor, back to the caves we had stayed in on the far side. Every other person in the space had gone. Had they retreated back to their respective caves or magically beamed off somewhere. Also, how long had I been looking at my reflection? The cavern was back to the same eerie emptiness it had had when we had first arrived so she had a clear path. I stared after her, again marvelling at what was happening to each of us but also at the fluid grace of her movements. I tilted my head to one side and watched, even as a monster, she still had it. That thought made a grin ghost across my face and I decided to catch her up.

I fell to all fours and started after her as fast as I could. Travelling on four legs when you are used to travelling on two is a very strange sensation. If you ever try it you'll know that your legs are too long for your arms thereby throwing out any really co-ordinated movement. You end up moving like a demented baby. My new form had remedied this problem. I tore across the cavern floor at high speed, my claws digging huge pits in the ground as I searched for grip. My speed was greater than hers so I closed in on her without much effort but before I could bring myself alongside her she leapt into the air in a full stretch dive, spread her wings and effortlessly speared through the air towards the roof of the cavern. I watched after her as she soared higher without any real effort. I didn't, though, stop running. With all of my attention focused on Andrea, I had stopped paying any attention to my surroundings. My speed continued and without any warning, I ran directly into the farthest wall head first.

I slumped over onto my right side and tried to regain my faculties. My head was now filled with a heaviness which felt like it still wanted to expand, despite the dimensions of my skull. My neck and back muscles were wound tight as the shock had passed through them. All in all, I felt like myself, just with a larger area now covered by the blanket of pain.

From above me I could hear Andrea's voice calling down to me in angry tones, "Lesson one. You must always be aware of what you are doing. If your concentration wavers you will be worthless to all of us." She artfully landed next to me with only the smallest amount of aid from her wings to slow her descent and I knew that the reality of the situation was here and now, the welcoming and back slapping of the ceremony to awaken my inner beast were in the past. We both looked at each other and Andrea continued.

"You are aware of the constant battle which is going on with followers of the various creatures we have imprisoned, but for you, it still represents something which is happening far away. Guardians are trained and taught from a very young age about the world they live in, about the responsibility they all have." Her gaze remained on me but her tone softened slightly, "Your Uncle broke with his duty by not training you in any way and I can see that you are totally unprepared for what is expected of you but that doesn't change the fact that you must be prepared to fight creatures like Tyus and others like him and if necessary things which are a great deal more powerful." She turned to face the obelisk again with apprehension etched on her face.

"Look, I don't understand the history. I don't know how awful the situation is. I don't know what it is I have to keep locked up or how but I do know that I am a quick learner and I am going to be pretty capable." The last part of the sentence was accompanied by me rising to my feet and spreading my wings. It was purely for show but it seemed to have the desired effect. Andrea looked me up and down and seemed to agree.

"We must return to the mansion to prepare you. You have been attacked here already so we will need to get you trained."

What about all of the others? Where are they? Can't they help?" I asked.

"They have been taken away by their people to rejuvenate after your Awakening. All the power the Mage channelled from them into you will need to be built back up. They all have long journeys to return to their respective homes." It was only then that I noticed that Andrea was breathing hard and that her legs were shaking slightly. I looked closer and could make out beads of sweat covering her head and running down her long neck. She had been one of the Circle who had 'donated' power to me so I could complete my changes but she was still going. The work load was starting to catch up with her.

She recognised that I had put things together. "The Mage gave the task of training you to me and I will make sure you are more than ready to take on all comers" she snarled through slight pants for air.

"You said we need to get back to the mansion, shall we make a move?" I asked trying to help. "First things first though, if we're going to start travelling over ground, I think a change of clothes might be in order." I waved a huge clawed fist at the two of us and Andrea nodded,

"Lesson two. Changing form."

Andrea was standing upright so steadied herself, closed her eyes and with only the barest hint of any effort, breathed out and began to shimmer. She took on the appearance of a desert horizon, all wobbly image and indistinct edges, then shrank down to the floor, morphing as she went. Her limbs changed and joints relocated. Her wings seemed to be pulled up and back into her shoulder blades and within a fraction of a second; she had returned to her human form and was standing at my feet. Naked.

I looked down on her and she seemed so far away, so small and so fragile. She carried herself with a calm assurance despite her lack of clothing and was breathing deeply, as if the effort was now starting to really catch her. Her body was covered in beads of sweat and tiny wisps of steam curled up from her shoulders. She looked back up to me and shouted with a slightly croaky voice "Close your eyes and focus your attention on your human self. Hold the image of yourself as you were in your mind. See yourself and picture your life force pouring back into you, coming from the giant you are now to what you were."

I breathed in deeply and looked down at my hands, taking in the details of the mighty claws which flexed and stretched before my eyes. Would I be able to feel this again, become the brute. I breathed out and trusted that Andrea and all of the others knew what they were talking about and that I was in good hands. I closed my eyes and focussed my mind on a picture of me. I looked at all of the detail of my face and created an image in my mind of a red mist leaving the Dragon and pouring into the human me. The image filled with a glow of deep red and stood there looking right back at me. Doing nothing. Saying nothing. And I felt nothing. There was no sensation, no shaking, no wobbly body, drunken sensation. I stood there feeling more and more self conscious. I shifted weight from one foot to the other and hoped to kick start something. My minds eye picture of me kept staring blankly at me and the nothing continued. Eventually, feeling bored and a little silly, I opened my eyes to find Andrea looking right into my eyes from her human height to mine. The shock of being that close to her without being ready for it made me stumble backwards and let out a far too feminine scream. I hit the ground in a heap and noticed that Andrea had a barely contained grin playing across her lips. My graceful fall and my lack of clothing must have added up to a quite compelling image.

Andrea reached forward with her right hand and helped me to my feet. Neither of us was wearing any clothing but there was no awkwardness, no feeling of petty fear at the openness of each of us. Instead Andrea looked up to me and informed me, "Now, we get dressed and head back to the mansion. We'll continue with the next lesson there." She held my eyes for a second, then turned and headed back towards the caves. I started after her feeling fired up to learn more but also, I was pretty keen to get some clothes on.

11

We both made our way back to the respective caves we had been using and hurried inside. As I strode in I could feel a pulsing force running through me. I stopped in the centre of the room and took in several deep breaths as I tried to reflect on what had just taken place. What had happened had been completely against anything my rational mind could have comprehended. The story that seemed like the strangest kind of fantasy had become a scorching truth and the ramifications for my family history were enormous.

I continued to breathe deeply and started to feel a pouring, buzzing heat through each and every one of my muscles. I felt suffused with sheer strength, an utter power that reached into me from what felt like thousands of years ago. A large smile spread across my face the more I thought about what had happened. A euphoria was building and I was being overtaken by an incredible sensation of wonder and confidence. I looked down at my hands and arms, taking in the familiarity of my human form, whilst at the same time, flexing my muscles and feeling a new strength and taughtness throughout me. As I looked myself over, I became aware that, like Andrea, I was covered in a thin layer of sweat. Steam was lifting from me in thick columns as the heat my body had produced during the transformations and the ceremony outside started to evaporate it. As the moisture reduced, it caused a chill to touch me and the small shiver which ran up my back brought me back to the reality of where I was, naked in a cave.

I snapped back to focus and looked around the room. The bed which I had been laying in before the ceremony was now freshly made and was offering up a new black suit for me, the clothes I had worn when I had arrived were nowhere to be seen. I smiled to myself as I thought about everything that was being done for me. I was really starting to feel every inch the powerhouse, with control over mighty forces of nature and people alike. The overt pull of it all was really compelling but that was what caused me to pause. Despite everything I had seen and all of the positives that were being thrown at me I could feel a slight seduction as an undertone. Was I being told everything? The more I thought about everything that had been taking place, there did seem to be a feeling of being swept along in a fast flowing river. Granted, I had seen some really peculiar things and had been put in very real danger. I had done some very unexpected things when I was forced to fight off that monster Tyus but I was still feeling that there were very large pieces that I wasn't aware of.

I carried that thought with me as I headed for the bathroom. I quickly showered in the pristine suite, all solid black marble and granite, cut through with frosted glass blocks and chrome, and wandered slowly back into the main room. The low, diffuse light cast a gentle glow around the room and seemed to be working with the suit on the bed to be creating an air of steady confidence. Everything just looked cool. Before I put any clothes on I took a few bites from the serving tray full of food which had also been left for me. Perfectly displayed meats, breads and fruit all beckoned to me. These few mouthfuls led to a great many more as my body moved to auto-pilot. Whatever I had just gone through, it had really burnt through my fuel reserves.

I dressed in the new suit, perfectly tailored and well fitted, and headed out of the door, still kicking the idea around that this could still all be too good to be true. Andrea was waiting for me when I emerged into the open of the cavern. She was now wearing a similar black suit to mine and had here white hair piled up on her head in an effortless bun, held in place with two jet black chop sticks. She was carrying the feel of someone who had just thrown their outfit together and wasn't really that worried about the results, but who looked perfect. Actresses and the like would have spent a ridiculous amount of money to look that good and not managed to get anywhere near. She looked me up and down and, despite her best efforts; she was looking at me in much the same way. Obviously this suit was *really* well tailored.

"Well don't we look like twins" I chided her as I sauntered up to her with a cheeky grin on my face (this look is what I relied upon when I was working, all disarming charm but with a hint of naughtiness). By the look on her face, it wasn't working. She rolled

95

her eyes and frowned at me. There was no appreciation of my charm there at all.

"Come on. We need to start your training" and she turned away from me and marched off towards the walkway around the cavern without checking to see if I was following her.

As we made our way back the way we had come in, all the time, I could feel a heaviness pushing against me, leaning into my mind and body with a cold force which made me feel distracted, unwell and unsure all at the same time. At the back of my mind, I could feel a familiar spinning sensation. It was barely there but I could feel something. The tumbling waves of barely restrained aggression poured out from the centre of the cavern, leaking from the obelisk and clawing at me to drag itself out. I was being spoken to. I shook my head and tried to push the sensation away, knowing where it was coming from but not too sure how it was coming at me. The spinning continued. I looked towards the obelisk and tried to focus my mind. I stopped walking after Andrea and started to feel my attention being drawn inwards. I could feel a whispering through my mind, an awful rasping noise which was being corrupted into words. The beast below us was reaching out to me and was calling into my head,

"Break my seal. Break your glyph. Free me."

The words repeated over and over. They were calm and melodic, thoroughly disarming and hypnotic despite the fury coming with it. I was relaxing as I listened to the continuing requests and I could feel the weight in my mind slowly increasing, creeping in without making me want to stop it. The spinning was still there but I was now not overly worried by it. The voice continued and I was suddenly feeling that it was really unfair that he was being held against his will and that I really should help him out. Luckily Andrea had been watching everything unfold and she moved to stand directly in front of me, making me have to look away from the obelisk to avoid her. This break in my attention was enough to snap me back to some level of self awareness. I knew immediately that she had just stopped me from doing something I really would have regretted. Suddenly, I wasn't feeling as invincible.

"That shows you another view of the weapons which will be used against you. You have seen the more direct approach which will be the most popular route with most of our enemies but you must also be aware of the more subtle." Andrea was holding my face and staring me directly in the eye as she spoke, forcing me to focus all of my attention on her. I focussed.

"That's always good to know but how am I supposed to fight off attacks I don't know are happening?" I was back to feeling like the only one who wasn't in on the joke and it was making my frustration rise again. The whispering voice was now out of my head completely.

"Excellent. Your mind is clear now, yes?" said Andrea and released her grip on my face.

"So."

"Your mind is a fragile place but you do have your own defences. The power of your Dragon comes from a certain aspect of existence. When you get fired up, passionate, angry, you are able to tap most clearly into that power. That in turn will allow you to raise your own defences and protect yourself most effectively. So, when you started to feel angry at the latest attack, it focussed your mind totally and put the barriers up." Andrea's explanation was making sense and as I began to relax, I could feel the volume of the whispering starting to rise.

"OK. Seems to make sense but that still doesn't help me to identify when the problems are starting, does it?" I couldn't stay in a constant state of fury just on the off chance something happened.

"You were aware of the attack weren't you?" said Andrea.

"Not at all. I just felt that I should do everything that was being asked. I felt it was making sense." Again, more riddles.

"At the back of your mind. A feeling that made you uncomfortable. Just think." Andrea knew but did I? I ran through the facts and started to realise what she meant.

"The spinning in my head? I've been feeling really rough for the last few days, head doing somersaults just for fun. It started when we were attacked in London and happened again on the surface here. It was there when the voice started to leek in too." The penny dropped. "You mean that my early warning system is feeling drunk?"

"The spinning is a perception of something that comes from a force which is a direct opposite to the power you hold. You see? Your body does have its own inbuilt defences; you just need to be able to listen to them. We'll work through some techniques that will

97

help to focus your mind to protect yourself but also give you some attacking threat." The last part of the sentence was accompanied by a small flash of something across her eyes. Whatever she had in mind, it looked like she was looking forward to it. It made me look forward to it, whatever it was.

We walked back towards the surface through a different tunnel from the one we used to get in. Andrea was obviously concerned that I was vulnerable to psychic attack so decided that we should get out of harms way as soon as we could. This tunnel was much nearer the rooms on the cavern floor than the first tunnel and was much steeper. It had the same feeling of smooth rock all the way round its floor, walls and ceiling and I was starting to work out what had caused the effect.

"The ceremony down there has happened once or twice before hasn't it?" I asked Andrea as she led us back out. She must have got her breath back because she was marching ahead at a remarkable pace and I had to really stride out to keep pace with her.

"This is the site of the beasts' cage and has been since the beginning. All of the power that was used to bind him has been seated here and will remain here for ever. It is the same at each of the locations. Every time a Guardian falls, the power passes to the next in their family line but it needs to be woken within the new holder. The Awakening is more than a rite of passage. You had an age of power channelled into you and your control of it wasn't strong enough to hold everything in, no-ones ever is" said Andrea, again without stopping her charge towards the surface. "You saw the wave of energy pour out of you didn't you? That hit every surface in the cavern and burned at the rough edges. It has been happening like that for the whole time our group have been doing what we have been doing so it does have an effect. My prison is the same."

"Are all of the prisons the same? Are they all buried underground?" I needed to try and find any kind of perspective on what was going on in the big picture as well as what was happening to me directly. Andrea replied over her shoulder.

"Not every prison is the same hole in the ground. There have been a differing range of the oldest magics employed in their construction which has resulted in them taking on very different effects."

I thought about pushing for more detail but by the way Andrea was moving, that was all I was going to get. I turned all of my focus back to the events touching me and resolved to pick her brain about the other Dragons at a later date.

I reached my hand out and dragged my fingers over the smooth wall and let my mind linger on images of crowds of people gathering here over the thousands of years this had been going on. As I continued to stride after Andrea, my mind still drifting, I started to see faces of people coalesce in my thoughts. Sounds and smells floated into my head in the same way as they had during my dreams at the mansion and before the Awakening. I was aware of what was happening in the tunnel but my minds eye was now more than a collection of random events and pictures. I was now looking over coherent events with clear information. I could see different people going through the same process I had, different people changing into a beast charged with the control of a monster which wanted to enslave the human race. As the montage of faces changed as the years rolled on, I began to understand what was being laid out ahead of me.

"The Dragon power passes through families. When one dies, the next one is called. How long does each Dragon live for, on average? How long do we have?"

Andrea must have felt that this was important enough to stop and deal with. She paused before she turned to me.

"It is dependant on so many things." She looked up to me and I could see that it was something she had thought of for herself.

The images of my predecessors continued to roll and change as the years passed through my head.

"We are all in the same position. Our power comes from years ago and puts us directly ahead of the charging forces which are always sniping at us. We are protectors to allow everyone else out there to carry on freely" she continued and despite her forceful manner and the icy calm of her voice, I could feel the sadness in her. It sat over her like a shadow but she was holding it back. She knew her responsibility and as such was going to follow through regardless.

She sighed as she spoke. "Some of the Guardians live for many years, others will last only days." Another pause and her expression showed the sadness she had been feeling. "Some will last only hours." That thought made me feel sick.

Without another word, she started to stride out again; forcing away the sadness which was building and I again fell into step behind her. My mind continued to run through the slides of the past and where I would fit into the great tapestry that was the Circle as we went but I was starting to be able to filter out most of the distracting effects.

We continued to climb in silence and eventually the tunnel came to a stop at a sheer wall with no sign of a way to the surface. The dark mood that had been hanging over us was still there but at least we now had a problem to work on.

"We should have used the tunnel we went down in" I chided, trying to lighten the mood. Andrea glared at me as she had done every other time I had asked a question or made a comment that she thought was stupid. There was still frustration in her expression but this time there wasn't the same icy blast. I like to think that my humour was appreciated.

"This is how to get out." With that, she raised her right hand towards the wall ahead of us and I could feel the crackling build up of force as blue sparks started to spit and fizz from her hand. The temperature around us started to climb rapidly and the tunnel began to feel like a very powerful sauna. It was a direct repeat of what she had done to open the way into the tunnels from the surface but having the effect of the heat channelled into such a confined space was startling to say the least.

The heat built and built to the point where I could see the walls beginning to glow and Andrea released the force she had been gathering at the wall ahead of us. With another burst of steam, a hole appeared between the surface and the tunnel we were stood in. Without a word, we both strode towards the portal, over the latest covering of magical ice, and exited onto the grass at the centre of the ruin of Neath Abbey, exactly where we had walked in. The weather hadn't improved despite our extended stay below ground and the low, grey clouds seemed to reach into both of us and suck away some of the positive energy we had been carrying. The temperature seemed to have dropped a few degrees and my breath was now visible.

I spun around, trying to work out how we could have come back to this point despite using a tunnel which should have taken us at least a mile from where we started out.

"We all have access to each of these prisons around the world at specific points. It doesn't matter which tunnels we use we will always end up in the same places. You'll get a feel for the subtlety of the magics we all deal in, it just takes time" Andrea explained as she looked around the area we had just walked into.

"OK. That's good to know" I replied and stared with my mouth open at the members of the public who were casually wandering around the ruins without so much as batting an eyelid in our direction despite the appearance of two people from a hole in the ground which closed up as magically as it had opened. They had looked directly at us more than once and seemed to be totally unaware of our presence.

"How are we going to explain it to them" I asked and nodded in their direction.

Andrea looked at the middle aged couple who were casually walking around the grounds and they, in turn, looked around us without any reaction. Their lack of interest continued and they casually wandered on their way.

"Did you feel the threshold when you got here?" Andrea asked without taking her eyes from the couple. "The barrier would have made you feel really muddled and probably quite sick. Each one of the prisons is surrounded by a wall of powerful energy which shifts the place just out of the reality of the rest of the world. People with no magical ability can pass through the threshold but can't see the reality that we are standing in."

"We have enclosed each prison with a power to stop creatures from our enemies forcing their way in which also means we can move around inside them without drawing attention to ourselves." As Andrea explained, the couple kept on walking without paying any more attention to us. "How can you attack something you don't know is there?" Made sense.

"When we cross the threshold, we have to be aware of people who could see us appear or disappear out of nowhere. There are some forms of magic we can use to make people less interested in us, sort of make us as bland and non-descript as possible, so they don't care what we do, but inside we are totally hidden and totally safe."

"If we're safe in here with a magical shield to keep the baddies out which keeps us invisible, how did Tyus get through to attack me?" The more facts were laid out for me, the more the holes kept appearing through the stories. There was a consistent flow of information which seemed to be spinning the entire situation to show the positive to me but there was always a black mark alongside what I was being told which I was starting to worry about. A serious expression landed onto Andreas face and I could see her mind furiously working to determine the answers to my question. Her lack of certainty made me feel worse.

"I don't know how he got in. These places have been strongholds for so long, they've never been breached."

We both stood still and stared at each other. Less than an hour ago I had been welcomed into a world where I was the fantastical, super powered monster but since then the shine was steadily being stripped away and had ended with a serious question which my guide through the magical land seemed to have no answer for.

"It is possible that Tyus has found a method to breach the threshold after all these years but it must have been draining his power. He is one of the most powerful of our enemies and is more than able to create enough havoc to be able to kill a Guardian like you before he has gone through the Awakening." Sounds positive.

Andrea looked at me matter-of-factly. She must have seen the blatant worry on my face.

"He should have killed you."

That was much better.

"Tyus has been fighting against us for thousands of years, trying to free his master from below us. He is a very powerful demon who is perfectly suited to destroying you and your line and he's someone who has personally killed twenty three of your predecessors. You faught him before you had undergone the Awakening so you had practically no power. You should have been torn to pieces." By the tone of her voice, she was certain of that fact.

Andrea started to walk towards the edge of the Abbey, towards the highly polished Aston Martin which was parked on the other side of the threshold. There was only one other car around and I assumed it belonged to the other couple. Their small hatchback did look dwarfed by Andrea's mighty machine. I followed her.

She paused at the edge of the grounds and looked round after the couple who had been walking round. They had moved away and were now looking at another part of the Abbey. I pulled up next to her and could feel the almost static pull of the energy field which was surrounding us. It almost felt like standing next to a pylon. I could practically hear the hum from the spell.

"Come on" said Andrea and pushed through the magical barrier without breaking stride. After my first experience with this thing, I was less than confident of getting through unscathed. I gritted my teeth and moved off. The sensation was much different this time. There was still the feeling of disorientation but this time it was barely enough to make me breathe harder. Whatever had happened below us had given me an antidote to this issue.

I passed through with no difficulties and again stood next to Andrea. The air on this side felt as if it were slightly colder than inside, and the wind felt a little stronger.

"OK?" she asked me.

"Feeling good" I replied and we both climbed into the car.

Andrea started the engine and pulled us back onto the small road which would lead us back to the mansion. The plush leather interior and superb workmanship of the car added up to making me relax back into the seat and again feel every inch the V.I.P. This made the slight dizziness at the back of my mind seem so out of place. I sat bolt upright and turned to look out of the rear window. I was starting to recognise some things and a level of fear was now crawling through me. Andrea noticed that I was on edge and accelerated without being told. Slowly, the spinning disappeared as we moved further from the Abbey, but before we had completely lost sight of it, I could see a large black shape stood back under the trees across from where we had parked the car.

Tyus stood still and let us leave without incident, but I still knew that he was watching us, and he was looking on with a wicked grin on his inhuman face.

12

The journey back to the mansion was fast but still calm. Andrea had kept her attention everywhere at once and had made sure that we didn't hang around, thinking that if we were going to be attacked, a fast target would be tougher to hit.

When we finally pulled up to the mansion, the light was slowly being drained out of the day as dusk approached. The majority of the lights of the old house were on and people could be seen moving hurriedly around inside. It certainly looked like everyone was on edge but I couldn't feel any dizziness. They weren't preparing for an attack so why was everyone going about their tasks in such a rush?

"What's happening here? Looks serious" I asked Andrea without taking my eyes from the activity ahead of us. I was starting to get the suspicious mind that seemed to be a prerequisite for everyone I had come into contact with so far. Trouble was most definitely afoot.

"They are all preparing for an inspection. Their Master is coming" Andrea informed me as she stopped the car directly outside the front door. She was already out of the car before I could ask my next question.

"Their Master? Is this something that we should be here for? I'd almost guarantee that we're not going to make this any better for them." Then as an after thought "Will this Master want to see me?" Without trying, all of my previous confidence had drained away to leave behind a nervous wreck.

Trouble was *definitely* afoot.

Andrea smiled, and held up her arm towards the entrance way.

Lloyd was slowly limping down the stairs towards us. He was carrying his right arm in a sling and was moving very gingerly. He had taken a monstrous pounding at the Abbey and was obviously still feeling the effects. Despite his blatant discomfort, he was still impeccably well dressed in possibly the sharpest dinner suit I had ever seen. He was dressed, not to attend a lavish party, but to work at one. He approached slowly and, from the open doorway behind him,

Mike looked on with a nervous expression on his face. He too was dressed to the highest standards.

Lloyd stopped before us and bowed in greeting to Andrea, "My lady." She nodded in return and Lloyd winced as her turned to face me.

"My lord. Your house awaits your arrival. We are here to serve you sir" said Lloyd and bowed down in a gesture of utter deference.

My chin hit the gravel driveway. This really was trouble.

"Wha, huh, fuer, wha?" was all I could muster.

Lloyd held still in the bow and I could see Mike fidgeting from one foot to the other as the silence expanded. Andrea leaned to speak into my ear.

"You have to acknowledge him, thank him and ask him to tour you round your seat of power." I could tell from her expression that I should have known that. Or maybe only she thought I should know that. Either way, I was embarrassed and Lloyd was in pain.

"Thank you for your efforts sir. Please show me to my house" I boomed out for everyone who may have been within earshot to hear. Lloyd stood up stiffly and let out a breath I hadn't realised he was holding. He gestured for us to enter the house and Andrea marched off in front.

"Sir?" I whispered into Lloyd's ear as we slowly climbed the steps.

"You're my boss bach. I can't go around addressing members of the Circle by name you know" he replied and winked at me.

As we moved towards the doorway, Mike straightened up and took on the posture of a butler awaiting an inspection. As we approached, he bowed in greeting and welcomed us to the house. Andrea was taking all of this in her stride but I was again back to feeling like the only person who wasn't in on the joke.

"My lady. Welcome home sir" Mike greeted us. "Refreshments are laid out in the Sun Room. Will you both wish to take dinner this evening?" Mike was now using the cut glass accent you see in films and period television programmes. It was further than a lifetime away from how he had behaved around me before this moment.

"Later on maybe Michael, thank you" responded Andrea without hesitation.

"As you wish." With that, Mike bowed deeply and hurried back out of the mansion entrance hall, I assumed towards the kitchens.

"Would you follow me please? Let me present your estate" Lloyd asked from beside me and started to limp towards the nearest hallway to our left. We were heading in the opposite direction I had travelled when we had first arrived, Lloyd must have thought that it would be more interesting for me to inspect parts of the estate I hadn't already seen.

As we slowly wound our way around the long corridors of the west wing of the house, we passed several people wearing service uniforms standing rigidly to attention. Every apron, every cloth, was pristine. Every tray and glass highly polished. Every detail was either shined or pressed to within an inch of its life. And it was all for my benefit.

Lloyd continued to lead us through doorways and archways, stopping occasionally to introduce me to a member of the staff or to show me a certain feature or item. He was leading me through the history of the mansion, history of the people through the ages who had held the seat of power here. The eyes of the pictures all looked down on me and I was again starting to feel the weight of history, the expectation that these dead eyes were heaping upon me. As we continued, every person I met greeted me with the same firm handshake or courtesy and the usual pleasantries which showed that each of them was both eager for my approval and terrified that I might find something which might not be just so.

After what felt like the millionth room of paintings and antiques, the millionth room of heavy history and expectation, I was starting to feel the need for some normal conversation. I asked Lloyd in as relaxed a tone as I could manage, "Why don't we just call this off for now and carry on tomorrow. You look like you need to sit down."

He turned to face me with a very worried expression etched on his face. The limp which had been slowing his progress had looked like it was getting worse and his face was also showing the strain. Most of the colour had drained out of his cheeks and there were several beads of sweat forming on his forehead. This tour had obviously been much more uncomfortable than he was letting on. His eyes flicked from me to Andrea and back again in quick succession, as if he was looking for help in an argument he wasn't prepared for. His reaction put me in much the same position and I soon found myself looking to Andrea for help as well.

"What? What did I say?" I asked.

"He must go through this protocol with you. When this tour is completed he will be cared for but he must fulfil your welcoming" Andrea informed me. I felt immediately very sheepish and the relief was visible on Lloyds face. Lloyd turned and started on down the next hallway and we fell into step behind him.

As we continued, I began thinking about what Andrea had said. How is it that someone who was so totally in control and confident when we were in London, utterly focussed when under attack and certain of everything he did become so subservient when someone snapped their fingers. I couldn't believe that Lloyd was being forced to walk me round this enormous building while he was obviously feeling the effects of the attack he had gone through while protecting me. The more we walked, the more I could feel the anger bubbling inside me. The utter injustice of it all. Someone who was looking out for me was being made to go through an awful experience that was causing him nothing but searing agony.

Lloyd continued to limp as he led us round the endlessly winding corridors which seemed to be leading deeper and deeper into a hole from which we were never going to escape. The anger kept on building. I had now started to clench my fists and I was feeling the tension, a growing pressure, building through my shoulders and leaking down my body into all four of my limbs. We all followed Lloyd regardless of what we were feeling as he led us into yet another cavernous room, filled with the now familiar musty smell of great age.

This room had the same dark wood and leather decorated shell that I had found everywhere else in the house but, unlike ever other ornately furnished room, here there was only one object in the room. On the farthest wall there was mounted a huge stone carving of a rampant Dragon. It stood in a classical battle pose, all teeth, claws and wings. At its base, on a large stone plinth, rested a leather bound book which was showing the effects of many sets of fingers rifling through it.

All around the room, on the walls, the floor and the high ceiling, set in closely packed and regimented lines, were small stone discs.

Each one was only three or four centimetres in diameter but they had covered every surface. I could make out on over half of them, very small, scratched writing. I tried to focus on the details of the stone coins but Lloyd's booming baritone filled the room with a mighty ceremonial crash.

"The past of the estate, sir. These are the fallen." He had raised his arms high to give the required ceremonial pomp but to also highlight the fact that these coins were on every surface in the room.

"All these are for someone who has died?" I took in the sheer number of coins around the room and felt sick. There must have been thousands of names shown in here but there were also about the same number again still to be filled. The Circle had lost people for years and years, and by the looks of this place, they were planning on doing it for years and years to come.

"All these people died fighting for the Dragon line?" It was such a huge number.

Lloyd looked at me with an expression that I couldn't quite place.

"No bach. These are just the Dragons." He dropped his head slightly and began to walk towards the door we had come in through, Andrea drifting slowly after him. I had seen everything that I needed to see apparently. Lloyd called out over his shoulder as he walked, a nonchalant delivery of a fact that he had come to accept a long time ago. "There are no records of the other staff that have passed in service, just the Guardians."

I stood in the centre of the room and felt as if I had been punched in the stomach. Only the head of the house had any kind of recognition of what they had done. Everyone else was written out of history regardless of their contribution. I stared at the gaping doorway that Andrea and Lloyd had strode through into the corridor beyond and tried to process the thought that Lloyd, like so many others would pass into nothingness when he died, just because he wasn't a Guardian.

I strode out of the memorial room to resume the tour but I could feel that my anger at the whole situation was building.

After only a handful of further steps, I couldn't take anymore of the pointless exercise. Making everyone stop, I asked to Andrea in a slightly too loud voice, "Why are we doing this? This is killing Lloyd for absolutely no good reason. I am not going to be led around

108

while someone who has been looking out for me is on the verge of collapse. I am not going to terrify the people here because history has said that it is what I am supposed to do." Lloyd had started to cower despite his mighty form as my rant continued and the volume rose. The realisation that a lifetime of servitude and hardship wouldn't even merit a badge of honour three centimetres across made me feel the imbalance of power personally.

"Andrea, we are not doing this now. Lloyd needs to rest and I really don't care about what some random painting in a room I'll probably never go into again has to show me. I certainly don't need to see that I am the only person who matters here. I will not grind people to collapse just because it has been done before. Lloyd, show me where my room is and then I order you to get some rest and have a doctor check on you."

As I finished, Lloyd had backed away from me by several paces which had created a large space between us. Andrea lunged through that space and grabbed me by the lapels of my new suit and thrust me up and backwards until I smashed into the wall. The impact shook the wall and the pictures nearest us fell to the floor with a splintering crack as the frames gave way. It also made the anger continue to grow within me and it was now on the verge of boiling over.

"Do not disrespect what we are doing here" she yelled at me through clenched teeth and she tightened her grip as she spoke. "This is part of the right of passage for every new member of the Circle and has always taken place. We are introducing you to the staff of your house and giving you a break down of the history and line you are entering into. If you had taken your training during your life then this would have been explained to you."

I was still boiling over and whatever she was saying was sailing over my head. Tendrils of vivid scarlet were now starting to snake their way through the edges of my vision and I could feel the need to give in to it. The temperature of my skin was climbing rapidly and I could see my hands starting to darken and take on a continuing reddening colour. I was starting to change and I didn't care what damage I did to the mansion, I wanted to show my anger at what was being forced on everyone. Lloyd could see what was happening and realised that something needed to be done, fast. He leapt forward to put himself between Andrea and I. She was surprised by Lloyd's appearance and that shock was enough to break her grip on me.

Lloyd forced her backwards and gripped me tightly with hands either side of my face.

"Come on bach, I'm fine" he looked at me with a pleading expression on his face. My fury continued to climb and I was just able to make out a ripping, tearing sound coming from behind me. My suit was giving way under the strain of my wrath.

"Focus Anthony. Look at me. You can't change here, you'll bring the mansion down and you could kill everyone in it, including yourself." All of the pretension was now gone from his voice and he was back to talking to me like he had before my induction into the Circle. Through the thunder clouds in my mind, I could make out what he was saying and listened.

"Breathe. Concentrate on what you can feel. Calm yourself and you'll ease back." Lloyd soothed me, continuing to hold onto my face and I could feel my mind starting to level out. I took several slow, deep breaths and my temperature started to fall. As it went, so did the red colouration which had been spreading over me.

"That's it bach. Just relax." As my breathing was becoming more relaxed, so too was the expression on Lloyds face. My suit was now a little more comfortable and I was feeling that I was now returning to normal. I took one final deep lungful of air and let my body fall limp as I leaned backwards, almost unable to stand upright without help.

"Anthony, everything goes on in a certain way, protocol has to be followed" Lloyd informed me as he relaxed his grip on my head. I could still feel the imprint of his hands where he had been holding me and that told me that he had been gripping me with some force. I realised that I was about to be unbelievably stupid at what I thought was a wild injustice. I was starting to be far too familiar with the embarrassed feeling of deep shame and I stood looking at Lloyd without knowing whether he would want to have anything to do with me again. That made me feel even worse. My first instinct had been to stamp my feet against what I didn't like, to rage against the machine. I hadn't even considered the thought that Lloyd may have understood completely what was happening and believed in it. I didn't like it so that meant that it was wrong.

I couldn't look at Lloyd anymore and turned my head to face Andrea, hoping to see some kind of understanding of what I was feeling. Instead, I was greeted by proof that certain rules and regulations must be followed and there was no room for argument. Andrea was slightly hunched forwards and had both her arms splayed out and back, with her fingers spread against the opposite wall. She now looked very different from the well tailored image she had been exuding when we first commenced our tour.

Instead of her usual skin tone, she was now a glistening white/blue and her eyes had turned the total grey they had been when she had been in her Dragon form. She was starting to move through the early stages of her own transformation. Her breathing was shallow and it looked as if she was charging herself, readying herself to drive forwards at me. The penny dropped. If I had continued to blow up, she had been totally prepared to rip me to pieces to preserve the safety of the mansion. By the look on her face, any weakness that might have been caused in the Circle by my demise hadn't even crossed her mind.

"He is calm my lady" Lloyd called out as he turned to face Andrea. All of the ceremonial tone had quickly returned to his voice when he talked to Andrea. She didn't take her eyes from me.

"My lady, please. He is calm" he repeated.

Andrea's eyes flicked quickly to Lloyd, then back to me. Slowly, her posture began to ease and she pushed herself away from the wall and lowered her arms. The colour began to return to her skin and the building tension in her posture ebbed away. I started to feel a wave of relief pour over me. Andrea's eyes were the last thing to return to normal. They had held their grey for a long time and served to remind me that she had been maintaining her readiness to attack for as long as she could.

We all stood still, taking in what had just taken place. We were all breathing deeply but for very different reasons. Lloyd was moving to the fumes in his body's fuel tank, I was trying to gather myself after my outburst and Andrea looked as if she was still on edge, ready to move in the blink of an eye. Lloyd spoke first.

"Shall we continue?"

I looked up to him and he had straightened his suit, calmed his hair, even his wild beard now looked like it was tamed and utterly presentable, and was now back to his almost regal demeanour in readiness to pick up where we left off. Without any fuss he shrugged off the effects of the encounter and was waiting for me. I looked down at my suit and ran a hand through my hair. I was a mess. The suit had split through the seams at odd points where my body had begun to alter shape and burst out. Both of my trouser legs had gaping holes in them down the front of my thighs and I could feel a great deal more movement from the back of the jacket. Had my wings done that?

Andrea wasn't showing any of the ill effects of her transformation preparation. She had returned to her usual appearance and was slowly smoothing down her jacket as I looked at her. She had regained her cool exterior and was back in character to resume the tour of the house. She didn't once meet my gaze though and I was left in no doubt that she wasn't at all impressed with my display.

The remainder of the tour took on the same pattern as before, row after row of dusty pictures and pointless small talk regarding the people they were depicting. The one thing that stuck in my mind was the fact that we were everywhere. Lloyd had pointed out that human history has images of Dragons of different forms all over the world, in civilisations that would never have met. It was only then that I had realised that the stories all came from the same place. The Circle was global and they had been doing what they had been doing for millennia. That thought seemed to weigh more than all of the house put together.

There were no more people to meet as we meandered along and after what felt like another ponderous thousand years, we arrived in the kitchens to be welcomed by Mike. He bowed in the same gesture of deference he had produced when we had first arrived at the mansion.

"Sir. May I present your kitchen and its staff. We are here for your service whenever you may need us." Mike had taken on the same regal tone that Lloyd was using as he spoke. He was also being weighed down by the same fear of my displeasure as every other person in the building. Everyone except Andrea.

Lloyd eased to my side and lightly coughed to attract my attention, "Protocol dictates that you should thank him for his efforts and accept a tour of the room." I quickly gathered myself, feeling chastened to the point that I would gladly take part in every aspect of the ritual that was expected of me.

"Thank you Lloyd" I responded in the most well to do voice I could muster and started to step forward.

"Don't worry bach, it's almost over" whispered Lloyd in reply, low enough so no-one except me would be able to hear. I whipped my head round in shock at the relaxed tone and Lloyd quickly winked at me as the slightest of slight smiles crossed his lips. I felt slightly less ridiculous and turned back to face Mike knowing that everyone here was being weighed down by the same expectation, the same history, only we were all covered by different parts of it.

Mike led me round the vast kitchen which would make several top class hotels look like the worst kind of greasy spoon cafe. Spotless stainless steel and tiled surfaces looked back at me as we moved around and all of the staff was presented with utmost care and attention to detail. Men and women from a wide range of shapes and sizes, from several ethnic backgrounds stood stiffly to attention as I moved. Mike even apologised profusely for the small pin prick size mark that was on the apron of one of the lower ranked members of the workforce. I hadn't even seen it!

"I am so sorry for my failure to present a clean welcome to you sir" he grovelled. I could feel that this was something that I shouldn't accept so responded in the way that I felt was appropriate for the situation. "Thank you for the welcome Michael, do not worry about the mistake, but don't let it happen again." I had hoped that that would be serious enough to sound like I was fully playing my part in this process but without making Mike and his team feel that I was really angry at them. By the look on his face, I had no idea if it had worked or not.

Lloyd walked forward to rescue everyone from the awkward silence that was now settled over the meeting.

"Thank you for your time sir. If you would follow me, I will show you to your room."

"I can remember the way, thank you Lloyd" I let tumble from my mouth without engaging my brain. Andrea growled from beside me.

"The room you stayed in is part of the guest quarters sir. Let me show you to the master suite where you will be staying from now on." With that, Lloyd quickly spun round and made a bee line for the door we had come in through. Andrea stormed after him with out looking back to anyone. She was obviously playing the role of the aloof lady of the manor but that was being augmented very strongly by the palpable contempt she was feeling towards me. The kitchen team seemed to take the smallest step towards relief as we made to leave the room, Mike included. As we left, I noticed that the limp that had been slowing Lloyd's progress during the tour had now almost completely disappeared. He was moving much more freely and was now not looking like he had been in anywhere near as serious an attack as he had. I made a mental note to speak to him about the whole situation when we could behave in a more normal fashion, protocol and all that.

As I followed Lloyd and Andrea away from the kitchen I could feel that I was treading in well worn footsteps. For the first time I stopped thinking about how this whole process was a waste of time. As we continued, I started to look at the whole process as something which had been done like this since the beginning. As I relaxed, my mind began to wander and fill with images from the past. Again, my mind's eye was being shown images of people from the past going through exactly the same process, reviewing servants and taking their place as the master of the estate. Images of centuries ago were folded in with those of a much more recent vintage. Rich smells of wood and smoke filled my nostrils and added more depth to the mental picture. Each person was being led through a tour of what they commanded but it was also a journey through the knowledge of the estate and the line. The colossal Dragons who had been here before had not only left behind their enormous power but they had given a spoken history of who they were, how they had lived. As I walked after the others it dawned on me that they were also leaving behind the details of their demise. I could feel everything hitting my mind at once as thousands of years of collective memory made itself heard. The details were missing in the roiling mass of information and sensation but I knew that everything that was going on had been done before and that it would be done again.

My mind was still being split between the information I was seeing in my head and the journey we were taking back towards the front of the mansion but I was still feeling the growth of understanding as we moved. The more I let my mind open to the

114

knowledge held in my family line, the more I realised what my life was going to be. There were no specific feelings, no details, no absolutes, but I was starting to understand the reasons behind the need for pomp and ceremony. Everyone had been through this before. I was just the next in line to be a part of the pool of power which would pass to the next member when I finally fell. I was now part of something which was bigger than I could comprehend but it was something that would only leave me when I died. No pressure then.

We finally reached the main entrance hall and Lloyd turned to face me, probably making sure that I was still following him. I snapped my head away from the images of the past which were filling my mind and focussed solely onto him.

"If you would like to follow me sir, the master suite is just upstairs." He raised an arm to show me the way. Andrea was already halfway up the stairs towards our destination. She must have been here before. We all strode up the grey slate steps and headed towards another staircase off to the left of the first floor wrap around balcony. These stairs spiralled widely up and around to open onto a closed door. The huge piece of polished mahogany hung within a door frame of stone and wood. Carvings similar to every other doorway adorned both the door and the frame but instead of the usual woodland and wildlife images, this time I was greeted by solid carvings of winged creatures in majestic poses. Dragons of various kinds were carved into the blocks at different points but they all surrounded the central image. Of double doors measuring roughly ten feet in height and at least seven across, the main icon took over an area of at least six feet by six feet. It showed me something that I recognised. It was something that I had seen very recently looking back at me from the mirrored surface of the cavern under Neath Abbey. I was confronted by a detailed rendering of my Dragon face. Razor sharp teeth, heavy, sweeping horns, scaled skin and piercing eyes all laid down with complete accuracy. This was obviously the master suite for the master of the estate.

Andrea and Lloyd were now stood on either side of the door and were looking down to me as I climbed the last few stairs. Lloyd reached into his pocket and produced a large polished brass key. "Welcome home sir" he said and placed the large key in the lock.

With a swift twist, he disengaged the drum and after several meaty clunks and a slight push, the door slowly swung open inwards.

"This room is sealed when the Circle is broken, we now open it again as the Circle has been reformed" boomed Lloyd and gestured for me to enter. I did slowly.

The room was enormous. It easily dwarfed the total floor area of my flat back in London but somehow, it still retained a feeling of comfort and warmth. There was a framework of dark wood throughout the whole area, criss-crossing the white plaster work between. There were several large paintings hung about but the majority of the wall space had been covered by thick tapestries. The ceiling stretched out above us at roughly double the height of a normal room – twenty to twenty five feet high. Evenly spaced throughout were deep set skylights which opened out onto the clear night sky. Around the edges of the room were various shapes and sizes of furniture, all of which was made of heavy wood and carved, again, with more views of the Dragon forms which were on the main door.

As I stood there looking around the room I could see that both paintings and tapestries depicted the same images of battle between Dragons and the forces lined up against them, demons and monsters of the worst kind. As I looked over the picture shown before me, I started to notice that not only death and destruction were being depicted. Woven in through the imagery of violence were pockets of normal life. The Dragon was watching over its charges. Its entire staff had the protection of the creature. As I focussed on the details I started to get more realisation of the position I was moving into. The Dragon, the entire Circle, represented more than simply a warmongering leviathan, unleashed only to do damage. It was more than that and now it was beginning to become clear to me. I had been told the history as to why the Circle had come into existence but I had totally missed the point. The Circle was in place as a mighty form of defence but it was there in service. They, I, had the responsibility for ensuring the safety of the human race. The power and the task had been moving onwards through time for thousands of years and would continue until any threat could be totally removed. Each new member would have gone through the same steps as I had and would have been feeling a mixture of emotions the same way I was.

I stood staring as more and more pieces of the puzzle fell into place.

Lloyd silently walked to my side and waited. I could feel his presence next to me but didn't know how to start. I looked back over my shoulder to catch a glimpse of what Lloyd was doing. He stood there unmoving. The expression on his face was calm as he waited for me.

"Welcome home sir" he whispered to me, echoing the words he had uttered before the doors had opened, but now they had been filled with so much more meaning.

I turned to face him and, from over his shoulder, caught the last glimpse of Andrea as she left the room, turning to head swiftly back down the stairway to the rest of the house.

"What am I supposed to do Lloyd? This is too big for me. I'm just a Personal Trainer who enjoys having a laugh. I can't handle this kind of responsibility. I can't even pay my credit card on time let alone stand guard over the human race." I felt like I needed help and that I needed it now.

"Anthony" Lloyd said as he checked that Andrea had left the room. "Andrea is here to train you. She is going to give you all of the awareness of the powers you have as a member of the Circle. She will open your eyes to what you can do." His tone was back to the familiar, conversational lilt and, strangely, that relaxed tone had started to sound a little alien. How long had we been walking around this place?

The thought of even more mystical surprises only seemed to make me slightly more comfortable.

"The members of the Circle all take the processes seriously. The tour of the estate, the meeting of the staff, everything. Andrea would have been trained from a young age, like everyone else, that things happen a certain way. Expectation for how to do things happens to all of us and we all take our responsibilities seriously. Andrea believes in what was happening because she has been trained to. Don't underestimate the power of belief." More feeling of what I was getting in to.

"What about all of the details that aren't to do with Dragons? With me stamping my feet earlier, I don't think Andrea is going to want to spend any more time with me than she has to and I am going to need a lot of help."

"That's what I'm here for bach" Lloyd grinned and took hold of my shoulders. "You didn't go through any of the proper training that everyone else does. You walked into this whole situation at the end and you've probably been struggling with all the detail."

I looked into his eyes and saw real concern for me. I began to relax out of the straight jacket of the protocol we had been working under during the tour of the mansion.

"I have been here for a great many years Anthony and I have held the position of Head of House for almost all of them. I looked after your uncle when he first joined the Circle and made sure he was ready for everything that was thrown at him." Lloyd had managed to pour a level of his authority from the tour into his voice now. It gave me the feeling of someone who was certain about their subject. His voice softened slightly as he continued.

"You will be fine. We are going to look after you." He smiled in reassurance.

"Thanks Lloyd."

"Don't worry bach. You rest here for the night and I'll get you set for the morning. Would you like me to send some food up?"

"No thanks. I'm good" I replied. I really wasn't even slightly hungry.

"Training will be great fun; your uncle always enjoyed it" said Lloyd finally.

With that, he turned and strode towards the door, still carrying himself with the utmost poise and precision. I watched him go and felt a gnawing sensation at my core.

My uncle had enjoyed it. The training. Would I?

This was the first time that someone had mentioned my uncle in terms of being in the same position as me, having the same experiences as me. I watched Lloyd leave and considered the thought of my uncle standing here, looking around the same room, taking in the same details and deciding what he was going to do. Had he welcomed the responsibility? Had he known from an early age that this was expected of him? Had he wanted to run for the hills? I stood in the dimly lit room and rolled the thoughts of my family round my mind. Had Steve known any of this? Was this why my brother had left, running from what he thought was nothing more than the ramblings of an obsessed old man?

I suddenly felt utterly alone again.

The room I stood in was the perfect display of wealth and comfort but it had been built on the bedrock of servitude and responsibility.

I turned and made my way towards the large double bed under the enormous window on the far wall. Plush furnishings of faux animal skin blankets and deeply padded pillows filled the bed and gave the impression of the kind of comfort that people like me can only usually dream about. I undressed as I looked out of the window and I dropped the lights to nothing, looking out over the front of the estate. Light was cast from the house out onto the driveway and the areas of scrub grass land. Long shadows were being cast over the overgrown lawns from the stone statues on the grounds and I was sure I could make out hordes of marauding demons coiling ready to brutalise the mansion and everyone in it. A chill spread through me and I couldn't help but shiver as the thought of monsters filled my mind.

I crawled into the bed and pulled the covers up over my head. I had seen everything to do with this estate, alongside the details which were coming from the Awakening and the realisation that I was a monster of epic proportions, and it was terrifying and intoxicating at the same time. Every part of me twisted in helpless fear and all I could do was scream for help.

My call of terror filled the room and beyond, but no-one came.

I unloaded all of the fear and uncertainty into my call into the darkness and knew that I wasn't the first to feel this way. The fear and uncertainty had been in this room before. It felt good but I knew that no matter what I did tonight, regardless of my fear, the real excitement would begin in earnest tomorrow.

13

The next morning came round much faster than I had hoped. I didn't sleep well at all and I spent most of the night tossing and turning. More and more vivid images of Dragons and monsters filled my mind. I couldn't be sure if I was dreaming or if the sensation was coming from another shared group of memories. Either way, when the sun came up I was in no doubt that I was really in need of more rest.

I dragged myself out of the bed and straightened myself up. Despite feeling like I could sleep for at least three more weeks, my body felt really good. I slowly made my way over to the bathroom which was over to the right hand side of the room. The suite was laid out in the same style and finish as the room deep in the cavern, black stone and chrome filled the space and more frosted glass blocks enclosed the shower area. I stood in front of the full length mirror and looked myself up and down, taking in the details of my physique. Things had changed.

I had always worked out hard to try and ensure that my body was at the highest standard I could get it. I was used to being fit and healthy but my reflection was showing me something slightly different. A week ago, I was someone who looked after themselves and probably spent a decent amount of time in the gym. Now, I had become the man who is the complete gym monkey. I looked as though I had put on at least fifteen kilos of muscle and dropped at least ten percent body fat. I now looked more like a body builder – thick shoulders and chest, massive arms and huge legs. My stomach was now covered in the lumps and bumps of an incredible washboard. My muscles were now bigger and more visible, the slight covering of body fat gone completely leaving behind the look of a sculpted statue. I looked at myself with my brow furrowed, not sure what to make of it all. I liked the feeling of flexing my new form and stood posing for a while, this look was great to get for free, who wants to have to put in that kind of time in the gym?, but it had also seemed a little extreme when I was training the accountant set, it scared people if you were too big.

I stopped twirling and stood still, staring into the mirror at myself. The realisation was dawning that this was yet another thing that was going on that I wasn't prepared for and that I had had no prior knowledge. It made me think. What else has been done to me or can I expect to see happen before this whole situation is over. The worry wasn't going to make anything easier and standing here looking at myself wasn't helping either. I showered quickly prepared myself mentally for whatever was about to happen.

I wrapped a towel round my waist and sauntered back into the main room. Lloyd was waiting for me.

"Good morning. Did you sleep well?" he asked breezily, still holding on to the formal tone.

"Awful. You?" was all I could manage in reply. Lloyd chuckled slightly under his breath and walked towards the drawer unit on the farthest wall from the bathroom. He opened the top drawer and cast a reviewing eye over the contents.

"We have provided a wide selection of clothes for you." He slowly closed the drawer and turned to face me. "I'll make sure that the kitchens have prepared your breakfast." He smiled, "Is there anything else you need?"

"Please will you relax when you are around me? I don't think I'm the lord of the manor type, do you?"

By the look on his face, Lloyd had been enjoying all the pomp and ceremony, and all of the discomfort that that had created in me. His rod straight posture softened slightly and his smile grew.

"Whatever you wish sir" he told me in a highly polished accent which was even more aloof than the one he had been using up to now. He bowed dramatically, throwing out both of his arms for the full effect as he practically scraped the floor with his forehead. He snapped back upright and looked much more like the Lloyd that I had met in London, even his beard looked like it had been mussed up during his enthusiastic bow. He looked like my friend again.

"I'll go back to the kitchens and get your breakfast sorted out; you've got a busy day." The last part of the sentence was accompanied by one of his trademark, slightly too hard, playful slaps to the shoulder.

"Come on bach, let's get you underway. What do you want to eat?" He made me relax slightly and it felt good. I started to think about food and what the kitchens could prepare.

"What's on the menu?" I asked.

With another grin, "Anything you want. We are very well stocked here."

I continued to think and I started to feel very cheeky.

"Since I have this newly pumped up body and I look as good as this, I think I'll have a full fried breakfast, bacon, sausage, beans, eggs, tomatoes and hash browns. Damn the calories."

"Tea, coffee, fruit juice?" asked Lloyd without showing any hint of surprise.

"I'll have a pot of tea. And some toast as well please." My mouth was watering at the thought of all the bad food that I usually steered well clear of. I was allowed to be as bad as I wanted and people were going to be preparing the food for me. Maybe I was the lord of the manor type?

"I'll bring your breakfast up as soon as it is prepared. It will be about ten minutes" and Lloyd strode out of the room, gently closing the heavy doors as he left.

Ten minutes? They must really be on the ball down there.

With the thought of rich food filling my mind, I pulled out some clothes from the chest of drawers and got myself dressed ready for a day of training. Images of miles of running and weights work fired through my head. Glancing out of the window, I decided that it was probably going to be cold enough for a full track suit. The mist and low cloud which had surrounded the estate when we had first arrived was back but it had pushed on and grown in strength. It was now seeping in through the tree line and was ringing the whole area in a halo of fog which was obscuring the bottom ten to fifteen feet of the trees. I started to think about what may or may not be in the pea soup mass, waiting for me to stray too close to the edge, but shook the thought away before I got too obsessed by it. Beasts or no beasts, it made for great training weather. At least it wasn't raining.

My attention was broken from the outside world by the door swinging open and Lloyd walked in, following a short, stick thin woman who was roughly forty years old. She had red hair, flecked through with strands of grey, pulled back into an almost painfully tidy ponytail. She was nervously bringing a large silver platter full of, what I could only assume to be, my breakfast towards the desk on the wall next to the bathroom. That was a very fast ten minutes.

The cutlery and crockery rattled loudly as she neared her destination. I looked at Lloyd hoping for some explanation as to why she was so nervous. His face was a cold mask of authority as he watched her progress, reviewing her every move.

"Will you be needing anything else sir?" asked the tiny woman as she finally set down her tray and looked up to me with absolute expectant terror written all over her face.

I walked over to the tray and looked over the meal which had been laid out for me, trying to look every inch the master of all I surveyed, protocol and all that.

"Everything looks delicious, thank you. Before you go, what is your name?"

"Wynn sir" she stammered as she shifted her weight nervously from foot to foot.

"Wynn. Thank you for bringing my food. How long have you worked here at the estate?" I really wanted people to feel more comfortable around me. The thought of everyone here at the mansion walking on eggshells every time I walked into the room wasn't something that made me feel that good. From the look on Wynn's face, she hadn't expected to be asked any questions let alone something about her personally. Her eyes looked to Lloyd and he nodded slightly to show that she could answer.

"Thirty one years sir" she replied and looked on hoping that her answer was acceptable. "Will that be all?" She was obviously really keen to leave the room as fast as she could.

"Thirty one years? You must have started here very young. Are you happy here?"

"Very sir. I enjoy being here" she stumbled through her reply, giving the response she hoped was what I was after. This was definitely something I would have to work on. I couldn't have fear being the motivator for everyone here.

"That will be all Wynn, thank you" said Lloyd from next to me and she scurried out, only just managing to keep to a fast walk. The door shut behind her and Lloyd and I were alone.

"Why is it that there is such a fear of me here? Has it always been like this, that the top dog is this monster who storms around the place making everyone else quake?"

"Times have changed a great deal over the years. It used to be that the lord of the manor was viewed as being the upper class and therefore better than the rest of the population. Land owners all over the country used to rule their estates with an iron fist over the years and we weren't any different here. Things may be different in the outside world regarding working conditions, but old habits die hard." Lloyd looked like everything was normal in that explanation.

"We'll have to make sure that that changes. I can't have people scared just to be in the same building as me."

Lloyd smiled again. "Sounds good to me. Now, eat and we can get you started."

I sat down at the desk and started to wolf down the huge meal which was laid out for me. The food was superb. All of the tastes seemed to be bigger and better than anything I had tasted before. I'd have to make sure that I didn't over indulge; my new super fit physique would get covered in soft padding in days!

Lloyd made his way towards the door as I ate, stopping before he left the room.

"When you're ready, Andrea will be waiting in the entrance hall downstairs. Have fun."

He left me to my breakfast and I pondered the events to come. What was Andrea going to put me through? Would I enjoy it as much as my Uncle had? Would Andrea just be waiting to torture me? She hadn't looked that happy with me the last time I had seen her and it seemed to me that this whole training exercise was the perfect opportunity for her to exact some kind of revenge on me.

I finished the meal and leaned back into my seat feeling contented but very full.

"You didn't really think this through, did you?" I told my stomach. If I started jumping around I would probably make myself sick so training would have to wait a while. The last thing I needed was for Andrea to think that I was totally out of shape because I was sick after the warm-up. I stood up and made my way back towards the bed, fully intending to have a lay down and let my body get to work on breakfast but as I neared the huge window I could make out the lone form of Andrea stood in what had once been a lawn off to the right of the roadway leading from the mansion. She was slowly and methodically stretching, preparing herself for the physical rigours of the day to come. Add to that, she was looking right at me. Her wintry stare was unwavering and I could tell, even from this distance, that she expected me to be at her side within the next five minutes. So much for a rest after my meal.

I left all of the dirty dishes on the desk and moved as quickly as I dared down the stairs. In the entrance hall, Mike was stood at the foot of the staircase with an expectant look on his face.

"I hope your breakfast was to your satisfaction sir" he asked me as I approached him.

"Top banana Mike. Everything was fantastic. Give my compliments to the chef."

Mike relaxed slightly on hearing the good news. "Mr Howells will be pleased to hear it." It felt good to give someone good news but it still reinforced the feeling of me being the ogre of the piece. As I started to tell Mike that he could relax around me my gaze drifted out through the open main door and landed squarely on Andrea. Her stretching regime had obviously finished and now she was stood with her arms folded, again looking icy spears at me.

"We'll talk later. I'll bring the dishes down when I get back in from whatever Andrea has planned for me. Wish me luck." Without waiting for any reply I bounded out of the door towards Andrea, all the while praying that my stomach could handle the exertion.

Andrea was stood amongst all of the weeds and mangled plants, some of which were standing well above her head height. She wasn't happy

"Good morning" I announced as cheerily as I could and looked on through the lifting clouds of our breath, hoping that she was going to go easy on me. "Sleep well?"

She snorted at me and planted her hands firmly on her hips. "Are you ready for training?" she practically snarled at me, ignoring my attempts at pleasantries.

"I'm fine. What have you got in mind?"

She paced slowly around me, looking me up and down in much the same way I had done to myself in the bathroom. She was less impressed by what she saw. She was dressed in a very loose fitting sweat suit and was wearing old dirty trainers. Her hair hung loose and was being blown around gently by the low wind which was streaming over the territory. She stopped walking and stood directly in front of me, and kicked off her trainers. Her bare feet settled onto the dewy ground.

"I have training in mind" she replied and pulled her suit trousers off, kicking them into a pile next to her shoes. "I will show you skills and techniques that you will need to survive" and off came her sweat shirt, again thrown to the side. As she stood before me, now completely naked, I was able to see again, the tight mass of muscle she was covered in. She was quite an impressive sight.

"But before we can begin, I'll need to know what you are capable of. Let us begin."

Without warning, there was an increase in the air temperature and Andrea screamed at me. The scream was piercing but soon began to change. In the blink of an eye, she had burst upwards to assume her Dragon form. Her head snapped towards me and brought all of her drilling glare with it. She reached out with her arms and her wings as she roared down at me and I could see that my breakfast was going to be on the field of play in no time at all.

"Your first task will be to survive me" Andrea growled and narrowed her grey eyes. Her pupils were barely distinguishable from the rest of her eyes, only the slightest shade lighter, but I could tell that she was intently focussed on me and that she meant business. The low crackle of a growl was rolling from her, sounding like she was gargling with rocks. She slowly twisted her body and lowered her head, bringing her gaze down, closer to my level. She looked like she was coiling herself up to deliver a strike of some sort.

A split second after the spinning in the back of my head started, a massive armoured hand flashed out from my right and slapped into my chest, pulverising all of the air from my lungs as I was flung backwards through the wild plants towards the house. I crashed to a halt underneath what was practically a tree of a weed and tried desperately to force air into my lungs. Pain wrapped my chest like a vice and there was nothing I could do about it.

I gasped at the shallowest of breaths and felt my mind spin again, another alert of impending danger or just my head going round the rollercoaster of disorientation. I couldn't take the risk that I was

126

simply dizzy and so forced myself to my feet. It was a good job I had. Andrea had taken off in what can only be described as being half leap and half flight. She had propelled herself upwards and forwards with one mighty effort from her wings and was now travelling directly at me in a large arc. I looked up to pinpoint her, struggling to hold onto the focus my injured chest was still trying to rob me of, and saw her fold away her wings and plant all four of her limbs forwards to land on the same spot – me. Every single razor sharp claw on her terrifying digits was aimed squarely at me and by the look on her face, even through the reptilian features; she was truly intent on tearing me to shreds.

I leapt forward as she neared the ground, pushing myself as hard as I could to clear the area she was going to land in. The pain in my chest stabbed at me in multiple spots and I could feel every one of them as a piercing from a rod of burning steel. This was going to be a short fight.

Andrea landed where I had been standing with an almighty thump as her talons embedded themselves in the turf. I pulled myself to my feet and started to run off in the opposite direction, back where my attacker had come from but my plans hadn't included an assault from her tail. The spinning in my head again appeared early enough for me to know I had a problem but too late for me to be able to do anything about it. The heavy appendage slammed into my back and I crashed through more plant life before coming to rest in the centre of a far too wide clearing. I tried to force myself back to my feet but my breakfasts return stopped me getting that far. My breathing was now starting to rattle in my chest and I was starting to consider giving up.

"You are soft. You have no awareness of any part of who you are and what you have to do. I hope your replacement is better equipped" roared Andrea as she started bounding towards my broken form.

"You are a waste. This estate requires a real leader" and with that she leapt at me again.

Her words had struck home and bored into me. I was seen as a waste? I would not allow her to carry that high and mighty attitude back to people I liked and rule them with terror. I would not be shown up by this station-driven mad woman and made to be the cowering fool she thought I was. The fury climbed within me. Red flashes filled my vision and the pain quickly drained away. I forced myself to my feet and span to face Andrea as she soared towards me.

"This is my house" spat wildly from me and I braced myself for her impact. As she landed on me the red flashes in my eyesight quickly coalesced and I roared out in defiance, reaching my arms up to catch her hands.

My transformation was lightning fast and left a deep frost on the ground all around me. I tore through my tracksuit, leaving shreds fluttering in the wind, as my body morphed into the giant from the cavern. She hadn't been prepared for me to change at that point and her attack was much weaker for it. As Andrea's claws swung at me, they met with my armoured form rather than my human skin and only scraped the surface. She crashed into me with the force of a speeding train but I was now much bigger than she was, and was able to catch her in mid flight. I held her at arms length ahead of me, struggling to be free, and looked her deep in the eyes. Her expression said it all. Again, through all the scaled features I could make out the feeling behind them. Andrea was pleased. That made me feel worse.

"Now it's my turn" I rumbled at her as I narrowed my eyes at her. Her expression changed as she realised that the game she started wasn't going to end where she had expected. She was angry at the behaviour of the upstart but she was also scared of me. She was trying to hide it but her fear was creeping onto her face and showed in her jerky movements. She wanted to get out of my grip quickly.

Without another word, I span and threw her across to the other side of the roadway, towards, what I hoped were very sharp thorned plants. She didn't land where I had intended. Instead, she twisted and spread her wings. This allowed her to glide gracefully away and bank round to face me. She landed softly about one hundred metres from me and held up both her hands in a gesture of apparent surrender. Her wings settled back behind her and her posture lost the murderous edge.

"First lesson over" she panted. I didn't trust her.

"What were you teaching me?" The anger was still simmering inside me but I would listen to what she had to say. I took a large purposeful step towards her, drawing myself up tall as I went. The spinning in my head had totally disappeared leaving me clear headed and free from the pain she had inflicted.

"I needed to see how you change and now I know. I can teach you how to control the transformation and be able to call on it at will, with a level mind." She started slowly walking towards me, still with her arms raised in mock submission.

"You are fuelled by rage. When you get angry enough, you find your power and can fight anything, that much was clear from the attack outside the Abbey, but I needed to find out how you really get fired up. You are going to have to learn to control that fire to allow you to wholly dictate your transformations. Eventually, you'll be able to change at will. This is something your line must master first, before any other skills can be added."

"My line?" Anger increased a level within me. She couldn't understand me. All the other people who had been here weren't me. They weren't the same each time. I was not going to be viewed as simply being the next off the conveyer belt.

She kept taking slow steps towards me, all the time with her hands raised. Her voice was coming out much more gently now and held a soothing edge. A small voice in my mind pointed out that she was acting in the way you would around gun wielding maniac, all calm and understanding, not wanting to antagonise or rile. I was too mad to really pay that voice much notice. She was probably trying to trick me so she could attack me when my defences were down.

That made me seethe. I braced myself for her inevitable betrayal and felt a thunderous growl developing within me as she paced a circular path around me. As the noise of my anger hit the air more clouds plumed up before my eyes but this time they weren't the usual white wisps of breath. They had now been replaced by dark grey towers of thick, sulphurous smoke. The acrid smell filled my nostrils and I knew that my anger was preparing a blast of fire within my stomach.

Andrea noticed the change in my posture and the rising smoke and knew that she would have to do something quickly.

"Anthony, you are the latest in a long line of Fire Dragons. You're different from me and most of the others in the Circle. My power is derived from ice. We are different but we are working together against a common foe." Her Russian accent was cut through with a deeper pleading now.

"Every one of your predecessors has gone through the same process, learning how to control what you are."

I wasn't a part of this history. None of these people knew me and I didn't believe that any of what she was saying would have any effect on me. The tiny voice in my head was engulfed by my growing rage and I didn't care what was going to happen. She was going to find out that no-one can make me do or be anything that I didn't believe.

For a split second, my vision was totally shrouded in a deep crimson and all of my climbing wrath poured out in a jet of white hot flame aimed squarely at Andrea.

She must have seen the attack coming. Before the gout of searing terror hit her she had spread her wings and with one almighty beat had taken herself straight up out of the range of danger. I followed her skywards, still spewing out flame, but I was always reacting to her movements, unable to truly cause her any damage. As she continued her aerial ballet I could feel the reserves of fuel for my breath depleting. The ferocity of the jet began to reduce as it swept through the foggy sky and it was soon burned out completely.

I stood looking up towards her as she held herself stationary in the air at the height of the tallest trees. My breathing was now much deeper and I felt a gnawing emptiness in my stomach. Andrea looked calm and collected and that all of the exertion of the previous exchange had had no effect on her. She was obviously much fitter than me.

"You are driven by anger so you will need to learn to control yourself" fluttered down towards me on the breeze, her tone playful. This time I decided that the voice in my head may have been right. I relaxed and immediately, the agitation I had been feeling, drained away.

Andrea watched from above me as my shoulders slouched down slightly as I relaxed my stance from one of combat readiness to one which could only really be called subtle bewilderment.

"Are you going to listen to me or should I stay up here?" I could hear the slightly playful tone to her voice again but I was also aware that there was a real undertone of concern.

"I'll play nice" I responded, hoping to highlight the fact that I was back in control of myself and the same relaxed Anthony had returned. Andrea considered that for a second and then slowly descended towards the ground. She touched down amongst a dense patch of brambles and maintained the cautious posture. Was she hoping for some cover from the plants if I went mad again? That thought tugged at me and made me feel very sheepish. Andrea noticed that my shoulders had just slumped even further so realised that I was not going to be any kind of threat. She eased her way out of the undergrowth and edged her way towards me in the same way she had before my barbecue session.

"Can you see that you need to control your emotions?" she asked as she came closer. I looked down at her and took in the details of the ground around me. Vast areas had been burned down to a blackened mess of ruined plant and earth, the victim of my lack of control. The worst sight was where Andrea had been standing when I had first let loose with my attack. A wide, jagged edged area of twenty feet square had been utterly destroyed. All of the ugly plants were gone, blasted away to nothing and disintegrated, but that wasn't where the carnage had stopped. The whole area had been dug out to a depth of six feet, forming an ugly crater in the ground. Its entire surface was roasted to a black, misshapen mass. Small fires were still burning at points within the rupture of the earth and were giving off an awful odour of rot and decay. As if to rub in the fact that I didn't know everything, Andrea slowly stepped through the crater on her way to stand with me.

The more I looked at what I had done, the worse I felt. The details of the carnage seemed to glow in my head as I stared at them, not wanting to take my eyes from them. Andrea eased up next to me.

"It's terrifying, isn't it?" she said quietly and was silent. We both stared at the damage that I had caused to the ground and I shuddered. Not only had I destroyed a vast area of this estates grounds, but I had been aiming that destruction at someone who, it would appear, had been testing me as a part of helping me stay safe. That reality twisted in my stomach.

"I'm sorry" was all I could think to say. I closed my eyes and bowed my head at the thought of the damage I could have done.

Andrea didn't look up at me, instead holding her gaze on the ruined turf before us,

"You aren't the first to react this way to the first trial of your training. I am going to show you how to bring out the best in your abilities, but without you needing to feel like you need to kill everyone in the room to do it." The last part of the sentence was greeted with a slight nudge. I opened my eyes and looked down to her at her playful gesture and saw her still looking straight ahead.

"Besides, I was never in any real danger. You couldn't hit me with your fire even if you wanted to." And she said it with a straight face.

I huffed under my breath at the release of tension and felt relieved that I hadn't ruined my relationship with Andrea and the rest of the Circle.

"How did you know that I was going to go wild and attack you? How did you know that I was going to go mad?" I started the conversation I hoped would give me some answers. She looked up to me,

"You Fire Dragons always do. You all think that you can beat the injustice of it all, you all feel too much, so all I had to do was push at that. You didn't hide the fact that you didn't really appreciate the way that everyone was behaving during the tour last night so I worked with that. You almost boiled over last night so I didn't have to think too hard about where to start. You don't like to be told what to do or how to think do you? All I had to do was tell you things you hated, things that made you feel weak and you did the rest. I did have other ideas but you bought into everything very quickly so I worked with it."

I felt like I had been utterly manipulated. The feeling of being the last person in the room to get the joke returned with a vengeance and felt like it was here to stay. My pride was dented both because of the way Andrea had moved me around at will to prove a point, but also the fact that I hadn't either seen it coming or been able to do anything about it.

"You've done this before haven't you?" I prodded, starting to get more of a feeling for the situation.

"I've trained one other but I have been tutored well by the Circle. We are all expected to teach the newer members of the group so you will be doing the same eventually." Andrea's response was heartening. Knowing that everyone in the Circle would have gone through much the same situation made me feel more comfortable with my behaviour, suddenly realising that maybe I wasn't too dissimilar to everyone else who came before me and that that wasn't really a bad thing. At least I wasn't the first to act like a complete jack-ass!

"So now what?" I asked after an elongated pause.

"We work on your control first, change the way you think so you can get the best results from your abilities" Andrea replied with a serious expression on her face. She wasn't out to kill me now but she still meant business.

"As you are now" she continued, "you are very different from being a human being but you are still thinking like one. When you were responding to my attack, you didn't even consider jumping or flying, did you? You were going to run around and spray fire everywhere but all I needed to do was use our greater proportional strength and flight to stay out of your range."

"I may not have been thinking like a Dragon but I don't think blazing fire breath can be called really human either" I retorted, standing my ground against being told that I was an utter novice with no skills at all.

"The fire came from your rage. You were so incensed by what I was doing that you completely let go of your human mind, of your rational control of yourself, to give everything over to the monster. It has happened before hasn't it?"

I was about to launch into a very forceful denial of her claims of me doing that before but I stopped and thought about it for a second. Some very unnatural things had been taking place since this whole situation started.

"The fight outside the Abbey?" The image of me spewing fire at Tyus filled my head.

"I also understand that your fighting posture became somewhat animal during that encounter." I thought back to the details of the encounter as I could remember them and was again forced to concede the fact that I had dropped down to all fours to attack when I was most wild with anger.

"Lloyd also informed me that the car he used to collect you from London was in need of some running repairs following an outburst on the journey."

133

"OK, I get it. You wouldn't like me when I'm angry" I said with a slight hint of humour. I don't think Andrea got the reference.

"But all of those things happened before the Awakening took place. How was I able to do all of those things before my inner killer was woken up?"

"The power was pouring into you the second the previous family member in the line to you died. The Awakening was there to unlock the final shackles within you so you would be able to access the creature and become it. Without the surge of power we were able to give you, you would never have been able to change, but you would also never be strong enough to hold the magics within you to keep your prison secure. Our enemies would have killed you and pulled the fortress apart."

"So we really are the keystones to this whole set up. If we go, then there isn't anything to get in the way of Tyus and anyone like him." I had been told this fact before but, here, in the grounds of my estate, it took on the final missing piece of reality.

"This means that I will always be in danger, doesn't it? There will always be something trying to kill me, won't there?" Resignation filled my voice and Andrea knew that there was very little she could say which would refute that fact.

Softening her tone, she looked back to the flaming crater. "We have all had that thought. We all knew that this was going to be a life of certain restricting conditions from a very early age."

"Certain restricting conditions is a very bland way of telling me I will have the Sword of Damocles hanging over my head for the rest of my life." That made me frustrated but this time I knew not to go mad. I would control what needed to be controlled quickly and I'd do it on my own as much as I could.

"And, you may have been aware of that fact from an early age but I wasn't. No-one has told me anything about any of this before Lloyd surfaced at my doorway. What is it that I missed out on? How much have I got to learn?"

Andrea sighed, dropped to all fours and slowly walked off through the scrub.

"That is a conversation to be held after our physical exertions are complete" she shouted over her shoulder.

"First you need to get to grip with the mechanics of what you are capable of, like how to fly" and with that she opened out her wings and with one thunderous effort forced herself skywards. This was the third time I had seen her fly and each time had built on the awe of the last. I just stood and watched her. She climbed quickly, banked and swooped with incredible speed and made the act of aerial movement look beautiful. Her graceful, flowing action looked effortless. It also looked to be totally out of my reach.

"Are you ready to learn?" Andrea shouted down to me.

I took in a deep breath, *in for a penny...*, and decided that I was going to out do her as quickly as I could.

"Ready when you are" I shouted back, dropped to all fours and started to run towards her. Maybe I *was* going to enjoy this?

14

When Andrea had finished imparting the wisdom she thought I had needed to know, it was very dark. The sun had long gone and the air had dropped in temperature by a very long way. The fog which had been ringing the wooded enclosure had remained for the duration of the days teachings but had now started to rise up the tree line and spill onto the scrub land, similar to the effect of a slow breaking wave.

The light in the arena was limited but came cutting out from the mansion. It jutted into the darkness with razor sharp blades of illumination which sliced through the blackness coming from the forest. Long, irregular shadows were being cast down on the ground and fell over what was left of the local plant life. The foliage had, for the most part, been absolutely destroyed. Small fires were burning all over the grounds. They were all my fault.

Andrea and I had slowly made our way back to the gravel filled expanse outside the main entrance to the mansion, her flying and me walking, and stood, looking back over the field of play. We had had a very busy day.

"Well Dragon. How do you feel now?" She asked the question, but she must have already known the answer.

"I feel good" I rumbled in a beastly growl which had come utterly from my animal side. Andrea knew that, despite my beastly response, I wasn't a threat now.

"Good" she replied, stretching out the central syllable with a wicked snarl of her own. We both looked into each others eyes with the effort of the day still pushing our heart rates. We were both breathing deeply after the activity of my first training session and knew we had been drawing heavily from the animal side of our personalities. We were both exhausted but we had both enjoyed it.

"Can you remember what I told you after your Awakening? Can you remember how to change back?" Andrea asked without breaking the stare we had developed.

"Just focus on my human self and let energy flow in. Easy" I reassured her, still locking eyes.

"Then I will see you in the morning. We have covered the foundations of what you are capable of today. We'll do more of the same tomorrow but take things much further, maybe even including weapons." Without another word, she closed her eyes and shrank down to her human form. There was no effort that I could make out, no light or sound. She simply shifted shape and shrank.

She looked up to me and smiled. Without another word, she turned and walked back into the mansion, completely naked. I watched her go and admired the poise and confidence she carried with her. She looked very; *confident*. Now it was my turn.

I closed my eyes and brought the image of my human form to mind. I hovered before my mind's eye with a completely blank expression on my face. Minds eye me was blank to what was going on! With a force of will, I conjured up a picture of the Dragon me and started to transfer energy from one to the other. Strands of deep red drifted from the animal form towards the human form and began to infuse a glowing energy into me.

I opened my eyes expecting to be back to my usual height but was surprised by the view from my Dragon body. I was still the monster. Great.

I closed my eyes and started the visualisation again. I ran through the same process again, exactly as I had in the cavern but when I opened my eyes for the second time, I was still where I had begun. This was typical. I couldn't call for Andrea's help, she had obviously thought that this was going to be easy for me so hadn't seen the need to hang around to check that I could transform. I closed my eyes and thought through the process three more times with the same results. All the positive feeling I had built up during the day's activities was starting to slowly turn into frustration at my inability to complete the very first magical task that had been laid down in front of me. I screwed up my face again and again with more and more concentration, trying to jump start my metamorphosis, but that seemed to make it even less likely that I would succeed.

I grunted out my ever climbing frustration and expelled two thick plumes of black smoke from my nostrils. The smoke settled over the entrance way to the house, totally shrouding the steps and the main door. Before it could clear, a deep, familiar voice boomed up through the obscuring blanket.

"Having problems there bach?" called Lloyd. As the smoke began to clear, I could make out my friend's imposing figure leaning casually against the frame of the open main door.

"No trouble. Just enjoying the night" I roared back at him in as laid back a tone as I could manage despite my Dragon form.

"OK. You enjoy the night some more and I'll be back out in about an hour to help you change back. When you're ready of course." He lifted himself from his relaxed posture next to the door and turned to walk back into the house.

"Wait." I was going round in ever decreasing circles and not getting anywhere. This was no time for stubbornness or pride. Lloyd slowly turned back towards me and casually wandered back outside.

"What am I missing? I'm doing everything that I did the first time I changed but nothing is happening. What aren't I doing?" My frustration was now replaced by a weak, pleading tone. I just wanted to get this done so I could have a shower, get something to eat and put my feet up. Lloyd recognised that as well.

"Start again. Close your eyes and concentrate. Hold the image in your head of your two forms."

I did as he said but didn't feel any closer to my goal. "I did this every time and nothing happened."

Lloyd ignored my protests and continued. "Before you start transferring energy from Dragon to man, stop, take a deep breath, let it out slowly, now continue."

I slowly breathed in exactly as Lloyd had said feeling every inch the fool. "Look. No different" I said as I opened my eyes. I was back to the same height as before, looking at Lloyd who had a very smug expression on his face. I jumped back with the surprise and couldn't believe that the same thing had happened again. Whatever the magic trick was, I would get used to it. I didn't want the same ridicule every time someone helped me change.

"How did you do that?" I asked as I tried to cover my nude form as best I could.

"Get cleaned up and I'll go through the details with you. You are a long way from finished for today. I'm going to take you through a crash course of Lore and magic. You've got a lot of training to catch up on so the sooner we get started. What would you like to eat? I'll get everything set up in the library so we can at least talk in a more relaxed setting."

"I'll have roasted everything with lots of vegetables please." I was so hungry from what Andrea had had me doing that I was going to eat Lloyd if he stayed still long enough. His grin returned as he headed back into the house.

"I'll have your food ready for you when you are cleaned up. See you in the library."

Wonderful.

I sprinted into the mansion, praying that no-one was waiting around in the hallways or on the stairs. Taking the steps two at a time, I felt surprisingly good considering how much energy I must have used during the day. My breathing wasn't strained at all and I felt strong, like I had just warmed up and was totally prepared for the main event. I was absolutely starving and needed to refuel, judging by the gurgling cramp in my stomach, but my body felt like I could keep on going for hours.

I started to take the stairs three at a time, bounding up and round towards the main room at the roof of the building, tearing past statuettes, doorways and paintings without taking in any of the details. Shadows danced up the walls as I continued onwards and my speed made some of them look like they were moving, leaning out to reach me in some cases and cowering back from me in others.

When I finally reached the solid carved entrance to my room, my head was buzzing with an almost childlike excitement. I felt superb.

I crashed through the double doors and slid across the polished wooded floor towards the bed. I finally came to a stop in the centre of the room and just stood there, breathing deeply but not feeling bodily tired. I had never felt better in my life and it was quite intoxicating. In the darkness of my private quarters, I rocked my head back and belted out a laugh which came from the very centre of who I was. I was powerful and strong and I liked it. There was no way I would be killed by any of the creatures who would come to try their luck. I was too strong and I knew that I was going to be able to beat everyone.

Eventually my euphoria was tempered by the ever increasing rumble coming from my stomach. I stopped laughing and began to return to the real world as thoughts of food filled my mind. A feast was going to be waiting for me downstairs and I needed to recharge my batteries.

I quickly showered and dressed, this time choosing jeans and a black shirt from the well stocked drawers. Whoever had chosen the clothes for me had very good taste. I checked my reflection one last time before leaving the room and heading back downstairs. I was looking good. Pulling the doors closed behind me as I left, I practically ran down the stairs as my hunger took control of my body. The same shadows were milling around the walls as I descended to the lower level of the house, dancing and whirling as I passed them by. If anything, I paid them even less notice on the way down.

I reached the end of the stairs and turned to my left and headed through the nearest corridor. After two more lefts and a final right, I pushed through the double doors of the library to see Lloyd waiting for me next to what can only be described as a banquet. He was stood, casually poking the fire which had been lit within the massive grate on the wall to my left. He looked every inch the lord of the manor as he tended to the fire, something I would have loved to have been able to pull off. My attention, though, didn't stay focussed on him for very long. Serving dishes and platters were laid out on a large table and were full of all manner of salad and vegetables. They were all crowded around the central display of joints of meat of various fashions. Chicken, beef, lamb and pork steamed in the middle of the display and their individual aromas mingled together to create an effect which was pulling me forwards without control. I was practically floating towards the food, pulled on by unseen hands hooking into my nostrils, every inch the personification of Wil E Coyote.

I was barely even aware of Lloyd's words but his relaxed tone was back and he was telling me to eat. I didn't need telling twice. I started to pick at pieces of the spread and began to fill my plate. Just like my breakfast, the tastes of everything seemed to have been magnified way beyond what my palate had experienced before. I made the most of the sweet meats and the tang of the vegetables.

"You must have been hungry" Lloyd pointed out as I sat down into a large leather arm chair and balanced my plate on the arm.

"Like you would not believe" I replied between mouthfuls.

He slowly made his way from the fire to sit in the identical chair at my side. There was a small creak as the leather of the chair reacted to him sitting down.

"You eat and then we can get underway." He then settled back into the chair and waited patiently for me to finish eating. It wasn't too long a wait.

After roughly half an hour of me chewing, slurping and gnawing my way through a much larger portion of the food which had been laid out than I thought I would have been able to manage, I wiped my mouth and settled back into the chair feeling contented but knowing that I needed to know what Lloyd was going to tell me. He made sure that I was ready to go, then began.

"How did you get here?" he asked and started at me expectantly. By his expression, he knew the answer I should be giving, and he also knew that I didn't.

"You drove me?" I probed, hoping that I hadn't just made that stupid mistake he must have been waiting for. He smiled. I'd made the mistake.

"How did you get from your room to here?" he clarified and again waited for the village idiot response.

"I walked, second corridor, two lefts and a right, through the double doors." I held my breath, hoping that this response was better than the last.

"Good" said Lloyd and adjusted his sitting position. I relaxed slightly.

"And how did you know that?" he asked, a split second after I had released some of the tension I had been feeling. It flew back.

"Uh, um" I fumbled. Come on.

After a pause that seemed to last hours, "The tour, last night." I felt triumphant with my response.

"We didn't come to this room last night, or through the corridors you followed to get here. So I ask again, how did you get here?"

I was totally lost. I thought back to the tour and what I could remember of it and I was confronted by the fact that I could remember practically nothing. I hadn't been paying attention and had been focussed on making a big noise about the pain Lloyd was in.

"I must have worked out where we were on the tour. Add that to the time before I became "Puff" and I saw what was where." I felt confident in that response and folded my arms defiantly across my chest. Lloyd took that in.

"Even in the dark?"

"What do you mean, in the dark?"

"Look out in the corridor, follow your footsteps back through the house. I haven't changed anything since you got here and all of the other staff have been given express orders to remain in certain areas so as not to cause any interruption to the lesson."

I shot out of my chair and sped to the doors. When I opened them, the corridor outside was pitch black. I looked back to Lloyd and he gestured to continue to verify his assertion. I walked back through the halls, reversing my route, and there was not one source of light anywhere as I travelled. More confusion settled onto me as I returned to Lloyd, again in the dark. I closed the doors slowly behind me as I re-entered the library, and this time felt apprehension as I approached Lloyd.

"Don't worry bach, that was a simple parlour trick, just to show you what history means to the Circle members. You will need to learn details of history, the names and the places, the details of who did what, but you have a connection to a shared instinct. You knew how to get here because the power has passed to you from people who have walked these halls before. Everyone else knew where to go; you didn't think about it, you just knew it."

The more I thought about it, the less impressive the story became, a shared, magical sense of direction. Let the world quake in fear! Before I could voice my incredulity at what Lloyd was saying, he continued,

"I know it may not seem like much, but it is the easiest, and safest, way for you to be shown that you are the latest link in a very long chain. Especially as you haven't been given any of the grounding people would usually have had before they take their seat."

Despite everything I had seen up to now, despite the transformations, the fighting and all of the magic, I still felt unsure of my place. I needed more. I needed to know the final piece of the puzzle for me.

142

""How did you know how I could change? Are you a Dragon as well?"

Lloyd shook his head slowly, almost letting some hidden feeling seep onto his face. Was it regret?

"There is only ever one Dragon in each house, the next member of that blood line which makes up the Circle. That means you are one of only twenty one, all charged with standing in the stead of those who went before them, standing guard over ancient prisons."

So everyone who had been involved in my ceremony, had been the entire collection of this group. Not much of a fighting force.

Lloyd continued, "I am the Head of House here. The position is basically that of the estate's overall manager. I oversee the running of the house and will be your point of contact, personal assistant and general manager rolled into one. I am a human being but, like you, I'm just a little more as well. My family line has been in service here since the beginning but where as you come from Dragons, I come from a line of beings called Tromin. They were a race of cat-like creatures that stood as tall as you or I. As a race, they made up a large proportion of the fighting group which defended the human race. They weren't the mighty creatures of destruction that you Dragons are but they were adept with weapons and magic, and they were incredibly cunning. I can't transform into the animal form like you can but I do have a pretty good control of magic, offensive as well as defensive. The Tromin were also exceptional healers too."

He took a sip from the crystal tumbler in his hand. It looked like he was drinking whiskey.

"As for me knowing how you work. I have overseen several new members here and for some reason, you all have exactly the same problem. You can't keep calm." I was about to tell him that I was very calm and that he obviously didn't know what he was talking about, when I looked at his face. His raised eyebrows and expectant expression told me that he knew what he was talking about. My comment died before it left my mouth.

"I told you to close your eyes and breathe slowly as you concentrated on the process. That was the one thing that you hadn't been doing on your own. Each time you tried it, you were just going through the motions, trying to get to the conclusion as fast as you could. You get frustrated easily and that disrupts your concentration, meaning nothing happens."

I pondered that for a second. I had been calmer, more focussed, in the cavern and I had been getting more and more wound up as I had continued in vain to master the process on my own. Maybe I did get a little short tempered.

"It must be something that runs in your family, your Uncle was just the same. He would get so wound up when things didn't go his way. He would snap at everyone if he didn't like what was happening when he first got here, but he did mellow as he grew into the role." Lloyd's tone showed a slight hint of pleasant reminiscence as he looked back into his memories.

There was my Uncle again, sounding just like me. I missed him.

I pushed the feeling away and started again. Lloyd continued to sip from his drink.

"What else have you got to tell me then Yoda?" I asked flippantly, partly to break the melancholy mood which was threatening to settle in. Lloyd smiled as well. He must have understood the reference. I hadn't expected that.

"The training you went through today, the flight, all the physical training, will only get you so far. You can become a ferocious beast with the physical abilities to demolish armies, but there are many more ways for you to be attacked than with brute force. Andrea doesn't have the same magics in her as you do. You are fuelled by a fire source; she isn't, so you will need guidance from someone who is used to dealing with your abilities."

"Why not just have another Fire Dragon run through my training? It would make more sense to have someone who can do everything work with me surely?" I asked question feeling like I d just fond the clear flaw in his plan and he would be devastated by my foresight.

Lloyd snorted with laughter!

"Two Fire Dragons training together!! You'd have killed each other out of sheer frustration and bloody mindedness."

I considered that and had to agree that, after what I had seen that day, two of me training probably wouldn't have been a great idea. I started again.

"So because you have done this before, you are obviously the man." I thought back to our skirmish outside my flat, to what Lloyd and Mike had done and began to think that maybe he was. Lloyd nodded his head slightly and settled himself into his chair as he began what he had to say.

"To manipulate magic, everyone needs to fuel it with something. As you are driven by fire, you pull in heat from around you to make things happen. This means that there isn't any heat left available around you. When you changed earlier today, after Andrea pushed your buttons, you were surrounded on the ground, by a thick layer of frost. You needed more power to transform and took it from the air around you. When Andrea uses magic of any kind, she pulls her power from an icy cold so she superheats the surrounding area as she removes the balancing force to the heat she leaves behind."

It made sense. I had left behind a very cold area when I had become the monster earlier in the day, and I remembered my journey up from the cavern with Andrea and she had turned the tunnel into a sauna when she opened the way to the surface. My mind continued back through every use of magic I had encountered as I tried to put all the information into context.

"The ice on the ground when Andrea and I first went into the cavern. Was that a result of the magical discharge?" It did fit.

"Very good. To open the doorway to the prisons will take a more explosive burst of power, hence the after effects. It looks like you'll get through all this pretty quickly."

"So what are you going to teach me?" I asked, this time without the humour. Lloyd had helped put several big pieces into this puzzle.

Lloyd rose from his chair and headed towards the drinks cabinet next to the fire. Poking the now dying fire, he slowly and deliberately refreshed his drink and returned to his seat.

"What I'm going to do is help fill in some of the blanks for you and work on some of the more delicate aspects of what you can do."

He settled back and began. "Firstly, close your eyes, breathe deeply and empty your mind." I followed his words to the letter, now trusting him to show me what I needed to know, but also that he knew the best ways for me to achieve what I needed.

"Let yourself see magic from the past. See the uses for magic which have come before. Feel the forces that you can command, from the smallest to the largest." Again, I followed his instruction to the letter and more and more images and sensations filled my mind.

It felt exactly like the other times I had been able to tap into the shared memories of the people who had come before me but this time, Lloyd had me looking for something specific. I had been looking at every page of the book before, trying to take in every detail. This time I was looking for only certain details amongst the collection in my very own reference guide. Snaps of colour, beautiful and revolting smells, surging sensations all bounded through my head as I struggled to identify what was what.

After a couple of minutes of sensory confusion, understanding boomed in regarding the single flickering flame of a tall candle. The image of the candle steadily drifted forwards in my head, coming into full clarity as the maelstrom of other details continued to broil behind it.

"I see a candle. I see the flame" I whispered, still with my eyes closed, holding tightly to the picture.

"Good" replied Lloyd. "That's where you should start. Hold that image in your head, focus on all of the detail you can make out. Now, open your eyes."

I carefully clutched the candle in my mental grip and opened my eyes. All around me, candelabras of all designs and sizes were holding newly lit candles. None of them were lit before my mental journey. I stared in wonder at the now burning objects. The main fire crackled and spat as its flames surged up into the chimney. Where there had been a weakening mass of flame, there now stood a roaring fire of renewed vigour.

"Another easy show but something which highlights exactly what can be achieved with magic. You thought of a lit candle and fire was called to your will." It was a simple explanation but it didn't really seem to do the process justice.

"The more you get used to the whole process of calling magic, the easier and faster it will be, and you'll have more control of what you are doing. Magical control is basically control of what you are thinking. If you want something to happen, just concentrate and go from there." Lloyd seemed to be happy with my first flirtation with Magic and the whole situation was making me feel pretty good.

I closed my eyes again, aiming to image the candle again, but this time there were no other images to work through, no other pictures to sift out. This time, all I held in my mind's eye was a bright blue/white ring of electrical energy, set against a thick black background. The ring sparked and discharged in all directions as large tendrils of blue/white force sank back into the centre of the circle. The smell of ozone filled my nostrils and I immediately felt wary of what I was seeing. Within my mental image, I could feel a very real pull of force, subtly tugging at me, drawing me in to the ring. I pulled my attention from it and opened my eyes again. I hoped Lloyd would be able to tell me what it had all meant.

I opened my eyes to utter confusion. Lloyd was still sat in his chair next to me but the rest of the room was gone. I looked around me to be confronted by vast numbers of trees, freezing air and above us, through the trees' naked canopy, the star-filled night sky. Hundreds of leaves were floating down on us from above, as if returning to their starting place after our disturbance. I snapped my head left and right and turned wildly in the chair as I tried to get my bearings. Where were we and how had we got here? I was feeling a strong urge to be sick and my head not only felt like someone had buried an axe in it, but a gentle dizziness was settling in to add to my nausea. Not only did I not understand, but I felt awful to boot.

My ignorance of the situation had started the engine of the fear inside me and I could feel the revs starting to climb. I turned to Lloyd, hoping he would be able to give me some clue as to what was going on, explain our location and my discomfort. From his posture, I didn't have anything to worry about. He was still in the same relaxed position in his chair but now he had started to laugh.

"I didn't see that coming bach" he spluttered through ever increasing guffaws.

"What coming?" I could feel the fear throttling back but that only left behind the pain and my favourite sensation at the moment, bewildered embarrassment at being the only one not to get the joke. "What just happened Lloyd?"

"Well," he began as he managed to regain his composure. "You just managed to create a cascade bridge, a pretty strong one too."

"A what?"

"A cascade bridge is basically a teleport. You open a gate where you are, one where you want to go, and off you go." Sounded simple.

"And you didn't see it coming?" Knowing that I had just done something that surprised my teacher set up more questions.

"That is a very advanced piece of sorcery bach. You have the power to do it, obviously, but I didn't think that you would have the control. Taking you through that tonight hadn't even occurred to me. I had been thinking along the lines of more basic stuff like the control of fire and concealment spells. I bet you feel like crap as well, don't you?"

"It's easing off a bit" I replied through gritted teeth as I ran the ideas through my head. Something which was above my station had happened before I had managed to complete the basics. It certainly sounded like something that my utter lack of patience would lead to.

"That sounds great, but where are we? Where did I take us?" I hadn't known what I was doing when I did what I did the first time so I was pretty sure that I wouldn't be able to repeat the feat. I wasn't that keen on making a cross country hike back to the mansion, at night. What if we were in a different country!

Lloyd settled back into the leather chair and narrowed his eyes. Under his breath, he began to mumble words I couldn't understand as he lifted his hands up to shoulder height, palms up. An undulating breeze began to pass through the small clearing we were sat in and I could feel a build up of static electricity rushing towards Lloyd, buzzing like an ever growing swarm of bees. Lloyd opened his eyes fully as his words grew louder to reveal his eyes had become fully grey, just as they had outside my flat, leaving behind no hint of colour. I didn't know what he was doing but I found myself starting to lean away from him in my chair and mentally brace myself.

It was at that point that Lloyd released his magic with a thoroughly underwhelming "Aha".

"I've found us" he declared proudly. "We're in the woods at the south edge of the estate." He turned his head slowly to his right and jabbed an arm out, pointing. "The outer boundary should be about fifty yards over in that direction." At least he knew where we were.

"How far are we from the mansion?"

"About a mile from here" Lloyd stated matter of factly as he stood up and straightened his jacket.

"Then how are we going to get back there?" My question had come from a place of logistical curiosity but it had also made a stop off at pure laziness. The thought of fumbling around in the dark trying to get back to civilisation wasn't something which filled me with feelings of delight.

Lloyd rubbed his hands together and a very mischievous smirk appeared on his face.

"You can jump us home. Fancy giving it another go?"

"I don't think that is a good idea." I would have usually just given it a whirl and seen where we ended up but the events of the last two days had shown me that my rashness and lack of control had the potential to land me in hot water. For the first time, I tried to consider all of the facts calmly rather than just rushing in.

"I'll help you with the specifics. We already know you can do it, now all we need to do is give you the finesse" Lloyd reassured me.

"Can't you do the honours this time and I'll work on the finesse when we're back indoors?" The more I thought about the possibilities of jumping to who knows where, the less appealing it got. And it hurt like hell!

"I'm afraid that I can't open bridges like that." Lloyd informed me and the ball was back in my court. "I can push small objects to one location only, the highlands of Scotland. I don't know why there but that's all I have. I used up every ounce of power to shunt Tyus there when we were in London, Mike stopped him moving and I did the rest. I used some of his power too, to slow him down and it took me an age to recover my strength. That's why he did me so much damage outside the Abbey."

He smiled at me and I knew that I wasn't going to get out of this.

"All you need to do is concentrate on the bridge ring in your mind, just like you did the candle and the picture of yourself." I closed my eyes and exhaled a deep breath in preparation. The ring sprang up in my minds eye again and crackled in the same way.

"Now focus into it what you want to take place. The ring is just a picture until you give it force to complete what you want it to." Lloyds tone had taken on the same reassuring tone of the candle lesson as he led me through the process.

I concentrated on what I wanted to take place, willing out the power to charge the bridge. The subtle pull on my subconscious kicked in almost immediately. The distinctive smell of ozone filled my nostrils as I pushed my focus harder.

"Finally, link where we are to where you want to be. Hold the two images in your head, either side of the bridge. When you have them, rush through the construct and release your built up focus. Make the jump." I pictured the library in my head and pushed towards it.

I slammed back in the chair as the axe in my head returned. It wasn't as big as the first time but it was still big enough. I gathered my senses together and opened my eyes, expecting to see the library surrounding us. Instead, we were in another clearing, being covered by another shower of dead leaves, surrounded by more trees. I coughed, my throat was suddenly very dry, my whole body felt sore and the dizziness was still there. I looked at Lloyd for an explanation but he didn't have one.

"You must have lost focus slightly. Let me find out where we are." With that, he returned himself to his mystical posture and began chanting for our location. After a long minute, he opened his eyes and declared that we had jumped about half a mile along the boundary of the estate but that we were still about a mile from the mansion. Great.

"Don't worry bach. This is pretty advanced stuff. I'm not expecting you to master this on day one. Do you want to give it another go?" Lloyd looked at me encouragingly but seemed to be wearing the expression of the boxer's corner man letting his fighter know that he was defeated but it was still his decision to call it a day. I reacted on instinct. It just fired me on to show him that I could do it. Maybe that was what he was after.

I closed my eyes and settled back into the leather chair again. I ran through the same process as before, Lloyd giving me the same pointers as I focussed and sent us jumping again.

The axe in my head was now down to feeling more like a large knife. I must have been getting used to it. Through the pain and disorientation of the 'landing', I opened my eyes and looked around us. We were back in the original clearing.

Lloyd looked at me with gentle confusion on his face and reached out to grip my arm.

"Don't worry bach. We'll walk from here. It looks like that first time was a bit of a fluke."

I felt annoyed that I had failed to send us back to the house. Annoyed that I had to now walk all the way back through the woods

150

to the mansion. I also felt glad that I didn't have to make myself feel even worse as I continued my fruitless attempts. Maybe I would enjoy the walk?

"Why don't I just turn into a Dragon and fly us back to the house?" I had, after all, just mastered the art of flight and I really didn't want to walk. Lloyd shook his head, "You're going to need to master control of yourself to really get the best results as a Dragon. The walk won't be that bad, we'll go through more lessons on the way back."

15

The woods surrounding the estate are very thick. Lloyd had explained that they had been planted to ensure both privacy and natural protection without drawing huge attention to what was inside. High stone walls covered by guards didn't give off the right idea.

"We have similar defensive magic cast over the estate as we do covering the Abbey. Our enemies can't pass through the estate boundary but here, almost everything is visible to the human race. We aren't covered by hugely powerful concealment magic so we have to do things the old fashioned way when we try to stop exposing what we are. It has been like this for generations, the only difference now is we have to shroud the whole estate to stop prying eyes from above, the down side of modern surveillance technology. Our safety is very fragile and isn't only at risk from demons." Lloyd was leading us onwards without any real difficulty despite the dense undergrowth and tightly packed trees. I followed as fast as I could but he seemed to be handling this much better than me. The winter air felt sharp in my chest as I breathed in deeply and I could practically taste the cloying smell of leaf litter as we continued. Cracking branches and squelching mud greeted almost every footstep, making me feel that I was being dragged at by the wood itself, this really would have put off anyone who wandered in. I just needed to concentrate my mind on what Lloyd was saying and just push through the undergrowth.

"I can understand why we want to keep the whole magic Dragon thing quiet but aren't we the good guys? Why would people be a risk? Wouldn't they be happy to have us doing what we do?" I could see the need for secrecy when talking about the details of huge mythical beasts walking across the countryside but surely that was only to keep the faces of the Circle off the front pages of the tabloids.

Lloyd stopped and let me catch him up.

"Where you grew up, what was the most common story you were aware of which contained a Dragon?" Strange question. I thought for a second.

"St. George and the Dragon. England's patron saint." As far as I could remember, there weren't that many stories in the first place but that was definitely the most well known.

"What happens to the Dragon in the story?" Lloyd asked with a totally blank expression on his face.

"St. George killed it" I replied before I could stop myself.

"Have you heard the story of the Lambton Wurm?" Lloyd continued. I remembered some sketchy details.

"The story ended with the wurm, a Dragon, being killed by the noble knight. Each story of Dragons revolves around the central point that the Dragon is there to do people harm, eat virgins and burn crops, and must be destroyed. The human race has hunted the Dragons the world over despite what they have done."

The silence hung between us as I considered what he was saying.

"If people knew the truth though, they'd understand what was going on?" I offered as a reasonable solution.

"Where do you think the stories come from in the first place?" Lloyd fired back. "In the past, we have made ourselves known to people and to begin with everything went well. We were left alone but advised kings, emperors and sultans when the territory we occupied was threatened. We never revealed the location of the prisons but our estates were opened up to the rulers. The problems always started in the same way after that. A country which housed a Hive prison wanted to attack one of their neighbours and the country's leaders knew that any army which marched with a Dragon at its head would be nigh on unbeatable. They would always plead the case as safe guarding the lands of the prison but it was always just an attempt at conquering."

He let that detail sink in for a long second before he continued. "It hasn't been like that in every case" he went on, perking up slightly. "We had a great deal of support from the early rulers here and they all seemed to realise that we would defend them against any and all supernatural forces so they left us alone. They even held the Dragon line in some real esteem, hence the national flag." I thought back to the huge flag that was waving over the estate when we had arrived. The huge Red Dragon flag was derived from a real Dragon?!

We pushed on through the darkness and Lloyd's tone grew sadder as he continued.

153

"Our position in this world is to protect the entire human race by ensuring the integrity of the prisons and destroying the forces which are sent to release the demons we cage. We are not here to further the ambitions of power hungry leaders."

"So when requests for aid in attacking another country were turned down, we were attacked?" I filled in the blanks.

"Not only by armies, but in stories. Looking at the position we hold now, the tales of evil Dragons have done more damage than any weapon. Even our reluctance to fund leaders over the years has been called into question. It's a classic image isn't it? The Dragon curled up in a cave, hoarding his gold from all others." I nodded in agreement, and then thought out loud, "Where does all the money come from? Who pays for the mansion, the cars, the staff, everything?"

"Spoils of war" Lloyd replied. "All of the treasures that had been amassed by the Hive demons in their attempts to conquer the human race were divided up between the twenty one Guardians. We took possession of all of their wealth but also the mines etc. where gold and diamonds were excavated. Over the years, we have also built up portfolios of land and business interests which furnish the Circle with quite a powerful income. Aside from the monsters etc, the Circle is actually a very powerful economic power."

This talk was starting to delve into some facts and figures that I could find out at a later date. I needed to get back to the meaty history before this became a financial report to the Board of Directors.

"So, St. George was really the bad guy of the piece. Do you know what really happened?" I asked as Lloyd turned and started back on the journey to the mansion.

"You obviously weren't paying full attention to the tour were you?" Lloyd shot over his shoulder with sarcasm practically dripping from every word. He knew I hadn't perfectly well. There must have been paintings or statues which showed it all back in the house.

"St. George was the lucky man who wandered across one of your dying ancestors and took the chance that was presented to him. He most certainly wasn't the bad guy. I actually like him for seeing what was before him and then making the best use of it." Lloyd pushed on through the woods in the utter blackness and I was back to struggling to keep up.

"The armies of our enemies, led by Tyus, were mounting a mighty assault to free their master so we were under attack constantly for months. Day and night, creatures were crawling out from their hiding places to break us down. The previous year, we had made ourselves known to the king, after a gap of roughly two hundred years; we were back in the world. The king of the Britons came to an earlier estate at that point of our battles and asked for funding from us so he could complete a vital quest for some religious object. We turned him down. He was looking for something that he wanted which had nothing to do with us or the protection of the prison so we refused." Lloyd broke from the story as he jumped over a small ditch which crossed our path.

"As he returned home, anger burning through him at our refusal to help him, his party came across the sight that would create a legend." Lloyd stopped and let me catch up again so I would hear the end of the story clearly.

"You see, Tyus and his forces somehow managed to free the beast. They managed to shatter your glyph stone and he burst free; very hungry. It aimed for a large population centre, hoping to feed and your ancestor followed him to put him back where he had come from. They fought in plain view of anyone who was nearby, the beast used multiple cascade bridges to try to escape but your ancestor, Gareth, I think his name was, kept with him all the way, regardless of who saw him. They jumped into view of the leaving royal party who scattered when they saw the beasts, terrified that they were under attack for asking for money. After hours of fighting, Gareth jumped the pair of them back into the prison and sealed the beast inside." His eyes were sparkling with excitement as he recounted the story, pride bursting from him.

"He had been the first who had been called upon to return their charge following an escape and he had done so with utter conviction and dedication." His tone then dropped.

"The fight, though, had been too much for him. He had been injured so badly that despite his success, he was doomed to pass. He had stood as a mighty force against things that would try to unmake the world and he had done his duty." Lloyd pushed his chest out and stood a little bit straighter.

"What about St. George?" I asked gently, trying to break the pride filled fervour that had gripped Lloyd. He blinked himself back to the here and now.

"The final cascade bridge jump that he performed, out of the prison, landed him just a mile from the fleeing royal caravan, in the fields of a farm, belonging to a man named George." A small smile played at the edges of Lloyd's mouth as he thought of the details of the story.

"Gareth had done his duty. He had laid down his life for the protection of the entire human race and he had done it knowing that he was doing good for everyone. As he lay on the field, bleeding from his wounds, nursing multiple broken bones, huge damage throughout his body, struggling for breath in his shattered Dragon form, a local farmer slowly approached. Fearing the monster that was on his land was going to attack him and eat his livestock, he plunged a basic, homemade sword into the Dragon's side. This tiny blow, combined with the severity of the other wounds, was enough to send Gareth on to what is beyond, but, at that exact moment, the fleeing royal caravan rounded a nearby hill and witnessed a local man slay the Dragon that had threatened to attack them earlier in the day. The king saw this man as a hero for ending the mighty monster. He saw that he had come under attack from the Circle, who had sent two beasts to destroy him and he had been saved by a farmer of strong belief in his king. George was knighted soon after, then canonised and the rest is history. The tale of the king's attack from an unwilling power, the monsters destruction, spread like a wild fire. Pretty soon, tales of Dragons eating and killing anything and everything sprang up all over the country. They were mostly false or could have been explained away had people wanted to look at the details but they were too exciting, too compelling. There was even one talking about two mighty Dragons, one red and one white, being locked together in a battle underground which shook the very land above. I think that was the closest to the truth that actually happened. The Dragon was soon the target of huge public hatred so the damage was complete. We end up where we are now, Dragons are the creatures which want

156

to eat people and tear cities asunder, and a scared little man from Oxford became the mightiest warrior in the lands."

Lloyd looked at me and I could feel the force of his belief rolling from him. That story had been more than just another collection of tales from a bygone era. He believed every word of it. He bowed his head slowly and turned towards the trail again. It was a big story and it looked like it was something that was hard for him to recollect.

I considered his tale and felt like I was being drawn in and hypnotised by the words. But that didn't make it real. Lloyd could see that I was unsure of the full details of the story he had told but moved to remove any hesitation.

"You don't have to take my word for it" he said with a hint of beligerance in his voice. "You have access to the entire collection of shared memories of all of the people who have come before you in your position so you will be able to see everything that has happened. If you focus your mind and look for specific details you should be able to find the Dragon's eye view of exactly what happened." He looked at me with expectation in his eyes. He wanted me to look into my collection of images of the past and pick out the exact details of what had happened. This must have been important to him.

"All you have to do is concentrate. I know that that seems to be the starting place for everything but the clarity which comes from being calm is something you are going to have to work at if you want to get the best results with magic." Lloyd read my mind as a pinch of frustration leapt up.

"Let your mind drift back in on its self and you'll find the memories."

Another deep breath to sweep away the now dead frustration and I let my mind drift. Instantly, all the images and sounds I had experienced during the journey out of the cavern flooded back. I was still aware of what was going on around us while I was calling up the past, like having the volume on an MP3 player down low. I could hear the music but it wasn't interfering with my attention on the outside world.

"What can you see?" Lloyd asked.

Hundreds of images floated before my eyes, like a snowstorm of family photographs, each one showing the events of a different time and place. "I can see everyone. I can't pick anything out."

"I want you to look for anything which has the prison being breached; there shouldn't be that many to choose from."

As I thought of what the prison being breached might look like, one by one, the images which didn't match began to fall away, slowly returning to my subconscious. Eventually I was left with images which made up the whole story.

"Now what?" I wish Lloyd could have seen what I could; it would have made this whole process easier.

"Let it play out. Watch what happened." Was it as easy as just pressing play?

I pushed my mind at it and with barely the slightest nudge of effort, the show began. The viewpoint was constantly moving but I could recognise the cavern and it was shaking violently. Through a bright flash of light, I could make out a huge white shape appear in the cavern within touching distance of me. I instinctively jerked back at the shock despite this only being a memory, albeit one which wasn't really mine.

"Are you OK?" asked Lloyd as I stumbled following my instinctive reaction.

"I'm fine, just got a little surprise." I could hear the expectation in his voice.

I turned my attention back to the mental image which was still playing. Without warning, a massive white arm flew into the edges of my vision and suddenly I was staring at the ground. My ancestor had been knocked down. As the picture returned to the action, I could recognise the burning corona of a cascade bridge formed against the nearest wall of the cavern. I could make out a large white tail disappearing into it and before it could make its way in completely, my viewpoint darted forwards and gripped it tightly with both hands. It wasn't enough to stop the movement but I watched as I followed it through.

We landed in a wide open field and the blows continued to rain down on my mind's eye. Each memory was more than just moving pictures; they had sounds and smells with them. The fight continued through a blur of bladed limbs and rolling roars from both leviathans.

This was most certainly the kind of thing which would have haunted the nightmares of anyone who had seen it for years after the event.

Another bridge opened, and again both creatures surged through. This time I found myself airborne when I exited, still under violent attack. As we twisted and writhed through the air, I could make out in the corner of the memory, a scattering party of people. They carried several flags and bore a huge standard. Was this the king's party?

"It's just like you said. Everything is just as you said." I couldn't believe that my memories were practically public record.

"I know. Keep watching." Lloyd didn't sound good. It was almost as if he was living it all over again himself.

I continued to watch as the fight continued. I watched as my ancestor was ripped open, his bones broken and how he kept doing everything he could to subdue his enemy. Eventually, the creatures were jumped back to the prison, and through a crackling of blue/white energy and rippling fire which made it impossible to make out the details, the beast was caged again just as the final bridge pulled the Dragon away to safety.

I could sense the pride building in me as I stared at the last few details. I found myself starting to stand straighter and push my chest out, exactly as Lloyd had.

The final fragments of memory showed, somewhat blurrily, a lone man walk cautiously up to the stricken Dragon and force his sword into its side before blackness took it. I had watched through my ancestor's eyes how the efforts of a Guardian of the human race were greeted. He had been utterly unable to defend himself from the scared little farmer who could have just left the beast to die of his injuries but instead saw the massive reptile as something to be slain. There was no fanfare at his passing.

I shook the pictures away and looked at Lloyd. He looked drained.

"That must be a pretty important story" and I could feel an ache in my soul that I hadn't been either expecting or prepared for.

"The history of the struggle we are all involved in is laid out in the estate but it is well known by each and every member of our group. Each estate is the same."

"But the Circle was doing exactly what it had to, to keep people safe. Gareth gave his life to protect the human race and was remembered as the worst kind of creature on the face of the earth. How can it be fair that his selfless act resulted in stories of him being a killer?" The fury was building in me as I thought about it.

"How can doing good give such terrible results?" I shouted and started to clench my fists. Around me, the temperature was starting to fall rapidly. Lloyd noticed and leapt to calm me down.

"Our group was persecuted for years, Anthony, because of ignorance but also because of a few isolated incidents of the hot headed Fire Dragon stamping his feet so to speak. The temper of the beast, while pretty useful in a fight, was less than useful when it came to diplomacy" he shouted. Strangely for me, I listened without much persuading. I must be growing.

"It has happened the world over. Every Dragon line has been persecuted over the years. I can think of at least two occasions that your Uncle lost his cool and made another Dragon's life just a little bit more uncomfortable."

I was calm again now and the mention of my Uncle came as quite a shock.

"Come on," Lloyd sighed. "I'll tell you on the way back. Come on."

We started off again, aiming for the mansion but I felt like I was carrying much more than when we had started. Lloyd also looked like the tales of the past had had an effect on him. He was still leading us along but I was now much more able to keep pace with him.

"When a prison is under attack or one of the houses requires 'military' back up from one or more Dragons, they call out and the help is sent. Everyone within the Circle is required to hold responsibility for their own charge but they are also a terrifying fighting force when they assemble." The tone was matter of fact but again, there was a slight hint of pride in his voice.

"My uncle went off to war? When?"

"The network of prisons is well protected and the estates have a great defence to them but each house is under attack from the forces trying to release their masters. We come under direct assault maybe once a year and through indirect means more regularly than that.

Each place is the same." The matter of fact tone had retuned. Lloyd continued.

"When battles take place we try to minimise our contact with humanity but I can remember David getting angry at the situation when Juan Martine's prison in Argentina was being assaulted. He thought they should have gone on a wild offensive against the enemy but the forces had hidden themselves in plain sight in a small town, passing themselves off as human. David wanted to tear into the whole town but, thank God, no-one else did. David went mad and became the Dragon when we were all still in Juan's mansion because he thought that one of the staff in the building was actually a demon. He brought the whole place to the ground because he couldn't control his temper. Sound familiar?"

I blushed for my Uncle. I, on the other hand, felt that my emotional control was at least improving. We were walking through ridiculously thick undergrowth in the middle of a cold February night and I wasn't moaning about it. Then a thought struck me.

"What do you mean 'we'?"

"What do you mean, what do I mean bach?" Lloyd shot over his shoulder as he strode on with purpose through the wood.

"You said "when we were all in Juan's mansion". Did you used to go out with him on 'missions'?"

"Head of House is more than just a Butler you know. As I said earlier, I do have some control over magic" and with that he thrust out his left arm and forced out a blast of fizzling, crackling power which burned its way through a tree directly ahead.

"The Dragons are always the head of the fighting force, they create most of the carnage, but the rest of the armies we can mobilize can use magic as well. We may not be as big as you lot but we can still do some damage." The tree he had attacked slowly toppled over with a steady, growing crack.

I thought about my Uncle. Thought about what he would have looked like going completely off the deep end at the forces which were lined with him and what a fearsome sight he would have been facing off against his enemies if he had brought down an estate house of a colleague because he didn't agree with him.

We continued our steady progress back to the estate doing our best to avoid the seemingly endless collection of exposed roots and earthy mounds which had been liberally sprinkled throughout our route. As we scrabbled and stumbled along I could finally feel the effects of the cascade bridges I had formed earlier on starting to ebb and fade away. The axe had been completely removed from the back of my head, the nausea had totally subsided and the lumbering dizziness was now almost completely gone. I took in a succession of long, deep breaths, pulling in as much clean air as my lungs would hold. I hadn't been aware of my body's reaction to the magical overload until it utterly left me.

The muscles in my upper back were like several tightly knotted bundles of twine; my chest had been weighted down by an invisible force which had in turn made my breathing much more laboured than it had been normally.

Suddenly noticing that these silent enemies were gone felt like an exquisite release and the deep drags of close to freezing air spread purity through me. It felt great.

With those distractions gone, I was more able to focus my thoughts on a clear chain of ideas.

"What was my Uncle really like Lloyd?"

"What do you mean, really like?"

"On a day to day basis. You would have seen him from the beginning to the end of his time in the Circle. You would have got to know him wouldn't you?"

"He did live with you for years, didn't he? You probably knew him better than I did." Lloyd was lightly joking with me but I wanted to know more.

"He was my guardian first so he would have acted very differently around me than he would have done with you. He may have been your boss in some way but you did say that he was a friend of yours. What was he like as a friend?" As more and more mythology built up around me and my family line, I became more and more aware of the fact that my Uncle had gone through the same things. I missed him and, knowing that there was a stack of stories about him that I wasn't aware of, I felt that I could almost bring him back into being just by finding out as much as I could. That gnawing feeling of family emptiness continued to work on my insides.

Lloyd slowed his pace and we continued our trek side by side.

"David was just like you when he first took his place here, full of righteous indignation and barely caged fury." I could here the tone of his voice change; get lighter, as he looked back through his memories.

"It was his father, Geraint, who had been the previous Circle member. He was killed by forces in Australia when our Uluru site was being pulverized. We won the battle but lost at least half our forces and Geraint, one of three Dragons involved. It had been a massive offensive but the Dragons did what they were built for. When word came through that we had won the day, David had been so proud of his father. When he was told of his death, it almost broke him. He was only thirteen years old and not only was he told that his father was dead, but that he was now expected to take on the same responsibilities in the defence of the world. That was what brought out his anger totally. We couldn't get the Awakening set up for around a month after Geraint's death, our forces in the houses which had made up the fighting force in Australia were too depleted to allow their Dragons to be away from their houses, and there wasn't enough power in each to keep the shields together. In that time, David was building up his power of the Dragon but before the Awakening, he couldn't unleash it. He felt like you did when you first got here, but it was for roughly three weeks, before we could open him up. He weathered the first storm of power but when the ceremony didn't take place, the pressure in him grew and he had to withstand some very nasty things."

I was already impressed by my Uncle and I had only heard the first piece of information. This was going to be a real eye opener on my family. Lloyd continued with his recollection.

"David saw the Circle as something that was there to do good but he had always pictured in his mind that it was going to be an elderly father passing the final secrets of the order to him from his death bed. He had assumed that he would only take his place in the Circle when his father died of age or some such other natural cause. Seeing the realities of what was now going to be his life didn't sit well with him. His father had trained him from an early age in the details of the Circle and what the order meant, making sure that he was aware of the importance of what he was doing and also giving him a full versing in the magical skills he would need but David always felt that the realities of death and destruction hadn't been explained to him. I tried to act as his friend from that point because that is what he needed. He needed to know that there was someone who wasn't going to let him down and that I would help him when he needed it.

He was mentored by The Elder in the beginning, the elderly Chinese lady. She taught him the details of what it was to be a Dragon in the same way that Andrea is doing with you but she was a great deal less forgiving when it came to any mistakes." I thought about Andrea and her overflowing forgiveness up to this point and winced for my Uncle. That couldn't have been fun for a teenager.

An owl hooted overhead as we walked and I could feel the ever advancing chill of a winter's night biting into my skin as the temperature continued to fall into the night. My shirt and jeans combo may have looked the part for casual discussions in the library drinking scotch but cross country hiking in the middle of the night didn't showcase the strength of the outfit.

"The years rolled by and we all tried to make sure that he didn't get sent on the big missions, that the other Fire Dragons took up the slack as he grew in confidence and ability. He had been filled with a wild anger for everything that he saw as being unjust and unfair. He saw that the Circle was a force for good but he felt that they were doing things wrongly. He didn't like the way The Elder had trained him or the way that his father had taught him. His natural fire had been stoked by what he saw as being an attempt to conceal the truth and then to make him toe the company line when he did find out." That sounded very familiar.

Lloyd seemed to leave the silence hanging between us for much longer than it needed, just to show that he thought exactly the same.

Something that Lloyd had just said suddenly burst out at me.

"The other Fire Dragons. There are more than just one?" For no reason that I could see, I knew that it was a vital detail for me to explore. Maybe this would mean that I wasn't quite as alone in my situation as I had first thought.

"In the Circle of twenty one there are five Fire Dragons, four Ice Dragons, three Water Dragons, three Life Dragons, four Earth Dragons and the Storm pairing, one of Thunder, one of Lightning. They all stand over creatures which their abilities can damage. All the Fire Dragons guard creatures which are vulnerable to searing heat and fire, Ice Dragons those that are vulnerable to the biting cold and so on. Each prison with one guardian, all except The Pit of Veema in Egypt. Thunder and Lightening stand together watching the creature there."

"Two guardians in one place? What's being held there?" More idle curiosity but the idea of something awful enough that it needed two guardians made my skin crawl a little more than the cold weather had managed. Lloyd didn't reply.

Lloyd stopped his explanation there and took an extra stride out ahead of me, daring me to catch up. I quickly matched his speed and drew level again; keen to continue down this road of information and learn as much as I could.

"And? Then what" I asked, trying to restart the conversation. Lloyd paused, staring straight ahead as he walked, as if his mind was stuck in thick mud. Eventually, he kicked off again with, "Your Uncle, yes." Apparently, the details of Dragons would have to wait and the previous line restarted as if there had been no interruption.

"As Dai got older, he seemed to want to do two things at once" Lloyd remembered. "He wanted to set himself two very different lives. He made himself the go to man for every violent conflict that happened across the globe. If any prison came under attack, if any Circle house or stronghold was threatened, he actively sought out the conflict. He travelled all over the world, unleashing all kinds of violence, all in the name of the protection of the human race.

On the other hand, he started a life of normality at home. He lived outside the estate, on a small farm further out west. He married a local girl in a small chapel out past Carmarthen, the same one his funeral was held in, and lived a life that everyone else had. He tried to be two separate people."

I thought over the details of the actions of my Uncle and, from what I had seen so far, I felt that I could understand his motivations. I had been very quickly introduced to tightly wound world of the Circle and of all of the expectations that they have on their members and I already felt that they were asking too much. Uncle David had lived his whole life in this environment, no wonder he wanted to have a piece of his life which was purely his.

"Did he tell his wife what he was? What he was expected to do?" I was reacting on instinct to the questions that presented themselves from what I was being told. A split second after I asked the question, I realised that in all of the years I had known my Uncle David, at no point had he ever mentioned a wife. I changed what I wanted to know.

"What wife? He never mentioned a wife when he was living with me."

Lloyd slowed slightly and we entered another small clearing on our travel back to the house. He found himself a small tree stump and sat down; making himself comfortable for what looked like would be a very uncomfortable story. I found a large stone and settled down to listen.

"David was married to a woman called Gladys. They met when he was in his early twenties. She was a small woman with long blonde hair who wasn't interested that David had a vast material inheritance or huge power. When they met, he said that he was a farmer who had only recently moved to the area. She loved him because he was David, not because he was Lord of this estate and a Fire Dragon of huge magical power. She showed him that an existence without the knowledge of perpetual death was achievable. She was the reason he left the mansion and lived in the farm all of his post went to. He loved her and the release from the terror that she gave him. He started to truly live the life of a man who was free of the responsibilities of The Circle."

Lloyd sighed before he continued.

"The rest of his family remained in the mansion when he moved out; I think making sure that the place was going to be ready for him should he..." I stopped him in his tracks.

"The rest of his family? Who else was there?" The idea of more members of the family that I wasn't aware of made me feel a churn in my stomach.

"His mother and his younger sister, your grandmother and your mother." Lloyd looked at me, sad at the knowledge that he was exposing a huge part of my family that I had no prior knowledge.

I sat dumb on my rock, thinking about my mother living inside the world I was now wading through. How had she coped with the death of her father and then the apparent abandonment of her brother? After two long minutes of silence, I gathered enough of myself and needed to know more.

"What happened next?" My tone was flat as I just needed to hear all of the facts.

"We called on him when he was needed around the world and when we were ourselves attacked but other than that, he lived a 'normal' life. He worked the farm. He drank in the local village pub. He followed rugby with a passion that bordered on obsession. He was normal."

I thought back to my Uncle drinking in the local bar in London and how his truly obsessive love of rugby had built up my own fervour for the sport. More pieces for the puzzle. Lloyd continued.

"When his son was born, it just reinforced the notion that he could separate the two roles he had."

"His son?" This was getting stupid. How many more massive facts about my own family didn't I know?

Lloyd waved his hands to calm me and show that he was going to explain everything.

"When his son, Matthew, was born he was the happiest man on earth. He told me that he was living the life he really wanted. None of this had gone down well with the Circle. The Elder had come to the house to find him and 'snap him back into line' as she put it. As you probably saw, she is a very serious creature. She believes utterly in the purpose of the Circle but she also thinks that each Guardian must always be on twenty four hour a day alert, just in case they are required. She made it very clear that what David was doing was against what was expected. It didn't matter what anyone else said to her, he was wrong and should be punished. That was probably why he tried to be the most fearsome warrior when he did go into battle, just to prove that his so called distraction wasn't affecting how he did his job." Another sigh.

"I always agreed with him. Why couldn't he have been happy in a life outside and still do his duty? For years I made sure that his farm was tended by people who actually knew what they were doing (your Uncle wasn't a farmer!), his new home had a decent early warning system and defences, and that he was safe when he was out of the mansion." Lloyd looked right at me and continued with slightly more urgency.

"His son didn't only change his life. When your mother saw that it was possible to have that life she decided that she wanted the same.

She had been cooped up in the mansion, learning of her importance to the Circle and that she should only marry someone from inside the house, since the day she was born and suddenly, her older brother was showing her that that wasn't the only way. She met a man from Swansea who didn't know about who she was and she was utterly enchanted by him. She quickly married and had two sons. I know I told you that I hadn't known about Steve when we first met but I didn't want you to think that you were the last person to find out all this. I know that you would have resisted what we had to say and we really didn't have time."

I sat listening in awed silence. A very bright light was being shone on the darkest reaches of my family's history and there was nothing that I could do but listen to every word, hoping that they would make my life more clear.

"Your father may not have known of the Circle and of the wealth of the family he was joining, but he was very driven to make money. He was sure that there would be a better standard of life for his young family in London so moved you all there."

"If my mother knew about what was really going on in the world, Dragons, demons and magic, why did she move?" From what Lloyd had told me, she would have seen that living just down the road would be possible but living two hundred miles away would have been pretty serious, both if she had been called back to the house or if she had been attacked. The shadow of past pain was now almost fully settled over his face as he began. This wasn't going to be good.

"Your mother was totally infatuated with him. She was in love. She saw what her brother had done and felt that anything was possible. I tried to keep an eye on her but it was the exposure, their distance from the house that eventually tripped them up." Sigh.

"I still don't know how, but Tyus and his forces found out every detail of both families. They knew who, when and where to strike. A regular family outing became the target. David, Gladys and Matthew were on a trip to a local lake to go for a walk, as they did every week, when their car was attacked. Magical forces pulverized the car and everyone in it. David survived the attack because of his Dragon qualities but Gladys and Matthew were killed, and not quickly." Sigh.

168

"We found David four hours after the attack; he had called to me with the last of his magic. He hadn't been able to do anything against the attack, no cascade bridges to escape, no outpouring of power to defend himself. He had barely been able to survive. When we tried to warn Clare that she could be in danger, we got nothing back, no magical response or phone call. We were too late." Sigh.

"Tyus had done the same thing in London to destroy you. He tore through your parents with a fury that still scares me. You boys had been left behind when they had gone out because you were both ill with some random bug. They would have got you all but for that illness." This time the sigh that Lloyd tried to let out was strangled by the low noise of tears. He had watched as friends of his had been killed by the enemies they had fought so long to defeat. They had been killed in car crashes rather than the heroic fields of battle which had been expected of them. Tyus' methods of killing had advanced with the times.

I sat looking at Lloyd as he bowed his head and let his grief at the memory spill out. Mine was doing the same. The creature that had been following me since I had lost my Uncle was responsible for the deaths of almost all of my family. Images of the Auntie and Cousin that I had never met filled my mind and I could feel the hot tears as they tumbled down my cheeks. As their imaginary faces floated before my eyes I could feel the fury growing in my chest. It wasn't growing to the point that would jump start my transformation; instead it was building a small ball of burning fire that was going to drive me. I knew at that instant that this was the first stage at channelling and focusing my rage. Tyus was going to pay.

"Then what?" I growled through clenched teeth. I was now on my feet, pacing back and forth in the clearing. I felt like a caged beast and reflexively flexed my fingers as I paced. The tension in me needed to get out somehow.

Lloyd looked up at me and my eyes were shot through with creeping fingers of red.

"As soon as he was fit enough, he went to you. He knew that you would be in danger when Tyus discovered that he hadn't killed you all in the one place. He told me that I was to keep the house running to the highest standards and left. He knew that he could throw up the defensive magic that was needed to protect you when he wasn't around and he swore that he wasn't going to let anyone hurt you. We watched him and you like hawks for the first year. We pushed back a couple of attacks without him even knowing that he was in danger. Eventually, as he was needed for the duties of the Circle, he would bridge jump at the last possible moment direct to where he was required, rip through everything in his way, and then jump back. He saw your protection as the only thing that really mattered. He knew he needed to prepare both of you for your roles in the Circle but he always knew that you needed his protection. He vowed never to let anyone hurt his family again."

The pieces fell into the final shape of the picture they had been shaping to display and an almost complete image of the life which had beset my Uncle was there for me to see. He had lost his family again and again. Each time he felt comfortable in his life, felt that he was finding contentment, his responsibilities from the Circle crept back to the surface and forces of the enemies he had had since the beginning of everything struck. I looked back over my life since David had come into it and I could see the reason behind each one of his actions. He had let me do pretty much what I wanted, let me explore the things that had made me happy without judging me or making me do anything that I didn't want. He had ensured that I had lived a life, one that was full and utterly lived should the worst happen. But more than that, he had created a lifestyle for me that would mean I would side with him as a matter of course. I instinctively felt a bond to him and believed everything he had ever told me. That had obviously been an attempt to make sure that I took up the position of Guardian with the minimum fuss should it ever be passed to me. I felt comforted by the knowledge of what my Uncle had done for me. Then I made the next step.

"Do you know why he and my brother didn't get on? He let me do anything I wanted and I loved him for it but why did Steve argue with him all the time?"

"When Dai first moved to be with you, he was convinced that Tyus was going to attack at any moment. Every shadow became a potential threat, every knock at the door a killer. He thought that the best way to protect you was to keep you under constant supervision; you were too young to suddenly be told that everything that you thought went bump in the night was real.

Steve, on the other hand, was old enough and Dai told him everything, hoping that he would dive into his training and protect himself. Steve, understandably, thought he was talking rubbish and was ridiculing his family. Dai kept pushing and Steve pushed back, both naturally angry because of their fire line, both utterly unwilling to cede to the other. The harder they pushed, the further they pushed each other away. There were several attacks over the years but they were always 'handled' before either you or Steve could get into harms way. Eventually, Dai told me that Steve had upped and left. He was terrified for him so I pulled some strings in the Circle and people from every Hive prison site kept an eye on him. He was followed all over the world to make sure that he was safe but he was never followed at all by any of the enemy. They let him go."

"Why did they do that? Didn't they see that he was a danger?" Again my mind swung back into the logistics of what was going on.

"I have no idea. We followed Steve around for years and nothing. It was only after Dai's death that we saw Tyus come anywhere near either of you, it was always smaller demons who were attacking when there was any trouble and, like I said, they were always easy to 'handle'."

"Will I be able to give my brother a proper funeral? At some point, pay my last respects and bury him? You said that you had organised the funeral but you never told me when." Family now felt like the most important thing in the world and I wanted, no, I needed to tie up the loose ends.

"We can have the funeral whenever you want bach. He is still in the hospital in London but we can make whatever arrangements you want, whenever you want."

Lloyd slapped me on the arm but this time there was much less force to his effort.

Both of us stood still thinking about everything that had been revealed. My Uncle was now a very different man than when we had started out. The only sound between us was our deep breathing, the effort of our journey being made very clear by the plumes of steam pouring upwards towards the moonlit sky.

"Lloyd. What am I responsible for keeping imprisoned?"

Lloyd spoke with a slight smile, trying to pour all the reassurance he could into his voice.

"Don't worry, that's for another day." He then shivered a little over enthusiastically.

"But I need to know what I'm up against. Surely all the magical training in the world is useless without having any idea what it is actually being used against." I set my stance in the cold and waited for Lloyd to respond. I needed to know and him trying to laugh off my concerns gave me a sinking feeling that he didn't think I was ready to hear what he had to say.

He sagged ever so slightly as he realised that I wasn't going to take no for an answer then began.

"You are guardian of The Zarrulent. The Indestructible." He paused as if giving me the chance to absorb that detail. This was serious.

"And he is?" I asked more as a prompt, reminding Lloyd that the name was meaningless to me on its own. Lloyd continued.

"The Zarrulent was, like his brothers and sisters of The Hive, an immortal titan of terrifying power but it was rumoured that he couldn't be hurt or injured by any person or weapon, let alone defeated. He was one of the more brutal members of The Hive and he was responsible for the taking of millions of lives over the years up to his imprisonment. He is a giant winged serpent of incredible power that the Fire Dragon has the ability to defeat." Lloyd stopped speaking and the silence sat between us like a wall. Images of warring monsters flew through my mind, all tearing flesh and bursts of fire and magic. I hoped that my imagination was pumping up the levels of gore but I think that was just wishful thinking.

"You will need to enhance all of your magical skills and your training to bring you to your peak so you can stand against this beast should you ever have to, but always remember," he took a step closer to me, grabbed my arm tightly and continued in an almost conspiratorial tone, "the Fire Dragon is the one that put him in the prison in the first place, and recaptured him when he broke free. You are built to beat him." The end of the sentence was accompanied by one of his wide grins and his customary too hard slap on the arm. It would have been great if he had told me how to actually beat him but at least it was start.

"Come on bach," he boomed into the night and straightened himself up again. "Lets get back to the house, we're going to freeze if we stay out here too long" he declared with a forced hint of humour and with another slightly too hard slap he was off and walking, back to civilisation, leaving me feeling that there was yet more to learn.

16

We could make out the lights coming from the mansion only when we were within fifty yards of the edge of the forest. Muffled sounds of voices came from ahead as well but they seemed to be much further away due to the natural camouflage of the forest. The thick wall of trees was very effective at blocking out all hint of the mansion beyond. Private lands they may have been with signs warning people from trespassing but there seemed to be little chance of people actually making it to the centre of the forest even if they did wander in.

As we neared the edge I felt a huge surge of relief. There was no real reason to be apprehensive of the woods but I could feel the irrational fear of the dark crawling all over my back. The stories that Lloyd had been spinning as we made our way back had made me feel very different towards the whole lifeline that I was a part of. As the details of what had been taking place over the years were revealed I found myself reacting in much the same way that Lloyd had when he had been telling me, I could feel a deep, surging pride filling me about everything that had gone on and I knew that everything that I had been told was true. The reality of the life that was ahead of me was now laid bare for me to see and I knew that I wanted to make everyone proud, knew that I was going to be dedicated to what I had to do.

The more I felt the need to push my chest out and stride with real purpose, the more I realised that the creeping fear was coming from the same knowledge of my life. The knowledge of what was lined up against me, that the monster under the bed was real, was magnifying my fear of the dark woods so the sights and sounds of the mansion made me feel a sudden surge of relief.

We finally burst through the tree line quite near to the south east side of the house. Our path had been reasonably straight through the woods despite the dark and the fun and games of the terrain. We were both breathing hard as we entered the clearing and I could make out lots of people rushing around the front of the house carrying torches. I could just make out that Mike was in the centre of the throng, calling out orders to everyone. As I took in more details of what was going on I noticed that torchlight was flashing through from the tree line, intermittently showing the locations of at least thirty others. Had something happened? Was this a search party? Lloyd stood still, catching his breath slightly and taking in the details of what was going on ahead of us. He seemed to understand as much as I did about the huge deployment of staff.

"What the hell are they doing?" Lloyd questioned the air and started to march across the expanse of open land surrounding the house. The journey wasn't actually that far as the crow flies but the effects of my Dragon aerobics earlier in the day were proving to be slightly awkward to negotiate. Huge pits and scorched earth were forcing us to work harder than we had during our trek through the woods. The acrid smell of charred everything was lifting eerily from every surface and worked its way into our heads.

Before we could get close enough to call out to the gathered crowds, we could make out the sound of rushing air coming from above us. We both looked up at the same time to see a massive winged shape glide out from above the trees behind us. It surged towards where Mike was standing at the head of the stairs leading up to the front door, quickly descended and landed at a run on all four legs, gracefully folding away its wings. As it neared the house and the light that was pouring out, I could make out that it was Andrea in her Dragon form. As she neared the house, she stood up on her back legs and morphed back into her human form, not even breaking stride as she went.

Mike wrapped a thick dressing gown around her as she walked to his side and from their movements, I could see that neither was feeling positive about what they were discussing.

"They're looking for us" I declared. Lloyd didn't seem that sure.

"They can find us easily. Ninety percent of the people in this house can run simple location magic and that includes both Mike and Andrea. Something else has happened." Without another word, he started off in a fast run towards the others hoping to help with whatever problem was causing all the commotion. I followed him and I could feel myself preparing myself for the worst as I went.

We made ourselves known by an ancient, time honoured tradition of waving our hands wildly and calling out Mike's name. When he finally noticed us, the look of relief that was on his face said that they had, indeed, been looking for us.

"Where have you been? We've been panicking here since you vanished from the house." Mike couldn't quite contain himself and came across as the relieved parent when a missing child is found. His relief couldn't quite contain his frustration though.

"Anthony opened a cascade bridge without knowing what he was doing and sent us out to the edge of the estate. I thought it would be better to walk back as we were going through some history. You couldn't see us?" His response was to both Mike and Andrea which would explain his full breakdown of the details.

"We have tried several times to locate you since you vanished but the whole estate was blank. We thought that you been taken so hence the search of the grounds, you couldn't have been jumped out by our enemies so if anyone was going to do it they would have had to take you in person." I knew that the final part of that explanation was for me and nodded towards Andrea in thanks.

Around us, more and more people were heading back to the house. The word must have got round that we were safe.

"Why couldn't anyone find us? Lloyd just told me that everyone could run the process to find people around here." It didn't seem like a huge problem but it still needed to be addressed. Lloyd answered.

"You probably masked us. It is a pretty taxing casting but you probably tapped into it during our unplanned bridge jump. Looks like you've been throwing random magic around all over the estate bach. We'll go through more of the specifics on another occasion but looks like you managed to scare the whole estate. I was starting to panic when we saw everyone scrabbling around." With a sigh and another too hard slap, Lloyd grinned at me and that seemed to be the end of that. Typical. I don't have any magical ability so therefore everything must be my fault.

Andrea looked from Lloyd to me and she didn't look that happy. I could read that she was utterly frustrated with me. I had sent the whole population of the estate off on a terrified hunt through the woods which included a Dragon flying overhead. What a way to waste resources.

The last of the search parties were now filing back into the mansion through various doors towards the rear and suddenly the four of us were alone at the top of the steps. Andrea was the first to move.

"I will see you here first thing tomorrow morning where we will go through more of your catch up training" she spat and with that, she span round and stormed towards the open doorway. As she approached the doorway she quickly looked back over her shoulder. She had a relieved expression on her face and a slight smile as she looked at me. I began to return her smile but she quickly snapped her face back forwards almost as a precaution, not wanting to show anyone that she was happy I was safe. She disappeared into the house without another glance back and I suddenly felt that maybe Andrea did actually like me. That would really be interesting. Mike looked back between Lloyd and I, flashing a knowing smile that was fifty percent understanding of the reaction from Andrea and fifty percent relief that we were safe. He then turned and made his way after Andrea.

"I had hoped to show you a few more magical details but I think we've had enough excitement for one night, don't you?" Lloyd wasn't looking that tired but his hair and his beard were now much wilder. He was showing the effects of the mini adventure in his grooming! I had started to fade a long way back but didn't want to show it. Fixing an expression of calm understanding and mock resignation I nodded my head. I was just starting on my way back to my room, the welcome heat of a shower and then the open arms of my bed. I needed the rest. I had made only two steps when Lloyd ruined it all.

"We've only got the one more thing to do and then we're done." He halted my progress by stepping in front of me. My shoulders noticeably sagged as the thoughts of comfort in my bed flittered away. My expression must have been a picture and Lloyd was quick to reassure me with yet another over enthusiastic slap, "Don't look so sad. This won't take long and we've really saved the best till last."

He wrapped an arm round my shoulders and led me towards the house at a reasonably brisk pace. It was slightly too fast for what I thought was going to be yet another magical trinket or trick as my tiredness took the last vestiges of my enthusiasm.

177

We marched through the entrance hall and round under the stairs to a small, plain doorway off to the left. Compared to every other doorway or design feature in this estate, this was the most boring and utterly blank thing I had seen. A tall rectangle of bland beige, totally without carving or design work, stood before us with the small round door knob being the only feature of note, but just barely. The shape itself was sunk level with the wall around it and looked very much like it would easily be missed by those people who didn't know where to look. My body's ache for the bed which was waiting for me upstairs grew as I stared at it. Lloyd was feeling very different. He was fidgeting excitedly next to me and you could feel the tension in him as he reached out to unlock and open the door. It opened inwards to reveal the top of a wide corridor which was leading down a wide staircase. Lloyd ushered me inside, followed, and then pushed the door closed behind us. As it closed with a low click, a string of bright lights winked on and shone all the way down the stairs.

"After you" Lloyd practically giggled. That made me curious. What on earth was down there that was making him feel this wound up? My curiosity drove up my energy levels slightly and I started down. The tunnel was very wide and at least twelve feet high. The whole place felt like it had been dug out with very strict dimensions to adhere to.

"There are miles of corridors and tunnels under the mansion" Lloyd chimed out from behind me. "The majority of the staff quarters are below the surface. That's why we can have a huge number of people at our disposal without it looking like the estate is a garrison." At least that explained how they kept the place so quiet despite the huge number of people who worked and lived here.

We continued down and despite the similarities to the journey into the cavern beneath Neath Abbey, this tunnel felt as if it had been machined rather than dug out by hand and magical power. The thought of the events under the Abbey stuck in my head as we continued. The last time we had ventured into the depths of the earth, I had been given a massive power. The memory of my day's training filled my head as we continued our descent and I felt good at the recollection of what I was now capable of doing. As each step came and went, I found my own level of excitement growing without knowing what I was going to see. After only another two or three

178

minutes we found ourselves stood before a pair of doors which were practically the double of the ones outside my room. More heavy wood carved with the image of the Dragon that I could now become stood as a silent guard for whatever was beyond. Lloyd stood close next to me and smiled.

"Are you ready for this?"

"Am I ready for what? You've led me down here without telling me why." I wasn't angry with him; my eagerness to find out what was going on had overridden that. Now my curiosity was running wild.

Lloyd unlocked the door and pushed them open. They swung with a smooth swish, no hint of time-aged stiffness accompanying these hinges, and we both stepped into the room beyond.

"Welcome to the brain of the estate" he announced theatrically and flung his arm out to emphasise our arrival.

I was greeted by more wonder at where we were.

Ahead of me was a large room of more machined stone measuring twenty metres by twenty metres. Its triple height ceiling loomed above us, shrouded in shadows. The lights that had lined the corridor we had used to get here were strung out around each wall like hastily hung Christmas lights, the wires hanging down between fittings. They were all directed towards the centre of the room from about halfway up the walls which left very little to beam upwards. They were all pointed at the swirling mass at the centre of the room.

Hovering in the centre of the room was what looked like a scale depiction of the sun. It had the same diameter as I had height and was gentling bobbing as it remained in place. Its surface was a deep red with what looked like waves of energy surging this way and that. Despite looking like the sun, there was no heat coming from the object, the room we stood in was the same temperature as the corridor we had just left and our breath could be seen in the slightly damp air. As it bobbed in place, I could make out a low hum of modulating sound. It was more than just the constant hum of mechanical power. It was ebbing and flowing with the waves which were passing over its surface and the more I looked at it, I knew that I could 'feel' it.

"What do you think?" said Lloyd from a position next to me. This time, he didn't even try to conceal his obvious pride.

"What is it?" I responded breathlessly. Whatever it was, it had really taken my breath away.

"That" he started "is how the big magic happens." Lloyd crossed his arms over his chest and stood staring at the floating sphere.

"The big magic? Come on Lloyd, you've got to tell me more than that."

He shook his head, looking like he was shaking himself back to reality.

"Sorry bach. He's very powerful and it can be a bit of a struggle keeping your concentration, well my concentration, you Dragons are immune in here but the rest of us are quite vulnerable."

"He?" I needed Lloyd to concentrate on what was going on. The excitement that I had built up during our journey down here was still calling out for answers.

"That is the one person who started it all. That is the one who commanded the Dragons when the battles for the human race first took place. That is the one who is linking each of the houses. That is the one who has driven the largest magics since the very beginning." He paused as he continued to stare at the sphere. He was losing himself again.

"Lloyd!" I nudged him – slightly too hard – in the shoulder.

He shook himself back to me and turned to face me, focusing on what he was saying.

"You met him in the cavern during your Awakening." He took a deep breath to compose himself.

"That is the Mage."

17

"The Mage? The man who oversaw what was going on in the Awakening? How can that be him?" I asked pointing at the light show.

Lloyd frowned as he concentrated on what he had to say.

"Look through the construct of the sphere. Focus on what is at its centre; look through the outer layer to what is inside. I can't give you any more than that I'm afraid, only the Dragon of the house can see what is beyond." His frown deepened and it became apparent that he was really struggling to control what was happening to him. I grabbed him roughly by the collar and started to shove him towards the doors. It was a calculated attempt to get him to focus his mind away from the source of whatever interference he was being affected by. It seemed to work as he began to complain at my treatment of him.

I called into his ear "Stay here and wait for me. If I don't come out in ten minutes, come and get me" and shoved him through the doorway and pushed the doors closed behind me. They thumped closed and the lock clicked into place without hesitation. I was now alone in an enclosed space with something that had made Lloyd lose his mental control and which was credited with being the magical equivalent of General Patton. Nice one Anthony.

I slowly turned back to face the sphere. It was unchanged as it stood still in mid air. The waves of colour pushed over its surface and the low collection of sounds coming from it continued. I walked up to the edge of the sphere and peered in through the edge as best I could. I couldn't see beyond the deep red skin covering the ball of power. I paused and tried to think. Look beyond the outer layer.

This time I closed my eyes and tried to imagine what the person who had been the centre of power at my Awakening would look like hanging inside the sphere. I focussed on the image and willed myself to see it clearly. I snapped my eyes open and let my mind bore its way through the outer layer of the burning sun before me. This time it cleared before me without any effort. I stood like a statue as the image of the Mage was displayed before me.

I had been unconsciously expecting to see the same hooded man from the Awakening sat in the lotus position, looking calm and serene as I looked through the veil of the sphere with his long wispy beard gently swaying as a gentle breeze tugged at it. The reality of the image was very different.

The Mage was floating, totally naked, at the centre of the sphere but he wasn't wearing the peaceful expression of the man at ease that I had expected. Instead, he looked like he was being pulled by each limb in different directions. His arms and legs strained against the invisible forces which were gripping him. His wasted body was being stretched in several directions and he was in agony trying to withstand it. His face was contorted in pain but it was only barely recognisable. When I had seen the Mage in the Awakening, his face had been concealed by his hood, only his beard was visible. Now I could see the true visage of the Mage.

He was completely human in his body but his head was an impression of each and every Dragon that I had seen during the Awakening. Scales, horns and bone of different colours were laid out over the expanse of his reptilian features and he was in agony through all of them. I caught my breath at the horrific sight of the crushed creature which was apparently holding the whole prison structure together.

As I looked past his ruined form I could make out more details of his supernatural prison. Snaking out from behind him were several long fleshy tendrils. They were of a slightly lighter colour than the rest of the sphere that he was encased within. They all reached up to the roof of the sphere and vanished out above and beyond. All of them were slowly moving in an ebb and flow with the sound that was continuing to spill outwards. The whole image was a world away from what I had expected to be shown.

I slowly edged my way around the sphere, all the time keeping my focus on the Mage as he hovered. As I reached the back of the sphere I could make out clearly the tendrils entering his body. They all looked like they had been there for years; there were no open wounds or damage from whenever they had been inserted into him. How long had he been like this?

I couldn't cope with any more of this. Yet another being who was serving the greater good, but who was imprisoned in agony. The Circle had noble ideals but their methods were proving to be blatantly dangerous. I made for the door without the Mage showing any sign that he had even registered that I was there. I got to the doors and pulled them open. I glanced back briefly and took one last fleeting glimpse. The surface of the sphere was now broiling with higher forces as wider and deeper waves thundered over its surface. The colour remained the same but the whole image was now tainted for me with the picture of the broken man within it.

I marched through the doors and pulled them smoothly back behind me. Lloyd was waiting for me. He looked up to me with a large beaming smile on his face from his seat on the bottom step.

"I'll bet you weren't expecting that" he boomed as he got to his feet. He was moving somewhat gingerly as he walked towards me and I could only assume that it had been an effect of the power that was locked in the room beyond. He had said that only the Dragon could enter safely.

His response surprised me. How could he be so dismissive of what was going on in there?

"Not quite" was all I could manage. Lloyd continued.

"He's the reason that we are able to do the things we are as a group all around the world. He is the power behind so much of what The Circle does. In each of the estates, he is able to augment the abilities of each and every member, giving us a much greater ability to communicate together. Yes we have mobile phones and first class internet connections now but for thousands of years, he gave the ability to communicate across the whole network of The Circle. That said, it's not everyone who can magically think to other members across the globe. It's only the senior members of each house, those who are the most powerful, who have that ability. With the right training, the higher members of The Circle can simply 'think' to each other." More pride poured from him.

"Although, it is a dying art with the arrival of the modern age of communication tools. He still augments and advances each individuals powers when they are within the estate." More pride.

I couldn't shake the picture of him from my head. He looked like he was being twisted and mangled in my mind's eye and I could feel a stab of anger at how he had been treated. I needed to keep calm. Ask questions Anthony. Find out as much as you can, you might be able to help him.

"If he augments all of the power for all of the prisons all over the world, why is he here? South Wales doesn't seem to be that central for what he is doing."

Lloyd locked the door behind us and began to lead me back up the stairs to the rest of the mansion.

"He is in each of the houses" Lloyd offered and looked at me with the expression of someone who had just explained the most basic problem with the easiest possible answer that any child should be able to understand. As always, I was still lost. Lloyd filled in the blanks.

"He is able to inhabit several sites at once. He can project himself into multiple locations and basically use the same magic to do multiple jobs. He casts one spell, if you like, and it happens in twenty places."

I considered that as we climbed. If you believed that you could be in more than one place at a time, then it not only made sense but was also a very efficient way of maintaining the Circle.

"What happens if someone attacks him? If you kill him then surely the whole Circle will collapse?" There was a flaw in the plan which I'm sure I wasn't the first to consider.

"When the Mage entered the link system, he built in some safeguards" replied Lloyd, again without breaking step. "Only the higher members of each house are granted access to the way to him and then only the Dragon can enter. If we lesser beings go in," he waved his fingers in quotation signs to accompany his lesser beings comment, "then we can't control our thoughts or what we do. No-one is strong enough to get to him but if they did, he is more than capable of defending himself. And, if we can't get to him, then our enemies have no chance. They can't even breach the boundary of the estate and that's a mile away from the house." He was still very calm about the whole situation.

"He put himself in there?" Lloyd's comment about that pricked at the back of my mind.

"He did indeed. He knew what it would mean to ensure all of the power remained in place and gave himself to the task without a thought. We explained some of that on the tour, about his selfless actions as leader" and with a nudge and a grin he reminded me that I was still very new to all of this and that everything had been going on for some time. Knowing he had done it himself did make me feel a little better about the situation, but not much.

"How did he get into the cavern under the Abbey to run the ceremony if he is locked into each of the houses?" My curiosity had taken over as I rolled the ideas round my head.

"He is linked to all the Hive prisons as well. He just 'beamed' himself into the centre of things for a short time and he was able to channel your power to you and still remain in control of everything he needed to. He is in possession of a great many powers and articles which can make this whole group function smoothly."

We were nearing the top of the stairs and Lloyd was still wearing a happy expression of quiet pride. He was really hoping that I was going to be as excited as he was. I tried to give off awe and inspiration as much as I could, I owed Lloyd that much, but the floating picture of a demolished old man somewhat sullied what I could express. Lloyd didn't seem to notice.

When we reached the top of the stairs, Lloyd paused before he opened the door.

"Despite us being confident that the Mage is safe, please don't explain to everyone what is down there. The fewer people who are aware of the full details of what's down there, the better we can maintain the power. The door is shrouded in boredom so everyone just looks past it meaning people don't even know it's here." Then as an after thought, "Besides, the more people who do know just cheapens it for the rest of us! Eh bach." The grin that flooded his face was more reminiscent of the Lloyd who had first greeted me and the return to him treating me purely like a man rather than the latest in a long line of supernatural monsters made me smile. With that he opened the door back into the mansion, the lights of the corridor we were in, winked out, and we made our way back to the house proper.

Lloyd secured the door and turned back to me.

"That concludes a long day of lessons." He checked his watch and whistled at what he saw. "That concludes a very long day of lessons." He stretched his arms out above his head and cracked his neck.

"I know that this isn't exactly how you would have chosen to spend a Friday night but everything that has happened today has been designed to get you in a position to defend yourself should you be attacked, and to guarantee that the Hive prison is defended. So far you have a solid grounding in what you can do as a Dragon, Andrea will continue the lessons tomorrow, and you have shown that your fledging magical ability is going to be something that is very powerful. You're going to have a busy weekend but it will be worth it."

Something at the back of my mind started to scratch to be heard. It was a tiny feeling to begin with but with each passing second I could feel the discomfort building as I fished round in the deepest recesses of my mind for a fact that was desperate to be heard. It felt like trying to catch smoke in a butterfly net as I pushed harder to work out what it was that was troubling me.

Lloyd picked up quickly on my discomfort.

"What's wrong?" he asked with concern in his voice which was only just masking fear.

"I know there is something but I don't know what. I can feel something at the back of my mind but I can't make out what. What did you just tell me?" I was starting to get more fired up as I tried to sift through my head to find what it was that was floating in the back of my head. Lloyd was looking more and more worried as the fear he felt overtook the concern and showed itself clearly.

"I told you that your training had been busy for Dragons and magic alike so you could defend the prison and yourself. That Andrea was going to do more of the same tomorrow and that you were going to have a busy weekend." He was holding me by both shoulders and was willing me to work out the problem. What the hell was about to happen.

With a flash of understanding, the issue rushed to the front of my mind. My eyes widened as the realisation hit me and Lloyd braced himself. I could feel him starting to bring in power to fuel whatever magic he may need to battle the on rushing threat.

"What is it?" pleaded Lloyd as he shook me, flicking his attention around him trying to find any sign of the invisible threat to us.

"You said that today was Friday and that I was going to have a busy weekend of training activities along the same lines as I have today."

"So!" Lloyd was getting desperate.

"Whatever Andrea has planned for me tomorrow, I think that we are going to be putting it on hold."

I looked down into Lloyd's eyes and knew that whatever they had planned for me wasn't going to be taking place like today.

"Tomorrow is the most important date of the year Lloyd and there will be nothing that stops me, gets in my way."

Lloyd looked lost.

"Tomorrow is the Wales versus England rugby international in Cardiff and there is nothing that will stop me from watching it, nothing!"

Lloyd slumped his shoulders as he slowly released the magic he had drawn in. He bowed his head and I could hear his breathing, deep and rhythmical, as the built up tension left him. After an age he lifted his head and stared me straight in the eye.

"The match." I could feel a huge amount of relief in him and suddenly realised that I really had looked like something was attacking. My fervour at following Wales play rugby had been likened to feelings of life and death but now I think that I had just proved it.

"I forgot about the match" Lloyd continued. "We'll have a word with Andrea in the morning to make sure she is finished by the mid afternoon. We'll both be watching the game, now get some rest, she isn't going to be happy at letting you miss any work for something that she will no doubt see as being utterly frivolous."

With that, he tapped me on the shoulders, gentle slaps which were much calmer than his usual efforts, and he slowly sloped off towards the stairs and his bed. His posture was that of a man who had just been taken on an emotional roller coaster. I followed him towards the stairs and tried to hold my mind focussed. It had been a very long day and I was struggling to keep my head together. I had pictures of my Dragon training, the walk through the woods, the Mage and the upcoming international swimming through my head and I didn't know what to focus on. I had learnt more about the Circle and how things happened and I had discovered the reasons behind why my

Uncle had been the man he was. All in all, it had probably been the busiest day of my life.

My paces seemed to be slowing by the second as I trudged onwards to some rest and I was now starting to realise that I was a little peckish. My stomach didn't feel cripplingly empty but I knew that I needed a snack before I turned in.

"Lloyd" I shouted up the stairs after him. "Can I just get some food from the kitchens? I think that I need to eat something before I actually turn in." Up to this point, all of my food had been prepared for me so I hadn't actually been near the kitchens to prepare any of the food myself.

"Of course you can bach, but I can get the kitchen staff to sort you out. There is always someone on duty." He began to walk back down the stairs with more energy than he had shown when he had been climbing them. I was about to stop him and let him know that I could sort out what I needed and that I didn't want to disturb anyone but I caught myself before the words left my lips. Everyone had a very real sense of position here and there had been a fierce pride in every department at the role they performed. The last thing that I wanted was to casually march into any part of the estate and disrespect members of the staff because I didn't want to put anyone out. That must have meant that I was growing.

I followed Lloyd back down the corridor towards the kitchens and started to feel a little more comfortable with the idea of everyone having a role to fulfil.

We pushed through the large port-hole windowed doors and entered the room and I expected to find the room empty. I was shocked to discover that a full team of kitchen staff were swarming through their business despite the late hour. Steam and smells rose from pots and pans and the sounds of banging dishes floated everywhere, mingled with the excited chatter of chefs and porter staff. I had seen the inner workings of a large kitchen before when I had worked in private health clubs. I was aware of the amount of activity that took place behind closed doors but seeing it happening here, at midnight, in a private estate, on the off chance that the one person who was 'in charge' might fancy a meal really blew my mind.

"Gentlemen." A voice trilled out from our left. Mike came striding confidently across the busy kitchen wearing the same razor sharp suit as he had earlier. I greeted him with a handshake and felt good to see him again. He and Lloyd had been the first people in this whole saga that had looked after me and they had treated me like an adult without bowing and scraping. They made me feel comfortable.

"Michael, can you and your team prepare some food for Anthony please, he's feeling a little empty!" Lloyd spoke with the same modulated tone he had used when he was on official business.

"Certainly. Would you like anything in particular sir?" Mike addressed me with the same business like tone of deference you would expect from a staff member when he spoke to his lord and master. That comfort at seeing him again faded as the reality of my place in things reared its head again. I still wasn't sure if I would ever get used to being called sir.

"Just a few sandwiches will be fine Mike, thanks."

Before I could say anything else, he nodded and spun back to the staff behind him and started to speak hurriedly, making everyone snap to their duties, presumably so I wouldn't have to wait for my food. Lloyd nudged me and whispered in my ear, "You can go up to your room if you want. Someone will bring your food up to you when it's ready."

It sounded like a good idea. Despite being hungry and tired, I was also in desperate need of a shower.

"I'll be in my room" I announced into the kitchen. It felt like something the lord of the place would say but it didn't feel comfortable at all. I turned round and made my way back out of the doors. As I left, Lloyd took a step into the room and started to speak with Mike. It looked like the head of house talking to the head of the kitchens and I paid it little regard, instead turning my mind to the hot shower and cool bed which were waiting for me in the roof of the building.

I shambled my way back up stairs, focusing what was left of my attention on the step immediately ahead of me. I reached one arm out and steadied myself against the wall as I climbed the seemingly unending stairs. The corridors and walkways were dark as I moved along them and made the journey seem even longer.

When I finally reached the doors to my room it was all I could do to just lean into them to force them open. Today had obviously been a very long day indeed.

I showered quickly and dressed myself in a light pair of sweat suit trousers and a black T-shirt and settled onto the bed to wait for my snack. The speed that the people in the kitchens were capable of working was quite startling so I hadn't wanted to hang around. It wasn't really in keeping with the image of powerful supernatural being for everyone who came in to give me food saw me wandering out of the shower wearing nothing but a smile! I didn't have to wait long.

Two very small knocks leaked into the room from the other side of the door. Then nothing. I paused for a second, confirming in my mind that I had really heard the tiny sounds but before I could decide either way, they cracked out again. They sounded almost apologetic through the heavy wood of the doors, as if they didn't really want to be heard so as to disturb me. They were waiting for a response from me. I jogged across the room and pulled the doors open, reflexively beginning to apologise for my delay. The same woman who had brought me breakfast was stood before me, bearing a massive serving platter of sandwiches, fruit, vegetables and dips. There was also a steaming pot of something that I didn't recognise. It smelt slightly like coffee but there was more to it than that – a thicker smell of fruit of some kind.

"Come in, come in, uh..." I snapped my fingers to myself as I tried to remember her name, "Wynn isn't it?" She quickly pattered into the room.

"Yes sir. Where would you like to have your meal?" Her tiny voice seemed to be lost in the huge space which was my room as it hunted for someone to hear what she was saying.

"Over on the desk again would be perfect, thank you" and I gestured for her to lead the way. She flinched back away from me slightly as I did, and then scuttled past me as if her life depended on it. She set the tray down and made for the door without looking back to me.

"Thank you Wynn, see you tomorrow." I floated my farewell after her but the door slam beat back at least half of the sentence. I was alone again. And I was hungry.

The food was superb. I had been prepared a selection of sandwiches of different meats, some cooked, some cold, but they all tasted first class. Whatever they were doing in the kitchens, it really

190

was something special. I wolfed my way through them in no time at all, had two cups of the fruity coffee and settled myself into bed. The food had hit me hard and I was now struggling to keep awake. I made myself comfortable and let the blanket of sleep draw over me. What a day.

18

No sooner had I shut my eyes and let sleep take me, the visions started up. It's said that dreams are the minds way of making sense of the activities of the day. I was watching visions, not dreams. Steadily, pictures of people and places floated through my head. It was much more ethereal than the way it had happened when Lloyd and I had been making our way back through the woods, but I knew that I was seeing snapshot memories of the past members of the Circle. I didn't try to focus on any one in particular or to look for certain details over others but I could make out several that I knew were coming from my Uncle.

Without trying, all the other pictures started to fall away one by one, leaving behind a collection of the person who had filled this position before it had been passed to me. The person who had had to die for that passing to take place. My mind was floating amongst the collection of memories and I wasn't drawn to one over the others but one started to reach out and pull me to it.

In it I could see the day that Uncle David was told that his father had been killed and that he was now going to take his place. He had been told in the library when he had been reading. He hadn't been surrounded by grieving family or worried friends, instead he had been told by Lloyd, during what felt like a lesson of some kind. Lloyd's voice boomed in the same way it had when I had spoken to him and I would have recognised that huge, wiry red beard of his anywhere. Despite the memory coming from decades ago, Lloyd didn't look any different. He must have aged really early. The room around him looked the same as it had when I first entered, although I think my trick with the chairs may have changed things slightly. I was suffused with smells and sounds that I could remember from my own time in the same room and that made the memory even more disturbing. I had walked in the same footsteps as my Uncle. I had seen the birth of my magical ability in that room where he had seen the death of his father.

Without warning, I suddenly bolted across to a new memory. This time, I was watching him spending time in a humble looking house. He walked between a large country kitchen and a very comfortable looking living room. Large, plump, well used furniture was dotted around the rooms as he walked and I could smell the rich aroma of roasting meat and the smoky produce of an open fire floating through the whole place. Without having been there, of knowing anything about where I was seeing, I could tell that my Uncle had been totally happy in this place, his contentment was almost palpable. A woman's voice suddenly called out from through a doorway off to my left and as the view point turned to face it, I was greeted by something that made my heart ache. Into the room walked a woman of roughly five foot six with shoulder length brown hair. She strode into the room with a subtle strength and confidence that anyone would have found hard not to be drawn to. She was woman shaped, with curves in all the right places, not a stick thin reed of a person with a head too big for the rest of her body. Her face was covered in freckles and she was beaming a wide, infectious smile across towards me. I knew that this was a memory and that she was looking at my Uncle but she made me feel immediately that I wanted her to be looking at me.

"He's awake" she said and nodded towards the small bundle in her arms that she was slowly rocking back and forwards. Her voice put me totally at ease and sounded like it was infused with quite strength. The view moved forwards and looked closely into the face of the small baby in her arms. I saw a hand reach out and watched as my Uncle had gently rubbed the head of the alert little thing that nestled in his mum's arms. I knew that I was looking at Clare and Matthew, the Auntie and Cousin that I had never met.

I felt like I was going to break as I watched the pictures which floated before me, the happy family life that my Uncle had so desperately wanted. The love that he had lost when his father was killed and his life was set completely to the Circle. As I looked on, I wanted to stay here and take part in this life. It all felt like the missing piece of my life since my parents were killed. Despite my want to stay, I then jumped out to another place. This time I didn't want to stay.

I found myself looking at the inside of a car crash. I knew exactly what was happening around me, Lloyd had told me earlier in the night all the details of my Uncle's life and I could recognise exactly what was floating before me.

I was strapped into the ruined car in the driver's seat and I could hear the shrieking sound of tearing metal as I looked forward, not moving. The smell of fires filled my nostrils and I could pick out different accents to the smell. The flames from burning upholstery were putting out a smell of heavy chemical coverage. It was wrapping itself around everyone who was nearby and I was aware of feeling like I was being held in place by it. The other odour which was mingled in with the damaged car interior was a sweet smell that made me feel somewhat confused. I couldn't recognise it through the chemical stench but I felt that it was familiar and that it was something good.

As I stared directly ahead, I could make out several black shapes moving slowly towards what was left of the car. Humanoid shapes which carried with them the real feel of menace and terror, skittered back and forth through my vision. And in the centre of the group was a shape that I would have recognised anywhere. His wide brimmed hat still sat down on his head to cover his face. Tyus was walking towards the car I was trapped in. His voice creaked out as he spoke.

"Who will take the line now half breed?" it was purely nails down a blackboard as he continued.

"We have undone the line to this cage. It won't be long before the place falls and my master is freed." He walked up to my side of the car and leaned into me. His voice dropped to a barely audible whisper of shards of glass and he reached out to grip my head.

"But I hope you will appreciate what we have done here for you? When my master breaks from his bonds, he will bring about the end of the human race, that pitiful breed that you are so driven to protect. He will free the others and destroy all of the Guardians, just as I have you, and the human race will be undone. Everyone on this planet will be pulled slowly piece from piece and they will all burn for us. You should be grateful that I have spared your family that." With a slow, deliberate turn of his hand on the top of my head, he turned my attention to the passenger seat. My Uncle had witnessed these events first hand and I could only pity the awful picture which must have been burned into his mind.

In the passenger seat, still belted in, was the charred and broken remains of Clare. Every inch of her flesh had been incinerated by a heat that I had never seen. She had raised her right arm against the force of the attack, a futile gesture of defence against the scorching attack which had come from the driver's side of the car. I realised as soon as I saw what was left her that the smell which had made me feel so comfortable earlier was the smell of burning flesh. It had reminded me of the image of the contented farm house from my earlier memory. I felt sick as the association would now be for ever tainted.

But the worst was still to come.

In Clare's left arm, covered as best she could from the force which immolated her, was the burned form of a baby. Matthew lay cradled in his mother's arms and had been finished at the same time as his parent.

I could feel a bilious charge run through my throat and I knew that my Uncle had been broken by what he had seen. From next to me, I could hear a sharp laughter. Tyus was enjoying the pain he was causing.

"They won't see anymore pain now. They have been released." His voice was filled with mock concern but quickly changed. "You can't move can you? You see, I can defeat you and you can't do anything to stop it. Do you want to be with your family again?" He snapped my view back to his horror face. He had stood over my Uncle and had gloated.

I could feel the fury building inside my own mind, a reflection of what had happened the first time round. Tyus' face registered that my Uncle was trying to break whatever it was that was holding him in place.

"You can't do anything about your bonds. We've got you held. Now, would you prefer that I kill you quickly, or that my" he paused and glanced around at the shadows which were still circling the wrecked car, "associates should send you off more slowly? They haven't eaten for a while so it shouldn't last too long."

The reedy laugh that followed was enough. My Uncle had roared out against whatever bonds were holding him and the sudden icing of the whole area in his field of vision showed that he was breaking free. Animal rage and the purest form of sheer violence ran through the memory and my Uncle did as much damage as he could. The image blurred and shook as whatever fight took place. Flames and beams of energy flew without me being able to pick out where they were aimed or who had thrown them. Shrieks called out through the melee until finally everything went black. I didn't know what had happened but knew that my Uncle had survived the encounter. The memory of his family being killed felt as if it had been burned onto the back of my eyes. I could feel the anger and the loss that it had brought as if it had happened to me. I knew that I needed to wake up and try to shake the memory away. Before I could push myself back to consciousness, another memory came to the centre of my head. My face appeared, looking right at me. Certainly not what I had been expecting.

My Uncle told me that he would see me later and turned away. He walked into the winter night and made his way off on a mundane journey through town. I didn't like the feel of what I was seeing. It felt like this wasn't a new memory to me. The lights from passing cars formed into a hypnotic train of illumination and I could feel the memory wandering along without really paying any attention to the surroundings. My Uncle was at ease as he walked along the roadside and some of the roads looked oddly familiar. As he rounded the next corner into a secluded roadway my familiarity of the situation cleared. A massive black shadow shot passed my view point and I saw a bright flash of metallic claw whip out. I could feel that it had found its target. I was watching the last memory that my Uncle had. The memory of his final attack by Tyus and that of his death.

The view point we shared dropped down, as he slumped to his knees. I could hear awful gurgling sounds as I watched him clutch to his slashed throat. Before us, Tyus dropped back into view from the sky above. He folded his wings back into place around him and he took on the appearance of the gunslinger he had worn when I had first seen him. He cautiously approached despite the injury to his opponent, flexing his clawed fingers.

"It's been a while, hasn't it? Let's finish what we started." Without any further sound, he lunged forward and drove both his hands into my Uncles chest. He looked directly into Uncle David's eyes as he twisted the talons in his chest, doing the most damage he could. They were finally face to face and I could feel the breath of the animal that had been killing my family for generations. The warmth made my skin crawl and I could feel the anger and fear in my Uncle.

"Now, let's see what the next member of your pitiful line can do."

With that, the edges of my vision started to blur and eventually the whole memory ended. I had just watched my Uncle die from his view point and I could feel the build up of a huge anger towards Tyus and all of the creatures who had ever worked against us.

I roared my way back to consciousness and sat bolt upright. My chest was heaving as I dragged wildly at the air around me, struggling to regain a level of composure as the memories began to fade. All over my bed, and on the floor surrounding, was a thin layer of frost and ice. It glistened in the low light from the moon which was pouring in through the wide windows behind my bed. As I felt my heart rate beginning to slow, as my breathing eased and the anger of the dream sequence dissipated, the sheen of cold began to melt away as the temperature rose back to normal. I sat still in the centre of the bed as I felt all of the rigid tension which had been knotting my muscles slip away.

Eventually, I was calm.

I checked my watch to find that it was just after two. Andrea and Lloyd would be asleep now, resting for the fun and games that I no doubt had in store tomorrow. I slumped back and tried to get myself relaxed, hoping that sleep would come easily. Outside, a steady wind was blowing past the windows and I could feel the gentle thrum of the glass as it quietly resisted it. The clear night sky outside allowed the light from the moon to pour in and cast more eerie shadows across the wide floor and walls of my room. I could still smell the metallic hues of my Uncle's blood and feel the fear he had felt at the very end. I could also still hear the scratching sound of Tyus' voice, taunting him as he clutched at his injury. The voice seemed to be holding firm at the edges of my mind despite my best efforts to push it away. After a further five minutes of feeling frustrated at not sleeping, I sat up in bed and decided that I could do with a drink of water.

I threw the covers back and swung my legs out, dropping my bare feet onto the cold tile surface. That jolt of cold really was going to help me get to sleep. As I stood up, a chill wrapped itself round my body and I started to shiver. Coupled with the dizziness of fatigue I was now feeling since standing up, I really wasn't going to be on tip top form in the morning.

I quickly padded over to the bathroom and filled a glass with water, gulped it back in one swig, filled it again and headed back to bed. I was absolutely exhausted and my head was starting to show more and more that I needed to get some sleep, if anything, the dizziness was getting worse.

I set the glass down next to the bed and was about to settle back to sleep when I noticed that my mind was starting to play tricks on me. I shook my head to try to clear it but it was at that point that a large shadow on the nearest wall to me moved, turned to face me, and lunged out.

19

The shock that the shadow drove in me caused me to stand stock still for a split second, not believing that whatever it was, was really running right at me. The dizziness in my head built rapidly and I finally worked out that it was my magical drunken sixth sense which had been calling to me. It was all I could do to just reach my arms out and attempt to grab the shape as it flew from the wall. It landed on me with the force of what I could only equate to a super charged, stampeding pillow. It had no distinct edges or hard mass. Any grip you tried to take on it seemed to contract under the force of constriction. We both flew back onto the bed and it landed squarely on top of me. I could now feel that, despite its peculiar make up, it weighed about the same as I did. That made it feel like it was smothering me without it having to move. But it did move.

Shards of inky tendrils flew from the centre mass and aimed at my face. One wrapped itself around my throat while the other pushed into my face and covered my nose and mouth. The smell of rotting flesh and decay filled my nostrils. In an instant, I could feel the air being pushed from me and the panic began to build. I flailed wildly at the assailant who had me pinned down. I struck out at the tendrils at my face but they seemed to be reforming around me wherever I aimed a blow, all the time maintaining a crushing grip on me.

The edges of my vision began to slowly ease in on me and I could feel that the shadow was winning. It was going to choke the life from me and probably destroy the whole house unless I could do something. I needed to break out to alert everyone else to danger that was inside the house. The edge of my vision sank loser together. It was no good. Wherever I gripped or beat the shadow it seemed to just absorb the force and keep on coming. I was going to be beaten in a sneak attack and killed in my bed. I was going to let everyone down. Pictures of the people who had been helping me bobbed helplessly in my mind, Lloyd, Mike. I'd never get to find out if Andrea really was as playful as she looked but I had let my Uncle down. This would be where the line ended.

The image of my Uncle was what did the trick. He had been killed when he was walking along a footpath in London, far away from the field of battle. He had been picked off without a fight. That wasn't going to happen to me.

Before the tunnel of my vision closed off completely, I felt my anger rising at the thing that was sitting on my chest. How dare it come into my house and try to catch me when I couldn't defend myself. The fury climbed quickly in me and I could feel the temperature around me beginning to drop. In my mind, I began to visualize a wide scream of flame that I was going to aim at my attacker. The thing had noticed the change as well. A panicked tension surged through it as the frost began to form around the bed. That was the distraction I needed and I didn't hesitate. Summoning all of my strength, I kicked up at it with both of my legs as I pushed with my arms. The combined force was enough to send it crashing back towards the wall it had erupted from. It landed with a gentle thud and then a crack as it hit the floor then slid into the wall.

I bounced up and focussed my attention on the shape that lay, scrabbling to right itself, at the edge of the room. All of the energy that I had pulled in to explode fire was still at my bidding so I poured it all out towards the shadow. I didn't care what damage was done to the house. I didn't care if my actions may have been questioned. I was going to destroy that thing and the almost animal need to totally undo it was intoxicating.

The flame lanced out and in a second, had totally engulfed the shadow. As the orange/white fire danced and leapt, I could now make out a stick thin shape within the mass of black. Its bony limbs were flapping wildly and its large head snapped back and forth with the force of the movements. It writhed and kicked against the force of the flame and I could make out a faint whine as it was burned away to nothing.

I stood over the bubbling corpse, prepared for the Hollywood villain 'leap from the flames', but it never came. The flames consumed every piece of the silent enemy, leaving behind only a charred stain, smouldering embers and a hideous smell of burnt flesh. I kicked at it and a sense of morbid pleasure ran through me. I had been faced with a very real threat and had dealt with it in the best way possible. I was safe and so was the house.

My head began to spin violently.

The sudden shock of it almost sent me stumbling into the still burning embers but I steadied myself before I fell. The danger wasn't over.

I scanned my way round the room, taking in as much detail as I could, trying to pinpoint where the next attack would come from. As I went I risked breaking off some of my concentration and calling out to Andrea and Lloyd. Lloyd hadn't actually shown me how to do it but I didn't have anything to lose did I? My mind called into the night for Andrea or Lloyd, pleading them to be awake and to come to my aid. Nothing happened. No-one spoke back and there was no reaction in my head. I kept looking around and backed myself into the nearest wall, into the first available space without a shadow of any description lying across it.

I slowly slid my way towards the door, hoping to get out as fast as I could and raise the alarm. It was at the door that I saw the first movement. From what I could make out, there were at least six different shadows smearing their way from the door into the room. They were moving along the floor and the ceiling as well as the walls and I found myself feeling more and more isolated as each second passed.

In desperation, I called out Lloyd's name as I tried to attract anyone's attention with my thoughts. Still nothing. No reinforcements were coming to my aid. The call into the dark did cause the shadows to stop in their tracks. They must have known that they had been noticed as one of their number lay a cindered mess near the bed. Before any of them could recommence their progress towards me, I caught a glimpse of something else, outside of the room, in the corridor beyond. All I could see was a small shape but I knew that it wasn't the same as the shadow creatures which were lining up to attack me. That object was someone standing in the dark.

That realisation was quickly locked away as the shadows all started moving again, slipping silently towards me. My eyes worked between each of the targets as they approached and back to the door. The small shape out there wasn't moving but I could make out more and more shapeless movement, as shadow after shadow came inside, if anything, each looking more threatening than the last.

Finally I had reached the point of fight or flight. My enemies were close enough now to be able to attack me easily so I needed to do something. But what? I reached in on myself and drew in as much power as I could and created a picture in my head of single candle. My head suddenly jerked with dizziness as the attack began. I pushed my mental force into the candle, willing it to light, as in the real world, I prepared for the impact of multiple foes as the shadows swarmed.

They all poured onto me with a speed and fury that I really wasn't prepared for. They had obviously seen their comrade fall and had been stung by how he had failed. I could feel a mighty weight slam me back against the wall and crack my head back. They all drove the air from me with the force of their attack and I could feel a growing constriction as they tightened onto me. This wasn't going to last as long as the previous fight unless I did something fast.

I pushed my focus back to the candle and willed it to light. As the blows started to rain down with concussive force, the flame ignited. Around me, each of my assailants burst into flame. The surprise caused them all to weaken their grip in an attempt to douse the flames which had sprung up over them. It was enough for me to push out against some of the shapes and break my arms free. I started to wildly swing at the others who had held me so I could avoid the flames but I could feel the need for payback growing. With each stroke, I had to concentrate on making sure that the candle in my mind was still lit, ensuring the magic did the damage I needed it to.

When I had finally pushed all of the burning shadows away, and they lay on the floor, life ebbing from them, I couldn't maintain the flame anymore. I had burned off a great deal of my mental energy and I was feeling the effects. My breathing was deeper than it had been, even during training with Andrea, and I was starting to feel my muscles tightening. My head span with wild abandon as my senses told me I was still in danger and my mental focus began to wane under the weight of concentration required to keep the magic controlled. I scanned the field of battle as my head continued to spin and I realised that I hadn't been dealing with the whole fighting force.

At least half of their number was still slipping around the room. They were all keeping back to a safe distance, circling me at a distance of roughly ten metres. None of them looked keen to encroach inside the perimeter they were creating.

I stood straighter and took on the posture of readiness. I was going for the Neo look of preparation, but I don't think anyone else in the room got the reference. I summoned up the fire again and tried to prepare the candle. The flame burst into life in my head and I willed the force outwards to attack everything around me.

But nothing happened.

I was surrounded by creatures that were aiming to rip me to pieces, and suddenly, the one magical skill I had had deserted me. The thought of the Cascade Bridge flashed through my head but was quickly snuffed out. If I couldn't maintain a flame on one candle, a bridge jump would be well out of my reach with my energy as low as it was now. My enemies picked up on my failure instantly and without a second thought, they all dived forward together.

The force pulverized into me and I flailed out at the group, hoping to find some weakness in the mass. This time the shadows were much more violent in their attack. Much larger blows were smashing me back and I could see an array of bladed weapons amongst the cloud, all slashing and stabbing.

I defended myself as much as I could, punching, kicking, biting. I threw blocks and defensive moves in all directions but they were all too much for me. White hot lances of pain shot over my skin at so many points as their blades made contact. My fatigue was slowing me and the ever increasing dark hoard was too strong for me. My pain started to light the fire of rage inside me and, despite the fatigue, I knew that I wasn't going to lose.

My blows flew round the mass and I could feel the temperature dropping quickly. I knew that regardless of where I was, I was going to do everything that I could to end this attack. The red flashed over my eyes and I could feel the absolute build up and release of my power. I was going to become the Dragon.

20

The swarm didn't react in any way as I roared out against them. My wild swings of defence had started to connect with individuals within the mass and I was now starting to force them away from me. Their bladed slashes were now not creating the same sensation of pain as they had when they had first started their offensive. My fatigue had now collapsed away from me as the ancient power surged outwards. My body began to change and shift. My skin colour darkened as the scaled armour plating of the Dragon spread out to encase me. Inside the melee of the fight, I could make out the sound of tearing clothing as my night attire was ripped open and I changed into the beast.

Despite their initial incredulity at my battle cry, the collection of shadows soon reacted when they felt me transforming. They all clung onto me as my size began to increase and I was aware of pin pricks all over my body. They were all digging in their blades and talons to secure themselves to me. They all maintained their hold as if they were scared to move and draw attention to their positions. It was at that point that the shape from outside the doors entered the fray.

It moved more into the open so it had a clearer view of me and raised its hands. The tiny shape looked like the weakest of the litter of shadows that were attacking me, almost as if they had brought it along on the hunt as a favour to their mother, promising to keep it safe. That thought played at my mind as I continued to swipe against the attackers who were now attaching themselves to me like limpets as I grew towards the ceiling. Despite my all-encompassing fury, the thought of the little brother being taken out by his older siblings because his mum had said so did make me laugh for a second.

That was as long as the thought lasted. Light began to gather at the shapes hands, spitting out shards of green brilliance as it did, until a tightly packed ball of green energy sat in the palms of each hand. My transformation had brought me to the apex of the room and I could feel my body straining against the structure above me until the black shape unleashed the power at its disposal and lanced out a searing fire at me. The bolts of energy hit me with a force I totally underestimated and which caused me to stagger back. It also caused a creeping cold to spread through me at the contact point in my chest and I could feel the transformation stutter. My body suddenly stopped pushing against the ceiling and I could feel that my enemy was using some kind of power which was completely against who I was. I had been told that Tyus was the perfect killer when it came to me and my people. Was this something that he was doing?

Another blast hit me as I stood distracted and it sent me staggering back towards the window at the front of the house. A third blast hit me in the chest and it lit up whole room as it did. The only shadows in with me were now stretched out over my body and were starting to swarm upwards, aiming at my head. I began swiping at them but then realised that the explosion of light had also exposed the true form of my assailant. The shape had moved forwards, out of the cover of the doorway and into the room, as it had been unleashing the magical force which had been sending me backwards. The last blast had been equivalent to a signal flare in my bedroom and I was now able to make out the details the darkness had been concealing.

Wynn stood in a similar posture to the one that I had been aiming for at the beginning of the fight but she had somehow made it look one hundred times more threatening. Her face was now constricted into a wicked snarl and her eyes had gone completely black. Whatever she was channelling, it wasn't coming from a good place. The previously timid woman edged slowly closer to me and continued to call up more energy to finish me off. She muttered under her breath and the power surged up again and she aimed at my head. She didn't look like the same person and I knew that there was going to be no talking with her.

She shrieked out as another blast poured out and that was enough to snap me back to the here and now. She wanted to kill me, probably more than the crowd of shadows that she had brought with her. That realisation of her betrayal was enough to fire up my transformation again as the anger flew through me.

"Don't. You. Dare" was all I could muster as she shaped to open up yet another attack. The rest of my transformation happened in seconds. I surged up and out, through the ceiling and smashed out through the roof of the mansion. As I burst out I threw my head back and let out a roar of utter savagery and smashed my tail, arms and wings out at the structures that remained around me. Masonry, glass and metal were thrown in every direction as I opened the whole room up to the outside world.

Wynn called out to the shadows which were still draping themselves over me, "Now. Go. Tear him to pieces. Do it now." There was a barely controlled glee in her voice, she was practically laughing at me as she willed my attackers on, the wild amusement of the utterly insane, her eyes wide with a broad smile at her lips, baring her teeth.

As the last of the debris I had created by demolishing part of the front of the mansion drifted down, the shadows restarted their attack and flew towards my head. They all arrived at once and began to both slash at me and attempt to smother me. They were not going to succeed. I started to surge out gouts of flame in every direction, aiming at anything which I felt was going to do me harm. The white hot beams of heat picked off the shadows which were unlucky enough to be in their way. Each creature that was hit by my fire was destroyed instantly, all trace of them gone.

Wynn could see that her force had lost their only advantage, surprise, and that they were defeated but continued to urge them on. One by one, they continued their attack, each hoping that they would be able to overwhelm me but their force was shrinking by the minute. Finally, the final shadow was torched to a cinder and I stood staring down at Wynn. During the fight, she had edged her way back towards the doorway, hoping for some cover from the massive frames. She raised her arms in a new gesture from her defended point and called up to me, "Your tyranny will end soon, *mighty* Dragon. Tyus will free our master and you and your pitiful little group will fall."

She drew her power in and I could see a cascade bridge starting to form behind her. She was going to make a run for it. I lunged forward and swung my right hand at her as fast I could, trying to grab hold of her and prevent her breaking for freedom. The ring snapped into life behind her, the leaping arcs of electricity booming out from the centre of the ring and licking outwards to earth themselves on the ground of my ruined room. She looked back at me and smiled, showing me that she wasn't afraid of me and leapt for the bridge and for the route to freedom.

She managed to travel around three feet towards the bridge ring before a blue/white scaled hand smashed down between her and the magical construct. Andrea gripped her tightly with her massive reptilian claws. The shock of Andrea's sudden arrival was enough to break all of Wynn's concentration and as quickly as it had appeared, the ring of energy dissipated to nothing.

Wynn struck out against the massive claw that was holding not only her with her fists but with her magic as well. Burst after burst of green power hit into Andrea's hand as she tried to break free.

"That hurts animal. Stop it before I do." Andrea snarled at Wynn and the words were practically lost within the sound of the beast. I stepped closer and Wynn stopped moving. She flashed her attention between each of the Dragons who stood against her and I could see that she knew she was beaten. She sagged slightly in Andrea's grip and accepted that she had been taken.

Lloyd came crashing up the stairs with energy burning at his hands and a collection of armed staff at his back.

"What the bloody hell has happened here?" he boomed as he led his force through the doors of my room and to what was left of it.

"I was attacked" I replied with reptilian snarls, "By one of ours and a band of shadows," and gestured towards the contents of Andrea's hand. Lloyd looked Wynn up and down and glared at her with the utmost contempt. She in turn looked back at him with a crazed expression of someone who wanted to kill everyone who was in her path. The change in her was quite unnerving. She had managed to become a crazed killer in the space of hours.

Lloyd addressed his troops, "Everyone, run the building and make sure that there are no other interlopers. Go." Without another word, his group of assembled staff drained away, back down the stairs, and spread out through the rest of the mansion, making sure that this was going to be the only surprise of the night. Lloyd remained.

Andrea gripped the now silent Wynn tightly and lifted her up. She was now held between the two Dragons who she had allied herself against and was now at least one hundred feet from the ground. She looked between the two of us as she frantically tried to put together some way out of the mess she was in. My fire was still burning inside and I could see that Andrea was barely able to stop herself pulling her to pieces then and there. We needed information.

Lloyd began.

"I think that it is easy to assume that you wanted to kill Anthony here so we don't really need to ask you that. First things first then. How did you get these wraiths in the house with you?" He craned his neck and shouted up to her. Wynn looked between the three of us, with fierce contempt plastered all over her face. She said nothing but maintained her grimace.

"Come on now Wynn. You've been discovered by the house. Every member of the staff here is now set as your enemy, through your actions. Your fighting force is gone. Your magic is contained. You have the Head of House as the best option if you want to try to fight your way out which, you know, is not a good option. And if you really still want to try to escape, you have two members of The Circle, in their, shall we say, battle attire, just itching for the chance to remove the issue you represent." Lloyd was now pacing back and forth around our legs, gesturing with wild abandon as if to emphasise his point. It looked to me, like he was talking to a conference hall full of people. Lloyd Jones, motivational speaker to the stars. Wynn seemed to take his points in and consider them, still looking furtively between the Dragons.

Before she could answer, the silence was broken by someone running up the stairs. The person stopped at the doorway, as if they were waiting for permission to enter. Lloyd strode over to the door and I could here a whispered conversation. They new arrival was still concealed in the shadows of the doorway so I couldn't make out any details.

Lloyd turned and strode back into the centre of the conversation, but this time he brought Mike, his shadowy messenger, with him.

"You are totally alone Wynn. There are no more of your friends anywhere in the house so you have very few options available. So. How did you get in?" Lloyd was almost showboating as he marched back and forth again. Wynn continued to look at each of us in turn until her eyes fell on Mike. He looked at her with a completely blank expression on his face and I could see her visually sag in Andrea's huge grip. The service element of the lifestyle that every member of staff here in the mansion lived with was more than just Mike being

Wynn's boss. From their reaction, it became apparent that there was much more to it than that. Mike was head of the kitchens and a very long standing member of his team was now revealed as a traitor to everything that he held dear. I could see that there was the air of failure hanging between them. Mike had failed the house by not seeing the fall of one of his staff and Wynn had failed, what could be called, her father. Mike was utterly disappointed at what she had done and it had cut him very deeply. His lack of expression spoke more than if he had started to shout and scream.

Lloyd reacted to the trading of glances between the two. He walked up to Mike's side and placed a reassuring hand on his shoulder. At the same time he beckoned up to Andrea to lower her hand down so he could talk to Wynn face to face. She slowly lowered her hand but didn't loosen her grip, still not willing to believe that her capture no longer represented a threat. Lloyd spoke much more gently this time.

"Wynn. We need to know how you got in here so we can defend everyone. I don't want to see all of your friends hurt in the crossfire if more of the enemy can find their way in here at will." She stared straight at him but the fight was gone from her. Mike stepped up and continued where Lloyd had left off.

"Help me defend the house. Whatever you felt to send you to this was a mistake. Your mistake has revealed you as a traitor but I want you to tell us how you got in here." The expression on his face was one of calm focus. He wore the mask of calm over the turmoil of emotions that he must have been feeling.

A thought suddenly jumped into my head.

"I saw where you came in didn't I?" I growled down at her. "My Cascade Bridge experiments jumped me between two clearings in the woods, out by the edge of the estate. I was being drawn to what you were doing wasn't I? That's how you got in isn't it?" All eyes burned into the tiny captive and she was utterly alone.

"Tell us!" Mike boomed.

Wynn jumped with shock at the huge outburst from her superior and finally agreed but when she spoke; she had a renewed fire in her voice.

"I have a lot more power than any of you know. I can breach the boundary of the estate to let the Wraiths in. I brought them all in at

the south edge of the estate earlier tonight, before you went missing."
The last comment came with a glance of daggers between Lloyd and
I. "We bridge jumped in from a couple of sites there and landed in
my room. You must have felt the magic. The search parties slowed
our progress, we couldn't move before everyone else was back to
where they were supposed to be. I didn't want to wake the whole
house."

It made sense to me. The realisation that someone close to me
was trying to kill me wasn't as bad a fact as I had thought it would
have been. I rationalised that so many people had been out to kill me
and my line that this was just the latest in a long line. I also thought
that I was getting the hang of all the magical business. How else
would I have been able to notice the bridge link?

Andrea spoke next, her growl was becoming harsher by the
second and I could feel a huge level of anger pouring off her. She
was a true believer of the cause that the Circle was fighting for so
having one of the people who was on her side betray her looked like
it was a crime that sat several steps above genocide. She was taking
this personally.

"Why did you do this animal?" Andrea was obviously viewing
Wynn as nothing more than a lowly beast. She had lost all patience
with her. It also looked like her grip was tightening.

"Please, please mistress. I will tell you everything." The
expression and bearing of the Wynn we had all seen before was now
back on display. Her voice had shrunk down, back to its previous
level and she looked terrified of everyone who was standing with
her.

"Now explain" yelled Andrea, getting more impatient by the
second.

Wynn took a deep breath and looked pleadingly at everyone in
turn.

"For His freedom." She screamed out her answer and raised her
hands above her head. In an instant, huge green energy tore through
the air, as if being drawn from any point from far and wide, and into
Wynn's hands. Her actions happened in an instant and caught all of
us off guard. Andrea tried to close her grip on her captive but the
power she was drawing in seared into her hand, flaying scaled flesh
as it bored down towards the bones beneath. Andrea reacted

instinctively and whipped her damaged hand back out of the way of the source of her pain.

Wynn was now free to move. Each person who stood around her reacted at once. Andrea surged a blast of purest white from her mouth at the same time I summoned up a blast of the most furious flame I could. Lloyd and Mike both dived for cover wherever they could find it and started to throw bolts of energy wildly as they went, covering their retreat. Wynn stood still and allowed all of the attacks to hit her. In a flash, she was engulfed by a torrent of power which buried her at the exact moment that she unleashed all of the power she had been drawing in. The impacting forces worked against each other but she had had a slight head start.

A spherical shield of green/gold energy slowly rose up around her. Inside the shell, I could make out Wynn's tiny body drifting slowly up, off the ground, so she hung about a foot from the floor. Her hair was being blown wildly inside her magical construct and she wore an expression of utter bliss. Then it collapsed. The walls of the shell fell back in on themselves and for a split second, took every piece of sound with them. All of the gathered power fell in on itself, taking Wynn with it, into a small pinpoint of light, hovering still at the centre of where Wynn had been.

Andrea moved in flash and scooped up both Lloyd and Mike in her strong claws and took off with a mighty beat of her wings. She called over her shoulder as she left,

"Move!"

I did by sheer instinct. My wings pushed me backwards as I didn't even try to turn to make my escape. The ruin of my room and the top of the mansion began to fall away as I thrust myself away but I was staring directly at the ball of light when it exploded out.

Shards of energy speared out at terrifying speed and brought with them huge pieces of masonry and glass. Andrea had managed to get further away than I had so she and the others were less affected by the force of the blast. I, however, took the full concussive blast.

A withering cold smashed into me as the wall of energy quickly caught up with me. My whole body went numb as it felt that each and every molecule of my being was freeze dried. The flying pieces of the mansion had a very different effect. Concussive punches from the masonry rained into me, giving me the feel of a very poor prize fighter while glass and other serrated material dug into my scaled skin. My armour was failing me.

I fell back and crashed into the ground at the front of the house. I was driven back and down, into the ground by the forces pouring out from the point of origin and the playing field from the training session with Andrea was taking even more punishment. Finally I came to a rest and the earth I had dug up fell back in on me and I found myself half buried.

My body was burning everywhere, seared by the cold force of the detonation. I tried to focus on the house but my view point was blurred. I could make out the vague shape of the house but there was something very large missing from the centre. Before I finally passed out, I remembered hearing a beating of wings and feeling the down draft as Andrea landed nearby. I was pulled about without being able to do much about it and I could only hope that Andrea was going to look after me.

21

I opened my eyes to see a bright white light floating above me. I panicked.

I sat upright as fast as I could and started to take a mental inventory of my body. I wasn't in my Dragon form anymore but I could still feel the pull of the multitude of injuries that I received in the explosion. My skin felt tight all over, as if it was now a size too small. As I looked myself over, I could see bandages and dressings everywhere. As I moved to check each of them I was introduced to a new and interesting slash of pain. All in all, I felt like I had been given a damn good hiding but that it could have been a great deal worse if I had been closer to the explosion.

I finally finished checking myself, so turned my attention to where I was.

From what I could see, I was in a private hospital room somewhere. There were very luxurious fixture and fittings all over the room which had all manner of beeping monitoring equipment dotted around. I felt well cared for but also slightly alienated.

Before I could do or think anything else, Andrea casually wandered in through the large bland door to my right. Her white hair was perfectly pulled back in a tidy ponytail and she looked like she was ready to walk into any top board meeting. She was again wearing a very expensive black suit and she was again making it look very good.

"How are you feeling?" she asked, her Russian accent slightly softer than I had ever heard it. Was she getting used to me? Was she concerned for me?

"You should see the other guy!" It seemed that a frivolous comment would be best suited here. Andrea rolled her eyes and her expression hardened again. Maybe not so suited.

"I feel like I've been hit by a bus. What happened?" Get back to business.

She pulled up a chair and sat down next to me.

"Wynn used a very powerful piece of magic to do the maximum amount of damage she could. It is very much the last resort. We've seen it done in the past but not by someone like her. The spell is called The Corpse and it is the last attack which will destroy everything around the caster but will take them with it. It is their suicide. It comes from a very dark magic that the Circle won't use but it isn't something that anyone can accomplish. The Circle only focuses its use of magic from the purest places of the magical spectrum. We don't resort to those kinds of castings. We are preserving life not destroying it. Only the strongest in the darkest magics can complete a spell like that effectively. The last time I saw it used, it was by a very powerful Freak who we captured trying to breach the prison in Australia. He took out the whole house after we moved him there. We didn't think that he was that magically able."

I considered what she had said, slowly. I needed to understand everything.

"Is that why I feel like my skin has shrunk? The impact of The Corpse spell?" I was settling quickly into the world of the magic now and needed to know what was doing me damage.

"You were burned by the 'death' of what Wynn threw out. The Corpse will absorb into itself, every piece of living energy it can, and then expel destruction and death. The energy will come from the life force of the caster, then the plague that comes out needs to suck in more. If you are within the blast radius of the Hex, you are going to be very severely damaged. You got far enough away so you got a good hit but nothing that will do any long term damage." She looked at me and tried to hold a concerned smile. She didn't look comfortable. To emphasise her care, she placed her hand on my arm, trying to reassure me. Her bandaged hand rested softly on my arm and my mind flashed back towards the events of the fight. She'd been hurt badly.

"How's your hand" I asked and gestured towards her injury.

She pulled her hand back and covered it with her sleeve. "It's nothing" she dismissed me. Her pride was still flying high. By the look on her face, that part of the conversation was over. I decided on another plan of attack.

"Where are we? Does the Circle have a collection of private hospitals around the world?"

214

"You're in the lower reaches of the house. The Circle does have medical facilities all over the world but each house is also equipped with the best we can offer. This is your medical facility."

I laid back and looked all round the room again. Now I felt odd again but only at the knowledge that I apparently owned yet another huge place that I knew nothing about. What else was going to be dragged out of the woodwork, secret underground lairs!

Then back to the here and now.

"What about Lloyd and Mike? Are they OK?" My last image of them was of them being scooped up and rushed from the house. If Andrea had had a similar landing to me then they would have bee in real trouble. Andrea's face relaxed slightly.

"They are fine. We were further away from the detonation so they were uninjured."

A relief that I wasn't wholly expecting bubbled up inside and the effect that they had had on me in such a short time was emphasised clearly. Andrea softened even further and touched my hand lightly.

"They are fine."

"I don't think I'd cope if any of you got hurt." I was glad that the few people who I trusted were all OK but I still couldn't shake the feeling of what losing them might feel like.

Andrea blushed at my comment. It was the first time she had been included in my thoughts in that way and I could tell that she was caught a little off guard.

"We will all have to look after each other. Agreed?" She tried to maintain her icy exterior but she had melted more than she had before. Maybe this life in the Circle would be OK after all.

Before either of could say any more, the door burst open and Lloyd and Mike came stomping in. Both wore the expressions of people who had been fighting in the trenches for hours and who were in real need of some sleep.

"Good afternoon both" Lloyd greeted us and practically stood to attention.

"Afternoon? What time is it?" How long had I been lying in this bed?

"It's just gone two sir." The stiff formality settled back onto Lloyd as he spoke to his superiors. When was he going to learn that I didn't react well to pomp and ceremony?

215

"I am ordering you to treat me like a human being from now on, understand? I want you to act like you did when we first met and not speak to me like you are scared of me. OK?" If we were all under attack from the forces of evil then I didn't want to have all of my soldiers bowing and scraping every time they spoke with me. Lloyd looked at Andrea, then back to me, looking for assurances that he really could do what I was asking him. I smiled at him to let him know that he would be in deeper if he didn't relax! He relaxed and continued, but still kept half an eye on Andrea, just in case.

"How are you feeling bach? Any serious bumps or bangs we should be aware of?" Lloyd spoke with his usual, more relaxed tone, despite Andrea's presence in the room. For a split second I considered the fact that she might just eat him for such insolence but she just sat and listened, looking relaxed.

"I'm all good. How is everyone else? Is the rest of the house OK?" It would appear that my concern was spread to cover the estate as well.

"The house took a battering but we picked off every member of the raiding party. All we have to do now is sort out the clear up." That sounded easy enough.

"We still need to discover how they got inside the estate boundary though" Andrea reminded us.

"I thought that Wynn had admitted that she jumped them all in from the sites I found in the woods. Didn't she?" I had thought that this line of questioning had been exhausted. Andrea didn't.

"That can wait for a while can't it" pointed out Mike from the doorway. "We'll get you two settled back in your rooms and we can start on the clean up. When you are feeling up to it we can examine all of the loose ends can't we." Lloyd agreed quickly.

"There is no point in you being run ragged with the life threatening details of sweeping and clearing is there. You two get some rest and we can get the house back to where it needs to be."

It did make sense to have the two Dragons well rested for any future encounters and not picking up debris from the house.

"Then I'll find a quiet spot and get ready for the match tonight if there are no objections. Would you like to keep me company Andrea?"

Of all of the things that Andrea must have seen and heard in her life, that last question seemed to have been the biggest surprise to her. She looked at me wide eyed with shock, her mouth agape. It was all a matter of timing.

"I'll just get some clothes on and we'll get under way." I delivered the final blow with perfect calm. How could she refuse?

She blushed a deep scarlet and dropped her head slightly, looking embarrassed and coy.

"We can watch this match of yours in the study down from my room." She looked at me through her eyebrows. "I'll see you there in twenty minutes. Gentlemen." With that, she slinked out of the room and down the hallway. The three of us watched her go, and then Lloyd and Mike turned back to me, each wearing the largest knowing smiles you have ever seen. Lloyd winked at me and turned to leave as well. He and Mike both burst out laughing as soon as they had left the room. The sound of their hearty guffaws echoed back into my room and I felt good. I had come through a very serious attack and everyone had survived, I was going to see the game, and I was going to spend some relaxing time with Andrea. So far, this was looking like a very good day.

22

I dressed as quickly as I could manage and headed up the stairs at the end of the corridor. I was running on the same instinct as I had when I had found Lloyd in the library, as I made my way through the house. Turn after turn followed as I made my way to where Andrea was going to meet me.

Exactly twenty minutes after Andrea had left my room in the subterranean hospital, I burst through the study doors with my very best casual look on my face. The room was empty. It was furnished in much the same way as the library, heavy furniture of dark wood was laid everywhere with the casual ease that could only have come with meticulous planning. The thick carpet under my feet looked like it was going to absorb each and every stray sound which may have come its way. The whole room looked like something from a stately home tour. Rich smells of leather and wood filled the air and gave the room the feeling of relaxed opulence. Exactly like the rest of the house, there was a feeling that everything was of the highest quality but that it was meant for comfort rather than show. People could really live here.

I walked in feeling a little let down. I had really hoped that she would have been there. I pushed that thought from my mind and set to making myself comfortable in preparation for the evening's entertainment.

There was a fifty inch plasma TV mounted on the back wall of the room. It had been displaying a stock image of a snow topped mountain landscape with bright blue sky and crisp detail of the grass and trees in the foreground. After a few prods at the remote control I managed to find the correct channel and left it playing in silence, it was still over two hours to kick off. There was a buffet spread laid out for us and I picked at some of it. It still boggled me how this much food could be prepared so quickly and with this quality. Whatever Mike and his team were doing, it was of the highest standard. I'll have to remember to ask him about that at some point.

It was at that point that the doors swung open behind me and Andrea sauntered into the room. Her hair was loose now and hung down either side of her face, framing her features and giving her the chance to look her most sultry. I stood agog in the centre of the room.

"Am I late?" she purred and closed the doors behind her. It really was all about timing.

I gathered in as much of my composure as I could.

"Have a seat" I offered and followed her to the leather chairs.

"So what is the match you are keen to see? Will I like it?" She folded herself back into the chair and reminded me of a cat curling up. She looked to be totally at ease but I knew that she was ready at a seconds notice to strike out if needed.

"The game is Rugby and it's a game of equal part strategy and brutality. You'll love it. It starts in a couple of hours so if you don't mind, I'd really like to have a chat with you, spend some time with you and find out some details. You seem to know everything about me so I'd like to even things out."

Andrea sank back into the large chair and watched me intently.

"I have been the Guardian of my prison since I was eleven. I have spent the last twenty years at the front of the war with those who are still aiming to destroy the human race." She dropped her gaze to stare at her intertwined fingers sitting in her lap. "My whole life has been spent training and fighting. I understand that my role is one of violence and danger," she paused. "I believe in what we are doing," she slowly lifted her eyes to bore directly into me. "My family let me know from an early age what was expected of me. Your training didn't happen in the same way so you are at a large disadvantage but you have seen a life that is totally alien to me. I have no idea how you have lived outside of the knowledge of what is expected of you."

"My Uncle didn't tell me anything but he did try to explain everything to my brother. He was the next in line after my Uncle and didn't want anything to do with it. He just thought that my Uncle was full of it so left when he got the chance." A conversation seemed to be breaking out and neither of the two of us seemed to be on edge.

"How could he just leave? David explained everything that is going on and he still left?" Andrea was utterly perplexed by this turn of events. She had spent her whole life living in the shadow of the expectation placed on her by the Circle. To hear that someone had just decided to walk away from their responsibility shook her whole belief system.

"What was it like growing up inside all of this?" Keep the conversation aimed at anything other than my family's failings, Andrea wouldn't ever trust me if she was always thinking that I might decide to one day just down tools and walk away.

She pondered and sifted back through her memories of childhood.

"Every aspect of my life was designed to prepare me for what was going to take place. I was schooled in magic and fighting techniques from an early age and I knew the theory of how to master my transformation, even before my Awakening. All the games I played with my family were designed to sharpen my skills in readiness for the day that I was called upon to defend what was entrusted to me."

"Sounds like it was a hard upbringing. It can't have been much fun for you, all work and no play." My life had been worlds away from hers. I was starting to really appreciate what I had had growing up.

"My life was always enjoyable. When my father and I played hide and seek around the grounds of the estate, I always had a great time. As I grew older and realised how he was always able to find me so easily, it became more of a challenge to try to beat him. I always enjoyed my time with my family."

"Did he cheat?" I was starting to see a very different side of Andrea as she recalled her childhood. She looked happy and I realised that despite the long hours of training and magic, she was still having fun spending time with her father. Maybe that was why my Uncle was how he was with me, just having fun.

"He used the tracking spells to find me. He channelled through the Mage and could locate me where ever I was." She wore a smile as she gazed back through her memories. She showed on her face that there was a warm feeling to what she was running through. Maybe there was more to her story than just ceremony and fighting. Before I could ask her any more questions about what she had seen when she had been growing up and about the life that was being prepared for me, Andrea's face clouded over and her happy memories disappeared.

"My father was killed when our prison was attacked. We were all in the house when the call was sent out that we were being attacked." She was staring into space as she spoke, not focusing on anything that was in the present. "It was a Sunday and we were preparing a family meal together. He told my mother and I to keep something warm for him and that he would be back as quickly as he could, he didn't think that there was any real threat to what was happening and said he would be back before I went to bed. He didn't call for help from any other members of the Circle. He thought that he would be able to defeat whatever it was." She smiled wistfully at the last comment. Looking back on what people say before an event can often make their viewpoints seem foolish. I wondered what Andrea's father would have said to her if he had known that he was going to die.

Andrea held her gaze on the nebulous past as she continued to flick through memories. She finally returned to now and locked my eyes.

"I have looked through my father's memories of the final battle several times, trying to discover the reasons for his death, but I can't ever make out what it was that had started the offensive. There were the usual collection of foot soldiers and assorted muscle but the thing that was pulling the strings; all I could ever make out was a black cloud, just off to the edges of my fathers' vision. It would strike from nowhere and retreat to nothing as my father swung to face it."

I had expected Andrea to be burning with anger as she recounted the story of her fathers' demise, but instead, she was calm and quite sad. There was no glittering oath of revenge, no hatred of the enemy. Instead, she had retreated back to being eleven again. She looked at me and I could see, worked deeply into her expression that, she was still just the same little girl who had seen her childhood come to a shuddering, shattering, premature halt. Perhaps, deep down, past all of the layers of responsibility and training, she too felt that, despite her station as a Guardian and top of the pile in her estate, she was just as much a servant as all of the others.

She shook her head slightly, breaking free from the shackles of the emotions that were leaking out.

"Whatever it was, it didn't do enough damage to kill my father before he had demolished the whole army gathered against him. He

221

took his fighting force and beat back the force that was threatening his charge. He died after the battle had been won. He didn't think that he had been dealt a mortal blow but the collection of injuries put together added up to be enough. He fell as the last demon was being driven from the grounds surrounding the prison. They hadn't even broken the boundary of the prison before they were driven off."

There was a sad pride in the final sentence. She was looking back to her predecessor who had done his duty and defended the prison. He had gone to fight off his enemies knowing that his life was on the line each time and he had gone on regardless. I kicked the idea around. Would I be that certain of my position that I would do the same as he had?

Andrea seemed to shrink back into the chair as she finished her recollection. She was shrouded by an air of the little girl lost as all of the layers of her position slipped from her. Maybe she was thinking the same thing?

"Have you gone into battle against the forces of evil?" I thought I'd aim for a more relaxed tone; I didn't want to make her dwell on the negative or make it seem that I was just after the morbid details. I think she took it in the right way.

"I've lost count of the times I have had to fight off attempts to free my charge or to destroy either me or my home. I think that I have been averaging about three a year but they have been getting more serious as I have got older. It's probably because I was shielded for so many years as I grew up. The Elder trained me and spent a very long time moving between her home in China and mine in Russia. She must have taken on a lot of the early responsibility."

That comment about the Elder was the first time that I had heard any of the members of the Circle actually do anything that resembled an act of compassion. That, more than anything, had made me feel off kilter.

"We all come into this role through the pain of loss" Andrea continued. "Each and every Guardian will have lost someone close to them otherwise they wouldn't be where they are. You may think that we are all far too obsessed with the importance of the past, but it can hold the secrets we all need to survive. Others will have seen things that you may need. Everyone in the Circle has gone through the same thing, so we all understand what is happening when each new

Guardian takes their place. We all take the details of the past very seriously because it can often be the only link we have to those who have been taken from us." That explained a huge amount to me and I felt like I was protected.

"I will be tough on you during the training so you can live longer. The faster you learn what you are capable of, the more able you will be to stay alive."

We both looked at each other and sipped on our drinks. Andrea had started to let me into her life a little and it had served to make me feel more comfortable about my situation. I could see that, despite the cliché, everyone was really looking out for me. My Uncle had tried to protect his and my family and made sure that I was ready to accept the role should it pass to me after he had pushed too hard with Steve. Loss had been flowing through my family and by the sounds of what Andrea was saying, she had gone through something very similar.

"It's not as bad as it looks then?"

She smiled and I could tell that I was starting to see the real Andrea.

"We have to fulfil a very important role in the world but, we can have some fun along the way." She looked through her fringe at me and I could see she was relaxed. Her smile was wide and her eyes were glinting. She sounded very appealing, her thick accent making each of the words sound just that little bit more exotic.

"Sounds good to me." I held her gaze and tried to match the tone of her voice. We had both started to lean forward in our chairs and I could feel that the tone of our conversation was changing. I couldn't tell if the crackle in the air was just something that was in my head or if it was really happening.

"Well, where should we start? More hide and seek?" I swear the crackle was real.

"As long as you play fair, I don't want every man in my life to have to resort to cheating." The words were practically hypnotic. She put her drink down and looked like she was about to climb from the chair. I watched her and studied every last detail, the curve of her body and the supple strength which was suffused through her. I hoped her father wasn't going to mind what I had running through my mind!

Her father. Hide and seek.

She slithered into my chair next to me and placed an arm around my shoulders just at the moment that realization crashed into my head.

I jumped to my feet and practically knocked her to the ground. I started to pace the floor and tried to organise what I was thinking.

"I don't think I care for this game" Andrea complained, folding her arms across her chest to really emphasise that she wasn't happy.

"I'm sorry, but I think hide and seek has just told me that we are all in real danger."

She sat straight up and frowned at me.

"What danger?" She hadn't been on edge before but she was back in battle mode at the flick of a switch.

"Come with me, and get Lloyd. We're still under attack." I gripped her arm and headed for the door.

"Under attack?" she questioned, her voice now rising to a much higher pitch. "Where are we going?"

We were now starting to run; my mind was pushing towards desperation. I hoped that I was wrong but too many pieces had just lined up. Please be an over-reaction.

"We've got to get to the Mage."

23

Andrea was now running after me as I twisted down corridor after corridor, aiming for the stairway down to the Mage's chamber.

"We need Lloyd to get to the chamber with us. How do we call him?" I was shouting over my shoulder as I ran and didn't stop to catch the response. I shot round another corner as fast as I could sure that I needed to be in the Mage's chamber immediately. I hadn't factored into the journey that there might be obstacles in my way. I crashed into a large suit of armour which had been displayed by the entrance to one of the many state rooms and sent assorted pieces of medieval armourment scattering all over the thick carpet.

I pushed myself back to my feet just as Andrea rounded the corner. She looked at me with a mixture of concern and annoyance.

"Lloyd will meet us at the chamber doorway. He is as keen as I am to know why." She helped me back to my feet and we both headed off towards the entrance hall of the mansion.

"When Lloyd and I were missing in the woods after my bridge jump, why couldn't anyone find us? You said that the Mage was responsible for ensuring the focus and power of all the magic that goes on inside the estates and that a tracking spell, like the one your father used to catch you as a child, was easy. If it was so easy, why couldn't anyone use it properly?" We rounded the next corner together but Andrea wasn't talking. She was turning the facts over in her mind as I made my case.

"When I was jumping around in the woods, I could only travel between two points. They were the jumping in points that Wynn and her troops used. I was drawn to them some how right? That means that they were in the house for hours before they actually tried to attack me. What were they doing? The easiest tracking spell you can cast goes dead the second that I find the sites they used to get in? Looks to me that they must have attacked the Mage first. They must have wanted to blind him to my whereabouts so they could do more damage. They could have jumped me anywhere in the grounds and started to do God knows what. No-one would have been able to find me. That's why no-one could locate me when I jumped Lloyd and I out into the woods." We were getting closer to the entrance hall and my apprehension was rising with every footstep.

"They would have killed the Mage if they could get access to him surely" questioned Andrea as we ran. She could understand my logic but needed to be sure.

"If they walked in the room, the Mage would have mangled their minds. I saw what a short exposure did to Lloyd. It's only the Dragons who can spend any time in there with him without losing it. Besides, if they attacked him in such a violent way, it would have alerted every single person in the house that something was going on and they would have lost any advantage they had. They did something more subtle than that. They poisoned him. Magically. I think."

We both sprinted out towards the bottom of the huge stairway to the upper levels of the house and rounded on the route to the chamber entrance. Andrea was really powering on now. I think my logic had made sense and she looked like she was going to tear the door down rather than wait for it to be unlocked. She continued questioning as she ran.

"What would they want to accomplish by only poisoning the most powerful magical force that we have at our disposal? It would still make more sense to kill him."

"If they tried to kill him, he would probably just 'walk' out through one of the other estates. If they had weakened him, how would we ever know? They would be able to send forces into the house at will, get around our defences, undo our attacks with ease and we wouldn't have known how. They would have been able to kill Guardian after Guardian until they had weakened the whole structure of the Circle."

"That all fits very well, but how did they all get through the boundary field? Our defensive magic was working when they crossed the boundary so how did they do it?"

"Wynn showed that she was more powerful than any of us ever thought. She must have been able to breach the power to allow the jump." The pieces had all fallen into place and I could see that there would be a massive variety of attacks to deal with in my role as Guardian, not just the full frontal violent assault.

All of my ramblings were enough to convince Andrea.

"What are we expecting to find in the chamber? More Wraiths?"

"I don't know but I would be pretty sure that the empty room that I saw earlier isn't going to be empty now." The image of the Mage in his sphere flashed in my head. The pain on his face was clear for all to see. Had he been tormented by those who had broken in?

We finally arrived at the door to be met by Lloyd who looked like he was ready to go to war. He was dressed in a pair of jeans, sturdy walking boots and a thick, checked lumberjack shirt with the sleeves rolled up above the elbow. He carried with him, a large, double headed axe and bobbed nervously from foot to foot. He was ready to go.

"What do you two mean we're under attack?" he shot at us. He wanted to kill something and all he needed was to be pointed in the right direction.

"I'll tell you on the way down. We've got to move, now."

"Shouldn't we be bringing a more powerful force with us? If there are things attacking the Mage then we could do with all the help we could muster." Andrea was running through possible strategies as we stood there and it looked like every plan of attack she could come up with would require a much larger force.

"We're the only people on our side that can go in the room and we're going to be dealing with an enemy in a very small space in the corridor outside. Besides, the enemy must have been in the corridor when Lloyd showed me the room last night before the attack. There couldn't have been a huge battalion of them, we would have noticed as we went in. There was probably only a small group so huge numbers on our part would be a waste of time."

The two of them listened to what I had said and then nodded their agreement.

It looked like the times I'd seen various captains of the Enterprise give these speeches of explanation had rubbed off.

Lloyd unlocked the door and led us all into the corridor beyond. I pulled the door closed behind us and the lights on the walls snapped into life. As we headed down the stairs at a fast run, we were all silently praying that we would be able to do something that would help the Mage.

I could feel a hum in my chest as we approached the end of the corridor. The power inside the Mages chamber felt stronger than during my first visit, it was more forced. Andrea and Lloyd could feel it as well. It was almost pushing the air from our chests as we continued down. We were roughly fifteen steps from the entrance to the chamber when the attack began. The spinning in my head alerted me to the danger a second before it hit.

One by one, shadows of inky black lifted from the walls and ceiling and dived for us. In total, five Wraiths had peeled from the edges of the corridor to create an angry wall of violence ahead of us. They each poured over the floor like a living liquid and took on the posture of battle readiness that I had seen them brandish when they had made a move on me in my room.

Lloyd pushed his way to the front of our group and raised his hands up to chest height. I could feel a build up of power as Lloyd chanted under his breath. In a flash, he had prepared all he had needed.

"Leave you filth!" he boomed at the gathered enemy and unleashed a sizzling burst of superheated light towards the nearest Wraith. Energy poured out from Lloyd and I could feel the air temperature rising around us from the heat of the attack. The corridor lit up like someone had ignited a flare. The creature saw what was coming and reacted. It collapsed down and flattened itself onto the floor as it avoided the magical attack. The one directly behind the original target wasn't as fast as his comrade. Before it could dive in any direction, the arm of magical fire hit it squarely in the chest and torched it to a cinder. Ash fell to the ground where it had stood and that familiar burning awfulness smell filled the space.

Our initial success was quickly forgotten as all of the four remaining Wraiths flew from their positions ahead of our group and dived headlong at each of us. They all started to wrap themselves around us and began to strike out as they constricted. They knew that we couldn't start throwing more wide reaching magical energy around at them if they were tied to us. We had become their human shields. Even Lloyd's axe had become useless.

We all continued to swipe wildly at our attackers as we tried desperately to break free. Punch after punch landed on the Wraiths but they all seemed to be dissipated by their fluid cloud bodies.

"How are you two getting on?" was all I could call out as the creature I was dealing with wrapped itself tighter and tighter around my chest. I hoped that the others would appreciate my sense of humour and I figured that the Wraith might succumb to the power of my positive propaganda. Andrea growled from behind me as she continued her own struggle and Lloyd laughed heartily as two Wraiths crawled all over him. Well at least he enjoyed it! Maybe he was starting to act like a human being around me?

The force from the chamber continued to buzz on and we could all feel the effects. The heavy sensation was leaning into us all as we fought against the Wraiths, continuing to show that something was going on in there that we needed to see.

The attack continued as blow after blow rained down from the three of us and the Wraiths continued to try to get a firm fix on each of us to finally strangle the life from us. But the final blow never came. The Wraiths seemed to be swarming over us and causing as much confusion as they could muster, but they weren't trying to kill us yet. In my room, I had seen a much more violent incursion which would have killed me had I not transformed. I knew that I couldn't change here as I would not only destroy myself but would also obliterate the core of the whole estate. Andrea and I had the most powerful weapons within the Circle at our disposal but everyone, Wraiths and all, knew that we couldn't use them. Maybe that was why they weren't trying to deliver the mortal blow? They were hoping that we would transform underground and do the damage for them.

"Does anyone else think that these creatures are nothing but a waste of our time? What do you reckon bach?" Lloyd was still on his feet and swinging against the two Wraiths that were attacking him but I could make out a small track of blood pouring down from his hairline. They were certainly doing him some damage but he was still swinging.

The fight continued, each side of the conflict seeming to be defending rather than going for any decisive killing blow but I suddenly caught the flash of blackness which passed us by. I don't think that anyone else noticed, but I couldn't be sure. I just knew that something had passed us by and that the Wraiths were opening a hole to allow just that.

Andrea was defending herself from the strikes of her attacker but she looked like she was quite comfortable in what she was doing. Had she felt the same thing?

"This is wrong. Both of you stay still. Don't move."

With that I could make out a huge increase of temperature surrounding us and I knew that Andrea was about to take a risk. So she had felt it. She crouched down and covered her head with both her arms as she prepared herself. Without any more warning, she bounced out a great blast of cold which flooded the entire corridor. The Wraiths that had been attacking us had all stopped their violence at the build up of temperature and had started to make a run for the doorway of the Mages chamber. They had poured down the corridor like a living oil slick and had crashed into Lloyd as they went, sending him spinning to the ground as they did. They each looked like they were trying to run from the impending attack and that they were going to use Lloyd as a human shield. The release of energy rushed outwards and at every point that it touched, pushed a shuddering deep freeze into the marrow of the bones. The Wraiths all halted within the blue/white hue of the frozen energy. One by one, they all hovered in the air as the wave took effect. Every last ounce of moisture within them was frozen solid. Their bodies slowly shrank in on themselves as they were practically petrified. The large cloudy appearance of their original forms shrank down to reveal the same spindly skeleton that I had seen in my room the previous night. Their faces showed the wizened truth of their existence. They looked like the faces of the malnourished that you see in photographs from all over the world during acts of genocide. They had the horror of their lives written everywhere but it had been joined by terror for what was coming. They had known that Andrea was going to do something terrible and they had tried to flee from it.

They all fell to the floor as one and smashed into a thousand pieces just like you see in the movies when someone or something gets doused in liquid nitrogen. Fragments of their ruined bodies littered the whole passage way.

I stood upright and shook myself off. An icy covering of crystals had totally engulfed the whole area and had given the impression of the inside of an industrial freezer. Andrea was stood bolt upright and wore the expression of the conquering hero. She had certainly vanquished her enemies. Our relief was short lived though.

Lloyd was curled into a ball further down the stairway. He was shrouded in a thick covering of frost and he wore the fixed expression he had when the wave had hit him. He had been terrified.

I flew to his side and started to shake him, willing him to sit up and tell me that he was fine. I began to brush away the blanket of ice crystals and shake him. He had to wake up.

"Lloyd. Come on, you can't just lay there." Desperation crept into my voice and I lifted him onto my lap as I cradled him, trying to get heat running back through him. I needed to get him back. Andrea dropped to my side and her apology was real.

"I told you both that you needed to stay still but he can't have listened. He must have been moving when I let the power go." She stood utterly motionless as I still called out to Lloyd, willing him to answer me.

"I'm sorry Anthony but I can't undo this." Andrea started to reach out one hand to me.

"Can I?" I screamed at her. I couldn't let Lloyd die. He was the closest thing I had to family left and I couldn't let him go.

"I don't know. We need to get him to the infirmary as quickly as we can."

I gathered Lloyd up in my arms and turned to run back to the surface as quickly as I could but Andrea stopped me.

"I just saw a shadow move under the door to the Mage's chamber. There are more of them in there with him." Before I could say anything she had started to sprint down the corridor. It was easy to see that she wanted to tear through that door and obliterate whatever was on the other side.

She reached the doors and started to push them open. As she did, the spinning in my head returned with the utmost force and signalled that what she was doing was going to unleash yet more danger.

My call to stop didn't have any effect.

Andrea crashed through the doors with blood fury driving her and revealed an awful fact. In the split second before all detail was obscured by the blinding explosion of light I saw that there was a small gathering of Wraiths crowded around a central figure. As Andrea opened the doors she had been hit by a blast of the purest

231

black energy. The impact had held her stationary with her arms outstretched and her head rocked back and had pulled out wave after wave of power from her. Inside the chamber, a wide circle of the brightest light had formed and framed each of the people in the room with a corona of utter white. A Cascade Bridge had been opened up inside the Mage's chamber and all those who had been infiltrating the house had just bought their ticket to freedom.

The light burst was burned onto my retinas and I snapped my eyes away from it as fast as I could. The pain of the light ripped through my eyes and into my head and I could feel the agony of what was going on seeping into my mind.

Inside the burst of light was a crowd of dark figures. Most were the Wraiths that had been attacking me for the past twenty four hours but at their centre was a different shape. It was one of the purest evil that I had encountered up to now. He stood there in the middle of the group of demons and commanded them all. Tyus wore an expression of the cruellest happiness as he looked towards Andrea and I. His team was on its way out, having done the damage it had intended and without suffering any vast losses. But that wasn't the worst part of my final image from the chamber. Settled at his feet, shackled by the demons and wearing an expression of pain and pleading, lay Mike.

24

After a final thump of sound and wave of light, the chamber had emptied and the heavy weight that had been pushing into us since we had arrived was gone. Andrea lay in a crumpled heap in the open doorway, small strands of black smoke lifting from her from at least ten different points. She was utterly motionless. I dropped Lloyd to the ground and rushed to Andreas' side. She had suggested that Lloyd could be saved if I got him to the infirmary but I had no idea what condition Andrea was in. Her face was a bright red, as if she had just been really badly sunburned in a matter of seconds. Her lips were cracked and she had small strands of her hair plastered to her face. She looked awful. I checked her pulse and her breathing to find that both were present, but weak.

As yet more relief thundered through me I snapped my attention back to the situation at hand. Both of my comrades were in need of serious medical attention but there was no time to go back up to the surface and bring back help. I would have to carry them both.

Straining as I hefted the two lifeless forms over my shoulders, I prepared for the journey back to the surface. I would have to deal with the Mage later, right now, my friends were more important.

Each step felt like a fresh blow to my head as the pressure built up. I throbbed behind my eyes and into my sinuses each time my foot hit the stairs. I was feeling like this with the magical infusion to my strength. Without it, it would have been impossible.

As I climbed, the frozen image of Tyus and his forces remained fixed in my head. They were always going to be after us. Members of my family had been killed for thousands of years by him and he was still coming. He wasn't going to stop until he had his master out of his hole and every shred of the Dragon line had been eradicated. He'd even spread his attention to people who worked in the house. He had somehow managed to turn Wynn against the Circle and now he had managed to abduct Mike from inside the heart of one of his enemy's strongholds. Was I going to be safe anywhere?

That thought punched out an increase in energy and I powered on despite the discomfort. Sweat beaded across my forehead and I could feel the first rivulet of moisture streak down my back. I was going to resolve this problem and I would not let anyone get in my way.

I reached the top of the stairway and kicked my way through to the corridor beyond. The door flung back and slammed into the wall with a splintering crack which suggested that I would need to buy a new one when this was over. So much for concealment. I called out for anyone to help me as I continued my progress towards the infirmary. After an age where each step seemed to be taking me backwards, floods of people started to pour out to my aid. Staff members from every area of the house crowded round us and started asking what had happened and where and how long ago. Both Andrea and Lloyd were taken from me and speedily transported away. I could still make out the sound of concerned chatter coming from the groups carrying them long after they had rounded a corner and passed out of sight. It felt reassuring that there were other people here who were as worried by the condition of the two stricken warriors. The people here weren't only here because they had to be.

"Are you OK sir? Do you need any medical attention?" a heavily accented voice enquired from behind me. I turned round to come face to chest with a mountain of a man who looked down at me with a concerned expression on his face. He was dressed in chefs' whites minus the hat and had both his sleeves rolled up past his elbows. His completely bald head perched atop his broad shoulders seemed to make him look more menacing. He too had a gargantuan physique but he looked like he could probably take on a Dragon without any help. His uniform was strained against his broad chest and was struggling to contain his massive arms. His very dark black skin seemed to suck in all of the light around him to the point that his serious eyes stood out as beacons of pearl. He must have been seven feet tall!

"No thanks" I stammered after regaining my composure from the shock of his appearance. Then the situation returned to focus and I snapped back to dealing with the emergency.

"Can you find out where Mike was around an hour ago? He's been abducted and I need to know if there were any more injuries. If he was working with anyone else when he was snatched it's probable that there will be others down."

The giant chef immediately nodded his head as a worried expression blossomed onto his face, turned on his heel and sprinted off back down the corridor. With everyone else now on an even higher alert footing, I turned my attention to the next problem. Now for the Mage.

When I made it back down to the bottom of the stairway, the doorway to the chamber was still open and the remains of the petrified Wraiths lay scattered where we had let them fall. The faintest smell of ozone hung in the air and mingled with the slowly retreating smell of rotting matter which seemed to accompany the Wraiths wherever they went. I slowly picked my way through the debris, trying to be as deliberate as I could when placing my feet amongst the pieces. Lloyds axe lay amongst the rubble where he had discarded it, an uncalled for reminder that he was seriously hurt and possibly fighting for his life.

Inside the room ahead, I could still make out the floating sphere of the Mage's containment. The red colour continued to bubble and boil at the sphere's surface as the waves of force continued to slowly pass over it. Inside, the Mage was still hung, helpless and in agony. His face was still wracked in a grimace of the utmost savagery but he looked to be even frailer than he had when I first saw him. His skin was almost transparent now and it looked as if every last piece of body fat had been peeled away.

As I paced around the sphere, I hoped that there would be something that I would just 'know' which would help him. Surely one of the previous Guardians would have had some kind of experience of this. I placed both my hands against the floating bubble and leaned into it, resting my head against it. Nothing happened. I looked into myself and tried to summon up the shared memories of the past that could give me some clue what to do. Nothing.

"Come on sunshine. Give me a little help!" I wailed at the sphere as I banged my head against the side. The Mage whipped his eyes down onto me and for the first time since I had seen him, he actually looked like he was seeing me. I couldn't let this pass me by. Maybe he could help me?

235

"What can I do? Tell me how to help you." I was shouting and mouthing my words with a huge exaggeration, trying to make him understand. He regarded me with pleading reptilian eyes, and then offered out his hand to me. His gnarled fingers were practically at the edge of the sphere and he seemed to be trying to push through the surface, but couldn't reach. I didn't understand. I placed my splayed hand on the surface, as close to his as I could, and called out to him, "What do you want me to do? You've got to tell me how to help you; I can't do this on my own."

He just floated there, again jabbing out his hand towards me, each time with more desperation than the last. This wasn't getting me anywhere. What was I supposed to do? I needed someone to be able to tell me the next step and the only person who could help me now was quite content to play charades. Andrea and Lloyd were injured, maybe dead, and Mike had been taken by the creatures that had been responsible for the deaths of my Uncle and my Brother. For God's sake help me.

I thrashed out my hands in sheer frustration and slammed them into the floating prison before me. This time though, there was a cracking sound which resonated through the chamber as I impacted the bubble. I looked up at the Mage and he was now looking much less pained. He waved his hand again and I realised what he had meant. Raising my hands above my head, I yelled out my rage and began to smash away at the sphere which held the Mage. I poured all of my anger into each blow and simply let myself unload everything I had. With each blow, the cracking sounds grew and the Mage looked less and less uncomfortable. I continued to hammer my way in, blow after blow as the red flashes filled my vision and my clothing began to tear.

Finally, with one final shattering split of power, the outer layer of the sphere gave way and disintegrated into the tiniest pieces of iridescent glass. They crashed down onto the floor and spread to fill the whole room, before they faded away into nothing.

The Mage called out to me in the same booming tone from the Awakening, "Stop! Dragon, I am free."

The huge voice shocked me and for the smallest second I felt that I was a naughty schoolboy being told off by the headmaster. That was enough to break my concentration. The Mage had been trying to

236

halt my transformation before I demolished the whole chamber. I stood, breathing hard as I stared at the Mage, who was now floating, sat in the lotus position, in the centre of a deepest green sphere. His pain was now gone and his body had taken on the look of a healthy man rather than a living skeleton. He looked every inch the serene spiritual master.

I raised my hands and looked at them. They were now covered in red scales and each of my fingers had huge talons sprouting from the tips. The rest of my body must have been the same as The Mage looked at me calmly and called out, this time in a much calmer tone "You have freed me. Breathe slowly and calm yourself."

I did as he said. His cool voice seemed to make you want to listen to him. The anger left me quickly as my gathered power drained away. It wasn't needed any more. I slowly returned to my usual appearance and stood before the Mage.

"What happened here?" I wanted to find out what had gone on and it did seem that I was always playing catch up. The Mage explained.

"Our enemies have breached the house. They have a very powerful ally inside our walls who helped them into this room."

"What did they do to you?" I still wasn't sure how I had managed to break the hold that Tyus had placed on the Mage.

"They covered me with their power and let it seep in to my atmosphere. I couldn't break away or push through it. It was designed as a defensive force so each time I attacked it, it made me that much weaker. The more I tried to escape, the harder it hit me."

"So you needed the most powerful force at your disposal to attack it from the outside. The spell wasn't designed to stop someone breaking in, just out, right?"

The Mage smiled slightly and I knew that I was right. He continued, "We have a spy in our midst and they must be stopped." His expression darkened at the mention of a spy in our group.

"I know that bit; we caught their mole when they attacked me. They blinded you somehow so they would be able to go about their business without being seen. I understand all of that but I don't get why they would take someone from the house with them as they left. What benefit would they have in abducting a high ranking member of the house?" The Mage considered that for a moment then his face

237

became a mask of worry. Even through the collection of Dragon features, I could make out that he had realised something terrible.

"The prison. The attack on you was meant as a diversion. If they killed you, excellent, but they also managed to limit the influence I could wield. The house would have been hunting for a fighting force of creatures aiming at killing the Dragon. No-one would have seen my situation because they were all looking in the wrong direction, expecting a different form of attack. By the time anyone realised that someone had been taken, they would have been able to force the prisoner they had taken to wield the power they needed to, not only to cross the threshold into the Abbey grounds, but to potentially break the glyph stone and release the Hive Master. The higher placed members of each house are imbued with more power than the others. It is possible that they are all able to use enough power to be able to shatter the magic which holds the prison seal together. With me affected, they could have done this at each house and no-one would have been able to see them coming until they were already doing the damage." His face was now hooded in terror as he ran through the possibilities of what he was suggesting.

"They are going to torture their victim until they give up the force to release the beast." His eyes flashed towards me and I could see that he was worried, really worried. "Get as big a force as you can together and head to the prison. They will have to cross our threshold but when they do, they will be able to unleash Armageddon."

I didn't wait to confirm anything with him. I turned and sprinted back up towards the surface.

"I will summon a Dragon force to help from the other houses. You won't be alone." The Mage called out from behind me as I powered on up the stairs. So far today, Andrea, Lloyd and now Mike were going through unbearable pain for helping me. I was going to make sure that they all got through this safely and I was going to make sure that Tyus and his boss would rue the day they even thought about taking me on.

25

I secured the door back into the wall when I got back to the surface and headed straight down to the infirmary to check on the condition of my friends. As I ran through the hallways, I was joined by the giant chef. He was easily keeping up with me as I ran and he filled me in with what he had discovered.

"Mister Christian was last seen as he left the kitchens around an hour ago. He told us all that he was going to continue his sweeps of the exterior on his own and that we should all get back to preparing food. He was certain that the danger had passed and that we should all get back to our jobs. That was the last that anyone saw of him."

We chicaned through turns together effortlessly as we neared the stair well which led to the infirmary. It also felt strangely comforting to finally find out Mike's surname. I didn't think he had looked like a Christian though.

"Thank you for that. I don't think that we've been introduced yet. What's your name?" I was glad for the information that Mike had been alone when he was taken only because it meant that no-one else was likely to have been hurt when they had grabbed him.

"My name is Mark Howell sir. I am one of the chefs but I'm also the Kitchens second member of security, behind Mr. Christian. If you have any requests please don't hesitate to ask. I'll be taking over for the back of house security effort now Mr. Christian is missing."

We arrived at the doorway down to the lower levels and stopped. I turned to face the giant chef who was quite prepared to step into the role that had found itself open without being asked or bargained with. I liked him.

"Thank you for stepping up. Mike will have left a big hole which needs to be filled and we really need to make sure the estate is protected while I'm away."

Mark looked at me, confused.

"You're leaving us? Now?" He had obviously expected me to circle the wagons and dig in.

"I'm going to find Mike and I'm going to bring him back. You will have to co-ordinate what you're doing with the other houses but I won't be long. If you hear from any other members of the Circle, tell them that they can find me in the prison chamber under the Abbey. Keep an eye on the place, will you?" Without waiting for his reply, I pushed through the door and started down to see Andrea and Lloyd before I left for the Abbey.

Both Lloyd and Andrea were in separate rooms, each surrounded by a swarm of different medical personnel. Medical instruments were still being clanked and clattered around when I walked into the first room. Lloyd was laid out on a bed with a glowing red blanket wrapped over him. He had straightened out but I could see that his limbs were still rigid, still under the influence of the casting Andrea had unleashed. He had tubes of varying colours leading from dressings on his arms and his neck, all linking in to at least six different machines which huddled over his bed like concerned relatives. The medical staff were checking and measuring and recording and generally looking like they were doing all they could. It didn't look good but it looked better than it had when I carried him out.

"How is he?" I asked the nearest person, a slight woman who looked like she was still at school. She had a very youthful face and looked slightly like a startled rabbit. Despite her age, she seemed to be the one in charge of the commotion in the room. She must have been a doctor. She nervously studied two or three pages of a clipboard on the end of the bed and declared,

"Mr. Jones was hit by a rapid freezing magic which had the obvious effect. He wasn't hit with full force but he was caught enough to result in massive injury to every part of his body. We are doing all we can but his prognosis doesn't look positive." She lifted her attention to me with obvious regret in her face. She didn't want to be giving me the news that my friend was in serious danger. She must have come into contact with Lloyd during her time at the estate so must have at least felt some kind of tug herself.

I gripped the end of his bed tightly and squeezed out my frustration, silently taking out my feelings on the frame. I didn't want to go off the deep end in here and demolish the place despite my feelings of anger. The doctor took a step backwards from me and looked nervously from my hands to my face, her mouth hanging open. I followed her eyes down, wondering what was happening, to see smoke leaking out from between my white knuckled fingers. I released my grip in a flash and looked down at the frame. It had been melted down into the perfect mould of my grip. Inside my hands was the solidifying proof that I had done the damage. The smell of burning chemicals filled the air and I could still feel a raised temperature coming from my hands. I looked up to the doctor, hoping to signal her an apology to find that the whole room was stood motionless and looking at me.

"Do the very best you can." My comment seemed to be redundant but I needed to get out of the room and underway. I headed out and made my way to the next room, this one holding Andrea.

This time, when I entered, I wasn't confronted by herds of agitated medical staff. Instead, Andrea lay in the bed in the centre of the room with only one intravenous line running into her arm. From what I could make out, the only medication she was attached to was a saline drip. She had her eyes closed and wore an expression of absolute serenity and calm.

As I made a small step into the room, she lazily opened her eyes and focussed her attention towards the sound. Her expression remained calm when she registered that it was me.

"How are you doing?" I asked her in as gentle a tone as I could muster.

"Empty. They used my power to open a bridge. They reached into me and burned at me to take it out." I could see that she was not only feeling the physical effects but also a weight of responsibility.

"I am sorry I helped them escape." She looked me directly in the eye and used the all too familiar tone of voice that she had been using since we first met. She sounded like a disgraced general who was about to offer to fall on their sword.

"You didn't know that you were going be used like that did you?" Time for the logic. "You weren't aiming to help them were you?" I sat on the edge of the bed next to her and slowly stroked her arm, trying to soothe her fears. Her eyes were slowly becoming more and more watery as tears crashed against her best attempts to hold them back. I could feel the utter discomfort in her so decided to leave her be. The last thing she would want is for her student to stand over her as she broke down.

I squeezed her hand and headed for the door. As I reached the frame, I turned and looked back to her, "The Mage is back to what he should be. He's calling for reinforcements from the other houses because we think Tyus is going to attack the prison now." As soon as I had finished speaking I knew that I should have kept that last detail to myself. Andrea threw the blankets covering her off and swung her legs out, heaving herself to her feet. She winced with pain as her feet hit the cold floor, her legs complaining quite violently at having to take her weight. I ran to her side just as she started to stumble back towards the bed.

"You are not going to help me if you can't stand up on your own." I helped her back into bed and pulled the clothes back up around her. "Stay here and recover. I'll take care of Tyus." I gave her a wide lopsided grin and, with one last squeeze of her hand, I bolted towards the door.

Corridors flashed past in a blur as I hammered on towards the front of the house and the waiting cars. I leapt right down the whole staircase and made my way towards Andrea's Aston Martin. I had managed to 'liberate' her keys when I was in her room. I turned the key and the huge engine roared into life. The last fragments of daylight were being dragged down behind the tree line and I could feel the night rising all around like an angry spirit. I flicked the lights on and put my foot down. The Abbey was far enough away that I would need to be enthusiastic with the accelerator if I wanted to get there in time to stop whatever was taking place. I had thought about flying the distance but it was still too light to conceal a forty foot Dragon tearing by overhead, even on match day and a bridge jump was too risky to rely on having only just picked up the skill. Any rescue would be scuppered if I couldn't jump to the correct location.

I skidded out onto the main road from the wooded track and threw every last ounce of power the big car could muster forward. As I raced through the roads, weaving past any and all vehicles in my path, all I could think of was the pain that had been inflicted as my friends and family had all been caught in the crossfire of an age old war, one which seemed to be hanging solely on my shoulders. Men and women had been fighting and dying for thousands of years and

Tyus had been doing the damage for my enemy for all that time. I could see the last image of my Uncle's memories hanging at the edges of my thought, the final snap shot of Tyus as he had finally completed what he had started. The pressure started to boil as, one by one, pictures of Steve, Lloyd, Andrea and Mike all flashed into my head. Their injuries and suffering showing in crystal clarity, all of which had been caused by one creature. And that same monster was now holding one of those friends captive while he tortured his way into the prison I was sworn to guard.

The Mage had told me to take as large a force as I could assemble when I went to face Tyus. The car was still roaring along at well over one hundred miles an hour as I pushed harder to get to the Abbey. I could see small flashes of red beginning to ricochet through the edges of my vision and I didn't care about the size of the enemy army, I knew that my army of one was going to make Tyus pay.

26

The last few miles of the journey proved to be the worst. As I had approached the built up areas of Neath town centre, the concentration of cars started to rapidly increase until I was forced to dive the wrong way down roads, passing lines of static traffic as they all queued at junctions. By the time I screeched to a skidding stop in the Abbey car park, I must have collected an impressive array of hand signals and derogatory gestures. It must have been sheer luck that the Police hadn't seen me.

I bolted out of the car and headed towards the edge of the Abbey grounds, where I had felt the disorientation the first time I had crossed it. I didn't make it as far as the boundary. I sensed the presence of the enemy broiling around me before I could even get close. I scanned the area as carefully as I could muster, taking in as much detail as I could of all of the surroundings. The last strands of the day had been pushed away now and darkness reigned. The bright spot lights which framed the Abbey at night cast out irregular shadows over every surface. I would be easy pickings out here. There could be any number of Wraiths in the shadows, waiting for me to wander too close to them. My head wasn't doing the usual early warning spin but I could feel the presence of a huge number of something watching me. The skin on the back of my neck was starting to prickle and I knew that this stand off couldn't last forever, I needed to get into the cavern below.

I sprinted forwards at the boundary and pushed my way into the area beyond. The boundary felt thick, as if I was pushing through a layer of marshmallow. The boundary felt wrong. The taste and smell as I passed through it was something which made me feel a deep nausea. The same rotting matter odour filled my head and I had the feeling that the magic that made up the boundary was somehow infected. I broke through the field rim and carried on sprinting. Despite being on the move, I lifted my hand and willed force into the image of the cavern entrance I had gathered into my head. The force built up quickly and lanced out to hit the ground at the centre of what had once been the floor area of the main Abbey. The grass which was there now was quickly burned away and a plume of crimson fire burst upwards like an angry firework.

I was running but was still at least twenty metres from the opening. It was then that my head began to spin wildly and I could hear a whooshing sound as all of the circling Wraiths aimed their attacks at me at once. My legs pumped harder as I risked a glance around me, trying to pinpoint the nearest of the onrushing creatures. My head was looking right when the blow came from the left. It felt like I had been hit by multiple trains and it not only knocked all of the air from my lungs, but snapped my neck in a violent whiplash. Several silent clouds were all reaching to grip me at once as they smashed me to the ground and started to constrict at whatever point they could find. That wasn't where the attack finished. More and more of the wispy phantoms joined the melee and started to drag me further from the open gateway into the cavern. It was no more than ten feet from me but they were working to drag me away.

Constrictions increased and were joined by slashes of blades as the ever increasing force used whatever methods they could to defeat heir enemy. Pain was filling every part of me as my vision shrank down to form a tunnel. My brain was being deprived of oxygen and I could feel them winning. That was what I needed.

The flashes of red burst out together and filled my eyes in one violent burst. I yelled out a roar of the animal inside me and poured out a thick blast of fire. I wasn't aiming at anything in particular; all of my attackers were in one place so I didn't need to be too specific. Cloud after cloud was caught in the incendiary force of my flame and were superheated to nothingness. I waved my head around wildly and took almost all of the force which was holding me down. The rest of the Wraiths leapt clear and moved back to form a perimeter around me.

The flame stopped and I was free. I stood up slowly and cast an eye out over the whole area.

"I don't have time for this." My anger was still fuelling me but I had managed to contain most of my transformation. My hands were now clawed and my skin was covered in red scales. I could also feel that I was now at least ten feet tall. My clothes had been shredded during the attack and I could feel the sting of knife cuts all over my body. My scales hadn't caught them all.

"Try and stop me, I dare you" I boomed into the night air and made a dart towards the open gateway. My head span again in warning but I wasn't going to be caught again. The candle in my head burst into life and this time was joined by a thousand others. I willed all of them to a brilliant flame and let the power of what I was doing pour out around everything. The whole Abbey went up in an all consuming flame that spread out from me and passed through the boundary. Every Wraith within the blast zone was destroyed instantly. As was every last piece of grass and vegetation which hung on the ruins of the ancient Abbey. I didn't look to check on the condition of the area. My only concern was to keep moving down.

I bounded down the tunnel, ducking to make sure my extra height didn't slow me down. The last time I had used these tunnels I had felt lost, this time I knew exactly where I was going. As I surged on I started to sacrifice finesse for speed. I bounced from wall to wall as my line of running started to become more and more ragged. My shoulders were starting to feel the effects of the impacts a great deal faster than I had first thought they would. The deeper I travelled; I could also make out more and more of the cuts that had been inflicted by the Wraiths attack. I looked at my hands to find that I had reverted to my human form on the way down. My anger must have faded as I had run so I had slipped back to my original shape.

I wasn't worried, I knew that I would be able to get myself wound up again with ease, but it did serve to show me that maybe I wasn't as strong as I thought I was. My pace slowed slightly as I adjusted my pace to steer clear of any and all jutting rocks and corners.

I reached out and laid my hand on the nearest wall and relaxed. I had seen snapshots of the past when I had done this on the way out last time, would I see anything else this time? I quickly revisited the fight that my ancestor had had when the beast beneath me was released. The same pictures and feelings filled my head as my mind revisited the scenes that my subconscious thought was going to be useful. I still couldn't make out the final scene of how the creature had been re-imprisoned. I re-watched it twice more before I gave up. I wasn't going to be able to see anything new. Releasing my hand from the tunnel, I turned back to my journey down.

I was still more than three hundred yards from the cavern of the prison when I started to feel the effects of Tyus crawling up the tunnel towards me.

It started with the faintest hint of an organic smell which can only be described as that of manure. It wasn't manure but that was the closest thing I could liken it to. The repulsive sweet smell grew stronger as I neared the source and it started to bleed into the back of my throat, making me want to gag. I pushed on regardless. As I continued, the walls of the tunnel started to show the physical manifestations of the evil that was at work at the centre of the complex.

A thin layer of moisture appeared on the walls but, despite its initial appearance, it wasn't water. I reached my hand out to investigate what was draped over every surface and found that I was being surrounded by a slimy concoction that seemed to further fit the feeling that the positive magic that was at work here was somehow being infected. I spread the mucus between my fingers, exploring it in every detail. The thick ooze swung between my digits, reflecting the light in the tunnel and looking a deep green. It was at that point that my head started to swoon. I recognised the initial sensation as being similar to the memories I had explored but this time, what I was seeing wasn't coming from my shared past.

Without warning, Tyus' face hovered before my mind's eye. It was his true face, not the leathery mask that he wore as a disguise. His far too wide mouth was spread out in a sinister smile underneath the shattered pit that should have been his nose and I could feel that I wasn't looking into a memory. He parted his thin cracked lips and started to speak to me, his usual knives down a blackboard voice slightly distorted by the form of communication but still holding the same effect of wanting to make your whole being turn and run.

"We're all waiting for you down here. Come and join the fun."

He hissed the words and there was no hiding the perverted pleasure in his voice. I gripped my mind and tried to remind myself that he was responsible for the deaths of hundreds of my ancestors and of my immediate family. He had spent a vast collection of lifetimes being one step ahead of whatever my line had to throw at him. If he wanted to goad me into a rage then that was just what I should avoid.

I shook my head at the beastly image and flicked my hand at the goop that was still dribbling from my fingers. I wanted out of this mind meld. Tyus must have felt my reaction.

"Oh, don't go. I have a friend of yours here who wants to say hello. He's just dying to see you again." Tyus laughed to himself as the last of the sentence slithered from his lips. He seemed to be enjoying the role of arch villain. His cackle remained in my ears as the image switched down and I was treated to the full glare of Mike. His face was swollen and bruised and his left eye was bulbous and completely shut. Blood seemed to be springing up from at least a dozen spots all over his face and neck as he carried the expression of a man who had seen a kind of focussed violence which would pulverise the mind of anyone unlucky enough to come into contact with it. Pleading filled his good eye but he didn't say a word. Swellings around his jaw line suggested that he had had his jaw broken in more than one place and that the damage was extensive.

The fury built inside me faster than I could control it and I could feel the temperature dropping around me as I drew in power from my surroundings on instinct. Tyus could sense the build up somehow and whispered out to me.

"That's what I want to see boy. Can you do better than the last two members of your line? I'm starting to feel lazy when I kill your kind, you do seem to die so easily."

That was enough to remove all of the protection that I had placed around my mind. I knew that I was being manipulated by the creature in the cavern below but I didn't care. At that point, all I could see was the face of one of my friends shrouded in absolute terror. He was pleading for someone to help him. He needed someone to end the suffering that he was enduring and help him to heal. I could see his broken spirit and I knew that I needed to get to him as fast as I could. I wasn't trying to prevent his power being used to undo the prison, I wasn't safe-guarding the Circle, and I wasn't even trying to save a friend at this point. As the shadow of Mike's face slipped from my head, all I could think of, all I could see through the gathering crimson tendrils in my eyes was ending the life of Tyus.

My speed rose to drastically unsafe levels as I hammered down the tunnels towards the centre of the complex. I had started to hit into

248

the walls of the tunnel again, only focusing on the events taking place below me.

The closer that I got to the cavern, the thicker the air became. I could feel the struggle to breathe as I continued and knew that I was going to be walking into an environment that wasn't going to be good for me. The closer I came to the cavern; the sensations that were engulfing me grew. With each step, the smell of rotting manure climbed and the taste of it became almost tangible. Added to this was the feeling of a weight that was bearing down on me. The feeling of magical force grew and grew as I closed in on the cavern but my rage was flying far too high to make that any real concern.

I hit the end of the tunnel at a full tilt run. My transformation was underway and I had done all I could to hold it together as I had closed on the open space. When I hit the freedom of the cavern, I could finally let go. With another roar that I had dragged up from the very pit of my animal self, I leapt from the stone walkway that ringed the cavern and surged towards the transformation. I could feel the Dragon straining against me, clawing its way out. I imagined the crunch of bone and the tearing of flesh that would accompany Tyus' death at my hands.

My fury was short lived. The feeling of knowing that I was being manipulated was something that I really should have listened to. Tyus had known that I would have been driven wild by the need to free Mike and exact a bloody revenge against the thing that had killed off my family. He had pushed me in exactly the right way to get me to deliver the result he had wanted. As I had reached the end of the tunnel, he had been waiting.

His mental connection had pinpointed my location as I made my way down towards the cavern so he had known where I was going to emerge. He then had more than enough time to prepare his welcome.

As I flew into the open space, a net of the sharpest white light wrapped itself around me and I couldn't move for the pain that was slashing all over me. The field of energy tightened on me, feeling like someone was winding it in. I was suspended in mid air, my Dragon form now firmly in place, unable to move for the pain that was washing over me from every direction. Every inch of my body felt like it had been dunked into liquid nitrogen, stiff and brittle. I suddenly worried that if I struck out and hit something, I would shatter into millions of tiny pieces, decorating the cavern floor with a morbid crystalline sheen.

All I could do was roar out my defiance against the grip Tyus had placed over me and spray fire in as wide an arc as I could muster, hoping to catch someone with a lucky burst. Anger made that seem like the best idea and I unloaded at anything I could. After a minute of blasting away, I realised that I had just as much chance of hitting Mike as I did of anyone else. I stopped and looked around me. Where was the attack going to come from? Instead, Tyus slowly walked up on the ledge to my left. I could just make him out in my peripheral vision. He had completely dispensed with the illusion of being human and instead stood there in his true demon form. His large bat-like wings were now held out rigidly behind him, adding at least another seventy percent to his size. His black, armoured skin was shinning brightly as the light of the cavern reflected from it and I swear his mouth of razor sharp teeth was now almost totally wrapped around his head. When he spoke, the sound of his voice was now almost lost in amongst his hissing and clicking.

"Now that was so disappointing. I do seem to be able to get under your skin don't I? I always have. The Guardians here have always had the same weaknesses." His tone was that of resigned disappointment. It sounded that he had hoped that this time would have been different but that everything had turned out the same way despite his hopes.

In defiance I belched out another lance of flame but achieved the same as the last time, nothing. Tyus continued.

"Now, now boy. I don't want to have to hurt you or *this* any more than I have too." As he spoke he heaved Mikes shattered form forwards from outside my field of vision and held him casually with one arm, suspended out from the safety of the ledge and thirty feet from the floor below.

I instinctively struggled against the bonds which were still cutting into me. More creeping agony rushed into me and my defiance soon seeped away. Tyus threw Mike back from where he had dragged him, out of my sight then turned back to me.

"You really are driven solely by all that anger you keep inside. You must understand that you are held securely. You can't inflict any kind of damage on me." Without any warning he raised his left

250

hand and summoned to him power enough to push me forward, towards the centre of the cavern and the huge obelisk that was the opening to the creature below.

There was nothing I could do. I was held so tightly that my breathing was causing me pain and I was being treated like a massive scaly balloon as I was floated down to the obelisk. In the distance, I could hear the sounds of Tyus speaking with someone or something else. Their whispered voices were too faint for me to be able to pick out but I concentrated anyway. I'm sure that there was some magical way of boosting your hearing but as with so much of the magical spectrum; it was something that I hadn't been taught yet.

I was gently lowered onto the surface of the obelisk and the force which had held me suspended in the air released its grip. The glowing netting which had entwined itself around me remained in place though. I risked one push against its hold but was burned back in the same way as before.

From above me, I could make out the sound of wings beating as Tyus approached. Before he landed I heard the crunch of bone on stone from next to me. I strained to look round and could just make out Mike. Tyus had carried him across the space and dropped him, probably just for fun or to highlight what he was willing to do to people who were putting up no resistance. What would he do to him if we fought back?

Tyus swooped down next to my head and landed with utmost grace. He looked to be utterly at ease but was always mindful of moving too far out in front of me. He knew that if he moved too far, that I would torch him. He had seemed to be able to withstand fire the first time we fought but that had been before I had become a Dragon. I must be too strong for him to handle one on one, despite his abilities. From a position that felt like he was talking from inside my head, his creaking voice started up again.

"Why do you want to keep my Master imprisoned?"

"That thing wants to destroy the human race. I'm human. Why wouldn't I try to keep him down?" I poured as much snarl into my voice as I could. I wanted him to know that I still meant business, despite my position.

"What if a hostile force had imprisoned all of your leaders? Would you have just left them to rot in their tombs?" I grunted at him, not willing to dignify him with an answer to his questions.

Tyus seemed to consider that. "Who told you that we want to destroy the human race? We want to be able to farm them just like humans farm other animals. Humans are a food source so why would we want to kill them all?"

"We are more than just farm animals. We are intelligent." The snarl remained and I tried to turn again to see him. Yet more pain.

"You say 'we', but you don't look very human, do you? Do you think that everybody in the nearest town or city would greet you with open arms if you walked down the main streets looking like you do now? You are as much a monster as I am but you have been broken. You protect that which would kill you at the first opportunity. That's why your group has lived in hiding since the beginning."

This time I had no comeback for him. He let his comments hang in the air for a long heartbeat before continuing.

"You have been set up to do the dirty work that the human race is incapable of doing. For thousands of years, human beings have been protected by your kind because they enslaved you, made you do their bidding. You have been given the trappings of wealth and power but you can't see the big picture. The most luxurious prison in the world is still a prison, and the one which holds you doesn't even have any walls. You have been robbed of your freedom for years and are too ignorant to see it."

This time when he spoke, there was no laughter or mocking, there was only a sadness. That made it even harder to take in.

I tried to focus on how to break free but all that filled my head was thoughts of what life could have been had my family not been tied to this responsibility. My parents would have been alive and Steve and I would have grown up with our family close to us. My Uncle and his family would have been safe in their farm and none of us would have had to spend their days always looking over our shoulders just in case the forces of evil chose that moment to attack. For years, my family would have been able to just live their lives without fear of the creatures in the dark.

Tyus picked up on the hesitation in me.

"You are more than the human race. You would be safe in the new world. You would be surrounded by beings just like you, powerful creatures who are stronger than the human race but have somehow been declared worse than them. All we aim to do is redress the balance in the world and allow our kind to take their rightful place in the world. We want to live in the world and not be scared of being attacked, is that too much to ask?"

His words were like honey being poured into my ear. He was telling me that he was exactly the same as me and that for years all he and his kind had wanted was to free their leaders and live a life away from violence.

"That is why I am hoping that after I free my Master, that you will join our forces. You won't have to live in fear any more. You will be able to have friends and family and live in safety."

"What about my friends and family? What is going to happen to the people at the estate?" The words had left my mouth before I had even registered that I was saying them. My body had sagged down and I could feel the trappings that were holding me down begin to ease their grip as my size started to diminish.

"This one here and all of them at your groups' strongholds will be the first to be 'farmed'. They are all the most dangerous of the humans so they will all need to be removed. We can't risk that your group will start up its misguided actions again. All of them will be made to serve us, as they should have been doing since the very beginning."

Tyus' tone had shifted as he had spoken and that had been enough to break the spell he had been weaving over me. He had started to show pure evil towards the human race as he spoke and his glee at the thought of turning me into one of his minions betrayed his true intent. Thoughts of the deaths of Mike, Lloyd and Andrea re-ignited my fury and I let all of the power that it was creating in me surge up and drive me.

I took advantage of the freedom my reduction in size had afforded me and struck before the magical trap closed tightly on me again. I coiled my neck towards Tyus and snapped my jaws down at him, all the time letting fire pour out in any direction. Tyus was taken utterly by surprise by my strike. He had been practically gloating over the thoughts of breaking the Circle and freeing his Master that he had lost his concentration on what was happening around him. Fire washed down over him and my jaws clamped down onto his left arm, just below the elbow. I could feel the crunch of bone and the tearing of flesh as my sword like teeth worked their way through his fragile limb. He screamed out in agony as fire engulfed him and his limb was mangled.

Before I could do any more damage, my transformation reached its conclusion and I was again trapped by a solid wall of slow slicing pain. I was forced to let go of my bite as the sharp pain returned and my head was again forced back into position, facing away from my enemy. I struggled out against the binding regardless of the pain and roared out to anyone who was in the cavern with us. I was again running on burning rage and I wanted everyone to know it.

"I will not betray the people who have looked after me. We all serve a purpose and I will not be the one who enslaves the human race."

Tyus was curled up on the floor next to me, again, just visible in my peripheral vision. He held his now ruined arm close to his chest, cradling it away from further attack. He stumbled to his feet and looked over the damage I had inflicted. His whole body was covered in large blistered patches where my flamed attack had covered him. Despite his armoured surface, I had managed to cause him some real pain. He moved slowly and winced as each part of him that had been damaged screamed for him to stop. When he finally looked up to me, he flashed out his intentions with the purest malice. His eyes showed that he was going to achieve his goals but that he was now going to do it in the most painful way possible. His attempts at seduction were now being abandoned, instead being replaced with brute force and torture.

"The rest of your life will be an agony that will spread out through time itself" he screamed out and rose what was left of his left arm, all the time supporting it with his right. There was no movement in what was left of his hand but I could feel the build up of force gathering at his fingers. I expected the web of energy that was surrounding me to start to constrict even further but instead there was nothing. No pain tore at me, no crushing vice compressing me. For a second I was filled with the knowledge that I had somehow removed his ability to use magic in a way that he was used to. That feeling was short lived.

Outside of my field of vision, Mike began to scream. It was more than the shouts and yells I had heard before in my life. That sound was one of absolute loss. The pitch rose to an almost inhuman level as Tyus made Mike pay for the damage I had inflicted on him. Mike was lost in the terror and agony of what was being done to him and I was powerless to stop it.

"Leave him alone" was all I could muster as a plead to the torturer.

"Never!" spat Tyus. He was grinning wildly as he twisted the wreck that was his hand and Mike was twisted even further.

"This human is going to die when I use both of you to open the portal to the prison. My Master will be hungry when he rises, you will make a good meal for him. He does so prefer to eat something that is still living." He followed that last revelation with a high pitched machine gun laugh. He was now totally lost in his own blood lust and was completely mad.

It was now or never. Whatever was about to happen, it was going to kill Mike and then I was going to be served up as a trussed up delicacy to the creature I was supposed to be keeping chained up. Tyus was using magic to hold me in place and all I had was brute strength. I would not let my whole family line be smashed like this. Mikes screams grew again, to a noise that I didn't think a human being could make. He couldn't have long left before whatever was being done to him got to be too much.

I pulled in every last ounce of energy around me that I could. I knew that Mike was going to die so I needed to get this done as fast as I could. I let my anger boil again and thrashed against the bonds again. They bit into me again, deeper and in more places than before, but I used that as more fuel for my building violence. The temperature suddenly crashed down to well below zero all around the surface of the obelisk and a massive layer of ice spread over everything. I thrashed and beat out against the netting with each and every last ounce of my strength, spraying out wide beams of flame as I went. The net was loosening. I roared and roared as I hammered again. I poured out every last ounce of anger and fear into what I was

255

doing and clawed at anything I could, determined to demolish the whole cavern if it came to it.

A small popping sound was the first indication that the web of energy was buckling. It was followed by another, then another and as I surged my Dragon form in every direction I could, I could feel that the end was in sight. I risked glances around the obelisk for Mike. I had heard his screams coming from behind me to my left but I needed to pinpoint him so when I broke free I didn't just step on him. He was lying on the floor, but he was arched into a violent full body spasm. His arms and legs were twisted in every wrong direction you could conceive and his face was spread in the mask of the worst pain imaginable. Stood over him was Tyus. Looking worried but still extremely smug, he was straddling his victim, with his ruined left hand resting on his chest. He must have been keeping the torment going from close quarters, not wanting to risk me getting free and simply incinerating him.

"Mighty Dragon" he shouted. I was still unloading all of my energies on my bonds so he was struggling to be heard.

"I give you my Master. The Zarrulent rises."

With a final pop-hiss, the netting that had held me down finally gave way and I was free. It was just at that point that Tyus reached out with his right hand and lightly touched my side. There was a sudden flash of light and more pain twisted out from where I had been touched. All I could do was stand up right, stock still as whatever Tyus had done to me, worked its course. After an age, I was released from the new bondage and I staggered back, unsteady on my feet. My head was fuzzy at the edges, feeling like I was trying to think my way through cotton wool. Mike was at my feet but Tyus was missing.

I twisted my attention all around us as fast as I could. I needed to locate him as fast as possible before he did something else to us. I didn't have to look far. His wide wings pulsed rhythmically as he hovered above the ground, out past the edge of the obelisk that we were standing on. He looked calm and was watching us closely, studying our every move. I took one step towards him, preparing myself to strike in as many ways as I could muster. That one step was as far as my offence got. Directly between us, from the edge of the obelisk, came a violent cracking sound and then a small puff of dust.

Tyus smiled.

For a second, I paused, confused by his reaction. The floor shaking violently signified exactly why he was so pleased. He had used the power of one of the senior members of the house and that of the Guardian to shatter my glyph stone which stood in the ring of symbols carved into the edge of the prison mouth. He had broken the ring of magic which held my charge in place, and by the sound of the ground, my charge was now on his way out.

27

Pieces of rock started to fall from the roof of the cavern. The missiles of varying sizes fell all over the space, littering the floor area with dust and debris. We weren't safe from them where we stood. We were directly in the centre of the room, completely exposed and Mike was in serious need of medical help. Forgetting Tyus and the rising monster, I scooped up Mike in my right hand and bounded off the edge of the obelisk and started to run across the cavern towards the rooms I had stayed in before my Awakening. I dodged boulders as they crashed to the ground all around me, listening to the spinning in my head as I instinctively knew when one was about to hit me. I had thought about flying but the risks of being hit by something when I was airborne were too high, especially with Mike cradled in my grip.

I reached the edge of the cavern and skidded to a halt. Without thinking, I shoved my hand into the first doorway and deposited Mike onto the bed in the room beyond. There was no spinning in my head so I reasoned that there was no threat in the room. As fast as I could, I pulled all the loose stone that was to hand, together and created a very thick natural wall to protect Mike. It wouldn't last forever but it would give me the chance to do some damage without having to worry about his safety. With Mike now out of harm's way, I turned my focus back out to the shaking in the cavern. Tyus was nowhere to be seen, but at that point, I was shown exactly why he was missing.

The surface of the obelisk in the centre of the cavern erupted, slowly at first, but after the first two or three seconds, with a violence that sent rock flying up and out to crash into all surfaces. Walls and ceiling were peppered with missiles as the surface of the obelisk was demolished for good. I covered my eyes against the hail of objects, but when I returned my attention to the centre of the cavern, I was confronted by an image that was equal parts terrifying and familiar.

Hunched at the rim of the stone centre piece, its arms holding up its massive, heavily muscled, armour plated, white scaled body, was the animal that I had been charged with guarding. Its four blood red eyes flashed glances round the cavern as it took in all of the details that presented themselves to it. It had a huge, elongated mouth which hung open to reveal four rows of curved teeth which looked like they would be able to make mincemeat of plate steel. From its back, I could make out the top of a pair of wings. Spread out all over its back were dark bony protuberances which flexed and throbbed as it breathed. I recognised the cold white scales of its hide from my mental attack by Tyus; this creature had been in the background, always pulling Tyus' strings. Its whole body looked like it was designed solely for the purpose of warfare. It reviewed the room with a frown on its face, its eyes darting from one thing to the next, independently of each other. It was obviously displeased with what it had found. Then its eyes settled on me and the frown turned to a sinister smirk.

"Tyus!" His voice was ocean deep and larger than the cavern could hold, making more loose stone fall free and crash to the ground. The sound curled out in an accent which brought to mind fragments of a hundred others but which was totally unique. This creature was as old as time and his voice hadn't been heard in eons.

"Is this for me?" The creature leaned forward towards me and leered at me, licking its lips.

I straightened myself up to my full height of forty feet, pushing as much brutality into my posture as I could. The last thing I needed to do was show any form of weakness to the beast.

Slowly, he pulled himself forward, out of the hole that had been the obelisk, and started to make his way towards me. Vast steely muscles throbbed and rippled under his skin as he came. I had expected him to climb out and look like me, a Dragon ripped from the pages of hundreds of fantasy novels. Instead, he revealed that, despite the similarities we shared in appearance from the waist up, from the waist down he was closer to the form of a snake. He poured himself out of the gaping space he had come from and heaved his massive bulk onto the stone floor. He slithered across the floor towards me, eyes focussed on me despite the movement. As he approached me I caught sight of a glistening collection of objects following on behind him. I tried to pick out the details of whatever it was but they seemed to be jumping from my field of vision. As the

259

creature pulled itself closer to me, I could make out the sound of metal being dragged across stone. They were chains being pulled behind him, but they must have been enchanted. They seemed to flutter into sight and then disappear again. They were wickedly barbed and seemed to run directly through and into the monster. They entered through at least a dozen sites. They all looked like they would be able to withstand a considerable force and were probably causing him severe torment. That thing really had been chained into his prison.

The age old horror drew up to me and stopped, pulling himself up to his full height, as if in defiance to my display of bravado. He towered over me by a huge distance and was at least half as wide again as I was. I could see why these things could only be imprisoned rather than killed outright.

He leaned down to face me more closely, practically touching his snout onto mine. His breath was searingly hot and carried with it the odour of burning sulphur. This creature was shaping up to be the absolute embodiment of the devil, well, behind what I looked like obviously.

"Are you here for me?" The question seemed to be laced with so much layered intent it made it even more uncomfortable. I pushed my chest out and flexed my wings out a little bit further, trying to exude confidence in my abilities; after all, he wasn't to know that I was only fresh into the position.

"David and, Steven, fell so easily. Will you at least make a fight of it little one?" Hearing the names of my closest family on the thunderous voice of the horror that had been attempting to enslave the human race was unnerving to say the least. How had he known anything about me?

I must have flashed my confusion on my face because he started laughing down at me.

"I have been in your head for quite some time boy. I have seen what my servant has been doing to you for long enough to see that you really are not ready for what you have to do. I'm very sorry to say that you are not going to survive the vengeance I am going to exact against your whole mongrel family line." He swung his tongue out and it swatted at the air between us, dripping large gobs of slobber as he did it. I stood staring up at him and realised, that

260

despite his eloquence, he had quite probably been driven ever so slightly mad during his time in the pit.

"Welcome to the new world" was the last sentence to boom out against the cavern before he struck. He must have decided that he had gloated enough over the tiny creature that was at his mercy. His dismissal of me as a credible threat made me angry. I didn't like to be told anything and him saying that he didn't think much of me fired me up.

The Zarrulent lifted his right hand and exposed the bony talons that were loaded onto each of his fingers, three per finger. Before he could drive his hand down and slash at me I leapt forwards at his face. The snarling roar flooded from me as I started clawing and raking in my own untrained fashion at his eyes. All the time, I was blasting fire out against his head where I was ripping, aiming to bore holes down into his skull. The surprise of my drive took a second to sink in as his serrated weapons flashed down behind me, where I had been stood. He drove his hand into the ground at high speed and caused yet more stone to tumble from the higher reaches of the cavern.

He let out a concussive yell of pain and frustration and surged even higher as he recoiled from the tearing force that was battering against his head before he reached out with both hands and gripped me tightly round my chest. His move had lifted me completely off the ground and I was treated to another point of view of the enormity of the task at hand. The floor looked to be at least a thousand miles away.

He pushed me away from him in an instinctive gesture that put the maximum amount of distance between us as fast as he could. His face was now covered in scorched flesh and torn muscle and he had lost both of his right eyes to my attentions.

Now that I was prevented from ripping into his face, he cradled his head with his right hand, taking stock of the damage I had caused. I started at burning into his hand with all my fury and began to slash at any and all available flesh with all the violence that I could muster. He screamed at me with his own fury building and suddenly, my attack was rendered useless.

His eyes flashed as a surging force was summoned from within the beast. My whole body seized to a standstill and a freezing cold spread through every inch of me. It was all I could do to whimper as the force hit through me like a very angry buzz saw. I couldn't move and I could feel every muscle in my body firing at the same time.

"You may be the creature who can do me the most damage, but that situation does work the other way." The Zarrulent was holding me at arms length and was concentrating every part of his focus onto what he was throwing into me. I strained against what his efforts were doing, willing my own anger in as fuel for a counter attack. His grip tightened both physically and magically and crushed more of my resistance. He was winning.

"Just think of the damage I will do to your whole existence. Every part of the human race will be shredded and your tiny little band will be ended for good." He drew me closer to his face, almost as a dare to me to try and break free. I tried but the pain was passing into realms I had never experienced.

"Now die. I will free my brothers and sisters from their bonds and your whole race will fall. Realise that your failure here is the beginning of untold agony for the human race. I've been in your head for some time boy. Maybe Andrea will like my advances, she does seem to be so, receptive." The mocking laughter was dribbling out through every word and he shook me with a mocking flick, almost as a final gesture.

The thought of Andrea being hurt in any way was enough to make the difference. The fury burning within me flashed out to a white hot heat in a second and I could feel the absolute power of who I was. I tore past all of the pain that was gripping my body and started to thrash wildly. I didn't care about the pain anymore and blazed out fire and violence to all I could reach. Sinking my claws into the flesh that was holding me, I burned into the gaping wound created and bored down to the bone. The Zarrulent reacted to my retaliation by pouring more agony into his own magical attack. It did no good. I was too far gone in my own fury and I didn't care. As I thrashed against his hand I could feel that I was moving towards an utter loss of self and I dived into the murky waters of sheer abandon. The temperature around us fell in seconds and I roared and roared.

My attack had been enough. The Zarrulent dropped me and coiled himself back away from the pain I was unleashing. He had been expecting to be able to end me there but the sudden counter offensive took him totally off guard. I thumped to the ground but was on my feet again quickly, dust clouding up around me as I rounded my attention at the animal that was threatening me.

"Tyus!" called the creature. His servant was quick to swoop down to his aid and hovered before his face.

"I tire of this. I need his power. Bring it to me now."

Tyus didn't give any signal of agreement but flew directly at me, his ruined left arm hanging useless below him as he descended. A glow of green sparks started to grow at his right hand as he fell and began to spit and crackle. He rushed at me but he was nothing more than a distraction.

As I focussed on him, preparing for the effects of whatever he was about to unleash, his Master made his move.

The giant shot across and behind me with a speed that I hadn't thought possible. In the blink of an eye he had taken hold of both of my hands and was holding my arms out to either side so I was held in a crucifix position. The force of the snap which took both of my arms out of Tyus' way also caused my head to snap backwards with a vicious kick. I had been held with my fire pointing in the wrong direction and my hands were in a position where I couldn't get any leverage to free them. In one swift manoeuvre, I had been disabled and Tyus now had a clear view of me. I was totally at their mercy and they knew it. I could feel the super heated breath of my captor cascading down over my shoulder as he was now pressed up directly behind me. Through the torrents of rancid air, I could make out a small laugh and it was growing.

I pulled uselessly against his grip but there was no movement at all. I tried to pour fire out by turning my head to catch him but I couldn't rotate far enough. My wings had been held down so I had no chance of using them to force my way free. If I started to kick against the creature behind me, or swing with my tail, it would rob me of the last of my balance and face down on the floor was the last place I could see being very useful. I hurriedly looked around me, hoping that there would be something, anything, that would be of some use. I quickly realised that Tyus had vanished. At that very second, almost as an exercise in perfect timing, another jolt of paralyzing cold was unleashed into my back. Each and every muscle in my body spasmed again and the shattering agony rendered me useless. From behind me, I could feel the voice rather than hear it as The Zarrulent called out "Good, give me more" in a long, drawn out command to his servant. Tyus obliged and, for the first time, along with the pain, I could feel that I was growing weaker. Panic spread through me and I started to lash out in any way that I could, flame and struggle, desperate to break free from what was being done.

The laughter grew.

"Excellent. Fight me. I want you to fight me." Each word was saturated with a twisted glee which made my panic soar. My strength and power was being siphoned from me and I was utterly incapable of doing anything about it. I wrenched again and again at the grip of the beast that was behind me but each time carried less force than the one which preceded it. My power was needed to break the chains and it was being taken from me by force. Finally, as all of my strength dwindled, I let my head slump forward and my body sagged down, my legs hanging limply beneath me.

With a mighty roar which shook the whole cavern like an earthquake, The Zarrulent released his grip and I crashed to the floor like a rag doll. From behind me I could hear the sounds of heavy metal being dropped to the ground. One by one, the last chains that had held the beast were being cast off. My power had been stolen to give him a jump start so he could force his way through the bonds. He had been running on empty and he had still managed to out gun me.

The Zarrulent then roared again but this time his tone was very different. It was angry.

"There are still two chains through me. Tyus I need more of him."

Tyus floated up from behind me and I realized that he had been the one acting as the siphon.

"He is exhausted my lord, look. He has no more to give."

That wasn't the answer that The Zarrulent had wanted to hear. He started to crash around the cavern, smashing and flailing wildly at anything and everything, his own frustration now pouring out like flood waters crashing over the top of a dam. He roared and roared out as he did. The noise filled my head to the point that, despite my weakened form, I felt that I wanted to turn and run from it.

Finally, the demon aberration came to a halt over me, breathing deeply after its outburst.

"You can't be useful, even in death." With his huge right hand, he swatted against me and sent me sliding wildly across the floor of the cavern. He had caught me squarely across the stomach from where I had been lying, prone on the floor and had made contact in much the same way as I imagined an articulated lorry travelling at sixty miles an hour would. What little air I had in my lungs was smashed out and the pain flashed out and through every part of my body. He slithered his frame after me and I could sense that he was going to pull me to pieces, just as a way of relieving his own stress. He brought his hand down towards me again, this time with the full intention of piercing my flesh. He was coiled over a half dead enemy who had nothing left to give.

It was the perfect time for my counter attack.

28

Using the spinning in my head as a guide to where my enemies attack was, I waited until his hand was almost onto me before I sprang to my feet and unloaded a thick volley of flame up and into his hand. I had realised that I was in no position to physically beat that creature when he had me held in such an awkward position, so I had gambled that if he saw me get totally drained, then he would let go of me on his own. I wasn't feeling one hundred percent and my head felt really groggy but at least I was free.

Shock at my attack caused The Zarrulent to let out a very short noise which sounded almost like a hiccup. That was soon replaced though, with a crushing roar which grew up into more of a scream when the pain from his hand finally registered. Before he could rip his hand from the source of the pain, I took a firm hold, burying my own talons into his flesh to anchor myself, and continued to unleash every ounce of flaming fury I had at my disposal.

Blackened hunks of charred meat started to fall from the demons hand as my attack continued. He struggled against the heat, trying to shake his hand free but I dug even deeper. I wasn't going to let him get a free shot at me.

My head suddenly climbed through the revolutions and I realised that my enemy had changed his point of attack. Rather than trying to remove his hand from the heat source, he was now going to remove the heat source. His left arm thundered through the air with a speed born purely of desperation. He had realised that he would be able to smash me to a pulp with his other hand if all my attention was focussed in one place, but I had already achieved my first goal. A fraction of a second before his blow landed, I let go of my grip, stopped the jets of fire and leapt into the air, clearing his arm as I went. When I reached the pinnacle of my leap, I opened my wings to their full span, and with two quick pulses surged away from The Zarrulent, past his left shoulder.

He wasn't slow to turn to face me, but now his right hand had been rendered useless. Most of the flesh had been utterly destroyed and what was left was burned to almost ash. He stared up after me and both his remaining eyes narrowed. I continued to retreat backwards through the air, all the time watching the huge demon, but also making sure of Tyus' location. Tyus hovered slightly away from The Zarrulent and carried himself like someone who was waiting nervously for the inevitable explosion from his master. But it didn't come in the way either he or I had expected. The Zarrulent spoke, but his voice was crackling with a seething hatred which I hadn't experienced before. Both he and Tyus had always been business like about their desire to kill me and my family. They had treated it as a job rather than some kind of sacred calling from thousands of years ago. In my experience, they had always been quite matter of fact. That was gone now. The voice that came from the coiled nightmare below was now filled with an unnatural fervour and the purest, white hot hatred and it was being aimed squarely at me.

"So, you had more power to give. My servant should have recognised that." He didn't once move his focus from me but could tell that he had been aiming that last remark of hatred at Tyus as well. "I'll make you suffer for this. Don't think that this is going to stop me in any way." He had lifted his right arm and was shaking his ruined stump at me, what was left of his hand was waving wildly as he did. But he didn't leave it at that. To really drive the point home, he raised his arm to his mouth, and bit down on what was left of his hand. The sound of cracking bone and the popping of tendons and ligaments filled the space as The Zarrulent removed his damaged appendage and ate it.

My stomach turned as I hovered watching what was taking place. The Zarrulent was exaggerating every movement of his oversized jaws as he chewed through his impromptu snack and I knew that all the time he was running through different scenarios and strategies, almost teasing himself with ways he was going to finish me off.

I needed to find a way to end this.

I looked inwards again and ran through the various stored memories that I hoped would be able to shed some light on how I was supposed to stop this thing when it really put its mind to the task of tearing me to pieces, and how to go one better than the only other Guardian who ever faced this situation, and survive.

As I sifted, the only image that really looked like it was going to be of any use was the shard of memory which related to the moment that The Zarrulent was re-captured. I could replicate all of the various brawling and burning moves that had been used before but the very instant that the fight was finally won could show me what skill or technique would be able to force The Zarrulent down. I looked again and again but all I could make out was the same collection of bright light and fire. There were no edges to make out and it all became a canvas of nothing in the blink of an eye as the final bridge jump took the Dragon out of the cavern.

Snapping all of my focus back to the two demons below me, I realised that I would have to rely on brute force and what little magic I knew to actually do any damage. The Mage would be assembling a fighting force which would be here shortly so all I needed to do was keep him occupied until then. Add to all of that that my power was seriously depleted and I was feeling dizzy without it being a warning signal and things weren't looking too great. The longer we stood trying to work out how to kill each other, the better my odds seemed to get.

The shared thinking time, though, was shattered by The Zarrulent. He had been running through strategies of his own. He had been slowly coiling himself up as we had been held, staring at each other, and now he was releasing that energy into a lightning fast strike which propelled his enormous frame up and at me. He roared out as he came and thrust out both of his white armour plated arms, bringing all of his remaining serrated claws to bear with deadly aim. The sheer speed of the drive caught me totally off guard. He was upon me before I could make any kind of evasive movement. All I could do was reach out my own arms and try to at least slow his surge forward and deflect the spears of his left hand.

He thundered into me, driving himself at my head and body. My wings were no match for the mass and velocity that he had thrown at me so we both travelled back through the air, over the mouth to the sub-terrainian prison that he had crawled through until we landed on the floor of the cavern and were sent sliding through the fallen debris and into the far rock wall.

The Zarrulent was laying over me, forcing himself down towards me. I could feel the tearing pull of pain as at least three of his talons had already found their mark and were embedded in my shoulders and right arm. I gripped tightly to his arms and tried to eliminate all movement. The agony grew each time either of us made the slightest change of position and it was starting to make me feel queasy. I tried to focus my attention and shake away the sensation but the smell coming from what was left of my attackers right hand was making everything seem just that little bit harder.

He lowered his face down so his nightmare appearance filled my vision.

"You had more to give me. Your fire is surging through me little one but I want to have it all." His voice was still enormous but there was still that steely rod of hatred running through it which served to make his threat more terrifying.

"TYUS!" The Zarrulent called out for his servant, but without moving his gaze from me.

From the very edge of my vision I could make out the small winged form of Tyus darting through the air towards us. The closer he got, I could make out his smile of insane glee. He wanted his master to end this and he wanted to be right there to see it happen.

He landed on my chest and without any further preparation or ceremony, I watched him lay one hand on my chest and one hand on the chest of The Zarrulent. I tried to move to swat him away but the feeling of tearing flesh buzzed through my body at the different sites that I was pinned and made it impossible for me to move. That pain was quickly replaced by the familiar sensation of full body paralysis and muscular burning which signalled that what little power I had left was being taken.

The Zarrulent closed his two remaining eyes and drew in a deep breath. I could tell he was enjoying the sensation. I, on the other hand, felt that my body was being turned to stone. I was growing number by the second and I couldn't see a way out. I was going to die here, The Zarrulent would take down the mansion and everyone there and then start working on the demise of the human race. The more I thought about the various scenarios which were going to be put into motion, the more I kept coming back to the people who had been working with me up to now. Would Mike be buried alive in the cavern? Would Lloyd survive to mount some kind of defence against the demon armies which would rise? Would Andrea recover to be able to defend the mansion as well as her own estate?

My mental image of Andrea floated ahead of me as I felt the last remaining fragments of my essence being drawn away from me. She was still lying in her bed in the estates infirmary. She was still wearing the same gown she had been when I had left her but she now looked strong and fierce, the same way she had when we had first met, not drained as she had been after her encounter with Tyus.

I flashed my eyes open and looked directly up at The Zarrulent. He still had his eyes closed and his head raised. He was comfortable in the knowledge that he was pulling all of my power from me and that he would soon be able to climb to his freedom. I looked up at him and knew that that image of Andrea was enough to make me realise how to get out of trouble.

Gritting my teeth against the pain of the draining magics and of the pain spears that were slicing into me, I focussed all of my remaining magical will into Tyus.

29

I drew all of my energy into my mind and focussed on what I wanted to happen. In my minds eye, the image of Tyus took shape and I started to focus my will on it. Despite all of the agony of what was happening to me, I built up my anger as a magical fuel source and created the picture of draining power through Tyus for myself.

The image Tyus stood stock still in the same position the real Tyus was in on my chest but this time I concentrated on the red and orange power that I had lost. I pictured it being drawn out in reverse, through him to surge back into me from The Zarrulent.

Tyus had used Andrea as a power source to jump all of his force from the Mages Chamber because he couldn't have been powerful enough to complete the casting. He was drawing magic from me to give to his master. It meant he was a good magical bridge, a conduit, who could take power from one place and put it somewhere else. He was drawing my power away from me but it meant that he could be used to draw my power back from The Zarrulent. He may have had a level of power to fight against humans but against a Dragon it would have to be his cunning that gave him an advantage. He had been able to hold me in a magical net but he hadn't really been able to do me any serious damage.

Tyus noticed almost immediately that something had changed. The Zarrulent was only a fraction of a second behind.

"My master" Tyus called out, his voice ringing with confused fear. "Something is wrong." He looked up to his master who swung his attention down to us at high speed.

"What are you doing Tyus? I am losing his force. What are you doing?" The Zarrulent was angry, all trace of any gloating gone for good now.

"I can't stop the drain my lord." Tyus was desperately trying to break his contact with me but he had been held firmly in place, his hand seemingly stuck to the scaled surface of my chest.

In my head, I continued to force more energy through Tyus' small frame, all the time wanting to rush the process to a conclusion. As pulse after pulse passed through my mental picture of the smaller winged demon, I could feel strength and power flooding back into me, practically re-inflating my chest as it did.

The Zarrulent, though, wasn't just going to let me take all of my power back without doing something in return. He began to twist the talons he had buried in my flesh, sending bolts of agony out as he did but they were to no avail. His right hand was gone so all he could muster was to beat me with his ravaged stump. Each blow felt as if it was being accompanied by a cry of almost pleading. He was losing the chance to remove the final enchanted bonds that ran through him and his enemy was getting stronger by the second as that chance went.

"I can't break free my lord. Help me, I beg you." Fear was dripping from each syllable of Tyus' plea and as my strength returned, I could feel a level of climbing fury coming with it. I was bringing more of my power back and I could feel the return of all of the accumulated anger that I had when I had first entered the cavern.

With the magical hold between us still in place, I was now strong enough to be able to strike out against The Zarrulent. Taking a firm grip of his left hand, I forced it slowly away from me and freed myself from the claws that had been spearing me. One by one, they each were slid from me until his remaining hand was suspended above me, my blood dripping down from the evil blades he had impaled me with.

With as much contempt as I could drag together, I threw his hand from me and onto the ground. He lurched forward towards me, no longer supported by his skewered victim. His expression had reverted to the quiet anger he had used after losing his hand and it served to highlight that he was still powerful, despite not having what he had been taking from me. He practically spat out at me, "You are stronger than I thought little one. You are a danger so I won't risk you being able to do me any more damage."

"Come on. Life's all about risk" I growled back. I couldn't help myself. I was feeling a level of confidence that I probably shouldn't have been feeling but I really enjoyed the sensation. I continued to goad him, hoping that I could make him as frustrated as I did Andrea with my own special brand of humour.

"We do seem to have gotten so close though." I flicked my eyes down towards Tyus as a highlight as more and more power slipped from The Zarrulent. He looked down as well and then lifted his eyes back to meet mine, only this time his face was shrouded with a black enjoyment that showed me my humour was probably best not used with anyone. The Zarrulent planted his hand and his stump either side of me, braced himself, then pushed himself up and away from me in what looked like a very precise press-up.

The two of us were held together by Tyus and the power that I was drawing through him. He had been anchored to both of us magically which had meant that neither one of us could escape the other. When he had been helping draw power from me, that hadn't been a problem, but now the flow of energy was travelling the other way, he was suddenly a liability to his master. His master therefore, took action against something that was doing him harm.

With a slow and controlled effort, The Zarrulent pushed himself up and away from me. Tyus had seen the movement coming but had scarcely believed that it was actually happening. His eyes widened and he began to struggle against the enchanted grip which was holding him in place, desperate to find some way to break free.

"Please my lord. Please!" He was slowly being pulled to the limit of his reach. I could feel the pull of his hand against my chest, in much the same way you can feel the skin being pulled if you take hold of a small cluster of hairs and tug.

I looked down at Tyus to see his arms straining against the force being exerted by his master. He looked back to me, almost with pleading in his eyes. He wanted to live and he didn't care who helped him do that. As I looked down at him I let my head fill with the different images of the ancestors I had lost over the years at the hands of this violent creature. Tyus had been a very painful thorn in the side of various members of the Circle over the years but here he was about to be ended. As I ran across the different pictures of memory I had relating to the deaths of my line at his hands, I ended on the last people he had managed to kill, my Uncle and my Brother.

Those last memories were enough to remove the small kernel of compassion that had been building inside me. The Zarrulent was not going to be the one to finish this stain on existence. Tyus was going to die at the hands of the enemy regardless of the actions of his master.

With a snarling roar which came from every last piece of fear and hurt I had ever felt, I raised both of my arms and both of my legs and dug my claws into the belly and chest of the creature over me, and kicked him away with all of the force that I could muster.

The Zarrulent flew back across the cavern and smashed into the remains of the obelisk. Stone pieces the size of houses flew out behind him. Still attached to his chest was half of his servant. Tyus had been pulled in two by the force of my drive against his master. His hands had remained bonded with the two giants either side of him leaving him no escape. The force of the separation had pulled him apart practically down the middle, except his head was still fixed to the piece of him that was still swinging from me. His black blood had cascaded down my chest and stomach to form a smear of awfulness that stood out against the red of my scales like a lone thunder cloud on a clear, sunny day.

I slowly stood up as the power finally drained from the corpse of the demon on my chest. When it was finally depleted, the bond between us was broken and Tyus' remains fell to the floor of the cavern in a wet puddle of his own entrails. The Zarrulent looked across the cavern at me as his half of his servant fell free. He was not amused. I took one step towards him and wiped away the mess on my chest, trying all the time to exaggerate the movement and to show my enemy that I meant business. The Zarrulent drew himself up to his previous imposing height and spread his wings.

"I have underestimated your abilities boy. This tomb will not hold me any longer and now you are going to live to see what The Hive creatures are really capable of."

His voice was hard and it showed his intent perfectly. I readied myself, expecting him to fly across the space between us, teeth and claws aimed in my direction. Instead he remained where he was but thrust out his arms directly at me. Two battering rams of black power wreathed in green shot from his open palms and thundered into my chest. They hit with enough force that it felt like they were going to break creation.

I was sent crashing backwards and into the wall of the cavern. I slammed hard into the rocky surface but didn't stop. The pile driving force that had smashed into me kept on pushing and the wall opened up behind me like a piece of wood accepting a nail being hammered in. Pain was spreading from the impact on the front of my body and from the shattering stone behind me, tearing at my back and wings.

Finally the force subsided. I clutched my chest and struggled desperately to draw in a much needed breath. My lungs fought the actions, as if they couldn't take any more movement, the agony was too much. I gasped and gasped through the dusty air of the hole that I had been forced into; knowing that I couldn't drop my guard for a second or The Zarrulent would make the most of the opening.

Air finally started to rush into my body. My chest started to send out explosions of bright pain which pierced every inch of my body. Whatever he had just done, it had been much more powerful than each of his previous attacks. His physical strength was only slightly more than mine but by the feel of it, his magical ability was way in excess of mine. I didn't linger on that thought for very long. The bright flash of blue/white light and the smell of ozone that was coming from the cavern told me that I would need to move and get back into the fight quickly.

I forced myself out of the cavern wall to be greeted by what I had feared. The Zarrulent had opened a cascade bridge, a massive one, and was disappearing inside when I hit fresh air. Instinct took over and through the pain of my injuries; I lunged forward as the tip of his tail slipped into the glowing ring. I was at least thirty feet from the bridge when I hit the ground but his tail wasn't my target.

I gathered up in both of my hands, the two remaining enchanted metal chains which were still passing through parts of The Zarrulents body. They had been clanking and skittering across the floor as they trailed after their host. I took a firm grip on the retreating bonds, holding as tightly as I could to the iridescent chains as they phased in and then out of sight. They snapped tight as I checked my foe's escape and I could hear a distorted howl coming from the other side of the bridge.

I heaved against them, pulling for all I was worth. That monster had seen all the freedom that I could risk. The longer he was out of the prison, the more chance that he would be able to do some real damage. The thought of seeing the potential end of the human race documented on twenty four hour news channels didn't seem to be the best way to keep the existence of The Circle secret.

Hand over hand, inch by inch, I strained every sinew against the monster on the other side of the bridge. Bursts of force came from the other side as I pulled. The Zarrulent wasn't going to give up easily. We both ebbed and flowed as we became locked into a demonic game of tug of war, neither one of us willing to entertain the thought of failure. I roared out against the exertion, letting my fury build. I could feel the blood lust rising inside me again with each passing second and it felt good. I roared again as I heaved and ahead of me The Zarrulent flickered into view as his head and chest were dragged back into the prison cavern. His head thrashed wildly as he struggled against the chains. He must have been in agony as I strained on the chains that ran through him. I could only imagine that it must have felt like someone picking you up by gripping one of your ribs. Despite that thought, I kept on pulling. Metre by metre, centimetre by centimetre, millimetre by millimetre, I was winning.

The Zarrulent, though, wasn't going to give up easily.

I had next to no time to react before he moved. The spinning in my head tore up through the revolutions in an instant. Both of his arms lanced out at me and more blasts of black energy ripped through the air at me. I jumped as high as I could, and, with one mighty pulse of my wings, was able to clear the thunder that had been unleashed at me. I still had a firm hold of both of the chains and The Zarrulent was still leaning through the cascade bridge. Then he wasn't.

I may have eluded the attack that he had launched at me but I hadn't thought about maintaining the struggle when it had passed.

When I was on the ground, I had been able to maintain a grip on the stone cavern floor by gouging out holes with the talons on my feet. I had been able to anchor myself in a way The Zarrulent was unable to match given his snake like anatomy. His superior size and strength were being cancelled out by my grip. As soon as I had taken off, I had surrendered my only advantage.

With a snap, the chains were pulled tight and The Zarrulent again vanished back through the cascade bridge, only this time he was pulling me through with him.

30

I hit the surface of the cascade bridge with my head bowed, trying desperately to offer some kind of defence to the attack which would no doubt come as I burst out on the other side. I didn't know where The Zarrulent had jumped out to but I had to expect that he would be aiming for a place that was familiar to him. Snap images of what a stronghold of The Hive followers might look like flashed through my mind. What creatures of horror were going to be waiting for me?

I cleared the edge of the bridge on the other side and braced myself for the worse as I tumbled into a forward roll which would bring me back to my feet as quickly as I could manage. The ground beneath my feet was deathly cold and my feet sank into a freezing ooze which was now smeared all over my back and wings as I had rolled. Wherever I had been brought, it was pitch black with a stiff biting wind surging up into my face. I could hear distant sounds but nothing sounded right. Everything was distorted by the space that was between its source and my ears. The one thing that I could pick out clearly was the sound of the chains I had been gripping tightly to, clinking from somewhere ahead of me. The Zarrulent was moving.

Without thinking I poured out a wide spraying arc of fire in the direction of the sound of metal beating against metal.

There was no scream of pain, no muffled call of anger, no hurried movement. I had missed my target.

From the darkness, creeping out of the very wind itself, I could make out the jagged sound of The Zarrulent laughing. I focussed ahead, peering into the emptiness and nothingness that was ahead of me. I pleaded with my eyes to pinpoint my enemy but there was just the sound of his voice.

"I have bathed in the blood of the innocent and unthinking, boy. For thousands of years I have dreamed of breaking free, to taste the flesh of the weak, to devour whole civilisations. I have feasted on flesh again here and I will have more. The strength that it gives me is intoxicating."

I span around, looking into the air and all around me as I did, still flailing in the dark to find my target. Still nothing. Where was he?

"There seems to be a much more plentiful supply of food here now than when I was last here. It would seem that you can farm yourselves just as effectively as we can. So much choice."

The final syllable of his speech was drowned out by a deep breath of down draft from behind and above me. I hadn't been able to find him in the dark because he had been flying above me. Still not thinking of all the options!

I thundered my wings out and lifted myself from the ground, acting purely on instinct, hoping that I would be able to see where he had gone. I climbed quickly and was soon able to pinpoint his massive frame. Understanding washed over me as I set off in pursuit of the monster. I hadn't been jumped into a fortress of the demonic evil that was set to end the human race. I hadn't been jumped anywhere that could be described as a place of evil. The Zarrulent had been listening to one of the most basic urges that he could have. He was hungry and he had jumped us to a muddy field in the middle of nowhere that had been full of food. Sheep. The sheep were gone now. I could smell the blood which had been on the ground and was now all over me, caked on with the wet mud. He must have gorged himself with mouthfuls in the seconds he was through the cascade bridge before I started to pull him back through. That speed to devour such a large number in such a small space of time let me imagine the massacre he would be able to create if he made his way to a town or city.

The Zarrulent had opened up quite a lead on me. I beat my wings harder and harder as the lights ahead of us grew brighter. My fear was climbing uncontrollably now as I looked ahead at the bright expanse that The Zarrulent as aiming at. He had whispered about how the human race had farmed itself. The population of the world had grown incredibly over the centuries, giving him a much larger choice of what to eat but we have always basically behaved in the same way. We are a social species that has always grouped together. He was aiming at the bright city lights ahead of us which he knew would be a large gathering of people, lots to eat and all in one place. He had jumped out of the prison into a field in the middle of nowhere but he had made sure that he would be very near a large supply of

278

food; the sheep must have been a happy coincidence. He was now surging through the night sky towards the city of Cardiff. Wales' capital city was about to be hit by a supernatural force from thousands of years ago which had decimation of the human race as its only goal.

I pushed on as hard as I could, my already aching lungs burning from the exertion. A city the size of Cardiff was lit up brightly against the night's inky blackness and stood out for all to see for miles around. It became a perfect beacon to guide The Zarrulent into his feast and he was aiming at the brightest part of the city. He was either being drawn by the lights or the smell of the population, but his target was clear. He was focussed utterly on The Millennium Stadium. The international match that I had been so desperate to see was well under way and that meant that there would be over seventy thousand people in a very large bowl, all held together with nowhere to go. He was hungry and was going to start a massacre.

So much for being covert!

I could feel the muscles throughout my back and shoulders beginning to cramp and seize as I forced myself harder than my fitness could manage. Andrea must have been incredibly fit having seen her in full flight not looking like she was under any undue strain. Despite the laboured breathing and the ever increasing need for a jumbo massage, I was closing the distance between us. The Zarrulent had been regularly checking behind himself and had been aware of my progress. He didn't seem to be that hurried by my closing in on him. His wing speed remained constant and his right arm had remained curled up under his chest, I assumed, carrying the phasing chains that were still bonded to him.

The freezing night air whipped at my eyes as I followed him in towards the centre of the city. We weren't flying over hills and fields anymore. Instead we were now surging through the sprawling outskirts of Cardiff. Below us, I could make out houses, parks and out of town retail centres. I was already passed the point of no return in terms of resolving this without the whole of the world being able to turn the battle into the latest spectator sport. All I could hope for was that I could minimise the damage.

I unleashed a short beam of fire at The Zarrulent as we continued. The distance that separated us had been reduced to the point that fire was now a viable option. The flames splashed against his tail briefly. My aim wasn't perfect on the move but it seemed to cause him some pain. His head flashed around and an expression of annoyance was etched across his face. He held his gaze on me as we flew and I could have sworn that I could feel the delight coming from him as he bared his teeth at me in a hideous smile and locked his eyes onto mine. All four of his eyes.

The shock of seeing the damage that I had caused to his face completely healed was akin to being winded. How could he have been able to regenerate himself in that time? How could he have been able to regenerate himself at all! I was so shocked that my pace slowed. The Zarrulent was pulling away from me again, taking full advantage of my hesitation. As he moved off, he lifted his right arm and flexed his completely regenerated hand in a triumphant wave. He was showing me that he was back to full strength and I would have to start all over again. The burning in my lungs seemed to grow by a factor of ten as that thought hit home and it felt like the air temperature dropped by roughly thirty degrees. I needed help. All I could hope was that The Mage had managed to summon as much help as was available otherwise I was really going to be in for a very long night.

Shaking off the feeling of growing dread, I pushed myself on again towards The Zarrulent. He was now well out of my reach and there was no way that I would be able to get to him before he arrived at the stadium. Even from this distance, I could hear the cheers and screams of the crowd inside, seventy odd thousand people can make a remarkable noise when you get them all cheering at the same thing in a confined space. The roof of the stadium had been left open for the game; one or other of the team's coaches probably thought that being open to the elements would give them an advantage, so everyone in there was open to the elements but also the slobbering attack that was shaping to greet them. Every beat of my wings propelled me on but it was no good. Ahead of me, through the black sky of a February night, I could only watch as The Zarrulent slowed himself with a single powerful beat of his wings, and landed on the top of the stadium at one end, wrapped his mighty tail around the nearest of the external structural supports that stand at each of the four corners of the building and leaned himself over the empty space and peered down at the people below.

The screams started up instantly. They began as singular beats amongst the huge noise of the crowd but they were fast to spread as more and more people realised what was above them. The sound that had floated out onto the wind had been replaced by something that was tearing at the edges of the night. Even the sound was utterly desperate to be out from under the gaze of that beast.

Inside me, I felt my animal fury building at an unbridled speed. This was my country. These are my people. He was threatening my whole race and he was doing it at what was practically a holy event in my family. All fatigue left me in an instant and I could feel the heat building throughout my body as I snarled and roared my way towards him. I had totally lost control when I reached the stadium and poured down a vast pillar of flame at The Zarrulent as well as using his body to reduce my forward momentum. I slammed all of the talons on my hands and feet into the exposed back of my enemy and dragged them all the way to the top of his body. He had been reaching into the stadium when I hit him so he had been totally exposed. He must have thought that I was further away than I was. He snapped his hand up and out of the bowl of people he had been fishing in and clutched at his wounds.

Inside the stadium, players and crowd alike had started to scatter from the giant creature that was scooping towards them. My arrival had done enough to force all attempts at reaching a meal to be discarded by The Zarrulent.

I steadied myself through the air and came to an ungainly halt on the far side of the stadium. I crouched myself down onto all fours and funnelled all of the brutality that I was feeling into a huge volley of flame. It tore through the night sky and burrowed raggedly into the face and torso of The Zarrulent. He tried to cover his face the best he could but he couldn't take all of the attack on his arms. The smell of burning flesh filled the air and spilled down to the people below, causing even more panic.

"You are a god to these insects" The Zarrulent called over to me, his breathing shallow. "You don't need to die in a pitiful attempt to save them all. You could rule them from your stronghold. The Circle has been deciding who lives and who dies for thousands of years by not aiding these animals. Are we really any different from each other?"

My fury flared up again at the mention of any similarities between us but what he had said did give me a good idea.

Without any more words, I leapt out across the empty space above the pitch below, belching out wave after wave of searing fire as I went, and landed on top of The Zarrulent. Concentrating as much of my mind as I dared, I focussed my attention. The Zarrulent bucked and writhed as I dug my claws into him to maintain my grip. The stadium structure creaked and moaned at the exertion of having to support the extra weight of two violent lizards and I knew that I would need to act fast.

A blue/white light snapped into existence behind the Zarrulent and the smell of ozone filled the air around us.

"We. Are. Nothing. Alike." I spat out through gritted teeth, dug both feet into the nearest part of the structure of the stadium, and pushed for all I was worth. I surged forward, taking The Zarrulent with me and we both tumbled into the cascade bridge that I had opened. The final sense of Cardiff that drifted into the bridge after us renewed my strength more completely than any magical construct or secret weapon. The terror that had been pulsing throughout the crowd below had changed. Just as we entered the bridge, I could hear that there were cheers coming up from the people below. They were cheering. They were cheering for me. No-one down there could have understood what they had seen but they must have known that one of the monsters over them was trying to harm them and the other was trying to save them. Regardless of anything else, they were all rooting for me.

The warm feeling I got from that knowledge spread through me and I could feel my grip tighten on The Zarrulent. I was taking a big risk jumping us but I knew that I was going to make him look back at this day and marvel at his failure. As we fell, still locked in our struggle, I hoped that I would be able to take him where I was aiming.

31

We passed through my cascade bridge in an instant and crashed out onto a wide area of pitted scrub land. The Zarrulent landed hard on his back, taking both the full force of the fall but also the added problem of my weight. I was still sprawled on his chest with every available bladed part of my hands and feet dug into him.

The bridge gateway snapped shut behind me with only the faintest sound of sucking air and the blue/white light that had been illuminating the surrounding area vanished, plunging the whole area into darkness. I readied another burst of fire, aiming to roast the animal at point blank range. I was going to show him what I was really capable of. The spinning in my head rose from nowhere but I didn't care. I was slowly ripping into my enemy at close range and I was going to sear his flesh from his bones. In my head, my attack would be the final flourish of the battle but in reality, The Zarrulent was too fast for me.

Despite the pain he must have been feeling from the multiple anchor points I had in his flesh, he was fast enough to take a snap grip on the two curved horns that swept down on either side of my head, and force my face up and away from him. When the fire came, it poured uselessly up and into space, setting small fires in the trees that were walled not far from us. I strained and forced against his iron grip. The spinning in my head was growing by the second and now I was listening to it. I needed to break free to be able to continue my attack but I could also feel that he wasn't content to simply hold my head away. The twisting continued and I could feel that he was trying to break my neck.

Again and again, he snapped my head from side to side. He was hurt but his strength was still more than a match for my own. I risked releasing one hand from its purchase in his flank and began to slice at his grip. If anything, his efforts to snap my head off grew more ferocious despite my attempt to break free.

I struggled though possibilities in my head without any of them really being plausible. If this continued much longer, he was going to tear my head off and be free to go about his business of enslaving the human race. The only option that I really had at my disposal was going to be to break free and start the fight again, despite the risks of having The Zarrulent moving freely in the open. My head was jerking even more wildly now as my strength was drained from the continued focussed attack that was being poured into my vertebrae.

I took in one final deep breath and mentally crossed my fingers. I let all of my talons slip free from The Zarrulent and I crouched on his chest. Then, summoning all of the power I could muster, I pushed up and away from my attacker, at the same time as I unfurled my wings and beat them hard, aiming to propel myself skywards and away to freedom. My hope had been that the surprise of the movement would be enough to release me from the vice like grip that held me, but I knew enough not to put all of my faith in that single fact. As I forced myself up, I started up another column of fire. If The Zarrulent was able to maintain a firm grip on my horns, then my head would be snapped to be pointing straight down by the movement of the rest of my body.

For a split second, I remained in his grasp. My head whipped down as the explosion of force propelling me skywards was contained. He still had a firm grip on me and I had relinquished my grip on him. I opened up with the flame burst and I could feel a bead of panic forming in my chest. I had been so fired up by the noise coming from the crowd at the stadium that I had got slightly overconfident. I had expected to win the fight. My bravado had been driving me and I was about to see the errors of my ways.

The fire poured out and I closed my eyes, not wanting to look into the eyes of the demon that was going to kill me.

With a sudden, mighty jarring crack, I felt my head bounce wildly to my left. As the excruciating, white hot pain flooded my consciousness, my only thought was that I had just had my neck snapped. Images of being helpless as The Zarrulent towered over me, before he finally finished me off surged to the front of my thoughts. All I could do was keep the fire pouring out for as long as I could before I lost the control of my body. A second later, well, a second that felt like an hour, The Zarrulents grip of me was released and I surged away from him, all the time wildly roasting down my counter attack, still with my eyes closed.

It took me a handful of heartbeats to completely regain some semblance of my composure. Pain was coursing to all areas of my head and neck as I hovered above The Zarrulent who was roaring now himself. His tone carried both pain and blinding anger. In the open night air, his voice sounded like the inside of a thunderclap and it was rolling out in all directions, spreading fear as it went.

"Come back down here!" he boomed up to me as he coiled himself up to almost look as if he was sitting atop a writhing pile of rope.

I shook my head wildly, feeling my fear burning at the edges of my mind, but also still wanting to give this demon from before time just a little bit of cheek. As I did, the pain that had been crawling all through my head flashed to a pinpoint on the right side of my face. It felt like someone was pouring molten steel into my ear and I instinctively reached my hand up to the site of the pain. My scaled fingers found the cause of the pain immediately. The huge, ridged horns that curled around from the side of my Dragon head towards my mouth had been what The Zarrulent had been gripping onto as he had tried to tear my head off. When I had broken free of his grip, it had been the horn on my right side that had given way. I gingerly probed the open wound and could only deduce from the damage that had been caused that it had been ripped from my head whole in the same fashion used by dentists when they remove wisdom teeth.

I peered down with my hand still clasped to the right side of my head to see The Zarrulent grinning up at me. I could make out large areas of charred flesh on and around his head but he was more concerned about gloating. In his hand was my missing horn, blood covered root and all.

"Now, come back down here" he roared angrily, dropping the macabre trophy and thrusting out his arms towards me in an all too familiar gesture. I started to move to my left, swooping through the air in preparation for the onrushing pillars of black energy that were being summoned. They flew up at me but I was moving fast enough that they didn't connect. They sliced through the cold air next to me, merely metres from their target and it was then that I realised that maybe my gamble with the cascade bridge from the Millennium Stadium had been worth it. The Zarrulent unleashed another blast, then another. They both missed me but did confirm my initial thought. I hovered still, watching as The Zarrulent prepared his fourth shot, breathing hard from the aerial exertions and the pain in my head. He had me still in his sights and fired. The beam hit me square in the chest, but nothing happened. There was no surging pulse of power sending me cart-wheeling through the night sky, no explosion of fire as I was cut in two. Instead, the black energy scattered when it hit my chest and dissipated into nothing.

Utter shock and confusion rippled across The Zarrulents face, but only for a second before he fired again and again. Each time the effect was the same, I remained unaffected by his attack.

"You haven't infected the barrier to this place, have you? Your magics aren't going to work here." I slowly descended through the freezing air and drew his attention after me as I went. I finally landed and took on a full battle ready posture, wings splayed to make myself look as intimidating as I could. Directly in front of the main door of my estate.

From behind me, I could hear running footsteps pouring out as the battle ready staff from the house formed ranks at my side and the thrum of barely contained magical energy built up around us all.

The Zarrulent hadn't been paying attention to where he had been jumped. I didn't know if I was going to be able to jump us inside the shields that were held up around the mansion but it did seem that mustering more help could only be a good thing.

I risked a quick look down at the people who were gathering at my side. Familiar faces from all over the mansion were everywhere. Waiting staff, butlers, odd job men and women and all of the kitchen staff stood looking like they were experienced soldiers rather than the etiquette masters they had been presented to me as. They were all clothed in differing forms of what looked like medieval armour, set against the horror that was before them.

At the head of the vanguard of my reinforcements was the giant form of Mark Howell, the acting head of security. He looked up to me and smiled.

"Ready when you are, sir." As the last letter of his sentence fell from his lips, both of his clenched fists burst into a deep blue flame which was duplicated in his eyes. One by one, I could see that each person in the assembled fighting force was readying themselves for the charge. Bright colours could be seen jumping to life at various points in the crowd and I knew that each and every one of them would lay down their life for the cause should it be required of them.

My chest swelled with pride and I lifted my gaze back to The Zarrulent. I lowered my head slightly and set myself ready for battle. The Zarrulent did the same. I felt a new form of fury building inside me and it made a wicked snarling smirk crease my face. With a low roar, I called to my forces.

"Let's tear him apart."

The yells lifted from the people who were gathered around me in a shuddering boom and the bank of people surged forward as one. Beams of bright colours started to lance through the air, all aimed at The Zarrulent. They all splashed into him and he let out another roar, this time it seemed more of frustration than pain. He levelled all four of his eyes onto the nearest flank of approaching people and pulsed out his left hand, releasing a singular volley of the black power he had wasted on me. I looked on in horror as the beam caught half a dozen of the soldiers and instantly turned them all into rotting, decayed matter. Their corpses fell to the floor in piles of gore that caused the nearest of the survivors to panic and dive for cover.

Mark had remained at my side when the troops had leapt forward at the beast who had invaded our property and he called up to me.

"All we will be able to do to him sir, is annoy him. We can cause him a distraction but nothing more. He will still be able to hurt us here despite the weakness our shielding will provide. You are the only one who is strong enough to withstand his power." With that, he turned to face the distant fight and fired out four blasts of buzzing blue light, one from each hand and one from each eye. They all connected with The Zarrulent and seemed to make him stop for a second. Mark was obviously one of the strongest members of the house, magically speaking, but, by the looks of things, he was only really able to do as much damage as a bee would stinging a person, an annoyance but nothing life threatening.

I didn't waste any more time. Again, my overconfidence had been shown to be utterly misplaced and this time, people had died because of it. My own anger was quick to burn hot again and I spread my wings and took to the sky. I wasn't aiming at climbing to a great height but, instead, of keeping fast and low and using myself as a flying battering ram. Beam after beam of black evil flew around the battlefield and I could hear the screams of the injured as they scrabbled for cover as I flew. They were intermingled with the low sound of clanking metal which was coming from The Zarrulent as his remaining bonds danced around him.

Mark had been right about his power but he had also been right about the power of the force that was attacking him. They were causing a first class distraction and The Zarrulent was now totally focussed on burning down each and every member of the fighting force of The Circle that was attacking him. He seemed to have forgotten about me completely.

I was practically on top of him before he even registered that I was still a threat. Before he could mount any meaningful defence, I blew out a mighty column of fire and crashed into him with as much force as I could muster. I hadn't tried to slow myself in any way but had stretched my arms out ahead of me; talons aimed squarely at The Zarrulents head. The flames and the violent attack with serrated blades combined to force The Zarrulent to collapse backwards and get driven back through the ground, gouging a huge chasm in the earth.

I held the burst of flame for as long as I could before I darted off the prone monster and moved clear of his slashing hands. My head was spinning a hell of a lot more than usual so I started to weave through the open ground, expecting to have to dodge incoming attacks as The Zarrulent flew after me. I risked a quick glance around behind me as I went, prepared to see the huge leviathan form bearing down on me. But he was still in the furrow he had created. He was up and ready to continue the fight but he was still where I had left him. I turned to face him, feeling a little confused. I was in the middle of a battle so the spinning in my head was going to be warning me of various attacks but why was my sixth sense going so mad, warning of immediate danger, when my enemy was a good distance away and not actually pursuing me?

I stood still and breathed deeply, only now noticing that I had been running on adrenaline for a very long time. My body was aching all over but my head was now pleasantly numb. The open hole in my head where one of my horns had been had slipped totally out of my realm of sensation. I shook my head, trying to remove the spinning which was still there but was now starting to make me feel dizzy. I touched my hand to the side of my head and felt the sticky liquid that was still oozing strongly down the side of my head. I looked at my hand and then down onto my shoulder and chest. I was covered in my own blood and more was cascading out of the wound that The Zarrulent had inflicted on me. Realisation dawned and panic took hold. The spinning in my head may have been partially a warning but it had mainly been brought about by massive blood loss. I was bleeding to death.

I had to end this fast and get him back in his cage before I was too weak to be able to do anything. I dropped to all fours and surged back at him, charging on for all I was worth. I narrowed my concentration as I went, dividing my mind between keeping awareness of the battle that was being waged around me and the casting I needed to complete the task at hand. Mark and the rest of the troops were still doing a remarkable job of sniping at The Zarrulents flanks but I knew that I wasn't going to have him as distracted as I had the first time that I flew at him. As I closed the gap, behind my target, a large blue/white circle of crackling energy snapped into existence. I knew where the bridge was aimed. I needed to drive him through the magical construct I had brought into being and send us both back into the prison cavern.

I shook my head as I made my final approach, willing the fuzziness that was filling my head to keep at bay for long enough to complete my task. With one final effort, I leapt forwards and braced myself for the impact. I was working on the fact that I would be able to simply crash into him and force him through the bridge. I smashed into him as hard as I could. He had been following his human attackers again, still trying to do the maximum amount of killing. He had seen me coming but hadn't been able to fully catch and resist my thrust. We both tumbled through the air, almost in slow motion, directly at the circle of power. It was at that point that the cascade bridge flickered once, and then winked out.

We both fell into a heap on the ground and I felt that each of my limbs was made of lead. I tried to stand but my legs were sluggish at best and didn't want to respond right away. Looking around, I had expected to see the wrecked cavern and the pieces of the obelisk that remained and it took me a long second to realise that we were still in the grounds of the estate. The Zarrulent had taken in exactly what had happened. He pushed himself back up onto his coiled tail and faced me, laughing slowly under his breath.

"My magic isn't as powerful here as it should be but natural strength and the rules of the body remain constant. For one," he leaned down to push his face closer to mine, "I am stronger than you." His tone was dark again, like he was dealing now with a cool fury rather than any driving madness. "But, two" he continued. "If you lose enough blood, then, you will die."

I wanted to attack him as swiftly as possible, just to prove that I was still a danger to him but my body barely registered my intentions. Instead, The Zarrulent surged forwards and started to swing wildly at me with both his hands balled into wrecking ball sized fists. Blow after blow rained down on my head, my chest, my arms, it even felt like he was evenly spreading the punishment around enough so that it included my wings. I staggered backwards under the unrelenting attack, dimly aware of voices calling out from round me. The remaining forces that were still attacking The Zarrulent called out to each other, trying to organise some kind of strategy which would prevent their Dragon being pulverised.

Finally, with one almighty blow, The Zarrulent sent me reeling backwards through the air, body totally prone and unable to mount any kind of defence, until I crashed down on my back on the stairs of the mansion. Blood was now leaking from me at so many points that the injuries seemed to feel that they were all connected. I coughed as I struggled for breath, the pain in my chest making even the smallest movements seem like I was being dragged through a field of broken glass. I knew that The Zarrulent would be advancing on me but I couldn't do anything about it. My body was broken and I could barely open my eyes.

I forced myself to look at my end as it approached, thinking that the memory of my death would serve as an important reminder to the next Guardian of how not to do it. They would need all the information that they had at their disposal if they were going to be able to re-capture this slithering horror.

My eyes blurrily opened but fell upon a very different sight than I had expected. Leaning over me, with one hand on the side of my head, was a very familiar shape.

"Come on bach. The cavalry is here" said Lloyd, his beard looking even more wild than usual, and he gave me a slightly too hard slap on the cheek, which considering the difference in size between us, was quite an impressive feat.

The shouts from the defending troops were still drifting through the air but I could hear a certain level of panic to them now. The Zarrulent was still moving towards me at the doors to the mansion but he had still been taking out any people he could on the way.

I looked up at Lloyd, feeling a deep sense of failure winding through me as I did, and smiled weakly at him.

"What have you brought with you? The holy hand grenade?" I spluttered.

Lloyd smiled broadly and winked.

"Something better. Give him hell bach, for all of us." He then raised both his hands into the air, practically taking a run up to what he was about to do, and slammed them both down, much too hard, onto the side of my head which carried the gaping wound. For an instant my head was shot through with the purest and cleanest cold. I was about to unfurl a roar of agony but before I could summon the sound, the pain was gone. Replacing it was a spreading feeling of relaxation and gentleness. It drifted through me and touched at all of my injuries and I was filled with that sensation we all get when we are kids, wrapped up warm in bed, a feeling of wellness and belonging. My head buzzed with a feeling of warmth and all of the pain that had been filling my body was gone.

My eyes snapped open and I climbed quickly to my feet, turning back to face the on rushing beast. The Zarrulent was slithering over the uneven ground towards the house with the simplest goal in mind; he was going to kill me. I readied myself for the on rushing attack and hoped that Lloyd had taken cover. He was just out of his hospital bed so whatever he had just managed to cast on me must have wiped out a huge store of his power. I touched my head gently, checking for the condition of my most serious wound but found that it was totally healed. I could feel ugly scar tissue covering a huge area on the side of my face but other than that, I felt as good as new.

I didn't waste any time posturing this time. Without any more pre-amble, I dropped down onto all fours and started to bound towards the on rushing beast. The Zarrulent hadn't been expecting me to get to my feet after the pounding he had just meted out, let alone start moving at him, and for a split second I caught a glimpse of shock working its way over his face like a dark cloud.

We smashed into each other at enormous speed which must have been equivalent to two locomotives hitting each other head on. The thunder clap that came with our collision was enough to smash through the trees as the edge of the grounds and shake their branches wildly.

Blow after blow was thrown by both of us, each trying to bludgeon their way through the other. I knew what I had to do to get my foe back into the prison cavern; the actual imprisonment would have to be figured out on the fly. The Zarrulent continued to throw out all manner of energy bursts at me but they were still being affected by the power of the shield magic we had raised around the estate. They had started to have an effect on me and I could feel large areas of my armoured skin burning with unnatural cold or feeling withered by the force of the point blank range attacks. Thank God for the dampening of his power or I would have been pulverized.

I responded to each attack with a volley of fire and slashes of razor sharp claws, whipping my hands and feet out at any available point of attack. We both continued to roar at each other as we struck out and I could feel my fury building to drive each blow harder and each strike faster. At the back of my head I could feel a build up of need. I was closing in on the point of totally losing myself to the violence and not caring if I actually got this thing back into its cage. The growing need to totally give in to the animal part of me and to totally lose control and rip The Zarrulent to pieces.

He must have felt something from me as I continued to hammer against him regardless of what he was throwing at me. He must have realised that inside the boundaries of the estate, the playing field was at best level but more likely slightly tilted in my favour. I could hurt him wherever we were but under these conditions, he was losing.

With a mighty surge of both his arms, he unloaded a thick volley of power at the same time that he smashed at my chest and I was sent up and away from him. I travelled less than twenty feet and landed easily on all fours again and started back at him as soon as my inertia allowed me. In that split second The Zarrulent was trying to escape. The bridge gateway opened up behind him and he heaved his enormous frame backwards. By the expression on his face and the fact that he made no attempt to defend himself from me as he fell towards the gate, suggested that he was using a massive amount of his magical strength to be able to complete his casting within the boundary. I didn't even try to catch him but instead aimed directly at the following magical chains. I had used them to drag him back to me before so knew that it was probably the easiest thing to do.

I wrapped the chains tightly around my hands and heaved for all I was worth.

The cascade bridge collapsed immediately I pulled on the chain and The Zarrulent let out a mighty scream of agony as the enchanted metal running through him bit down hard, shattering the magic he had been trying to wield.

I kept on heaving against the force of the chains and inch by inch, The Zarrulent came closer and closer. He was gripping tightly to the insertion points of the chains on his body, trying to minimize the pain they could cause him.

"Now we go back to your hole!" All my fury was driving my efforts now and I was pulling him harder and harder with each surge of my own.

Concentrating as hard as I could through the physical exertion, I summoned up the picture of the Cascade Bridge in my mind again. It flickered into existence to my right as I forced as much power into the casting as I dared. I needed to get us through the gate as fast as I could otherwise it would collapse just like the last one had. The Zarrulent could see what I was doing and reacted by changing his focus. He stopped trying to reduce his pain from the chains and instead started to pull on them against me. For a split second, we were, again, locked in a titanic tug of war.

"You are right little one. This skirmish does need to relocate." Again, his voice thundered through the space around us like he had just exhaled a sonic boom. Only this time, with the slightest nod of his head, he opened up another Cascade Bridge opposite mine.

Immediately, I could smell decay and putrification pouring through into my senses. Wherever that gateway led, it was the basis for the forces of The Hive. I could just make out the sounds of skittering and clacking coming through with the odours which were assaulting my senses. Tyus had retreated there when he had attacked us outside the Abbey before I had gone through the Awakening and the sensations of a walking nausea coming through were far too familiar.

"I can see that you have an advantage here. How would legions of my forces fare against your little band?" He was breathing hard and grimacing through each and every word. I was having an effect on him and he didn't like it but I also knew that I had to get him through my gate as fast as possible before the whole estate was over-run by any number of slimy, greasy monsters.

As if to highlight the point, the end of that thought was accompanied by a collection of flashes from my Cascade Bridge. I needed to concentrate hard to hold it open and by the looks of things, holding a conversation while I was doing it was still beyond me.

"You're going back in your box" I roared out and sent a crash of flame out at The Zarrulent just to prove my point and started to heave against the chains again.

Nothing happened. He didn't start to move my way again. Instead he remained totally stationary, straining hard to counteract my force, and managing it. He smiled slightly at me and I could feel the force of the bridges between us shift as his became stronger and mine became weaker.

"Now, as I said" The Zarrulent gloated. "Let us relocate" and he made a dart for the open gateway to his reinforcements. I pulled as hard as I could, aiming to drag him away from his freedom. He boomed out to me, "You're coming to my territory now!" and pushed on.

I closed my eyes to hold my bridge open and I tried to summon up as much magical fire as I could. I had to stop him getting to that bridge.

Before he could reach the threshold of the Cascade Bridge there were three massive explosions directly at its mouth. Steam, flame and earth flew up and out in every direction and covered both of us in a hail of debris. I struggled to see through the clouds that were slowly drifting away, hoping to get a good look of my enemy but also to see the damage I had somehow just managed to unleash.

There was a huge pit where his gateway had been but now, all of the power had been released. The Cascade Bridge to wherever he had wanted to go was gone. Mine was still in place but it was now much bigger and much brighter. I could feel a buzzing force washing out from it and the energy seemed to be leaning ever so slightly into me, making it harder to breathe. It was now a much more powerful construct.

What the hell had I done?

Ahead of me The Zarrulent had brushed himself off and had set himself into a ready stance. He was prepared to fight again. I set myself and waited for the violence to recommence.

"You are correct. This fight does need to leave this place." The voice boomed out from behind and above me. The thick Russian accent very familiar.

I turned around to be greeted by Andrea in her Dragon form, hovering in mid-air with both of her hands out-stretched. She was accompanied by Dragons I recognised as Eugene and Wagdi, both of whom had smoke coming from their mouths, showing that it had been a combined effort from them that had taken out The Zarrulents Bridge.

I turned back to The Zarrulent and I could feel a wave of fresh fury surge through me.

"Come with me" I growled out with renewed venom, snapped my head round, and headed for the new Cascade Bridge, back to the prison.

32

I gripped the chains as tightly as I could and heaved myself towards the gateway at the same time that my reinforcements all unloaded volley after volley of energy at The Zarrulent. Beams of the cleanest cold from Andrea, boiling steams from Eugene and searing fire from Wagdi all crashed into The Zarrulent as he tried to defend himself and escape all at once. I heaved him on and reached the horizon of the Cascade Bridge. Without checking for further details, I dived in, yanking hard on the chains as I went.

Behind me, The Zarrulent was firing back beams of his own and they were all crashing home to their targets. The three Dragons that were aiding me were now under attack from this brute. Despite all of the advantages that we had, The Zarrulent was still able to have an effect as he continued his assault. My final effort put an end to his resistance though.

As the chains pulled tight, The Zarrulent was dragged quickly after me towards the hungry mouth of the Cascade Bridge. Letting out booming roar after booming roar, he struggled wildly to grip onto the ground. Furrows large enough to conceal hoards of men were slashed through the ground as he was dragged against his will towards the magical doorway which led back to his cell. Andrea, Eugene and Wagdi continued their bombardment, each time aiming at The Zarrulents hands as he tried to slow his progress, preventing him from having any effect.

Sliding across the cavern floor, I reached the other side and set myself to continue the effort. I dug all of the talons on my feet into the ground and dragged violently against the chains. Around me lay the ruins of the obelisk and the debris which had been shaken from the cavern roof by The Zarrulents escape, and in the centre of all of that was the huge hole that I needed to get my foe back into and somehow seal behind him.

Through the gateway, I could hear blasts of power and furious roars as the fight raged on despite my efforts. I continued to heave against the chains and I could make out the sounds getting closer.

Then, without warning, the chains in my grip went suddenly slack and I stumbled backwards at the removal of the tension I was straining against. A split second later, my enemy came smashing back into the cavern and the gateway fizzled out the second he had arrived, leaving the other Dragons back at the mansion.

Regaining my momentarily lost composure, I started to surge against the chains again, and began to drag the hulking beast back toward the obelisk. Only this time, he didn't move.

I turned to face him and found him slowly moving back to his fully upright position. He had wrapped the chains around his right hand and was leaning back against them, forming the other half of a gargantuan tug of war. He closed his eyes and took in a deep breath. It was only then that I remembered that the magical energy around and inside the cavern had been tainted by The Hive and that this would tip the scales back in his direction. He levelled his eyes back onto me and I could see a deep hatred pulsing behind all four.

"This will have to do" thundered across the cavern from The Zarrulent and he let out a volley of black energy from both his hands. The destructive power had returned to the blasts and smashed into me with unnatural force.

I took the blows in my chest and was thrown backwards. I slammed into the cavern wall and sent deep cracks splintering through the rock. In a second, The Zarrulent had blurred and was on top of me. He began to rain down blows with his huge hands, punching and slashing at me, while he unloaded yet more magical energy from his mouth and his eyes at close range. He was going to pulverise me at the very site that I was supposed to be at my strongest and I knew that I wasn't going to survive. Even if I somehow managed to get him back in his prison, there was no way that I would ever be able to get out from here. The best I could hope for was a suicide mission which would probably bring the whole cavern down on the pair of us. But there was no guarantee that that would be enough to hold The Zarrulent. I had seen him regenerate a lost limb so he would probably be able to put himself back together again after a cave in.

I sent out bursts of flame as a token gesture but the blows that were raining down didn't slow or weaken. I could make out the smell of burning flesh from above me but he was obviously pushing through the pain.

Agony was crashing over me like ocean waves during a storm. I could feel that my head was drifting away now and I started to think of my family and friends. Images of my uncle and my brother floated through my mind's eye and were quickly followed by pictures of Andrea, Mike and Lloyd. I hoped that they would be able to put some kind of defence together and that I wouldn't simply be remembered as the weakest link in The Circle who was responsible for the fall of the human race.

"Look at the past, bach" floated through my mind. It was Lloyd's voice. *"You are built to beat this animal. It is what you are – a Fire Dragon. Energy and attitude. Just know you can imprison him."*

The Zarrulent, seeing that I was lying limp on the ground, injured and defeated, had stopped his assault and leaned down to me and dragged me up the cavern wall by my throat so my lifeless body was at eye level to him. "You are weak" slithered from his lips. "You don't even know your true name, how were you ever going to defeat me?"

I heard what he said but just couldn't afford to let my mind focus on it.

Inside my head I shuffled through the shared memories of the previous Dragons, looking back to the single memory that showed this creatures defeat. As quickly as I could, I replayed the image of the defeat of The Zarrulent and this time, listened to Lloyds' words and didn't focus on the pictures. Funnelling as much of my remaining awareness into what I was doing, I pulled the mind of the Dragon to the forefront and became the warrior of the past.

And there it was.

With blinding clarity, realisation washed over me and the pieces that I had been struggling for fell into place.

The roar began in my mind but was soon washing out into the reality of the fight.

The Zarrulent hadn't been expecting any response from his prey so was utterly taken aback by the roaring outburst. I quickly followed the sound with a wild explosion of fire. The Zarrulent shielded his face from the heat as he was forced away from me. My focus was purely on him now and I pushed myself away from the wall of the cavern with all of the speed I could muster. I stretched out my arms before me and aimed all of the razor sharp talons on my hands towards his face. I slammed against him and began to tear and slash out with a wild fury that I had, up to this point, been trying to control. He struck back at me, sending more physical and magical blows out but I had truly lost myself in the realisation of what I had needed to do.

I slashed out wildly and kept on throwing fire for all I was worth. I had realised that what I was doing was going to be the end of me in the same way that it had for my ancestor all those years ago but I finally realised what the missing piece of the puzzle had been. The Zarrulent had nearly killed me but I was going to pour every last shred of myself into one final massive attack. Neither of us was getting out of here.

I could feel all of my anger and fury being channelled into my attacks and began to recognise that I was hurting The Zarrulent. Blow after blow landed, and with each attack, I could feel the destructive force of my enemy dropping. This spurred me on and I could feel the heat inside me rising as my arms and legs sped up their attacks. My vision was now completely clouded by a red cloak and I liked it. I roared out against the hot air which surrounded us and continued to strike out, faster and faster.

It was at that point that there was a blinding flash of orange flame and the truest form of the Fire Dragon showed itself. Flame erupted over the whole expanse of my back and spread out to totally cover all of my mighty Dragon form. The Zarrulent desperately tried to scramble away from the searing heat I was emitting but I followed after him, still tearing and slashing after him for all I was worth. I was going to end him.

He screamed out against the flame as I smothered him and heaved him backwards towards the open chasm in the cavern floor which led back down to his prison. I could faintly make out the sound of metal being dragged over stone but it was only just noticeable through the whirlwind of surging brutality which was driving my efforts. The enchanted chains which were still passing through The Zarrulent showed that there was more than just putting him in his box.

I wrapped my arms around The Zarrulent, pinning his wings and his arms as I did, I dug all of my claws into his chest. He roared out a booming scream of agony and desperation as he was pierced but also as he was being seared all over his body. His wings began to wither and shrink as my fire licked hungrily over his body, eating through all of him.

I responded to his screams with roars of my own, but they sounded now to be much different to what they had been. My calls had become deeper and much more 'animal'. I was truly letting my humanity fall away. I heaved the massive bulk of The Zarrulent up and slammed him as hard as I could back into the ruined hole under what was left of the obelisk, ripping my arms away from him without pulling my talons from him. I could make out his screams being punctuated by the new sensation of the smell of his blood as his bleeding body hurtled down back to his prison.

I stared down after him, watching as his battered body bounced and crashed through outcroppings of thick stone as he fell towards the deepest of deep places we could have mustered to hold him. I could feel the violence surging through every fibre of my body as I breathed deeply, showing the effects of the conflict that had taken place. It was at that moment that The Zarrulent showed that he was still far from defeated.

He reached out with both of his hands and dug his massive claws into the very walls of the chasm. Huge pieces of rubble were gouged out as he slowed himself, leaving two channels to show his path. He stared up at me and I could make out the hatred in his eyes. Despite his burned body, his ruined wings, I knew that he was still a threat so readied myself for whatever he was going to attempt.

"You can't simply throw me in here and expect me to sit still. You can't hold me because you are ignorant of what we are. You are so young, little one" was thrown up and out of the pit by The Zarrulent. He was looking at me and had seen me as the young upstart who was barely trained and that I wasn't able to do what needed to be done to hold him. The actions of Tyus and all of the agents working for The Hive had been designed to free their Master but also to coincide it with the arrival of a new Guardian. They had been hoping that the latest Guardian would be unprepared for the task they were being charged with and that that naivety would give them the advantage. Everything that had happened, almost through my entire life, seems to have been orchestrated by them. That thought fuelled the fire crawling over me like a living wave and I set my stance ready for the next step.

The Zarrulent smirked and heaved his left hand upwards to start his long climb back to the surface. It dug into the stone wall and anchored him firm.

"Maybe I'm not as young as you thought" I roared out down the tunnel to him and started the final part of what I needed to do, what I knew was going to be my final action in this whole conflict.

Reaching out my arms to my sides, I focussed as deeply as I could muster on the largest, most fierce, all consuming flame that I could imagine. The fire that had been writhing over my body like a caged animal waiting impatiently for the chance of freedom, poured down my arms and engulfed the remnants of the obelisk. I forced out more and more fire and screamed out to every last inch of the cavern surrounding us as I did. I knew that my family's work was going to be taken care of. I knew that all the effort that my Uncle had put into his charge not only as Guardian to The Zarrulent but also to me, as Guardian, was going to be worth it.

The cavern filled with a living flame and I could feel the temperature climbing to almost unimaginable levels. Roar after roar joined the dancing flame and before me I started to make out the super heated stone of the obelisk starting to soften and melt. The Zarrulent could feel the heat even from his lowly vantage point but he must have recognised what it all meant. With growing desperation he climbed, hand over hand, towards the surface.

The fire was surging around the base of the obelisk now, and it was doing it without further driving force from me. Reaching down, I took hold of two soft chucks of stone and raised them in front of my face. It felt like I was holding two negatively charged snowballs. Focusing all of my concentration onto the stone in my hands, I slammed them together into a molten mass and began to drag a single claw though the shape. With several quick strokes, I traced out the image of my mystical glyph, all the time pouring my internal fire into the casting. In ten seconds, it was finished.

The effects were instantaneous.

Deep within the pit, The Zarrulent let out a call of agony.

He had been making fast progress towards the surface but with the completion of the new glyph stone, his progress had been suddenly halted. He screamed out in pain and terror as the remaining enchanted chains that were still passing through his flesh seemed to jump to life. They were suddenly coursing with unnatural animation and seemed to be set on only one goal, the re-imprisonment of The Zarrulent.

They jolted straight down, as if pulled by a massive electro-magnet. The Zarrulent gripped tightly to the wall and resisted the force of the pull for all he was worth. He was incredibly strong but the effort of having to hold himself against the power of the ancient magic that was dragging against him was beginning to prove too much.

Above him, I walked slowly through the circling fire with the now completed glyph stone in my right hand, and leaned over the gaping hole that was the pit chasm and glared all of my power and contempt down towards him. The strain of resisting the effect of the age old magic pulling against him was clear for all to see but I could see that the fight was going to be short lived. With the last of all of my flaming energy, I heaved the new glyph into the form of the obelisk and completed the binding spell.

From below The Zarrulent, I could make out at least twenty writhing chains climbing out of the darkness below, each flickering in and out of sight as the magic that was driving them rippled over their surface. They made no sound at all, despite their heavy construction so they gave no forewarning to their target of their approach. The Zarrulent was focussed solely on me.

"We are legion. We are all immortal in The Hive" he spat out. "We will have you all."

It was at that point that the chains crashed into him.

The Zarrulents head rocked back under the weight of the multiple attacks and a dark blood spurted from his mouth. All four of his eyes focussed directly on me and for a split second, all time and motion seemed to stop and he was held suspended in mid-air. Finally his grip failed and I knew that the conflict was over.

The living chains seemed to pass effortlessly through him until there was as much length of metal visible on each side of him. He was pierced through his body, his arms and tail and even through his head but I was now totally aware that he was in no danger of death from his magical bonds. They were only going to be able to hold him but they would guarantee that he was unable to move far. The Zarrulent fell backwards, screaming as he went. The last I saw of him was his pain contorted form snapping wildly against his magical bonds as, around me, the waves of magical flame surged upwards and dragged with them the stone pieces of the new obelisk. Stone grated its way back into position and built the structure back to existence.

After thirty seconds it was complete.

The obelisk sat newly reformed and all the other glyphs were as they had been but they were now accompanied by a new, slightly rough looking, design. My handy work stared back at me from the wall of the new stone structure in the centre of the room and I realised that I was now woven into the history of The Circle.

Before the blackness took me and all of the flame that I had brought to my will had died, I could make out flashes of blue/white light and vaguely familiar voices calling out to me. I felt good that whatever voices they were, they were looking out for me but I couldn't make them out more than they were my friends. All except the deep voice at the back, slightly out of reach, whispering, out beyond the confines of my mind. Whatever that voice was, I was certain that it didn't like me at all.

33

Was I dead?

If I was, where was I?

If I wasn't, where was I?

My mind sat inside a magical marshmallow and relaxed back into it. There were no edges to poke in at me or make me have to concentrate. That would have been evil in the first order!

I could feel my mind drifting slowly through a gleaming white landscape of non-descript design. There were no features for me to orientate myself or identify what was happening.

I could sometimes make out smells of something I had recognised once before, then pictures of faces and places I thought I knew and voices that were still familiar. Nothing seemed to bolt together into a whole though so I wandered aimlessly through death, or at the very least my own sub-conscious.

"WAKE UP!"

The tone was very familiar. They were tired of having to wait for me. I recognised the sentiment but I recognised the thick Russian accent even more.

Very slowly, I forced against the gum that seemed to be holding my eyes shut and looked out onto the world for the first time in what had felt like a thousand years.

Andrea was staring down at me with that most familiar expression of mild annoyance etched across her face.

I looked up at her and grinned. "Your bedside manner may need a little work."

She rolled her eyes and turned her head away. She tried to hide the smirk on her face but she didn't get anywhere near.

I lifted my head as slowly as I could, not wanting to risk any pain from unknown injuries, and looked around my surroundings. Where was I?

The pristine white room was instantly recognisable as one of the medical suites back under the mansion. The tiled walls wrapped themselves around everything like a protective shield and I started to notice that I was hooked up to at least three different machines, all beeping or humming as they completed some medical measurement or procedure.

I wasn't alone in the room. Not only was Andrea sitting on the edge of the bed, but Mike was stood leaning against the wall on my right hand side of the room, looking none the worse for his violent abduction. The giant form of Mark Howell stood, almost to attention in the doorway. He was still wearing his chef's whites which now looked even stranger on him than they had done, after his displays of magical fighting. I laughed to myself at the blatant ridiculousness of one of the estates most powerful fighters dressed as a cook. Steven Seagal he wasn't.

The laugh brought me back to reality. I hurt like hell at every part of my body. Every inch of me felt like it had been doused in boiling hot, flaming oil and then someone had tried to put the fire out by beating at it with a wrecking ball. Not a good place to wake up.

I slumped back into the bed and took in a deep breath, trying to regain my calm. I was covered in bandages with some of them carrying varying size patches of seeped blood. I reached my hand up and touched gingerly at my head where, as a Dragon, one of my horns had been torn out. I had been expecting to find ugly scarring or at least a seeping wound. Instead, there was just a small patch of dried blood. It felt like it was barely there in comparison to some of the other injuries.

Andrea noticed me rubbing at the site of my injury. "You won't have any lasting scars and the horn will grow back for your Dragon form." I didn't say anything but I think she could see that I was relieved to hear that.

"How are you sir?" called Mark from the doorway. I looked at him and he was still rod straight and all business.

"I feel like I was beaten up by you." I let him know. By the look on his face he didn't seem to know how to take one of my sarcastic comments. I put him out of his misery. "I feel awful, but I suppose that the fact that I can feel anything is probably a plus." Mark tilted his head slightly and I knew that he agreed with me. Mike made his way slowly towards the bed and looked like he was the condemned man about to admit all of his sins to a priest. He fidgeted uncomfortably and didn't seem to know which way to look.

"I owe you my life sir" he started, reverting to the 'proper' greeting and ceremonial speak that everyone had been made to follow. That seemed to highlight the fact that he was feeling somewhat sheepish about what had taken place. He had been getting quite relaxed with me as his boss, which I liked, but the weight of responsibility was making him revert to his servant persona.

I gripped his arm and looked him in the eyes, "That was my job, and I would have done it even if it wasn't. Just remember that the creatures who are set against us have been at this a very long time and that they are going to keep trying. This wasn't the first time that The Zarrulent has escaped so we'll make sure that he doesn't do it again. You are part of my team here Mike, always remember that." Mike dropped his head and seemed to take in what I had just said. Maybe I was more capable as a Guardian than I thought.

"Ah" I added before Mike could walk away. "You can also remember that I don't like being called sir. You too Mark." Both of the men stood chastened, as if they had just received a serious dressing down. So much for the relaxed air. This was going to take a long time to work through.

Andrea stepped in before any more social discomfort ensued from my attempts at humour. She thanked the other two men for their efforts and quickly shooed them out and shut the door. We were suddenly alone again and I couldn't help my mind drifting back to what had happened the last time we were in a similar position. I'm not sure if it was my imagination, but Andrea seemed to slink her way back to sit on the bed at my side. I could feel a nervousness hovering over her as she made her way to me. Was she thinking the same thing?

She sat down slowly, this time much nearer to me than she had been earlier. She gripped my wrist lightly and I could see that she was showing a deep concern for me. I covered her hand with my own and looked into her eyes. Her apparent concern seemed to highlight my situation. I could feel a frivolous comment wanting to form in my mind but there was now a shadow cast over where it wanted to grow. I could feel in my mind that something had changed in me and that Andrea could understand what had happened. I knew she was the one to fill me in on the details.

"What happened to me?" It was the only way I could feel to start and I could sense that there was a great deal to go through.

"We didn't see the end of your fight" she began. I was reasonably sure of what had happened myself but it would have been nice if someone else had witnessed my victory, ego and all that.

"We were finally able to bridge jump in after numerous attempts and we found you in Dragon form, collapsed at the edge of the ceremonial platform. The power of the binding was strong and in place and we all knew that that must mean that The Zarrulent was back where he should have been."

"Eugene, Wagdi and I carried you out through a new bridge but you were fighting us in a delirious state all the time, shouting about imprisonment and stone and Mike. Wagdi worked out what you were trying to say and we pulled Mike out as well. You have been in the infirmary ever since." She looked around the room as she completed the tale, just to emphasise our location.

Ever since? How long was 'ever since'?

"How long have I been here?" I asked feeling a cold dread building in my stomach and crawling up my throat. Thoughts of months or years having passed filled my mind and a subtle panic took root.

"You have been here for twelve hours." Andrea stated in a matter of fact tone but I could tell that she was enjoying the fact that I had been expecting to wake up a million years later.

I slumped back in the bed and felt stupid. Andrea smirked again and felt superior. The shadow in my head didn't go away though.

"How did you finish off The Zarrulent?" she asked and the 'all business' tone had returned. She looked as if she was interested on the human level of how a member of her group had succeeded but it did look like she wanted to know all of the details so she could be better prepared if she was ever called upon.

"I remembered all of the lessons – and did the opposite."

She sighed and frowned again. Still not the right time for jokes.

Taking a fleeting second to attempt to wrap some kind of order on my memories, I began.

"Lloyd's directions had led me to look at my memory of the earlier fight here in a different way. Every time I had looked back through the details of the previous fight, I had focussed solely on the moves that the Dragon had used, what techniques he had employed. This time I looked inwards, into the mind of the Dragon and it all fell into place. I am a Fire Dragon and at my heart, as people have been telling me from the beginning, is a boiling, fiery rage. I am the servant of my fury. I had let it get the better of me in the past and had almost gone off the deep end in the mansion when I was on the tour." By the look on Andrea's face, she remembered that event clearly.

"I've been told that my Uncle had had the same issue when he took out another Circle members mansion by transforming inside because he couldn't control his temper. Despite all of the magical ability and flight training, at the very core of what I was, was an unbridled violence that was passed down through the Dragon line. I could summon fire to my will and control it and that was something that could severely damage The Zarrulent. I could burn him down but I needed to really let go of my human mind and become the wild Dragon to defeat him. Every lesson I have had so far has centred around me being calm or having pure focus so I could complete the castings. Lloyd led me to see that I needed to go wild. I had been getting wildly angry during the fight but I had never really let go."

"As I had examined the mind of the previous Dragon to fight this fight, all I found was the overflowing animal mind. He had totally let himself go to re-capture this beast but at the very heart of him, the only thing that I could make out, was a single image, one that was feeding all of the animal fury. It was the picture of a woman. The Guardian had been thinking about his wife."

Andrea looked at me with a blank expression on her face. She still didn't understand.

"He knew that he would never let anything happen to her. He aimed his fury at The Zarrulent and had been able to defeat him because he knew that he would give everything he was, unmake himself utterly, to make sure that she was safe."

I adjusted my position in the bed slightly as I had found the excitement of the tale such that I was moving around a little more than was comfortable.

"In every lesson I've had," I continued after I had found the most comfortable position I could, "I had been told to keep calm and focus to get the best results. If I wasn't focussed, I managed nothing. That was good advice for magical control as a beginner, but when I was faced with the fight my whole family line was picked for, I had to totally lose control. I had to really let my temper go to really do the damage. No-one knew this before because the only other Dragon from this line to have this fight died before he could tell anyone what he had done."

Andrea regarded me quietly and I could see on her face the questions that were lining up in her head, all fighting to be the first one asked.

"What did you do to defeat him? How did your Fire Dragon line fury show itself?" The purely business part of her mind won the day.

I thought back to the sensation of watching an almost living, malevolent flame pour out over my body and for it to want to react to my every command. The sheer power of it, the real fury. How do you describe the feeling of having one of the most destructive forces on the planet aching to do your bidding? How can you tell someone that an ancient force had been bent to your will and that a very real part of you that you didn't even know was missing, was given back?

"I summoned fire to me. I called at so much of it that I was able to melt the very stone of the cavern. I reached so far back through time to drag every inch of any power I could to my hands. The Zarrulent tried to run from the fire but I didn't let him." I recounted as close as I could in a serious tone. I knew that this power wasn't something to joke about.

The answer hung in the air for a handful of seconds. The only sound in the room was coming from the medical machines as they went about their tasks regardless of the activities around them.

Andrea sat stock still with an expression of what looked like awe on her face. She finally re-gathered herself and leaned a little closer.

"But how did you find that power? What was it that allowed you to really let go of your human self to become that power?" She really was all about the details.

I shifted my weight in bed again. I knew that this revelation could leave a lasting effect.

"I thought about everyone that would be in danger if I failed. Everyone who is important to me and what would happen to them. I knew that I would tear every piece of The Zarrulent apart to protect my loved ones." I lifted my hand and took hold of hers. "The thought of anything bad happening to you was all I could see. I did the same as the first Dragon and focussed on someone I cared for. It was a purely animal need to protect that was fuelling my fire."

We both looked down at the sheets nervously, neither of us really sure of what to do or say. Andrea was the first to react.

She slid her hand from mine and stood up from the bed, straightening her clothes as she did. She looked nervously around the room and back to the door. It looked like I had read her signals wrongly.

I straightened myself and scrambled for a way to re-start the conversation before the silence became too wide to cross.

"How is everyone else? How much damage did The Zarrulent do?" Keep it focussed on business.

Andrea looked me in the eye but her expression seemed to grow even more sad.

"We lost forty two people. Twenty nine from magic from The Zarrulent, twelve from physical injuries from the attack and," she paused "one person to a life casting."

"A life casting? What's a life casting?" Back to not knowing again.

Andrea took a step backwards and straightened her clothing again. She looked like she had developed a very odd nervous habit.

"A life casting is a massive healing spell. The caster will infuse a mortally wounded victim with their own life force to save them but it will drain a massive amount of power from them. Only the strongest of healers can cast it with any kind of safety."

"So the caster wasn't strong enough to do it safely. Why did he do it then?" Keep it business Anthony, focus on the details.

A single tear rolled down Andrea's cheek as she looked back up to me.

"You were dying. He knew that you would be the only one who could stop The Zarrulent. He knew that he was going to die but did it anyway."

I looked back through the memories of the battle and scanned through the events to sort out the details. Pictures bounced through my head and the final fact hammered all of the air from my chest. Through the haze of rolling, grief driven madness, I could make out Andrea leaping at me and crashing us through the newly formed Cascade Bridge she had summoned at the head of the bed. I thrashed against her and screamed for all I could as we both crashed into the muddy ground outside the mansion, both transforming as we went. I had realised what had happened the previous night and Andrea had known that it would make me react in this way. She had been prepared for the need to jump us out.

I had looked back to the fight and had realised who it was.

The person who hadn't come to see me.

Lloyd.

34

Our Dragon forms writhed on the ruined lawn of the estate as I unloaded my anguish. All the pain was gone from me as I roared into the clear blue February sky. Andrea tried to control where I was aiming my outburst but she, for the most part, just let me vent.

Lloyd had been the first person to lead me into the hidden world of The Circle. He had been the person who had let me see the full picture of my family and of where I fit into the big picture of the safety of the human race. He had been the one person who had tried to really get to know me on a human level rather than simply as the new head of the house. And now he had died to safeguard me. Another life lost to a mis-guided sense of what was 'proper'.

After what felt like hours, I crashed down into a whimpering heap of leathery scales and pointed horns. I heaved in breath after breath as I struggled for air as I cried. Andrea changed her grip on me to reflect my state. She had gone from a firm force, ensuring that I never got close to hitting anything important, to now cradling me next to her, rocking slowly back and forth as she did.

There was no reaction from the house at my actions. No crowds of people came streaming out in reaction to the explosion of reptile cries. They must have all heard about what had happened and been waiting for me to get word. I must have been the last to know. Everyone in the infirmary had been on edge, reverting to type and hadn't even vaguely reacted to my humour. They were all feeling the loss of the house. It wasn't just my loss to bare, but they did all need their Guardian to stand up and give them a focus.

Andrea spoke softly into my ear.

"He knew what he was doing when he went to you. He was casting to safe-guard life." Her voice was enveloped in the rolling low sound of thunder but I could hear the tenderness coming from it despite all of the unnatural elements surrounding it.

"He knew that you were the only one who was going to be able to stop the beast. Other Guardians could have done some real damage to The Zarrulent but it was only going to be you who could defeat

312

him." Her accent curled itself around all of the words and reminded me that I was part of something bigger. I straightened myself up and stood staring at Andrea.

"So, another person had to die for me." The words growled out and I could see that Andrea was taken aback by the venom coursing through them. She took a step towards me but I pulled away from her before she had the chance to touch me.

"Anthony. You will see a great number of people die during your lifetime; it is a drawback of your own survival. People here are all aware of the roles they fulfil. You need to understand where you are in the big picture." Her voice was pleading now, gone were the hard edges of her more familiar tone.

"The people at each estate are the same. They have all come from a family line of people who have sworn to serve The Circle and safeguard the entire human race." She stepped forward again but this time I let her rest her hand gently on my left arm.

"Since you have arrived here, you have been angry at what you see as the useless servitude of everyone here as they follow traditions and conventions that you don't understand or see as relevant. Those traditions are what drove Lloyd to do what he did." Her grey eyes focussed deeply on mine, showing me that she was pleading with me to understand.

"Everyone in The Circle can feel where they fit into the whole and can feel that they are a vital link, regardless of their position. We all know that we are reliant on the actions of those around us to complete our task of chaining the worst of the enemies of the world we live in. We are all ready and willing to fall to complete what we need to."

I looked in her eyes and felt my budding anger start to fade. I had seen Andrea become a fearsome beast of untold power but now she was talking to me like someone on an equal footing – a colleague even.

"Lloyd believed in you utterly, as he believed in The Circle and everything that we are trying to achieve. He looked on you like a member of the family and as such was going to do everything in his power to protect you. We are all in a fight that seems to be destined to last until the end of time. There have been so many people who have fallen already and there will be so many more to come. We all share the same task. That is what makes us all family."

Her final words felt like a needle point shot of understanding. My family was splintered by forces outside of our control but I had been protected from the horrors of the world by Lloyd and the other members of the house, my extended family. Lloyd had shown his pride in the Dragon line when we had been lost in the woods of the estate and I was re-living the past memories of a former Fire Dragon but I hadn't understood why he was so caught up the past. Every single person in the mansion was going to die if I asked them to. Not because I asked them to, but because they would give everything to protect what was being done. Everyone could feel the roles they had at the very core of who they were. And that meant that I hadn't lost everyone in my family. My new family was all around me in The Circle.

I felt a little off balance as I came to the final conclusion but I could also feel an emptiness inside me, which I hadn't really acknowledged, filling up. I laughed to myself as all of the previous fury left me and I was left with a feeling of long sought after belonging. Andrea dropped both her arms from me and moved slightly away, obviously wary of what I was going to do next. I didn't let her worry that long.

Lunging forward I took hold of both her arms and lowered my head so that we were staring nose to reptilian nose.

"This house is in mourning and as such we will respect *all* of the members of the house who have fallen today" I growled, pouring as much ceremonial pomp into my voice as I could, trying to mimic the power that Lloyd had been able to muster. She looked back at me, trying to work out what I had meant.

I let go of her arms, whirled round and headed back towards the entrance of the house, filled with a purpose I hadn't expected to feel. I could finally understand the facts that had seemed so alien to me ever since I was first told of The Circle's existence. Focusing my mind on the mental image of my human form next to my Dragon form, I closed my eyes and dropped myself back down to the man I was and strode with a naked purpose back into the entrance hall of the mansion. I didn't know how long it would take to achieve, but I knew that, as Guardian of the estate, I owed it to every single person within the boundaries, to provide the fallen with a proper burial.

The Circle was bigger than just the Dragon Guardians and should be viewed as such from now on.

My wishes were carried out at lightning speed by each and every member of the staff that was involved. Mike and Mark had been the driving forces behind what I was doing and they made sure that everything was in place in less than six hours.

As the sun set on a very cold February day, a snaking column of people left the house by the main doors and made its way across the pitted and scarred surface of the grounds towards the largest crater in the former lawn. Each and every member of the household was dressed in well tailored formal attire as would befit a ceremonial funeral. At its head, Andrea and I led all of the staff out in mourning. We both wore long black ceremonial robes with the hoods raised. Mark had dug them out of some deep stores but I don't think anyone was that sure what they were really for. We led the line of people down inside the rim of the crater, leading everyone down towards the edge of the water which was cradled at the bottom.

One by one, the staff from the mansion filed into the crater and took up their positions. All eyes were fixed intently on me as a low murmur began to roll around the bowl of the crater. Raising my hands above my head to signal that we were beginning, everyone fell silent and looked on.

"The Circle has won a massive victory here and every single person here should take pride in what they have achieved." My voice boomed out into the gathering dusk, vapour from my breath curling out with every word. The crowd remained silent but I could see some heads nodding.

"We have all lost someone close to us here, and it was the actions of each and every one of us that have led us to this point. I vow, as Guardian, that we will honour everyone who has fallen in our service and as such, this monument, on the very field of our greatest victory, will bear witness to all those who have fallen in service of The Circle." This time there was a strong wave of agreement from the gathered crowd, growing louder as more people voiced their feelings.

"I ask each of you to honour those who have fallen by casting their names into the water. Let them be held dear to us all and be remembered!" My voice climbed in volume and I could feel an intensity of feeling that would have seemed alien to me only a week ago.

One by one, the surface of the water in the crater erupted into ripples as small stones hit. Pride filled me as I watched every single fallen member of the house honoured by their comrades. I had spread the word that everyone who had fallen was going to be remembered as the Dragons were, and that each and every member of the house would be able to show their respect to their family and friends. Mike and Mark had made certain that the area I had chosen for a memorial would be both safe but also respectful. Their efforts in the crater were perfect. They had carved steps and balconies in the exposed stone walls and made it usable as a lasting memorial to the whole staff of the estate. Leading down from the rim of the crater at numerous points were ornately lined stairways which bore the same style of ornamental decoration as the main stairs in the mansion. The stepped viewing platforms all had heavy slate guards to them which made me think that in another time and place, they would have been perfect for the balcony scene from Romeo and Juliet. The whole area had been transformed from a site of destruction to a place of remembrance.

Now we all watched in silence as small stone coins baring the name of the person who had died were cast into the pool for history to watch over. Every family line within the house would now be able to remember those who had fallen in their duty. Behind me, the mighty slate statue that Mike had been responsible for stared down at everyone. A huge duplicate of the Dragon in the room of stone coins had been placed to stand guard over the memories of our dead. From now on, everyone would be remembered and everyone would be honoured.

As the water finally settled back to stillness, I looked down at the small stone coin in my hand. Lloyd Jones was carved deeply into it. I smiled to myself and ran my thumb over the letters. I hadn't known him very long, but in that time Lloyd had certainly made a big impression on me. As I heaved the stone into the water, the last member of the armies of my house who had done what they needed to do was cast to rest. With no sound, Lloyds name sank into the blackness and settled for ever. I watched the ripples fade and felt the cold air crawl over me, making me shiver.

Lloyd Jones wasn't going to be the last name I would have to cast into the water.

Looking out at all of the staff of the estate, who were now much more than just staff, I could see that they all looked back at me with the same burning fire that I had curling through me. We all knew that we would do anything for each other. That we were home.

The people were dismissed and slowly started to drain their way back to the mansion. I watched them go and felt glad. I had a family again.

Andrea slowly slid up to my side and we watched everyone drain away.

"I will need to return to my house Anthony. You did a good thing. I will speak to you soon." Her voice was calm, but sad. I could feel the resolve in it, that had seemed to be a solid building block of Andreas personality no matter what she had to do but I could feel a hint of distant longing, just at the edges of her accent. What was she feeling?

I turned back to face her, wanting to ask her all the questions that were forming in my head and to pull her to me a hold her against whatever she was feeling, but she had opened a small Cascade Bridge behind me, and had stepped through before I could make any comment. With a bright snap of light and a boiling smell of ozone, the bridge closed and I was left alone.

I stood looking at the space that the ring of power had held, blinking away the burned after image from my eyes. Andrea had never run off before. She didn't have the same cold certainty to her as she had in the past. Maybe I was making her think? That would be a first for both of us.

As the last of the gathered people left the memorial, Mike casually drifted to my side. He settled next to me and we both looked out over the waters and towards the house. The cold breeze which had been lazily circling the area was now beginning to pick up speed and drop in temperature. The sun was gone from the sky and was dragging the last remains of light after it. At the nearest edge of the wooded ring which encompassed the entire estate, a low mist was starting to form and climb up the tree line. I could feel every film ending come to mind as I casually scanned the tree line. Images of ghostly warriors watching over us filled my head. But there was no-one there. Focusing back to the departing mourners I brought myself back to the here and now.

Mike spoke first.

"They all appreciated what you have done here sir." Neither of us took our eyes from the departing crowd.

I could feel a level of pride developing as I finally felt more at home in what I had to do but that was quickly followed by a twinge of shame at having to be called sir by Mike. Turning to him, I knew exactly what needed to be done.

"You're never going to stop calling me sir are you?"

He half smiled back at me and replied, "I may do one day," and with extra force, "sir".

It made me smile.

"You're promoted" I blurted out. Mike stood silently before me and didn't move or react in any way. I moved quickly to put him at ease.

"Lloyd was Head of House. I need that position filled as fast as I can and the person has to be someone I can trust but also someone I can actually get on with." I placed a hand on his shoulder and smiled at him, trying to look reassuring. He looked back at me, his eyes flicking around wildly as he obviously ran through different thoughts and emotions in his head.

"Lloyd was my friend. So are you. I think you're qualified and I think that Mark will be able to look after the kitchens, don't you?" My voice had no trace of forced ceremony to it as I tried to speak to Mike on a more personal level.

Eventually, his face cracked into a huge, relieved grin and he boomed "You're on!" and he slapped me on the arm, just a little too hard. The position of Head of House had just been passed on.

"I believe you have one more duty to attend to sir." Mike was straight to business. I scanned through everything that I had asked him to take care of and came up with nothing that was still outstanding.

Before I could ask him what he meant, he dug into the pocket of his jacket and reached out his closed hand to me, offering me whatever was in it. I held my hand out and waited. Mike dropped the two stone coins into my hand and was already walking back towards the mansion when I realised what they were. David Davies and Steve Johns had been intricately carved into the stones. I had completely forgotten that these names had a place to hold here as well as where they were to rest in the real world. I let the tears fall without even trying to stop them. I could feel the loss of the two people whose names sat in my hand but I was also happy that I had found so much more, an extended family here in the mansion and The Circle as a whole.

I pulled my robe off and draped it over the stone balcony next to me. Pulling in all of the power I had at my disposal, I threw my head back and roared out at the night as I became my Dragon self. I kept a tight grip on the stones in my hand as I did and screamed out for everyone to hear that the former Guardians had passed but that I was more than ready to take up their burden.

The animal cry floated out through the evening and reverberated around the bowl of trees at the edge of the estate. There was no other sound around as I roared. It felt as if all of nature had stopped to allow me to give my family the respect their positions had deserved. After a minute, I fell silent and breathed heavily into the air, just looking out over the estate.

Shrinking back down to my human form, I dressed myself in the robe again and started my way back to the mansion. Everyone else had disappeared from view and the night had fully enveloped us all. The stones in my hand were going to hold a place in the memorial for ever and I felt good knowing that my brother and uncle were always going to be with me. All that was left for me to do was lay Steve to rest back in London. He may have travelled all over the world trying to get away from what he thought were the ramblings of a crazy old man, but his home had been in London.

Mike stood in the doorway as I climbed the stone steps towards the ruined facade of the mansion. He greeted me with a shallow nod.

"Can you prepare a car for me please? I need to get back to London as quickly as I can."

Mike looked worried for a split second but seemed to realise what I had in mind.

"Not bridge jumping sir?" He was aware of what I could do even if it hadn't even crossed my mind.

"No, I think I'd like to do this the old fashioned way." I strode into the house and Mike made his way off to prepare the car.

An hour later I was heading down the gravel driveway in a pristine Mercedes Benz. I was wearing a very expensive charcoal grey suit with a black shirt and I felt very different to the man I had been when I had first entered the estate. I had left the names of my Dragon family inside the memorial and was now heading back to my old life to prepare for yet another funeral.

35

As it had turned out, Lloyd had been much busier when he had been making arrangements for Steve's funeral when we had first met. All I had to do was follow a list of names he had left on my kitchen table and everything else had been taken care of. As such, I had found myself walking up to the front of the Bar where this whole series of events had seemed to start from, after the small funeral for Steve, at a little after lunch time. I had seen how a shared knowledge of the Dragon line could direct me so the feeling of autopilot bringing me here didn't seem out of place, I had a whole library full of good memories from this place, and they were just from me.

The front of the place had been repaired very quickly. Lots of new paint and glass formed the doorway but it still looked like they had a way to go before they were going to be finished. There was still some bare plaster board visible and all of the new construction was missing the final coating of paint. Still, it was looking more like the place to spend time again rather than the site of an accident.

Easing in, I could feel the uncomfortable memory of my brother's death here, sitting in the corner of the room. No matter how many good memories I had had here, this bar was always going to be coloured by the image of Steve after the attack. I pushed that away and dragged up the memory from the cavern fight instead. Seeing Tyus, the creature responsible for the pain of the last memory, being pulled to pieces did soften the edges of the previous image.

Drawing myself up a little taller with the feeling of triumph, I made my way to the bar, nodding to the few familiar faces that were dotted around the space. People looked me up and down as I strode to the bar. I was always a jeans and t-shirt kind of a guy so the expensively tailored suit must have seemed a little out of place on me. As I strode on though, I realised that it didn't feel out of place.

Behind the bar stood a different woman from the last time I had been here. Seeing a man die on one of your first nights had obviously been too much for the previous barmaid. I thought to myself that I would have reacted in the same way had I not then seen the magic and monsters I had.

"What can I get you?" she asked brightly, a casual smile playing across her lips.

"Double Whiskey please." Not my usual but it felt more like that kind of a day.

"And for your lady friend?" and her eye line lifted from me and passed to my left. I turned to follow her gaze and my eyes landed on the perfectly tailored form of Andrea as she drifted in and sat down on the stool next to me. We must have looked like we belonged together.

"Iced water please." Her accent seemed to be made of treacle it was that thick. Maybe just hearing her here made it stand out a little more? The barmaid nodded and prepared our drinks.

As she left us, I sat down next to Andrea and took a sip from my glass. The warmth of the Whiskey felt good on my throat. I'd kind of got used to heat over the last few days.

"This is a pleasant surprise. What brings you all the way to London today? You left in quite a hurry the last time I saw you." I faced her and smiled. I had hoped to hear an explanation for her rapid exit from the memorial but by the look on her face, she wasn't going to bite. She stared straight ahead and dropped a newspaper on the bar.

"You had quite a night on Saturday, didn't you?" she whispered and pointed at the paper. Across the front page was a crystal clear image of a massive white clawed hand swiping into the bowl of the Millennium Stadium while a fire breathing red Dragon was crashing into the monster who owned it from above. The feeling of fear and embarrassment surged through me at high speed and I could feel the beads of sweat breaking out all over my body.

What had I done?

Andrea didn't turn to face me but rolled her eyes in that all too familiar way. She wasn't happy but this time I could see why.

"Anthony, you will need to be more careful in the future. All our efforts to continue the world as it is are bound by keeping our existence a secret. Staging part of a magical battle between demons of fantasy at an international sporting event is not wise. What's next, the Olympics?"

The last question was covered by a very slight laugh. That made me stop and think. Before I could start asking all of the questions that were swimming through my head, she turned to face me finally and continued.

"The Circle is very powerful Anthony, and in more than just magic. We have been spinning the whole event as being a staged show as part of the game. The world thinks that it was a puppet and light show and the various powers involved are all trying to take credit for what has been widely agreed as the best stage show ever. We even managed to explain away the fire at Neath Abbey as being an act of isolated vandalism." She sipped from her glass and let me feel like a chastened child.

"We're still hidden? The Circle I mean." I scanned through the story as fast as I could, trying to glean as much information as I could from the text.

"What is easier to believe? Would the public believe that they had seen a pair of magical leviathans fighting in plain view or that a show to celebrate the game had taken place which had contained radio controlled puppets? People as a whole 'know' that Dragons don't exist. Science has told them all that there must be a simple explanation to the issue." Relief washed over me as I slumped down into the stool. I could feel the celebrations start to build now. The paper had also explained that the sight of a fire breathing red Dragon had inspired the Welsh team to a rousing victory.

Andrea sipped from her water again, but this time stood up, straightened her jacket, and made her way towards the doorway.

"We can continue this conversation in a while but for now I need you to come with me." She stood with her weight on one hip and flashed me a very seductive smile. All of the guys in the place who had heard her speak that last sentence to me from across the bar started to giggle ever so quietly. I even got one knowing wink from a bearded man in his sixties who was sat by the door. He wasn't someone I knew but even he could see what was going on.

I threw the paper down on the bar, finished my drink and started towards her, aiming to look like I was moving in a very cool and detached way. To everyone else in the place I must have looked like a dog being called to heel. The giggles got louder. Barry and John even managed a wolf whistle amidst the now barely contained laughter.

I followed her outside and we started to make our way towards the back of the building, her swaying her hips as she went to really sell the idea of seduction.

"Where are we going?" I called after her. Andrea stopped and let me catch her up.

"We are required elsewhere by The Circle." She spoke with a very thin veneer of confusion to her voice. Her expression let me know that she had thought that point to be obvious. "We need to continue your training and both of our skills are needed in Peru. There is still an enormous amount for you to learn, and remember, we are at war. We live to serve The Circle" Her voice was barely a whisper and I almost lost it as she opened up a cascade bridge for the pair of us. She half turned towards the magical construct and looked back at me.

"You are a very new presence in The Circle, Anthony. You have no preconceived teachings to work with. You are looking at us all with a very fresh perspective. Your view point could allow us to grow in ways we haven't thought."

I didn't respond but let the words slowly sink in. For the first time, Andrea was trying to entertain the idea of change. So I had had an effect after all.

For a very long minute, the only sounds that hung in the air were the sounds of cars passing on the distant road and the low crackle/hum of the bridge gateway. Andrea broke the stand off.

"I can see why your family liked this place so much" Andrea called as she stepped through the crackling ring of power to who knew where, nodding at something behind me as she went.

I turned round, not knowing what she had meant, to see exactly why she thought my uncle had been drawn here. Swinging gently in the cool breeze for all to see was the board which bore the name of the bar and a small picture. 'The Red Dragon' and a picture of a mighty crimson reptile with flame pouring from its mouth was hung on the side wall of the building. I looked up at the sign and realised that my uncle had ensured that I had always been drawn to what was buried deep inside me.

Smiling, I turned back to the bridge gateway, took a deep breath, "In for a penny..." and ran through.

About the Author

Owen is a fan of all forms of storytelling and enjoys books, film and TV, as long as there's something compelling going on. He's worked in different roles over the years, but has always had the spark of creativity lurking in the back of his mind. A Welsh rugby supporter, he lives in South Wales with his wife Joanne and they are protected by their loyal guard cat, Baggins.

Visit Owen Elgie on Facebook, Twitter, and Wordpress.